SUMMER
DARLINGS

BROOKE LEA FOSTER

Gallery Books

NEW YORK   LONDON   TORONTO   SYDNEY   NEW DELHI

Gallery Books
An Imprint of Simon & Schuster, Inc.
1230 Avenue of the Americas
New York, NY 10020

First Gallery Books hardcover edition May 2020

GALLERY BOOKS and colophon are registered trademarks of Simon & Schuster, Inc.

For information about special discounts for bulk purchases, please contact Simon & Schuster Special Sales at 1-866-506-1949 or business@simonandschuster.com.

The Simon & Schuster Speakers Bureau can bring authors to your live event. For more information or to book an event contact the Simon & Schuster Speakers Bureau at 1-866-248-3049 or visit our website at www.simonspeakers.com.

Interior design by Jaime Putorti

Manufactured in the United States of America

10 9 8 7 6 5 4 3 2 1

Library of Congress Cataloging-in-Publication Data is available.

ISBN 978-1-9821-1502-9
ISBN 978-1-9821-1504-3 (ebook)

To John, Harper & Emi for everything

and our Vineyard summers

SUMMER
DARLINGS

{ ONE }

$\mathcal{J}$ackie Kennedy sails these waters. In fact, the First Lady might be looking at the same sunlit cliffs as Heddy, and the thought of Jackie in her big black sunglasses, placing a kiss on the president while their boat rounded Vineyard Sound, tickled the corners of Heddy's mouth and made her peek over onto the deck of a wooden sailboat bobbing in the harbor. Heddy waved back at a man, shirtless and barefoot, holding a fishing line. He was no Jack Kennedy, but he wasn't half bad, either.

Pastel-striped umbrellas lined the beach as the ferry neared the dock, and the colors were familiar, even though she'd never stepped foot on the island before. Martha's Vineyard had become an obsession for Heddy that year at Wellesley after she'd overheard friends comparing where they'd stayed when they'd gone. But when movie star Gigi McCabe—*the Gigi McCabe*—posed in a barely there bikini for *Look* magazine, sunbathers oiled and stretched out on chaise longues around her, Heddy simply knew she had to go. (She and her roommate hid the magazine from their housemother, who called it "cheap trash" and forbade any copies in the dormitory.) Heddy had been drawn to the photo like a mosquito to a light, not because of the actress but because of all those patrician noses and straw hats, white Keds, and elegant tanned wrists. She wanted to know this fabled summer culture, those beautiful people who sailed in the morning, dressed formally for dinner, and sipped champagne at sunset at the famed Island Club.

Heddy pulled a small black notebook from her purse, pausing to take in the row of colorful Victorian houses lining the approaching town, and began to write. She was overwrought at arriving on the island, not only because she would live amid the wealthy, watching how money could take the edge off the sharpest points of life, but also because her job as a nanny would insert her into the home of a real family. There had been other well-paying options for summer jobs, of course, like the all-girls summer camp in the Catskills. *But living with a family*, she wrote, *particularly an illustrious one, offered something the other jobs didn't: a peek into a well-tended marriage.*

When she snapped her journal shut, an envelope tucked inside drifted to the rounded tips of her sandals. She'd delayed opening the letter long enough, she thought, snatching it from the cement floor of the ferry. The enormous boat bumped against the dock as the crew began tying long, thick ropes to the pilings. She turned the thick parchment over in her hands.

To think, this whole mess was because of a boy. A Harvard boy. Maybe the scholarship committee would overlook her mistake, forgive her one small misstep and focus instead on everything she *had* accomplished. She was the only woman from her Catholic high school in Brooklyn to go to college. Her beloved literature professor, a mother of three who looked like Carol Burnett, had spent hours helping her to revise a short story last semester and had even written an appeal in her favor, attesting Heddy had "promise." *Promise*. And now . . .

Heddy exhaled, slipping her finger under the envelope's tongue and tearing it open.

Her eyes went straight to the first line: *We regret to inform you that your scholarship for the 1962–1963 academic year has not been renewed due to . . .* She didn't read the rest, crumpling the paper up in her fist. She hadn't believed they'd actually revoke it.

She chewed on a fingernail, then another. Maybe it was what she'd deserved. Girls like her didn't get a do-over. Getting in to Wellesley—where the quad smelled of fresh-cut grass and the simple act of walking to class bestowed on students a responsibility to make something of themselves—had been prize enough, and receiving the check allowing her to go had been a coup. How else would she have paid? She dabbed her eyes with the back of her wrists and stared at a departing ferry, this one transporting a crowd of vacationers back to the mainland.

"A fool's paradise," said a young man who came to stand next to her, pushing his tortoise-rimmed glasses up his nose. He rested his elbows on the metal. Below them, a passenger ramp was fitted to the ferry's doors, and he watched it pointedly, fidgeting in his burgundy letterman sweater, a large "H" on the lapel.

She tried not to look at him. "Looks pretty perfect to me."

"It's your first time," he said, pulling on a baseball cap that was stuffed in his back pocket. "I knew it."

He smirked at a group of college boys throwing footballs on the dock. "Pass it to me, Bobby," he yelled, a smile in his voice.

His friends lobbed the ball toward him, making tourists on the dock duck out of the way.

He caught it and threw it back. "This island fooled me, too, once," he said.

She smiled plainly at him, taking in the clapboard houses with tidy shutters and the charming row of ice-cream shops and clam bars near the dock. "Well, it's just as I imagined," she said, picking up her suitcase and bidding him goodbye.

As Heddy stepped onto the dock amid car horns and beginnings of conversations, she saw women of all ages in the latest summer fashions, many in the requisite dress of the wealthy and Jackie-obsessed: ballet flats, a pillbox hat, and clutch—all in the same color. Many were trying to catch the attention of arriving friends and relatives, so Heddy scanned the crowd, looking for anyone who seemed to be looking for her. Her eyes followed the man in the maroon cardigan sweater as he met up with his buddies, a porter wheeling his trunk behind him. He saw her staring, and his eyes crinkled, sending Heddy's gaze down to her feet, the corners of her mouth turning up.

"Don't worry, there are plenty more of those," said a slim woman in navy capri pants, her loose blond curls pinned back on either side of her ears with small red clips in the shape of anchors. They matched her ruby lips. "You must be Heddy. I'm Jean-Rose, and this is my husband, Ted."

Heddy willed herself to shake the slender fingers of her new boss, a large emerald-cut diamond on the woman's ring finger. She'd babysat for neighborhood kids aplenty, but she'd never worked for someone so well-to-do; she hoped Jean-Rose didn't notice her clammy palms.

"Nice to meet you. I'm excited to be here and to, you know, get to know your family."

Jean-Rose tilted her head toward the man in the maroon cardigan. "That's Sully Rhodes. Handsome, a little peculiar. Still, everyone's angling for him."

Heddy nodded, pretending to understand, feeling a flash of excitement—her new boss was already talking to her about well-connected young men.

"Now, Jean-Rose, we don't want to lose our babysitter to someone tall, dark, and handsome on the first day." Ted winked at Heddy.

She'd never seen someone with such dark eyes—his were nearly violet. "But you do need to meet our little prince and, of course, the queen." Ted placed his hand on the bony shoulder of a scrawny boy standing next to him and then motioned to the little girl in a poufy dress with a towhead of curls.

The boy threw the soccer ball he was holding at Heddy's feet, harder than he should have. Heddy pretended not to notice the ache in her toes, bending down on one knee with a smile plastered on her face.

"You must be Anna and Teddy." Heddy extended her hand out to the stuffed monkey Anna was clutching and shook the primate's fingers, which made the little girl chuckle and jump right into Heddy's arms, nearly knocking her backward. "Oh, aren't you a doll?"

"Oh, aren't you a doll?" The boy snickered, making Heddy shift uncomfortably.

She tried to noodle him in the belly, murmuring that they'd be friends in no time, but he bit his cheeks to keep from smiling.

Ted pushed the boy's back, which made him lurch toward Heddy. "Mind your manners, young man." Ted reached for Heddy's suitcase, exaggerating a groan upon lifting it. She'd packed a stack of her favorite novels, plus two biology textbooks to study in case the scholarship committee allowed her to retake the final she'd failed that awful morning that led to that awful letter. Good thing she'd waited to open the letter until this morning with Anna in her arms, Heddy couldn't cry; she would look certifiable.

"This bellhop must have something else of yours?" Ted pointed to a squat man in a white-buttoned jacket walking toward them holding a purse a different color than her shoes, and she blushed. With all her nerves, she must have left it on the ferry. She took the frayed patent leather handle, watching Ted pull out a wallet thick with bills and hand the bellhop two dollars.

Two dollars. How she'd learned to stretch two dollars over the years. On their leanest days, she and her mother squeezed ketchup packets into hot water for instant tomato soup.

"I can get it, Mr. Williams, thank you." She picked up her luggage, but Mr. Williams insisted. She was just relieved the bag appeared shiny and new. Her roommate, Beryl, had never even used it.

He pushed through the crowd, and they all followed, the sound of seagulls and laughter and good-natured greetings all around them. "There's no point in being formal. We prefer Ted and Jean-Rose."

"If you call me Mrs. Williams, I'll feel like my mother-in-law." Jean-Rose rolled her eyes. "I don't want that woman's voice whispering in my ear all summer."

"Be nice, Jeannie." Ted checked to make sure the kids were behind them. "Mother means well. Besides, it's the children she's most concerned about."

"It's control she's most concerned about," Jean-Rose quipped. She sighed, as if there was a lot more she wanted to say, but she seemed to remember then Heddy was walking next to her. She threaded her elbow into the crook of Heddy's arm. It felt warm and friendly, and Heddy hoped she and her new boss would always be this chummy. "It's going to be a wonderful summer. You'll love our housekeeper, Ruth; she's about your age. And there's this new craze now, surfing. Have you heard of it?"

"Oh, sure." Of course she had. Who hadn't seen *Gidget*?

"You have to see these guys. They use a special board to ride on waves. Maybe Beryl told you about it. Anyway, Beryl tells us you're great fun."

With Anna's arms wrapped about her neck, Heddy felt the corners of her mouth turn up again. "When I'm not studying. Thank goodness for summer break." She still hadn't told her mother about what happened the night she and Beryl went out, how she'd met that Harvard boy and arrived for her final an hour late. Sometimes Heddy couldn't bear the sound of her mother's disappointed sighs.

"Everyone is doing something utterly fascinating on this island. I run the bridge group. Even Ted, here"—they stepped past an old couple stopped in the middle of the dock, luggage splayed at their feet—"he made sure the old lighthouse works, giving more to that falling-down eyesore than I ever would, and he's considering a state senate run." Heddy raised her eyebrows conspiratorially, making clear she was impressed. "But enough about us."

"She's like a windup doll," Ted laughed, and Jean-Rose grinned. "Heddy, how was your voyage in?" He was tall, skinny, a man in a boy's body, an unfortunate upward tilt to his eyebrows. Not her type, but she'd never be interested in a married man anyway. That pain had been unbearable for her mother.

"Like glass—not even a bit of chop." Heddy didn't know where the word "chop" came from, perhaps from reading *Moby-Dick* last semester in American lit, but she liked how experienced she'd sounded. Heddy had been on one other boat, if she counted the Staten Island Ferry.

By now they were standing in front of a shiny red convertible. The Williamses had parked in front of the Landing Luncheonette, a small ferry-side soda fountain with a lunch counter in the front window. Two teenagers sat sipping milkshakes, pointing and giggling at a boy walking off the ferry.

"You play?" Heddy asked Ted, pointing to the tennis rackets in the back of the trunk. Heddy, who had always been a swimmer at the Y, had recently taken to tennis—she'd seen it as a prerequisite to fitting in at Wellesley.

"I'm afraid I'm the tennis enthusiast in this match," Jean-Rose joked, taking Anna from Heddy's arms. "Even when I get him on the court, his backhand isn't the most, hmm, helpful."

"But I can be helpful in other ways, can't I, love?" He tapped Jean-Rose's bottom before opening the driver's side door and getting in.

Her cheeks took on a shade of crimson. "You could say that."

Heddy darted her eyes away. "Maybe you and I could play sometime," she said, positioned in the back seat, her face hopeful and pleasing. If she couldn't return to Wellesley in the fall, then she needed this job more than she'd realized.

Jean-Rose cocked her head, like she was pondering Heddy's suggestion, maybe a little too much. "I'm not sure I could get you into the club, but there *are* public courts. It would be fun, wouldn't it?"

"I warn you, my serve needs work," Heddy said, willing herself to stop being so self-deprecating. It had worked against her at the hearing with the scholarship committee back in May. She'd been too intimidated by the row of suited men and women sitting at one end of a hulking mahogany table to be convincing, too afraid of interrupting one of them or saying the wrong thing, so she'd been quiet, meek, a scared mouse on the other side of the table. And it didn't help that every question they'd asked was an accusation: *If you were that ill for the final, then why can't you provide a doctor's note? Did you skip curfew the night before? Then why didn't anyone see you leaving the dorm that morning?*

"There's a great pro at the club." Jean-Rose directed Teddy into the car, then plopped Anna on Heddy's lap, while Ted fiddled with the radio.

She slipped into the passenger seat, purring as she settled in next to Ted, running her hand along the back of his neck. Heddy wasn't sure she'd ever met a pair who looked as radiant as the two did at that moment, sharing the front seat of a convertible on a perfectly sunny summer day. Her new boss put on white cat's-eye sunglasses, tied a sheer red scarf around her head, and tapped the side of the car door. "Now, let's get Heddy some lunch."

The car drove by storefronts housed in charming cottages, each one's sign more colorful than the last. A line of families waited to buy tickets for the Flying Horses Carousel, old-fashioned music chiming from inside. Ted swerved to avoid bicyclists, all of them with a basket attached to the handlebars, pedaling through town.

Ted hollered to one, a man in his forties with slicked back hair and shapely tanned calves. "Watch it, Edison."

The man waved, and Jean-Rose smiled wanly. Traffic moved on, the bicyclist vanishing into the distance. Ted pulled Jean-Rose toward the center of the seat, nestling her under his arm.

"Now don't get all upset again." His voice was soft, but Jean-Rose turned up the music, resting her head on Ted's shoulder.

Heddy's purse had fallen open on the floor at her feet, the crumpled letter from Wellesley sitting atop her wallet. She'd prepared for her meeting with the scholarship committee as best she could, but maybe she should have enlisted help. She racked her brain, trying to remember her answers, what she'd said to the committee, how it may have been perceived. One of the members, a bald and bespectacled man, had given a speech at the start imparting Wellesley's motto, "Not to be ministered unto, but to minister," and how that meant that college wasn't just a place where students learned, it was a place where students passed on the highest morals. Maybe he believed her lowly economic status was to blame, her irresponsible actions contaminating the student body.

"Jean-Rose, do you do your shopping there?" Heddy tried to distract herself from her thoughts, hollering over the music. She pointed to a gas station with the words "Groceries and Meats" on the sign.

"With the dead flies in the windowsill? No, thank you. I'll take you to Cronig's in Vineyard Haven. Two brothers run it, and everyone adores them."

They zipped by a harbor lined with bobbing sailboats, children walking the jetties. Farther up, there was a handsome lighthouse, white with a black tip. Ted stroked the back of Jean-Rose's hair— cornflower blond, bouncy and soft. Beryl had told her more than once the Williamses might as well be the Kennedys. They were rich, in love, and the envy of their social circle.

Teddy bounced up and down on the seat, slamming into her thighs. "Up, down. Up, down."

"He loves the way he flies up when Ted drives fast over the bumps. But not too fast, right, Ted?" Then Jean-Rose whispered: "One day last week, Teddy nearly flew out the window." She giggled.

The crunch of the gravel driveway alerted Heddy they'd arrived. The rambling cedar-shingled Victorian was magnificent, backing up to lush rolling hills with abundant views of the sea. It had aqua shutters, little crescent moons cut out of the tops, and a front porch with four rocking chairs, each looking freshly painted, as crisp and white as a laundered shirt. A housekeeper shook out the doormat, while a gardener, a black man with a ring of sweat around his neck, clipped the layers of red rosebushes that lined the front of the house. The hydrangeas along the brick walk were a deep cerulean blue, and a small sign hung over the front door, white with block letters: "Elysian Fields." Home for the next nine weeks.

Heddy labored to remember the meaning from her freshman-year Greek mythology class and made a note to look it up. *Wouldn't it be grand to be so rich you named your summer home something most people had to read about in an encyclopedia? That's steel money for you.*

"Welcome to paradise." Jean-Rose smiled. She strode off behind Ted to the front porch.

"Or hell, depending on your perspective," a young woman about Heddy's age wearing a chambray collared dress and white apron whispered, reaching into the trunk. Heddy checked to make sure her new bosses hadn't overheard what the housekeeper had said, which made the woman grin. "Sorry, I shouldn't be so crass. I'm Ruth."

"I'm going to tell my mom you said a bad word." Teddy wrinkled his nose.

"Then I'll tell your mom about the chocolate you snuck into bed last night." Ruth tugged at Heddy's suitcase.

Teddy stared at his feet, then took off with Anna, a mischievous look on her face.

"Gosh, let me help you, Ruth. I've got books in there." The two of them pulled at the handle with all their strength, not getting it out until they lifted the corners of the boxy Louis Vuitton suitcase up in their arms. They dropped it to the ground, both jumping back to save their feet.

"Where's Mr. Helpful when you need him?" Ruth said quietly. Then she smiled sweetly at Ted, who was walking toward them with golf clubs slung over his shoulder, neat and angled, like his side part.

"I would have gotten that out." He winked at Heddy, still standing by the car, as he tossed his golf clubs where her luggage had been. "Make yourself comfortable, sweetheart. I'm off to the links."

The children emerged on to the porch, watching their father, and Anna, barefoot and hair loose around her shoulders, yelled to him, "I love you, Daddy."

Ted glanced at Heddy, a stupid grin on his face. "That child has me whipped. She's more charming than her mother, and I didn't think that was possible." Heddy felt her breath catch as he returned to the porch, planting a kiss on Anna's rosy cheek. Then he hoisted Teddy up, throwing him over his shoulder and spinning the boy, who erupted into giggles, making Anna jump up and down begging for a chance, too. Heddy loved seeing fathers play with their kids rather than treat them like flies that needed swatting, but she could be undone by dads who tipped the chins of their pouting girls with a single finger or dads who made an effort to listen to what his teenage daughter rattled on about. Those men made her weepy. At least when she'd seen them on television shows.

Moments later, Ted was back in his car, pulling on his driving gloves and peeling out of the driveway, kicking dust into their faces.

Ruth glanced at her watch. "Seven hours till dinner. If he's home by then, she won't ask any questions." Heddy followed Ruth to the porch, lugging her suitcase behind her. She would have carried that suitcase anywhere if it meant getting out of her and her mother's tiny Brooklyn apartment for the summer.

"Children, will you show Heddy her room?" Jean-Rose clicked down the columned veranda in heels, her head scarf untied and fluttering in the breeze.

"The ladies are coming over in an hour for bridge, and I want to serve the canapés out here. Did you make the lobster salad?"

Ruth was at Jean-Rose's side. "Two pinches of salt, four scoops of mayo."

Jean-Rose ran her hand along the surface of the outdoor table, a diamond eternity bracelet dangling from her delicate wrist. "Smells like Lysol. What would I do without you, Ruth?" She flitted off. "I'm going to change. I'll be down in five, and we'll set the table."

With her gone, Ruth formed a pistol with her finger, holding her hand to her alabaster temple and pretending to shoot.

Heddy didn't know how to respond, so she opened the home's French doors and stepped into a formal living room with high wing-back chairs and a tufted sofa. Beryl—who happened to be the heir to the Bethlehem Oil fortune and happened to ride horses with Jean-Rose's cousin and happened to insist on getting Heddy this job—had stuck her neck out for her. She wouldn't embarrass her by getting caught up in some childish antics on her first day.

"Come on, babysitter." Teddy swung around the intricately carved newel post. At six, he was slight enough to be mistaken for younger. "Follow me."

"Her name is Heddy." Ruth's eyes pinned him.

With Anna's soft hand in hers, Heddy followed the boy. "Nice meeting you."

"Don't let these two gang up on you," said Ruth, balancing an armful of dishes. "They're brutal when they're in cahoots."

Once in her sunny square bedroom on the third floor, the kids pulling out the dresser drawers and trying to unzip her suitcase, she sat on the edge of the bed and took the rumpled letter out of her purse. She flattened it and placed it in her top drawer, while Teddy, a doll tucked under his arm, showed her the musty corner closet and Anna sat at the small writing desk with a paper and pencil.

"And this is where you'll pinch a brown loaf," Teddy said, pointing at the toilet in a small adjoining bathroom; he rubbed the doll's yellow hair against his lips. Above the bathtub was a stained-glass window, two lovebirds chirping at each other.

"I'll wash your mouth out with soap if you speak like that again." Heddy snapped at him from her perch on the bed's patchwork quilt, the sinking feeling in her stomach having nothing to do with the boy, and he was taken aback, she could tell, but still he stuck out his tongue. Anna hugged her brother protectively, and he pushed her off hard enough that she burst into tears. Heddy scooped the child in her arms mainly because she needed a hug herself.

All she'd wanted was a chance at being the kind of woman her mother sold scarves to, rather than the woman stuck behind the Tiffany's counter. A hunger had always been in her—to live a plum life, yes, but also a genuine belief that something better lay just around the corner.

Then she'd met that boy, the son of a custodian at Harvard, who was attending the college on scholarship. He was just as much the outsider at school, and after meeting him at the bar with Beryl, Heddy had gone home with him, skipping her ten o'clock curfew in the dorm; Beryl had secretly signed Heddy back in, while distracting their den mother with tears about a pretend heartbreak. Heddy and the boy had stayed awake on his frayed corduroy sofa talking about how lonely it was to live with the pressure of their hardworking parents, how it colored every experience they had at college. She'd drunk a few beers, which wasn't like her, and even with her final the next day, she stayed, even though it was 2:00 a.m. by then, because she'd never realized anyone else felt as weighted with the future as she did, let alone a man. She was ready for her final, she'd told herself. She'd ace it. And then she'd snuggled in bed next to him, under a blanket he said his nana knit—they'd made out, and he'd put his hand up her shirt, but they were both too tired for much more and had fallen asleep, a sense of satisfaction in their shared experience. Then she'd overslept for her final, and he'd looked at her like her sandy brown hair was on fire when she started to scream: "Shit. Shit. Shit." She'd pulled on her fuchsia-colored pants, slipped on her flats, and run out to catch a cab, crying the entire way home. He'd called later, but she was too upset to talk. And that was the end of that courtship. The end of everything, really.

Well, not quite everything. Not yet, anyway. No one had to know. Besides, she was already here, they were paying her well, and the money she made this summer would at least allow her to open a savings. And prepare. For what, she wasn't sure.

She arranged her books in a neat stack on her nightstand: *Jane Eyre*, *The Golden Notebook*, *On the Road*, *Franny and Zooey*. She arranged everything she had in the two top drawers and hung her three dresses in the closet. Pleased, she crossed her arms over her chest and stood by the children, who were fighting over who got to sit on the desk chair. Heddy wasn't going back to Wellesley— that was clear—but it didn't mean she couldn't have a good summer. There were plenty of people to meet on this island, plenty of men to make the acquaintance of. Perhaps, she thought, she could win the bet that she and Beryl had made on their last day of school, and just the possibility gave her a lift.

She cupped Teddy's head with the back of her hand. "Who wants to show me their room?"

❧ TWO ❧

*H*eddy was downstairs and dressed in a simple mustard-yellow dress with knee-high matching socks by seven the next morning. She considered the pairing her most fashionable outfit, and the chilly morning temperature had cooperated, allowing her to pull the socks onto warm her legs. Uncertain where she should wait for the family to wake up, she chose a sunny window seat in the formal living room where she could see the stairwell.

She crossed and uncrossed her legs, bit at her nails, and adjusted her ponytail while taking in the room's oriental carpets, the polished mahogany furniture and ornate floor lamps, the gleaming brass bookends holding together neat rows of colorful spines. Just sitting there made her feel regal. The house even smelled of money. And Chanel N°5, which Jean-Rose used like deodorizer, leaving a bottle of it in every room and spraying it as she traveled through the house.

Heddy heard the children coming down the steps and stood.

"Come, I'll make you breakfast," Heddy said cheerfully, her heart warming at their tousled hair and bright eyes.

"But you're not supposed to give us breakfast." The girl adjusted the top of her darling baby doll pajamas.

"Of course I do." Breakfast was one of her specialties, and the thought of busying herself frying eggs gave her familiarity in this house of foreign smells and unsettling nighttime creaks.

Teddy curled up in a floral wingback chair, his pudgy toes dangling off one brocade arm. "Ruth gets us breakfast, dummy. You just follow us around."

Heddy plastered a smile. She glanced at the grandfather clock: 7:12 a.m. She wouldn't let them sock the energy from her that quickly.

The back door latched shut, and they heard footsteps, the coat closet opening and closing. Ruth stuck her head into the living room. "You're up already?" she said, taking in Heddy's outfit. "What's with the socks?"

Heddy swallowed. "Everyone wears them on campus." She tried not to sound defensive, or worse, snobbish.

Ruth shrugged. "I'll put out the cereal. The coffee, too. I'm sure you're going to need a cup."

Heddy put her hand on the small of Anna's back, leading the child into the kitchen. She felt strange living in a house with a servant, and she wouldn't let herself be waited on. She didn't want Ruth to confuse her with the family but didn't want to get too comfortable living in a home with a housekeeper, either. If her mother instilled anything in her, it was how to be self-sufficient. Heddy took in the row of white mugs hanging from hooks along the faux-brick-veneer walls, the spices stacked on a rack, the singed potholder. Curious, living in someone else's house—it was like parachuting into another person's life, landing smack in the middle of a home with its own culture and mores. She'd have to study the family closely, finding a way to fit right in so her sudden appearance at their kitchen table was seamless.

"You don't have to serve me," she told Ruth, who was pouring her coffee, "and I insist on making my own bed and cleaning my bathroom."

"I don't mind the work, actually," Ruth said. "My mom used to work here, and she told me if I keep sand off the floor and dishes out of the sink, I'd be okay, and it has been." Ruth moved about the kitchen a moment. "Thank you, though. That's lovely."

Ted came down for breakfast soon after, inserting himself at the small kitchen table and lifting Anna onto his lap. He was unshaven, his short hair unkempt, and the sight of him gave Heddy a chuckle, she'd never seen a man before his shower and pomade. It was adorable really, even if he smelled of sleep. Ruth tipped the percolator, pouring him jet-black coffee.

"Maxwell House . . . 'it tastes as good as it smells.'" Ted yawned.

"Perk, perk, perk," said Teddy, feigning the deep authoritative voice of the announcer in the ubiquitous commercial. "Listen to it perk. Look at the coffee as it gets darker and stronger. But will this cup of coffee taste as good as it smells?"

"I don't think I've seen a commercial as often as that one," said Heddy.

Ted picked up his newspaper, which Ruth had set before him. "But I'll give it to Maxwell House: the coffee does taste good."

Heddy, sensing an opening with Ted, like maybe this was her chance to make an impression, said, "Oh wait, who knows this one? 'Plop plop fizz fizz. Oh, what a relief it is.'" She'd actually sang it in the quiet of the kitchen.

"Alka-Seltzer," Ruth called out, the kids beginning to sing the popular refrain, while Ted opened the business section of the paper. She'd wanted him to guess, felt disappointed he'd ignored her.

"Now we're going to be singing it all day." Heddy grinned at the children, who continued to sing the jingle on repeat.

Jean-Rose padded into the kitchen, her hair set perfectly in waves, her makeup expertly applied, and Ted leaned over to kiss her good morning lightly on the lips without looking up from his paper. Later, when recounting her first impressions, Heddy would write in her journal that Ted kissed Jean-Rose like it was on his to-do list, and she wondered if a morning kiss from one's husband was different from an evening kiss, which may be less perfunctory.

Jean-Rose said that Heddy and the children would go to the beach that morning, so Heddy returned to her room to peel off her socks—she'd wanted to from the moment Ruth made the comment—and change into her bathing suit. It was an easy walk from the house to the family's private beach, the winding path twisting through a grassy clearing lined with lush and flowering beach roses. Once there, few houses dotted the beach and she rarely saw anyone else. After swimming for an hour, Heddy's calves stiff from the cold water, the children barely registering its cool temperatures, they emerged onto the sand.

Heddy toweled off Anna, who was by this point pruned and shivering, while Teddy draped his towel across his shoulders like a superhero cape. The air smelled salty and fresh, nothing like back home. "Who wants to go for a walk?" Heddy asked.

"Walks are stupid." Teddy kicked at the sand with his foot.

"Think of it as an adventure." Heddy held out a thermos of water, but he pretended not to see. Next week, the kids would start camp, and Heddy would need to plan only their afternoons—rather than their entire days. "We're exploring, like the astronauts."

"C'mon, Teddy," pleaded Anna, her pointer finger in her mouth. She was four, much too old in Heddy's mind to be sucking on her fingers.

Heddy and Anna ambled on, collecting slipper shells. When Teddy sprinted by, Anna dropped the bucket and took off, too.

"Teddy, wait—" Anna, her pigtails wet and curling, was gleeful.

"Don't go far," Heddy hollered to their bobbing heads. The sea stretched before her, a giant expanse of deep blue, with twiggy-legged piping plovers running the shoreline. The beach was a wonder. At Coney Island, people sat so close you could smell the hot dog breath of the guy next to you, and the crowded boardwalk was as busy as a city avenue. Growing up, the beach was where she learned that men had hair in their armpits and that women's legs sometimes grew dimples.

Heddy placed a piece of driftwood into the pail and laid down to feel the sun wash over her, listening for the children's reassuring chatter. Tired from rising so early and lulled by the peace, she closed her eyes for a minute. Maybe they could collect more driftwood and use it to make stick puppets. She envisioned various animals, lost in thought, when she noticed the children's voices fading. Heddy bolted up, looking far down the curving beach, then scanning the water, but there was no sign of the children. She hadn't fallen asleep—she would never. It had been seconds. Maybe thirty.

"Boo!" She jumped behind a large boulder, where she thought they might be hiding, but saw nothing but a rotted horseshoe crab.

Heddy's heart lurched. She wondered if they'd doubled back and she hadn't noticed, but she knew that was impossible. Her bare feet took off against the rocky sand, and she was thankful now she'd been practical in her swimsuit choice. When her Wellesley friends purchased bright-colored fast-drying bikinis at the Jordan Marsh department store in Boston, she pretended nothing suited her. Later, she'd slipped off to the drugstore near campus to buy a navy wool crepe halter suit on clearance. With its straight hem across her upper thigh and stiff fabric, it was more old-fashioned than she liked, but it had been only $1.25, and sensibility was needed as a nanny.

"Anna! Teddy!" she called. She imagined Anna crying and lost in the hot sun. A flash of Jean-Rose's face, scowling. "Anna!" Heddy yelled.

Losing them hadn't even entered her mind: it was a private beach, no one was around, and who took children? They weren't the Lindberghs, for goodness' sake. Maybe they'd run back to the house?

"Children! This isn't funny."

She froze. Voices: a little girl's and a man's. Heddy surged forward, spying a weathered cottage just above a thin line of dunes; the fishing cabin she could see from her attic bedroom. Anna and Teddy were eating strawberries at a picnic table, their fingers stained red. They were with a stranger, a man maybe a year or two older than Heddy.

"I was looking everywhere for you!"

Anna's terry-cloth beach dress was soaked from her bathing suit. "This is mama's friend Ash."

Teddy ran onto a flipped surfboard, balancing with his arms out. When he locked eyes with Heddy, the boy shrugged.

"Take a deep breath," the man said. Heddy had barely noticed she was panting. "Looks like they gave you a scare."

She ignored him. "Children, you cannot run away from me. What if you couldn't find your way home?" Embarrassingly, her voice didn't sound as firm as she'd intended.

Teddy rolled his eyes. "We live here."

"And Mama lets us come whenever we want."

Firmer now. "Well, I'm in charge of you, and it's my job to get you home safely or I'll . . ."

"Or what?" Teddy sassed, meeting her gaze. The children she'd minded back home didn't talk back; they would have been dragged to their room by the ear. She couldn't possibly tell two little rich kids they couldn't have ice cream ever again. And she didn't want to start her first week on the wrong foot. She looked away, and the boy began to sing "Lollipop."

"Or else," the man interjected, turning down the volume on his transistor radio. "Miss . . ." Here he stopped, flashing her a sunshiny grin, whispering, "What's your name?"

"Her name is Heddy," Anna whispered.

"Right, or else . . . Miss Heddy won't be your babysitter anymore. And boy, would you miss her."

"I wouldn't miss her," Teddy mumbled.

Anna climbed onto the man's lap, all monkey-like, wrapping one arm around his neck. "I would. We found a crab in the sand and made him a home."

"Don't give me that malarkey, Teddy. This beautiful woman right here is your funmaker in chief."

Now that the man had called her beautiful, Heddy turned to look at him. He was shirtless, a wetsuit folded at the waist, droplets of water dappled across his muscled chest. His sun-kissed hair was still wet, maybe from surfing, and he'd pushed it back off his forehead, giving her full view of his emerald eyes. *This is what men in California must look like*, she thought, although she had no idea where he was from at all.

"I'm Ash." He didn't stand up from the director's chair in which he sat or hold out his hand. "I'd be a proper gentleman, but Anna here is a bit of a snuggler." The sight of him made her uneasy. She was standing on his deck, in her bathing suit, which felt much too intimate. She remembered the fabric along her bathing suit's cup seam was threadbare—that's why it had been on clearance—and it exposed a sliver of the plastic boning. She shifted Anna's beach towel to her chest. She'd also forgotten about the unfortunate way the bottom sagged off her rear, until now.

"Smashed to meet you." That he was good-looking guaranteed she'd say the dumbest thing possible. "I mean, nice to meet you. Thank you for keeping the children."

At least she hadn't let her Brooklyn accent slip. She'd worked to perfect her Wellesley voice, the cadence she used when talking to classmates of means, speaking in such complete sentences you could nearly hear the punctuation. Her mother teased her when she'd visited and heard Heddy describe something as "lahv-lee," instead of "love-lee." At times, when Heddy was angry or anxious, her accent would slip, and her classmates would do a double take, as if they were seeing her anew and for the first time.

Ash shot her a disarming smile. "They show up here all the time, you know. I'm not sure they're looked after very closely." He had three small brown circles on his arm, pocks the size of quarters, and he caught her looking there.

"Me and some buddies, three a.m., cigarette stubs, hurt like hell the next morning." He smiled.

"We all do dumb things when we're young."

"Who are you calling dumb?"

At first, she thought she'd offended him; his tone had a hard edge, but then he laughed, making her laugh.

"You here all summer?" he said.

Heddy tried to look busy, gathering Anna's bucket. "Yes, until I go back to school. Do you surf?" Wasn't it obvious, considering he had surfboards leaning against the front of his cottage?

"It's like flying. You ever try?"

"City girl." It came out like an apology.

"No kidding." Ash grinned. She met his crystalline eyes for a half second, then darted her gaze away. "You been to the island before?"

Heddy was certain Jean-Rose wouldn't approve of her having the kids on this man's patio, but perhaps she shouldn't rush them back to the beach. If she didn't marry in the next year or two, the girls at school said she'd be stale bread. And then what? Heddy imagined her mother pulling her wire grocery cart down Atlantic Avenue in Brooklyn, struggling with the groceries up the stairs.

She shook her head. "My first time. I typically stay close to home on summer break. My mother says I'm the only person in New York who likes the city in the heat."

He laughed heartily. "Is it the stench of the overfull trash cans or the lovely smell of the subway that appeals?"

The corners of her eyes crinkled. "It is terrible, isn't it? No, it's Prospect Park. I could sit and write there for hours. Do you come to the island every summer?" Heddy eyed his ring finger but found no band. If only she were one of those girls who knew how to prance before a boy, rubbing suntan lotion up her thighs while asking him to light her cigarette. Women in the movies got men interested in them by taking charge. Instead, Heddy tended to wish men would want to know her, sense her quickening pulse, note her cheerfulness or the way she twisted her earring as she imagined kissing them. But men never looked that hard, she supposed.

"I came once or twice when I was a kid, but I'm a Jersey boy. My parents had a place near Atlantic City. Dad wooed clients over cards; Mom would take us to the beach."

"I'm a Coney Island girl myself. Is that where you learned to surf?" *A Coney Island girl?* She cringed.

"That came later." He had a glint in his eye. "So you write?"

Heddy flushed all over again. Why did he look at her like that, like he couldn't stop? The boys at mixers approached her regularly, but after talking with her, they started looking behind her, like they had somewhere else to be. This man, though, he kept chatting. Her neck began to itch, but she couldn't figure out how to scratch it without letting the towel drop and revealing her fraying bathing costume.

"May I use your powder room?" she asked. Inside, she'd figure out what to say next.

"Through the living room, first door on the left," he said. She assumed it was the *only* door on the left; the cottage looked about as big as an Airstream trailer. Mismatched blue couches in the sunny living room and a cluttered kitchen table gave way to avocado-green appliances in the small kitchen; despite its rustic facade, it had the fancy electric stove she'd seen in magazines.

She posed in the bathroom mirror, trying to assess how bad the bathing suit was. Possibly terrible, she decided, trying to re-center her breasts in the top so they looked fuller. Opening his medicine cabinet, she noted the brand of his shaving cream (a red tube of Old Spice) and his neat row of colognes in serious dark bottles. She was about to pee when she saw there was only a shred of toilet paper stuck to the roll. She could practically hear a sitcom laugh track, the ubiquitous joke about the things *only bachelors* do. Clearly, if he had a wife, she wasn't here now. No woman would let the paper run out without replacing it.

There weren't any rolls under the sink, just an electric razor, so she popped open the bathroom door and leaned into the small closet she'd seen on her way in. Two tissue rolls sat on the white-painted shelf in front of a stack of folded navy towels. She reached for one, and behind it, next to the Windex, there was a gleam of silver metal, something shiny poking out of a navy hand towel. Outside, through the screened door, she heard Ash and the children clapping, singing a nursery rhyme. She edged the towel back, just enough, curious if it was the grip of a microphone or the lens of an expensive video camera, or God forbid, one of those handheld machines—Beryl said they vibrated—you used all on your own.

Heddy stood on tiptoe to peer onto the shelf, but the silver handle wasn't what she'd expected. It was a barrel, the nose of a pistol.

Staggering backward into the bathroom, toilet paper in hand, she pressed her thighs to the cool porcelain of the toilet seat. *You're fine. Jean-Rose knows him. He's the neighbor.* Then she considered if she should replace the toilet paper on the ring at all. If she did, he'd know she went in his bath closet and might have seen the gun. If she didn't, he might remember there wasn't toilet paper and wonder if she was a slovenly girl who didn't wipe. That was worse than being nosy.

She squirted soap into her palm, rubbing her hands vigorously under the faucet. *Why would anyone on Martha's Vineyard have a gun?* This morning, the police blotter in the paper reported a teenager had been stopped for bicycling while holding a bottle of Coca-Cola; the officer thought he wasn't paying attention. Jean-Rose snorted with laughter reading it aloud.

"I better get these two home." Heddy stepped outside, working to sound nonplussed. *A gun.* She wondered if it was loaded. Reaching for Anna, careful not to let the towel drop, she let her bare arm graze the man's wrist, which sent a jolt of excitement—and maybe a little fear—through her. Was he a police officer? An adventurer who hunted sharks swimming too close to shore? "Sorry."

"What are you sorry about?" He lifted Anna off his lap, right up into Heddy's arms. She was sorry for knowing his secret, for finding the gun, but she couldn't say that.

He looked at her funny, like he might be done with this conversation, but she wasn't sure, so she prattled on. "My psychology professor says women should stop being so apologetic or we won't ever get what we want. . . . Well, I'm sure your wife does the same thing. Anyway, sorry to ramble." She cleared her throat, then laughed.

"Stop saying sorry!" He grinned, crossing his legs at the ankles, his hair shiny with sun. "And no, no ball and chain yet."

With the telephone ringing in the kitchen, he went inside to answer it. Heddy stared out at the dunes, straining to hear his conversation. "Just put it in the bag," he said, losing the chipper tone he'd used on her. The kids began singing loudly, and she couldn't hear anything else until he said, "Don't worry. We'll get him."

Heddy smiled at the gentleman when he came out, taking Anna's hand and following Teddy, who was already running ahead down the path back to the beach. "Nice to meet you," she said.

"Same." His breezy tone returned. "Come over and surprise me again sometime." There was something in his eyes, a softness. He hardly seemed like a murderer.

Maybe he had the gun because he was on the president's Secret Service detail, taking a day off from the mayhem in Hyannis. Maybe the cottage *belonged* to a Kennedy and he was renting it.

"I'll see you at the beach, Ace," Ash hollered to the child's back.

"Really?" She blinked innocently. "Ace." He seemed to enjoy her attempt at being cute and started to follow them, walking next to her through the dunes.

"I'm teaching Teddy how to surf. I told his daddy the younger he starts, the better."

"Like skiing, I suppose," she said.

"Only who would trade this for snow?"

She glanced at the cobalt-blue horizon, then back at Ash, who was shielding his eyes from the sun and looking at her, waiting for her to say more. But what came to mind was a line from a Salinger story, something about how every man has at least one place that at some point turns into a girl. She'd written a paper on what that one line meant, and still, she hadn't understood until she happened upon this surfer on Martha's Vineyard. *Perhaps, for every woman, there is at least one place that at some point turns into a boy.*

Heddy walked off, feeling Ash's eyes on her, knowing he could see her rear end. She rewrapped Anna's beach towel around her body. Just before the trail descended into the marsh, her racing heart forced her hand and she let the towel go, curious if she'd catch his eyes on her. But when she turned, he was dragging the hose over to his surfboards.

He was handsome, charming, a bachelor without any serious intentions. Someone she could never trust, the kind of boy who convinced a girl to skip a Wellesley mixer and make out in his car instead. And that was not the kind of boy she wanted.

She wanted someone like Ted Williams.

So why had she gone out of her way to make it clear she was interested?

* * *

The surfer was still on her mind that evening when she was putting the children to bed. Even after dark, when she was alone in her bedroom, sitting at her desk and penning her first letter, she thought of him. But these were not details she'd share with her mother.

June 24, 1962

Dearest Mama,

When I was a little girl, you and I would daydream about buying a cottage with a view of the sea. Well, the Williams's home is one hundred times grander than any of our fantasies, and the view from my bedroom window is equally sublime. Sailboats glide along the silvery waves in the morning, the sky a painting of pinks and purples in the evening. Jean-Rose, even the children, take everything about their lives for granted, whereas I appreciate every detail. We all have our very own bathroom. There was an actual handheld hair dryer left in my closet. Even the freezer has three choices of ice cream flavors.

I met a nice girl named Ruth—she's the housekeeper—and I feel comfortable with her in a way I don't with the others. You were right. The Williamses are not like you and me, but I'm still trying to understand how. Is it because she poured the last quarter of the milk down the kitchen sink, just because there was a fresh bottle in the keep? Is it because the husband spritzes himself with cologne or because he flips through a book at two in the afternoon, a square of sun surrounding his wingback chair?

But they are lovely together, and I would love to find myself in my own version of this life.

Missing you,
Hibernia

✦{ THREE }✦

*J*ean-Rose was filing her nails in a rocking chair on the porch when Heddy and the kids returned home from a nature walk around noon the following morning, their buckets full of feathers and rocks, tiny crab skeletons and oyster shells. As soon as she saw them, she dropped her file and sang out: "I have good news." She shimmied her shoulders like a jazz dancer and beamed. A Bloody Mary sat empty on the small table beside her, a chewed-up celery stick at the bottom. "I hope you don't mind, but I love playing cupid. He'll pick you up at seven."

Heddy crinkled her nose. "You set me up? On a date?"

Her boss's dainty jaw gaped with self-satisfaction.

"Sure did," Jean-Rose said. "On your night off next week. Did I tell you you're free to do as you wish on Friday nights and while the children are at camp?"

"We're thirsty," Teddy whined, tossing his thermos at his mother's espadrilles. The smell of honeysuckle wafted by. It grew in a tangle up a white-painted arbor over the bricked path to the porch.

"Come, I'll explain," she said, and they followed her to the kitchen, Heddy carrying the thermos. "He's a waiter at the Clamshell, a friend of a friend, and he's thrilled to meet you."

A waiter! Heddy tried to hide the disappointment on her face when she turned on the faucet to fill the water bottle.

"But he doesn't even know what I look like," Heddy said.

"Who, Mama?" Anna tugged.

Teddy snatched the thermos like a basketball, and Jean-Rose rolled her eyes.

"You think I didn't show him a picture?" She scooped Anna into her arms, balancing her on a hip; Teddy kicked at the table leg, slurping. "I passed along the lovely photo you sent us with your application."

Oh God. Her high school senior picture.

Ruth, who was standing at the counter with her back to them, spooned chicken salad onto Wonder bread. She wiped her hands on a tea towel. "That's the second night of the carnival. I was hoping to take Heddy."

"Sugarpuss." Jean-Rose tapped her fingers against her crossed elbows. "Can we finagle a double?"

"Who's the boy?" Ruth asked.

Jean-Rose whispered in Ruth's ear, then handed Heddy a wet washcloth to clean the children's hands.

Ruth grinned. "Oh, that's easy. Jerome works at the Clamshell, too. They can come together."

Jean-Rose balled her hands into fists and cheered, her shoulder-length hair bobbing over her shoulder. "Ruth knows everyone. Did I tell you that already?"

Ted ducked into the kitchen, literally, since he was nearly a foot taller than his petite wife, pulling Jean-Rose to him and kissing her sweetly on the top of her head. He threw his voice so he sounded like a girlish teenager. "I can't wait to hear how it goes."

Heddy and Ruth laughed, probably harder than they would have if he weren't their boss.

"Jeannie, can't you let our babysitters focus on minding the kids?"

Jean-Rose flipped her hair, smiling. "I'm good at matchmaking! Look at Shipley and Lindy."

"You simply picked two people with ridiculous names and got lucky." The lines around his eyes wrinkled, and Heddy laughed along with them.

"He's classically good-looking," Jean-Rose said.

"Ahem, I'm sitting right here." Ted pointed to his seat.

Jean-Rose rubbed the top of Ted's hand. "Well, everyone knows Ted Williams is the most handsome man on the Vineyard. But you're taken."

Heddy sipped her water, hoping to mask how disappointed she was that Jean-Rose wanted to set her up with a waiter. That wasn't much better than the boys back home happy with their hourly jobs at the shipyards; didn't anyone think she was worth the guy in the necktie with the degree in accounting?

"My skin is like an oil slick." Jean-Rose opened the glass cabinet and reached for a juice glass, then poured from a can of 100 percent Hawaiian pineapple juice. "Can you believe my cold cream melted right in the bottle? How are you smoking that thing in this heat?"

Ted pulled the cigar out of his mouth and examined it. "I paid a mint to have it shipped."

Jean-Rose made a show of waving the smoke away from her face, and even though Heddy didn't like the smell, either, she felt Jean-Rose was being a little dramatic.

"It smells of caramel." Heddy inhaled, pretending to like the acrid scent. The children sniffed at the air, erupting into coughs.

"At least someone appreciates a fine cigar." Ted smiled at Heddy. "I'm going up to the Old Light to see how my money is being spent. They want another five grand. Do you want to come, dear?"

"We better get prime seats at the benefit. Otherwise, what is the point?" Jean-Rose sat down at the kitchen table, crossing her legs, shiny with baby oil. Ted's hands went to her shoulders, massaging them over her linen blouse, and Heddy supposed that was what she envied most about their relationship—the small affections they traded. At first, she'd categorized Ted's morning peck on the cheek as lacking, but after watching the couple the last few days, she realized there were lots of quick kisses and hand squeezes, moments when their bodies brushed by each other, like they were two magnets that couldn't help but be drawn together, then swiftly pushed apart.

"You hear that, girls? Philanthropy at its best. Give only if you can get," Ted hollered.

Jean-Rose flicked her head back, laughing, and Ted kissed her bow-like lips. The kids pretended to throw up.

"What's gotten into you today?" Jean-Rose raised an eyebrow.

"A good morning at the Big Top," Ted said, grabbing one of the sandwiches and tearing off a bite. It's what he called his company, but Heddy knew from the manila envelopes delivered by water plane that morning that it was really called Sky Top Steel and Financial. "We're about to swing high."

"Well, I can't come to the lighthouse. Monday is market day, and Heddy and I need to pick up groceries. Then I promised I'd give her a quick tour of the island."

Heddy nearly said they could skip it, hoping to please Ted again, but she really wanted the tour. Since she arrived two days ago, she hadn't seen much besides the house and the beach.

Ted disappeared into his study, while Jean-Rose went into the kitchen pantry, holding a small notepad and pencil. "I swear we just bought a box of Frosted Flakes, and where is the macaroni?" She slammed the mauve-painted door.

"Maybe Ted ate them?" Heddy didn't want Jean-Rose to think she was hoarding a box in her room, perhaps because she'd been tempted. As a girl, she hid Sugar Daddy candies she took from a bowl in the school office under her bed, just in case of what Mama called "a lean week."

"Ted hates cornflakes."

"I told you, Mama—there are aliens on the island stealing stuff." Anna pretended to fly her sandwich around the universe.

Jean-Rose added cereal to her grocery list, then grabbed a mason jar from off the refrigerator, placing it in front of Heddy's plate. "Have I told you about the fun fund yet?"

Inside the jar was a tight swirl of twenty-dollar bills.

Heddy shook her head. She couldn't take her eyes off the money.

"How did I forget to tell you? Say you want to take the children to the movies or for an ice cream after camp. It will always be full." Jean-Rose tapped Ruth on the arm. "You can use it, too. For small stuff."

Heddy stared at the money, swallowing hard. She wondered what those twenties added up to, guessing there was several hundred dollars right there, enough to pay the rent on her and her mother's Brooklyn apartment for the year. She needed two thousand for next year's tuition, which seemed like an astronomical number, but there it was. A little less than half that in a glass jar set aside for entertaining the children.

"I know, it looks like a lot," Jean-Rose said, reading her expression, "but children are expensive." She threw the keys against the jar. "You don't mind driving to the market, do you?"

Driving hadn't been in Heddy's job description. She didn't think it would come up until she'd arrived and seen how large the island was. She watched Jean-Rose flip a page in her date book, the hum of the refrigerator kicking on.

"Jean-Rose?" Heddy waited for her boss to look up.

"What is it, Heddy? You sound panicked."

Heddy pushed the keys back across the table. "I never learned."

Jean-Rose looked at her in that tender way Heddy's own mother had hundreds of times. "Oh dear, don't worry, this is the summer you'll learn. You're hardly dropping an A-bomb."

"But I don't have a license."

Jean-Rose clapped her hands twice. "C'mon, children. Let's teach Heddy how to drive." She grabbed her Hermès purse. "Don't worry about being pulled over—all the cops here are college kids."

Heddy bit at her cuticles, then forced her fingers out of her mouth, remembering how her mother would grab her arm and hold it by her side whenever Heddy bit her nails.

"If anyone stops us, we'll remind them you're *our* babysitter. The only reason this island functions like a first world country is because Ted pumps dollars into its measly economy."

On her way out the kitchen door, Ruth tapped her on the shoulder: "She's set me up with so many duds, but you might actually like this guy."

Heddy spied her unfinished sandwich on the table, her stomach growling. "That doesn't sound promising."

Ruth smiled. "You'll see."

"Well, now you're going, too, so at least I have an escape hatch." With that, Heddy grabbed her sandwich, shoveling half in her mouth before letting the screen door slam behind her.

Heddy tried to seem upbeat as she opened the convertible's driver's side door with caution, as if the car might implode at her touch. Driving a car, let alone owning one, was so distant from her daily life, she'd never considered learning. She knew it took twelve minutes from Union Square to the Upper East Side, twenty-five from Atlantic Avenue to Grand Central. She'd been on a train when she first decided to apply to college. She'd been on a train when she got the courage to confront her mother about her father's identity.

With her thighs on the warm leather seat, Heddy gripped the steering wheel, which was skinnier and more slippery than she'd imagined. The kids settled into the back, and from the passenger seat, Jean-Rose slipped the key into the ignition and turned over the car.

"Just remember three things: the brake is on the left, the gas is on the right, and the steering wheel is in front of you. Go ahead, give it some gas. You're still in park."

Heddy looked down at the gearshift and pressed down on the gas pedal, listening as the engine responded with a loud rev. She rubbed her lips together. A bead of sweat dripped down her neck, and she wanted to rub it away but was too nervous to take her hands off the wheel.

Jean-Rose eyed Heddy. "Ready?"

"I'm not sure if this is a good idea, Jean-Rose."

Jean-Rose banged the side of the door like a drum. "Nonsense. Put the car in drive."

"I thought all grown-ups could drive," Teddy said.

"Not everyone in the city learns," Jean-Rose told him. "Mr. Parker doesn't know how."

"But Mr. Parker drives the bus," Anna said.

"No, dear—he rides the bus."

Heddy put the car in drive, waiting for the car to lurch forward, but it remained still.

Jean-Rose leaned toward Heddy, whispering. "You have to lift your foot from the brake."

"Everyone knows that," Teddy sassed. "Right, Mama?"

"Right," Heddy said. She glanced at the kids in the rearview mirror, then angled up her foot and the car began rolling forward, creeping right toward the rosebushes. Heddy turned the wheel to the left, then felt like the car might tip, and slammed her foot on the brake. In the back, the kids flew forward, slamming into the back of her seat, erupting into belly laughter.

"Can Heddy drive every time?" Teddy snorted.

Jean-Rose had her eyes on the driveway in front of her, lighting a cigarette. "The car wants to go, Heddy. It's your job to control it. Keep the wheels straight, brake by pressing the pedal ever so gently. It needs a soft touch, not a swift one."

Heddy swallowed hard, lifting her foot from the brake once more. Pressing the gas, she felt the car go, allowing herself to steer it slowly down the driveway; it was going better this time.

"Let's pick up the pace." Jean-Rose blew smoke into the open air. It filled Heddy's nose as she stared hard at the road. She pushed on the gas some more, zipping the Bonneville down the street. They passed a biker who had sped by minutes before, causing Heddy to look at the speedometer: she was going twenty-five miles per hour. A car behind her beeped the horn, passing her on the left.

"The speed limit is forty, lady," the guy hollered. Jean-Rose grabbed on to the windshield and raised herself up, waving over the glass, like it was all a big joke.

"It's my babysitter, Hal. She's learning."

"I thought you'd had one too many cocktails at the club." He winked, zooming away.

Jean-Rose popped a piece of gum, slumping back in her seat with a chuckle. "He and his wife are going through a nasty divorce. She doesn't even come to the club anymore. God, I couldn't bear it if Ted and I split. Sad how quickly you can fall off the list." She spun the silver knob of the radio until the static turned into the clear voice of Chubby Checker: "Come on, baby, let's do the twist." Jean-Rose wiggled her hips in her high-waisted white shorts. She seemed her thirty years then; music had a way of dating people.

"The list?" Heddy was fascinated by the ways the upper crust organized themselves. She'd seen it at school, how different degrees of wealth were delineated, resented, talked about. How people dropped hints by comparing where they liked to stay: Chicago's Drake Hotel

(Judy Garland's favorite) or the Palmer House (which had gilded-peacock doors). Then there were small details, like the girl spotted wearing a skirt without a satin lining, or a girl whose boyfriend had to walk to a date instead of driving since he didn't own a car. No one did it to Heddy, at least not in front of her. This kind of heckling was often reserved for girls *with* money, the unlucky ones the cooler, affluent girls had decided just had cheap tastes.

"The list—" Jean-Rose said as the car bounced over the dips in the road. "It consists of people you like, people you pretend to like because you have to, and people you make plain you don't like. It's all about invitations. Who is inviting who? And it changes every summer."

"How do you make the list?" Her mother would have told her this kind of thing reeked of rotten cabbage, but Heddy wasn't so sure. She was convinced wealthy women were different from her mother and her friends, and knowing how—really understanding their manners and mannerisms—might help catapult her into their carefree lives.

"The question is: What kicks you off the list? A divorce is never good. Susanne and I hate those new-money girls who come in with the gaudy jewelry piled around their necks, but we often have to make exceptions, especially if, you know, our husbands are connected in business."

"It sounds stressful." In the rearview mirror, she could see Teddy and Anna wrestling in the back seat.

"It *is* stressful. Obviously, you can't get invited to everything, even though Susanne and I always do." She chuckled. "But we figure out who should sit next to who, and everyone is always calling one of us to say: 'If so-and-so comes, then do I have to ask so-and-so?' I mean, who wants to ruin their summer with the omission of one person?"

Heddy slowed, a milk truck in front of them, heading back to the dairy with the morning's empty bottles.

"This summer, Ash made it. On his name alone. Who wouldn't want to fraternize with Harrison Porter's great-grandson."

The surfer. Why hadn't Jean-Rose set her up with *him*? She was about to ask who Harrison Porter was, when Jean-Rose's face lit up like there was a string of bulbs around her neck. "You do know Ash, from when you lost the children the other day?"

Heddy's cheeks burned like one thousand stinging bees. She was going to *kill that boy*. "I'm sorry, but I had no idea they would wander up there. It was just minutes."

"It's okay, dear. Anyway, we all love Ash. He's really something, isn't he?"

Heddy stared at the black pavement, wanting to steer the conversation away from her mistake with the children, even though she was dying to know who Harrison Porter was.

"Let's go back to the list," Heddy said. "So if I was a Mellon or a Carnegie, I'd make it, even if I smelled like mothballs and painted dreadful artwork." Heddy imagined her mother sitting in the back seat, rolling her eyes at this conversation, calling Jean-Rose "Lady Muck," which is what she and her Irish immigrant friends called the rich and pretentious.

Jean-Rose yelled at the children to sit with their backs against the seat, then ran her tongue along her teeth. "You have so much to learn, dear girl. You must think about the friends you keep and what they can do for you. Powerful people weave complicated webs, but if you can make yourself useful to them, they may weave you right in."

Heddy steered the car past a farm stand selling strawberries and geraniums, excitement building inside her, like she was standing in an airport with a plane ticket to anywhere in the world. Jean-Rose had passed her a hint, a secret she could have scribbled on lined paper and passed in class. *Make yourself extra useful, and you'll be rewarded.* Heddy's eyes crinkled, even as Teddy kicked his feet into her seat. If she made herself indispensable to Jean-Rose, if she took care of the children better than previous babysitters who were there just to collect a paycheck, maybe she'd be invited to be part of the family. Jean-Rose had already set Heddy up. Perhaps she'd offer to write a scholarship appeal for Heddy, or, in a few weeks, Heddy could ask Ted for a loan to return to school.

Heddy marveled at the woman beside her: "Jean-Rose, you're a true doyenne."

Her boss opened her compact, checked her lipstick in the circular mirror. "It's just experience. My mother used to organize these morning teas at her house in Darien, inviting women over after they dropped their kids at school. I thought it was so boring, but my mother taught me how to separate the shiny apples from the bruised ones."

Darien. Heddy had a friend at school from Darien. The girl wore these large diamond studs in her ears every day, and Heddy thought they must be fake until she heard her complaining to Beryl that her father refused to buy her a full carat until she was twenty-one. "Then he'll make your husband buy them," Beryl deadpanned, and the girl pouted: "You're so, so right."

Jean-Rose was still talking. "On my wedding day, she told me marrying Ted was the best thing that ever happened to me, but now I had three jobs: keep a fine house, organize an enviable social calendar, and be a tiger in the bedroom."

Heddy swerved, the car nearly taking out a white fence. Jean-Rose cackled, throwing her head back. "I'm just joking, dear. I love keeping you Wellesley girls on your toes."

Shingled houses with charming gardens and picket fences lined Main Street, and Heddy made a note to include details about them in her journal entry tonight. It was all so curious to her. She and her mother had taken the bus to City Island in the Bronx once to eat fried clams, passing high-rise buildings on the parkway, then emerging over the small drawbridge to the island's busy sidewalks.

But Martha's Vineyard was different. There were pristine pine forests, unspoiled craggy cliffs, grassy meadows rolling into dunes, tidy clapboard houses with shutters. Last night in bed, she waited for the wind, so the buoy would rock in Vineyard Sound, chiming, and she watched as the sky faded to pink, the water shimmering. She couldn't have imagined any of this a few weeks ago, and Heddy relished the mental image of herself driving this car. Sunglasses on, the convertible blowing wisps of hair about her temples.

"See, you're a natural at driving. You know, I bet you're capable of so much more than you think. More than your mother even knows." Jean-Rose reached over to squeeze Heddy's forearm, but she flinched, making the moment awkward rather than tender. She didn't like what Jean-Rose had said about her mother. Heddy's mother knew exactly what Heddy was capable of; she'd been the one to encourage her, helping her study vocabulary and math, even if she didn't know the answers herself.

More than your mother even knows. When you grew up with a parent short on rent most months, when a budget taped to the fridge accounted for every penny of your mother's income, you *knew* what you were capable of because you had to decide early on if you were going to fight against the tide pushing you downstream or simply let yourself sink. You knew that when your mother collapsed from exhaustion on the subway steps after working nineteen hours straight, that she was the definition of the word "tenacious." Or when she fell into a funk and cried for hours on the couch, the shades drawn and dinner hardly a thought, then you believed your grandmother when she told you, "Times are hard, but this, too, will pass." You believed it because you had to. It wasn't whether you were capable in life that mattered, it was whether you got a chance, and her mother's lies about Heddy's father had given Heddy a legitimate chance.

Heddy sucked in a deep breath, pushing her shoulders against the warm seat leather. She had to relax. Jean-Rose didn't mean any harm by what she'd said. Besides, Heddy would have to swallow her pride a bit to keep this job. Everyone in service had to.

With its robin's-egg blue clapboard siding and neat maroon awnings, Cronig's Market occupied a double-door building on Main Street in Vineyard Haven, near a women's department store, a candy shop, and an electronics store selling portable radios with large handles and televisions set into shiny mahogany cabinets standing on four legs. The ferry down the hill had just let out, and people were coming up every street from the water. After circling for a parking spot, they lucked into one next to a bright aquamarine Thunderbird, the white steering wheel wrapped in a panel of turquoise leather, a pair of driving gloves on the dash.

Jean-Rose clicked her tongue. "My, my. Look who's here." She pushed open her car door and went to peer inside the aqua car. "How ridiculous—who needs air-conditioning in a car?"

Heddy had never seen a car with a cooling system. She felt like those sliding chrome knobs were as high-tech as the inside of the Apollo spacecraft. "I wonder if you need a sweater when you turn it on. . . ."

Jean-Rose reached for a metal shopping cart in front of Cronig's, motioning to Heddy to follow her. "Ted asked me if I wanted it in the Bonneville, but I like fresh summer air."

Heddy wiped sweat from her brow. *On a day like this, it might feel as refreshing as ice-cold lemonade,* she thought. Anna and Teddy headed to a toy section at the front of the store, while Jean-Rose examined netted bags of oranges. Apparently, shopping was something she considered her job as head of the house, like meal planning, even though she hadn't prepared breakfast, lunch, or dinner since Heddy arrived. The market was filled with other women like Jean-Rose, some in kitten heels and pencil skirts, others in sundresses or scallop-hem shorts. Jean-Rose knew them all. "How are the kids doing in swimming, Muffy?" "Susan, are we still on for bridge?"

Heddy was in awe: Jean-Rose made grocery shopping look like a fabulous day in the park. While she was fetching her boss a carton of eggs, she overheard two women, their grocery carts nose-to-nose at the end of the aisle, talking quietly. One said Jean-Rose's name, which made Heddy's ears perk up. "She must be in denial," the woman said. "I mean, he hardly even looks at her."

Heddy hurried back to Jean-Rose's side, and the eggs went into the cart alongside two boxes of cornflakes and a carton of Minute rice. Heddy mentioned they were low on Tang—the children had to have it every morning at breakfast or they'd throw a fit; she'd learned that much already. While putting the canister of Tang in the cart, Heddy felt an elastic ping her ankle—something about her shoe had given out—and her sandal was now loose, dangling off her foot. She reached down to reseal the closure, but it was missing. The tiny buckle had popped off.

Oh brother, she thought. She couldn't possibly wear the sandal without a strap and buckle, and these were the only shoes she'd brought. For the entire summer.

Jean-Rose tossed in a can of Cheez Whiz. "Have you ever tried this? It's just divine. The bridge ladies love a smear on a Triscuit."

Heddy tried to hide the foot with the broken strap, dragging her foot behind her to keep the shoe from slipping off.

"Why are you walking like that?" Jean-Rose pulled a bag of potato chips off the shelf. "Are you limping?"

"It's my sandal." Heddy pulled the silver metal clasp out of her shorts pocket; there was a small square of elastic hanging from it. She opened her palm and held it up for Jean-Rose to see. "Do you have a safety pin to hold it in place?"

Jean-Rose pursed her lips. "Let me see the shoe."

When Heddy held it up, her sandal, damp with sweat, appeared more battered than she realized. You could see just how much leather had worn away by the crisscrossing straps, how battered the sole. Her heart was racing the way it did when she was called on in class, like she needed to prepare an answer.

Jean-Rose placed the shoe on a shelf lined with canned green beans, opened her purse and removed a handkerchief, wiping her hands clean. "There's a safety pin in my wallet, but it's probably time to retire this pair, dear."

Heddy grabbed the shoe, slipping it back on her foot. "I think I can sew it." She took the safety pin from Jean-Rose, balanced on one foot for a moment and pinned the elastic in place. How could she tell someone like Jean-Rose she owned only one pair of shoes?

Jean-Rose sauntered ahead, Heddy following behind. "I'll dig through my closet. I'm sure I have *something*." In the refrigerator case, Jean-Rose reached for a glass bottle of orange juice when they overheard a booming voice in the next aisle.

"Yes, you should bring Meriwether. That would be just fabulous, sugar pie."

Jean-Rose froze, cocking her head to one side, shameless in her eavesdropping, so Heddy listened, too. A click-clack of heels inched closer to them. Jean-Rose pulled out her compact, rushing a few strokes of Chanel rouge onto the tops of her cheekbones, when around the corner walked a woman whose full lips were familiar, whose legs seemed to go on forever, and all at once, Heddy knew who it was.

Gigi McCabe, *the* Gigi McCabe, and she was walking straight toward them. Heddy had never seen a movie star before, let alone one as famous as Gigi. Only those photos of her in *Life* magazine, where she'd posed on the island, her shirt unbuttoned just enough to tantalize the imagination. A butcher clerk in a white uniformed shirt, blood splattered on the front, leaned up on the counter, leering.

Jean-Rose, who had thrown her compact in her purse in a panic, took on a contented stance, like she'd been deep in thought about the cookies. She clasped her hands together at her sparkly neck. "Gigi! I was hoping to see you here this morning. You look amazing, as always."

Gigi did that thing Heddy had seen her do a dozen times in the movies, when she tilted her chin down and turned her coquettish eyes up. "Oh, this? I wore it in Cannes," she said, sizing up Jean-Rose's white shorts, the pink espadrilles.

Gigi wore a black-and-white gingham, knee-length skirt popped like a tutu below a fitted black short-sleeved sweater tank, pushing her large breasts up and out, which was precisely the point. A golden snake buckle clasped a thick elastic-band belt at her tiny waist, while oversize black sunglasses sat atop her head. Gigi flicked her wispy reddish-brown hair over her shoulder, like she was annoyed by it. "Are you coming to the party?"

"We have it on our calendar." Jean-Rose put down her basket of groceries, opening her arms in an embrace. "You'll have to come to our clambake in mid-August, too—it's become a highlight of the season, you know."

Gigi didn't loop her arms around Jean-Rose, and Jean-Rose awkwardly hugged her middle. "If I'm here," Gigi said. "Who's this pretty little thing?" Gigi looked at Heddy just as she was working to hide her damaged sandal.

Heddy sputtered. "I loved you in *The It Girl*. I want to write a movie like that someday." It was true. Her dream, the dream she'd never admitted to anyone, was to write screenplays with an actress like Gigi in the starring role. Why she'd chosen this moment to blurt it out escaped her, and her cheeks flushed with heat.

Jean-Rose rolled her eyes, and Heddy wished she hadn't said anything at all. "This is our babysitter, Heddy. She's staying with us for the summer, on break from Wellesley."

Gigi craned her head a bit to look around her, and Heddy swore she was trying to see her shoe. "A babysitter from Wellesley? And you want to be a writer? How interesting. I thought you were all debutantes perfecting your backhands."

She was waiting for Heddy to answer, so Heddy stopped chewing on her nails long enough to say: "Not all of us, Ms. McCabe."

Jean-Rose smiled broadly. "Gigi and I are old friends from Darien. Your neighborhood was still considered Darien proper, right?"

Gigi held her head still, her eyes boring into Jean-Rose. "It's nice to reconnect every summer, isn't it, sugar pie? Reminisce about the old days, before you married that buffoon."

Jean-Rose breezed right over her statement. "Gigi bought the house two doors down from ours."

"I'd say it's more than a house."

Jean-Rose turned to Heddy. "Remember the three driveways at the end of the gravel road? The first is Shirley Q's. Oops, I mean, *Gigi's*. Ash lives in the cottage in between." Heddy pictured the house with the three brick chimneys she could see from her attic bedroom. She'd been staring at those chimneys more than usual since her mind wandered whenever she tried to read *Revolutionary Road*—she preferred to look out the window than dive into a book about marital discord. Why hadn't Jean-Rose recommended a love story?

Heddy willed the actress's eyes away from her sandal. Of all days, this was the one she had to be walking around with a busted shoe. Fate could be so cruel.

"Have you ever tried writing a screenplay?" asked Gigi. "It's not exactly a growing field for women."

Heddy, the hair on her arm prickling with nerves, wondered if she should tell. It was silly to even admit. Childish.

"There is one, but . . . it hasn't amounted to much. Not yet, anyway." Heddy licked her lips, her thoughts all mixed up, like swirling paint in a can.

"Don't write about anything you see in my house." Jean-Rose chuckled, but the way she held her gaze, Heddy could tell it was a joke based in truth.

"Jeannie, I have a swell idea. Why don't you bring Heddy to the party?" Gigi's eyes flicked.

"How thoughtful of you." Jean-Rose coughed. "But she'll be watching the children."

Gigi twirled a piece of her hair around her finger, addressing Heddy. "It's a Midsummer Night's party the second-to-last Saturday in July. You'll need a proper dress. Come over to my house next Wednesday, around two. You and I look about the same size."

Heddy wished that were true; her own boyish figure was more gamine than sexy, her bust line a constant source of disappointment.

"That won't be necessary, Gigi," said Jean-Rose. She glided past her, the other shoppers pretending not to notice the movie star.

"I'm sure someone else can stay with Anna and Teddy for one night." Gigi tapped one of her black heels impatiently. "Or perhaps there's another couple who would prefer your place. . . ."

Jean-Rose froze. The air chilled for a second, and Heddy tried to think of something to say to offset the silence, an apology for mentioning the screenplay. It was the only reason Gigi was inviting her.

"And she can bring the children to my house next Wednesday, Jeannie."

"But, Gigi, it's the Fourth of July."

"Okay, Tuesday then. I picked up presents in Cannes."

"But I don't think our babysitter needs an invite," Jean-Rose said.

"Oh, Jeannie, just let her come."

Heddy looked from Gigi to Jean-Rose, like they were smacking a tennis ball back and forth. Then Jean-Rose's hard look softened. "It's a swell idea," she said.

"Really?" Heddy had a mouth full of sand. "Me?"

"Yes, you," Jean-Rose said, her voice high-pitched. "Isn't that wonderful?"

"Don't be such a baby, sugar pie. The party is going to be outrageous. Hollywood types will be there." Gigi picked up another lock of hair, twirled that one around her finger, too, pleased with herself.

Hollywood people. Gigi had been connected in the tabloids to Cary Grant, controversial since he was at least twenty years older and not yet divorced—was he going to attend? How would her friends at school react when she told them about the party? She wouldn't have to listen silently to all the other girls' lavish reports; she was going to a real-life movie star's party! Then she remembered the letter. The scholarship. That unless she found a way to get two thousand dollars, she wasn't returning to school at all, and her knees felt like Jell-O.

Gigi kissed Jean-Rose once on each cheek, then turned to Heddy to do the same, but Heddy turned her face the wrong way at the wrong moment, slamming her nose right into Gigi's lips. "I am so sorry. Thank you, Ms. McCabe. Thank you."

Jean-Rose pushed past Heddy with a peevish sigh, walking toward the cashiers, where the kids were playing tag with another child. "Let's check out."

Gigi waved, closing one finger at a time into her palm. Her peach lipstick was so lush it looked painted, her eyebrows arched with interest: "*Au revoir, mes enfants.*" Heddy had been so awestruck she didn't even notice her sandal flopping off her heel as she walked to the registers.

"Not so fast, miss." It was Gigi's husky voice, and when Heddy turned, the actress was dangling something shiny and silver from her fingertips. For a moment, Heddy mistook it for a sardine. "I think you lost something," Gigi said.

Heddy pushed back her shoulders and reached for the safety pin; this would go down as one of the most humiliating moments of her life. "Thank you. The strap popped. I'll just grab another pair from my suitcase. Maybe the red ones with the little bows." She'd cut pictures of those shoes out of a catalog and glued them in her journal. One day, she'd wear shoes so chic no one would ever guess she'd once had only one pair. She backed away, the safety pin buried in her palm. "Thank you, Ms. McCabe. Thank you very much. I'll be going now."

Gigi's voice was breathy. "Don't let her fill your head. She's the destroying type."

Heddy curtsied, then laughed at how idiotic it was, like Gigi was royalty. She hurried to Jean-Rose, who was at the cashier, the steady ding of the checkout ringing up the groceries. "Twenty-three dollars," the cashier announced.

Jean-Rose hollered to the kids, and she and Heddy carried the paper bundles out to the convertible. Heddy got in the passenger seat, looking back at the double screen doors of the market, wondering what it would be like to be Gigi McCabe. That's when she heard the driver's side door of the convertible swing open, slamming the car next to them. Jean-Rose had pushed the driver's side door open with all her might, hitting hard into the aqua Thunderbird's glossy passenger side door. A small dent shined next to the silver metal handle.

"Oops," she said gaily. She jerked her door shut, scooting herself into place behind the wheel. "I can be so clumsy."

Heddy squinted from the passenger seat, trying to see how much damage she'd done. "Gosh, maybe you should tell someone."

Jean-Rose spit through gritted teeth. "If people knew who she really was! The things she did." She smacked the steering wheel, started the car. "And this nonsense with you. Why would she be so interested in *you*?"

{ F O U R }

That Saturday, Heddy found herself helping Jean-Rose organize an elaborate luncheon. Ted smoked a cigar and made notes in a lined yellow notepad on the wraparound porch while Jean-Rose flitted around him in periwinkle satin shorts, preparing the tables set up for three dozen guests. She wanted every napkin folded into an accordion fan and spread across a lattice-patterned salad plate, which was stacked on top of a larger coordinating dinner plate. From inside came the clatter of spoons stirring pots, the refrigerator door opening and closing, the busy swing of the porch door as caterers in pressed black dresses ran items in and out of the kitchen.

"There's still no sign of Ruth?" Jean-Rose phrased it like a question.

Heddy had just tried her. "No one is picking up." She returned to setting the table with heavy silverware from a box lined in garnet velvet. She wondered if the children, or the guests for that matter, would be able to lift these forks to their mouths.

"She'll be here soon." Ted cleared his throat, and perhaps to distract Jean-Rose, he spoke to Heddy. "Where do you live at school?"

Tickled that he'd asked, she replied, "In that dreadful dormitory with Beryl." Her classmates often griped about Tower Court, so she never let on she loved that housekeepers vacuumed the couches daily and shined the floors with lemon Lysol (actual housekeepers!) and there was nary a cockroach in sight. Her mother had stared at a photo of the Gothic brick building in awe.

"Living there must feel like a million bucks," her mother had said, and Heddy nodded, because it did.

"I've done business with Beryl's father, and by business, I mean we both smoke cigars at Cincy's Supper Club on East Thirty-Second. He's a bit of a lout, though, I think his wife hikes her skirt for someone else." He blew his cigar smoke upward, a grin on his face, and Jean-Rose scolded him for being crude.

Heddy forced a smile. She'd overheard him on the phone earlier bellowing about how he didn't want to look at *that inbred monkey* anymore, referring to his secretary.

"By the time I get back, have one of those cuties in typing waiting for me," he'd said. She didn't like the way he'd said, *cuties in typing,* like the woman was something for him to enjoy, rather than a professional doing her job. Fathers shouldn't talk that way; as Heddy saw it, once a man had a child, particularly a daughter, he should tamp down any vulgar aspects of his personality. But boys will be boys, she supposed.

"Beryl and I considered moving off campus together, but living in the dormitory is closer to class." It was also cheaper.

Jean-Rose came over to them, lovingly smacking Ted in the shoulder with a napkin. "It's true—Beryl's mother is a bit wild, just like Beryl—but she can be great fun." Jean-Rose was refolding every napkin Heddy arranged, making her self-conscious about whether she was placing the silverware to Jean-Rose's liking.

"We've been best friends since freshman year," Heddy said. At first, they weren't the obvious match. Beryl had tried to win Heddy over minutes after she twirled into their room, a string of bellhops following behind. She invited Heddy to the movies and on shopping trips for dresses for the mixers, but Heddy had made excuses—she was too proud to admit she had only enough money for books, and even then, she'd had to ask one professor to lend her a science text-book. Soon, Beryl stopped asking her to come out, smuggling gin into their room instead. While studying, they began to commiser-ate about how greasy the eggs were at the commissary, how hard it was to do their business in the bathroom with so many girls coming in and out. That's when they promised to guard the door for each other. "Don't let anyone in until I flush," Beryl said, and the first time, Heddy had had to chase away pouting Anjelica Smythe with her toothbrush already pasted.

Jean-Rose examined the floral tablecloths, the mauve place-mats, the lattice-patterned plates centered on top. "I want it to look like this *Good Housekeeping* spread, but something's missing." She thrust the magazine in front of Ted, his head buried in a newspaper cover story: "Is President Kennedy at Fault For the 'Flash Crash'?"

Jean-Rose elbowed him, causing Ted to glance up: "Ash Porter's a salesman, Jeannie, not an ambassador, and I'm not interested in buying the swampland he's peddling."

Ash? The handsome bachelor. Coming here.

"Don't be such a sourpuss." She pouted. "We have the china, the linen napkins, the peonies." Jean-Rose's eyes followed Heddy's hands placing the silverware. "Let's put them a bit farther from the plate edges." Jean-Rose moved a fork and knife a millimeter, if that, and Heddy adjusted each one.

"Do you think Beryl will marry Phillip?" said Jean-Rose.

Rich and handsome. Of course she would. She and Beryl made a pact before they left school that they'd return engaged in the fall.

How that would work in Heddy's favor now! No one would even question why she didn't come back to school if she were engaged. "She thinks he's going to ask this summer."

Jean-Rose cut hydrangea blooms from over the porch railing with a scissor, then arranged them in vases Ruth had left out the night before. "Okay, this is serious now. Where is Ruth? She was supposed to be here an hour ago."

"I'll call her again," Heddy said. Inside, she tried Ruth's number, but an operator came on, her nasally voice announcing the number was out of service. She sometimes heard a similar refrain when she called home from Wellesley, gripping the lining of her woolen skirt pocket when she heard the operator's voice, imagining the woman was pock-faced and full of judgment.

"Still no answer," Heddy said.

"It's strange . . . she's usually very punctual." Jean-Rose downed a glass of water. "We have the entire club coming to hear about Ash's plans. I need her."

"She must be on her way." Heddy made a mental note to check her makeup before the bachelor was set to arrive.

Jean-Rose disappeared inside, then returned a few minutes later with a glass of champagne, mumbling that she needed to relax. She followed Heddy as she fixed and folded. "What do you want to do after Wellesley? Clearly, you're not writing a movie."

Heddy didn't look up, a little stunned by Jean-Rose's blatant lack of faith but also because she was probably right. "Maybe something in teaching," she said. Teaching would make her mother happy, after all.

"Oh, I thought I'd go into education, too. My parents made me go to UPenn—I didn't want to be one of four girls on campus. But I liked it enough. I was a columnist for the women's newspaper. We may have been the only paper in the country to publish engagement statistics like batting averages." She sighed. "But I covered serious topics like the integration of women into the men's cafeteria and such."

Ted guffawed. "Sounds serious."

Jean-Rose smiled. "Anyway, keeping house was more important to me, dear. And it will be for you, too." Heddy liked that Jean-Rose expected her to follow in her footsteps, like they were equals somehow. "Senior year is all about future setting."

Jean-Rose checked her wristwatch again, a rush of panic tightening her cheeks. "Guests are set to arrive in forty-five minutes—we need to find Ruth."

The kids came out on the porch arguing, Teddy holding his sister by the ponytail, his sister gripping a doll.

"Teddy, all you do is terrorize your sister. Go to your room." Jean-Rose pointed at the front door.

"Yeah," said Anna. She crossed her skinny arms across her embroidered blouse.

The boy's voice cracked. "But it's my doll. She can't just take my—"

"*Now!*" Jean-Rose yelled, slamming her champagne glass on the table. "I can't believe Ruth is doing this to me. Thankfully, I had the good sense to cater, considering my housekeeper is *nowhere to be found.*"

Ted stood, patting his pocket for his keys, then pulling them out. "Relax, you'd think we were having a wedding. We'll pick her up. Heddy and I will go." With the grown-ups ignoring him, Teddy went out to the swing set.

In the car, Ted prattled on about his Yale days while Heddy took in the curvy roads, how they cut a path through the island's rural center. Here, modest shuttered farmhouses, the paint peeling and chipped, gave way to lawns that looked craggy and dry with sun, the picket fencing in various states of disrepair. He told her of a party where he threw a mattress out a dormitory window, and the story he spun for the campus cop to get out of it, and while he made her laugh recounting the shenanigans, she considered that he wasn't too different from the men she'd met at mixers at school. One of those silver-platter boys, entitled and aimless in conversation, purposeful only in getting to the part where he stuck his tongue in her mouth. She was glad to know him now, as the responsible family man, rather than the drunken frat boy.

They pulled into Ruth's dirt driveway, parking outside the small ranch, the screen door unhinged at the top, hanging sideways, like it had been blown about in a storm. Ted parked a few car lengths away from the house, nodding her on. Heddy opened the screen door, which squeaked on its rusted hinge, and knocked.

A squat, flushed man who smelled like liquor and cigars opened the door, leering at her from the other side of the screen: "Well, Ruthie never told me her new friend was so pretty." Inside, a couch with a gaping tear in the cushion was piled with laundry. A red-haired woman was sleeping in an armchair, snuggled under a crochet blanket, an oxygen tube in her nostrils.

"I'm Heddy." She reached out her hand for a proper shake, but Ruth shoved the man aside, stepping outside and slamming the door behind her.

"Sorry about that." Ruth picked a beer bottle off the step, tossed it in a can by the front bush.

Heddy forced a smile. "Is that your father?"

Ruth rolled her eyes, red and puffy from crying. "He's pleasant, I know." She crossed her arms, becoming interested in her cuticles. "Mom got sick last year." She said it like it explained everything, but Heddy wasn't sure what it explained at all.

"I'm sorry."

Ruth shrugged. "It is what it is." She noticed the car idling in the unpaved drive then, her cheeks turning ashen. "Jesus. I didn't know Ted drove you."

Heddy turned her back to the car and whispered. "He means well, that's all. She's freaking out. The luncheon is today, and she doesn't trust me to mix the drinks. You need to come."

"It's my bike. I couldn't fish it out of Sengekontacket Pond. The damn fool." Ruth kicked the concrete steps. "Then my ride didn't show up."

Through the screened window, Heddy could hear the TV blaring, a laugh track bellowing out every time the actor delivered a punch line. *The Honeymooners.*

"You could ask Jean-Rose to borrow a bike."

Ruth exhaled with force, like she was blowing birthday candles. "I'll be right back." From the steps, Heddy heard Ruth's father yelling about "her fancy friends," so Heddy got in the car, wanting to avoid any more unpleasantness. Ruth emerged in her apron.

"Sorry, Ted," Ruth said, her childlike frame sinking deep in the back seat.

"A phone call next time, miss." He emphasized "miss," causing Ruth to look out the window, where a junked car bumper and loose tires were tangled in a garden hose. Ruth couldn't fault him for worrying. The family had been expecting her, and she didn't show; of course, they deserved a call. Heddy wondered if Ruth's own father would notice if Ruth didn't return home one night and whether that meant the Williams kept closer tabs on her than her own family.

"The operator said the lines are down," Heddy said. "Half the island."

Ted spat out the window. "That's curious. We haven't had a storm in weeks." They drove on in silence, Ted puffing his cigar until they pulled into the drive, the neatly trimmed hedges calming her nerves. Perhaps it did the same for Ruth. The tidiness of the house, the gardens, the way their roles were so defined. Working in service made it easy at times to forget your own problems.

As he put the car in park, Ted said, "God dammit, girls. If she's unhappy, I'm unhappy."

At the sight of the car, Jean-Rose stopped pacing the porch, placing her hand to her forehead like she might faint. "Ruth, everyone is arriving in fifteen minutes."

Ted eased back onto his porch seat. "Why do we care so much what everyone thinks?"

"Don't razz me. Ruth needs to know *how* to serve the drinks." She'd applied her makeup while they were gone, her cheeks thick with foundation and blush.

Ruth stepped behind the bar, threading her fine strawberry hair into a tight ponytail. "I'm sorry, really. Lime rickeys. I got it. A shot of gin in each highball. Go upstairs and change."

Jean-Rose admired her, like she was her eldest-born child, and Heddy hoped Jean-Rose would come to see her as indispensable, too. "Oh, Ruth. You're such a doll."

Ruth squeezed the limes into a glass, a smile spreading across her face. "You want them passed?"

"On the silver platters. Maybe Heddy can help." Jean-Rose pranced inside.

The day was overcast, and it was cooler than the heat wave of the previous week. Still, Heddy planned to take the children to Vineyard Sound after lunch. Jean-Rose wanted them seated at the luncheon with the adults, which Heddy thought ludicrous but didn't question. As her grandmother always said, "When it comes to work, put your head down and nod." Anna and Teddy, now dressed in coordinating sailing suits, sat on the lush grass below the porch, their crayons and scrap paper spread around them.

At crunching footsteps in the driveway, Heddy looked up to find Ash Porter holding a shiny black briefcase. His tan sports jacket was cut short and slim in the latest fashion, and his navy tie, freshly brushed saddle shoes, and crisp white button-down shirt made him look like an advertisement. His hair rippled like a wave to his right temple.

"Ash Porter is here," Heddy announced, hoping Ted didn't notice the teenage pitch of her voice. Gun or not—the sight of him did something to her.

Ted folded his newspaper and handed it to her; she dashed upstairs to reapply her blush. On her way back out, she took a platter from Ruth holding two drinks with lime wedges. Ruth, noticing her lipstick, glared: "Don't make a fool of yourself."

Anna was already in Ash's arms, Teddy pulling on his pants leg in that annoying way kids did when they wanted attention.

"Lime rickey, Mr. Porter." Heddy handed him a tumbler.

"Please, it's Ash." He smiled, sipping the cocktail. It did feel strange to call him a formal name, since they were nearly the same age.

Ted signaled to the other glass. "That one for me? So useful, these college girls, aren't they?" He winked.

Heddy logged his patronizing tone, looking pointedly at the children. "Let's give Ash some space." Only Anna followed her to the bar, where she stole a handful of orange slices. "Get Teddy and finish your pictures in the grass," she told her. "I'll be right down."

"Not sure how it's going to go with these two," Ruth whispered, gesturing toward Ash and Ted.

"I thought they were friends."

Ruth put four more glasses on the silver tray; another couple had arrived. "No, Ted and Jean-Rose are. I think she's sweet on Ash."

"But she's so much older . . . and she and Ted are in love."

"Are they?" Ruth said.

The porch grew crowded, a steady hum of chatter all around, while Heddy roved about serving lime rickeys. Edison, who they'd seen on his bike the day Heddy arrived, reached for a drink, introducing himself, "You must be Ted's summer girl."

It wasn't how she'd characterize herself, but she smiled. "Nice to meet you," she said, noting how physically fit he looked in his pressed white shorts, how fashionable his round white sunglasses.

Edison spun on his heels, looking back at her. "Don't worry: Ted will take good care of you." Heddy thought it an odd thing to say, but she nodded and moved about with her drink platter.

Standing at the center of a few women, Ash held up his finger to signal he wanted another, and she slowed, handing him a cocktail with the flourish, she imagined, of a Pan Am girl.

He softly elbowed her middle. "We were just talking about last night's full moon. Did you see it?"

The expectant looks of strangers, their faces awash in polite smiles. She realized he wanted her to answer.

"I read by it longer than I should have," Heddy said.

A disgruntled sigh. "It kept me up half the night—I hate the full moon," said a squat coed whose pug nose gave her the look of those stubby dogs that waddled down uptown sidewalks.

"Thank God for blackout curtains," joked a wispy middle-aged woman, tight curls crowding her head.

"I find it rather mysterious, actually." Heddy looked to Ash to make sure disagreeing was okay, and he moved aside, allowing her to step into the circle. "I like to stare at it, the ridges and craters," she continued. "It makes me wonder what I look like from up there. What John Glenn saw when he looked down at us."

"What Glenn saw was a wonder." Ash smiled.

"He's lucky that thing didn't explode. I would never do such a ridiculous thing as shoot myself up over the earth." It was the woman with the nose.

Heddy longed to sip one of the drinks on her platter, like she was a guest, but she didn't think Jean-Rose would like that. She straightened as Ted came over. "To circle the earth like that, to see us all as we've never seen ourselves . . . ," she said.

Ted threw an arm around Ash, his eyebrows in sharp angles at Heddy. He peeked over the side of the porch, where the children, on a picnic blanket in the grass, colored. "We're all set here, Heddy."

She snapped her mouth shut, curtsied awkwardly, and nodded vigorously, like an actress told she no longer had a part. "Excuse me," Heddy managed, still holding the platter. She longed for him to act fatherly to her—take an interest in what she was saying or introduce her to someone he thought she'd liked to know. But to him, she was the help.

"Sorry about that," Ted told the guests.

Had he apologized for her presence? She'd assumed she should be quiet unless spoken to, but Ash had engaged with her. She didn't want to be rude. Maybe she hadn't had to go on quite so much about the moon, but still.

At the bar, Ruth mouthed "I told you," sending a ping of shame through Heddy. She wanted to explain, but then Anna started to scream. Teddy was trying to write on her with black crayon, forcing Heddy to snatch it away.

"Let's have a drawing contest." Heddy rushed to redirect them, dabbing Anna's eyes with the corner of her dress. They were sitting close enough to the porch she could hear the guests talking, and everyone could hear Jean-Rose, with the way her voice carried out over the crowd.

"Ash, we're so happy you agreed to do your presentation here," said Jean-Rose, dressed in a blush-colored, collared sheath and matching wide-brimmed hat.

Ash kissed her on the cheek, her lipstick leaving a pretty smear of red on his cheek in return. "You shouldn't have worked so hard. You set a beautiful table."

She shot Ted a look, batting her false eyelashes, and he shrugged.

"You're making me look bad. She was in a tizzy all morning I didn't remark on it."

The trio laughed heartily, and Jean-Rose slipped off to welcome someone else.

Ted led Ash to the front of the porch, where a long rectangular table sat twelve. "You take the head, sir."

They seemed quite chummy; apparently, Ruth was wrong.

A plume of Chanel N°5 enveloping her, Jean-Rose leaned over the railing where Heddy was sitting in the grass. "Heddy, will you be a dear and help Ruth serve the drinks?"

"Ted sent me away." Although, he hadn't told her to go to the children. She did that on her own.

Jean-Rose's lips drew a tight line of red. "Don't listen to Ted. Our guests need drinks."

"Of course, I'm coming." Heddy raced up the porch steps, hoping Teddy stayed immersed in his drawing of the ugliest monster he could think of.

Ruth mixed drinks into several glasses, arranging them on platters. She wiped her forehead with the back of her arm. "Didn't you see me waving you over? I can't mix and serve."

"I'm sorry. Ted said—"

"Ted doesn't know his ass from his elbow when it comes to entertaining. Here." Ruth placed the platter in Heddy's arms.

The women stood in tight groups making small talk, while the men sat at the table smoking cigars with Ted. She wondered who Emily Post would serve first: the men or the women? Heddy stepped in the direction of the cigar smoke.

Ted patted a friend on the back. "Ernie, we need you at the Big Top. Things are a bit hairy right now, but don't believe the papers. It's temporary."

The conversation turned serious; men huddled over their collective anxiety about the markets. Heddy's tray empty, Ruth handed her a fresh set to deliver. Jean-Rose tapped her on the back, pressing Anna's hand into Heddy's. Anna was bawling, the front of her dress soaked. She'd had an accident.

"I thought you could do both." Jean-Rose's smile was all Miss America, but Heddy felt how hard she pressed Anna's hand into hers.

Despite her wet bottom, Heddy picked her up, pee staining her waist. "I'm sorry, I was serving, like you said."

Jean-Rose smoothed the front of her dress. "Change her, please. Lunch service is about to begin."

One of Jean-Rose's friends sidled up to her, and Heddy heard her say: "Oh, Lila, sometimes I feel like I have two more children. These girls, they're . . ."

Out came a snort. "Service isn't what it used to be. But you get what you pay for. They're hourly girls, right?"

Heddy's jaw tightened. Is this what she was to these women peacocking in their pastel-colored cocktail dresses—nothing but a punch line in a joke about the help. An "hourly girl"? The thought cut like a razor, and for the first time, it made her resent these women in updos and strappy sandals. If Heddy ever had money, she'd never make anyone feel like less because they worked in service. Her mother taught her to be thankful for any kindness the world showed her, and the two of them often listed three things they were grateful for over breakfast each morning, no matter how hard times were. She wondered what Jean-Rose was more grateful for—having two beautiful children, or having two servants, even "hourly" ones? Sadly, she guessed the answer was the latter.

Encouraging the kids to the house, she passed Ruth. "Can you cover me? I have to change Anna's clothes."

Pinching her cheeks for color, Ruth emerged from behind the bar, the corners of her eyes damp. "You can't tell I was crying, right?"

"No. You look great." She couldn't tell Ruth the rims of her eyes were still red.

Ruth arranged the drinks on the tray and was off while Heddy carried Anna up into her bedroom, Teddy running ahead up the stairs.

"Why was Ruth crying?" Anna asked. Heddy pulled her dress overhead and slipped a new striped frock on her.

"She wasn't."

Teddy dove onto Anna's bed. "Ruth has runs in her stockings."

Heddy eyed him. "Maybe she needs a new pair."

"Can't she afford any? I mean, we pay her enough." Heddy had noticed the run, too, a subtle pull up the back of her leg. He was just mimicking his mother, but still, she thought, that she'd raise children to have empathy for others.

Anna wrapped her arms around Heddy's neck while she straightened the hem of her dress. "The sooner we eat lunch, the faster we can get to the beach," Heddy said, eager to escape the luncheon herself.

"We can see if we trapped any lobsters." Teddy pushed his belly into Anna, knocking her over, and Anna pushed right back.

Outside, Heddy could see the guests were still milling about.

Heddy held a single finger in front of the boy's face. "I need better behavior or no beach. You understand?" She ran upstairs to swap her dress, too—the pee smelled acrid in the heat—immediately regretting snapping at Teddy. Someday he'd grow up and understand what kind of money he had, how that separated him from the other children and defined every last bit of him. But right now, he was a child, and she needed to be more patient.

She had the kids walk in single file onto the porch, where guests were taking seats at tables, husbands and wives placed more formally next to each other. Ash was in between Jean-Rose and her best friend, Susanne, who leaned into him, blowing smoke into the air and crinkling her nose, like she knew how adorable her pixie cut was. Heddy immediately hated her.

Jean-Rose stood to get everyone's attention, using her largest fork to make a chiming sound against her glass. "Ted and I would like to thank you for coming today," she told the crowd. She glanced at Ash. "As I've told many of you already, we met Ash at the beach."

Ash piped in. "I nearly beached a whaler I'd borrowed from a friend. That would have been an expensive ride home." Everyone laughed.

Then Ted: "Next time, take the surfboard." The crowd chuckled, Ash grinning.

Jean-Rose, hands clasped at her chest, waited for everyone to quiet. "After he ditched the boat and swam in, we realized we were neighbors. And what a neighbor! To imagine that the great-grandson of Florida's original developer is in our midst. Harrison Porter is responsible for Palm Beach, and now his great-grandson has a dream of his own."

Heddy saw a few couples whisper and point in the direction of Ash's house, even though they couldn't see it through the trees.

"Ash is working on a new luxury community in Florida that we're so excited about. So, without further ado, I present to you the man bringing surfing to the Vineyard, Ash Porter."

To light applause, Ash stood in front of a poster featuring photographs of a spectacular pool surrounded by palm trees and Corinthian columns, a woman lying on a beach blanket on powder-white sand, the water so clear people could see to the bottom. "Welcome to the Coconut Coast" read the caption.

He slid one of his hands in his pocket. "When the weather turns cold, Palm Beach is my paradise. My friends are there. My favorite restaurants are there. And when I swim in the water, there's nowhere else in the world I'd rather be." He moved to the other end of the porch, and everyone followed him with their eyes. He was a natural public speaker, unlike Heddy, who could agonize for weeks over giving any kind of presentation.

"I could look at him all day," an elfin woman with studious glasses whispered to a friend.

"Don't get any ideas—he's taken," the friend said back.

"No, he's a bachelor!"

"That's not what I heard."

Ash put his foot up on a chair, leaning toward the crowd.

"On the shores of West Florida, the sand is as powdery as the snow of Aspen. The water, as turquoise as this beautiful woman's bracelet." Ash was behind the woman with the glasses, and he gently asked her—"May I?"—and after a nod, he held up her arm to show everyone her turquoise-stone bracelet.

"I got this in Santa Fe," she told people at her table.

"The Coconut Coast is what Palm Beach was ten years ago, the next big resort town, the most spectacular development of our time. Your children will thank you for buying here, so will their children's children." There were murmurs, nods. Ash began handing out a stack of folders, each one decorated with the same photographs as the poster on the easel behind him.

"Here, houses aren't just houses. They're sprawling estates painted in a rainbow of pastels, each one surrounded by their own piece of the West Florida jungle, the smell of hibiscus drifting by as you sit next to the pool and wonder if it's snowing back in New England." Ash sipped his cocktail as everyone opened their folders, sifting through the color brochures inside.

"As kids, we spent some winters in the Berkshires, skiing a cold day away. But air travel has put paradise within everyone's reach. Why not jet off to the next big thing? A resort created with the distinguished young family in mind."

Heddy looked at the brochure's sprawling Mediterranean-style estates, a golf cart parked in front of each one. The woman in glasses raised her hand. "Can you tell us about the community? Palm Beach has theater, fine restaurants."

"If you're asking who bought in"—he smiled, with mischief—"well, let's just say we have six founding members: two work in film, one is a jazz singer, and the others are in finance."

A rush of excited murmurs, whispers about who the film stars were.

Ted's voice rang out over the hush of the crowd. "When will the houses be complete?"

Ash toasted his glass to Ted's. "We'll be toasting again when we open our community center at Christmas, 1964. We're on the hunt for people with refinement and taste who can help us build this area into a world-class community." Ash paused for emphasis, staring into the horizon, where storm clouds hovered. "Have you ever looked around a club or a resort and thought, *I could have done this better*? Why didn't they think to do this or that? This is your chance." His eyes were full of magic now. "Don't be a part of someone else's paradise. Build your own."

Ted tipped his chair back, his legs spread open, his feet anchored to the floor. "But why would I buy a house in the swampiest part of Florida? All the bugs. It's making me itch just thinking about it." Ted itched his forearms for comic relief; the crowd laughed.

Ash took in the faces around him, like he was charmed. "You're not going to let a few bugs scare you away, are you, Ted? All of Florida is swampland, but we clear-cut, plant palm trees, make sure there's no standing water. To keep away those pesky bugs." Ash turned to the other side of the porch. "Any other questions?"

Ted's voice broke the quiet again. "Let's talk dollars and cents. How much for one of these beauties?" Ted pointed to a large manor house, yellow stucco with white shutters.

Jean-Rose pressed her hands into a prayer. "What Ted's saying is: Should we or shouldn't we?"

Ash's face was unruffled. "I'm glad you asked. To get started, we need a significant contribution. But remember, it's the first step in building your dream house."

Ted, on his feet now, patted Ash's back, letting his voice carry out over the din. "So what is the buy-in? Specifically?"

Jean-Rose took in a sharp breath. "Ted, perhaps he wants to discuss it privately."

Ted put his arm around Ash's back, feigning innocence. "It's sales, darling. Everything has a price. So tell me, dapper fellow. What do you want for this piece of paradise?"

"Seven thousand dollars." Ash's voice was clear and unapologetic. "To reserve your land."

The crowd erupted into chatter. Ted, a smirk of satisfaction on his face, raised an eyebrow, looking around at the others at the table.

Jean-Rose clasped her hands together. "Well, I want in. That yellow house with the shutters—I can't shake it."

Everyone clapped, and Jean-Rose broke into a grin, holding her clasped hands at her heart.

"A quick reminder: Everyone save the date for our annual clambake on August eleventh. Now let's all thank Ash Porter for dropping by today."

Heddy looked at Ash then, taking a bow. When he came up, his eyes scanned the crowd, and when he locked on Heddy, he smiled—a dashing smile.

She felt the earth under her shift.

Later that evening, Jean-Rose and Ted hardly noticed when Heddy slipped down the emerald-green stair runner to meet Ruth outside for a smoke. With the stink of a cigar wafting through the house, Ted watched Walter Cronkite, while Jean-Rose chatted away on the telephone. After worrying all afternoon that Jean-Rose would fire her for messing up at the party, her boss had been in good spirits when she and the children returned from the beach.

"I can't exactly let her go," Jean-Rose gossiped into the receiver. "From what I gather, her mother doesn't have much time, and her father is always laying into somebody at Rooney's. It's a mess."

Ruth sat on a small boulder by the garage, and Heddy could hear Jean-Rose's voice there, too, but Ruth was unfazed.

"They finally asleep?" Ruth picked a bouquet of hydrangea and held them in a wet paper towel.

"They were exhausted from swimming all afternoon."

The two women walked together down the driveway. At the end, Ruth crouched her spindly legs onto the grass near the mailboxes— she had the look of a person who was ill as a child, whose body never quite caught up.

"I thought this day would never end," Ruth said, lighting a cigarette.

"Do you think these people ever see themselves through our eyes?" Heddy took a long drag, grateful for the buzz. Her hair was wet from her shower, her skin smelling of Ivory soap. "If only they could hear themselves, a recording played back on the radio. 'They're hourly girls, right?'" She mimicked the woman from the luncheon.

"Someone said that?" Ruth ashed in between her knees. "Jean-Rose was going to kill you! Her eyes were so narrow, they nearly touched."

"You were the one that had to be fetched."

Ruth looked down, exhaled. "I know." Heddy remembered Ruth's mother sleeping in the chair, the crooked screen door, the beer bottles on the stoop.

"Weren't you worried she'd fire you on the spot?"

Ruth shook her head. "We have an understanding."

That Ruth and Jean-Rose knew anything about each other beyond their formal relationship at the house made Heddy uneasy. "I wasn't aware you were such good friends."

Ruth took another drag of her cigarette. "Friends? I'm her charity case. Do you know she sent me to the bank to make a deposit yesterday? I looked at her balance: $107,000."

"One hundred thousand dollars!" Heddy had yelled it. It was enough to buy a mansion, a couple of cars, too.

Ruth nodded. "One hundred and seven. It wasn't even a joint account."

Heddy didn't know what she'd do if she had that kind of money.

Perhaps she'd buy a steamer trunk, board one of those fancy ships that left out of New York Harbor. No, she'd buy her mother a house in one of those pretty Westchester suburbs. After she paid for school, that is.

"Ruth, are you in a bad way?"

The girl darted her eyes. She knew what Heddy was asking. "I'm fine."

Heddy reached her hand out to rub Ruth's back, pulling it away before it touched. "It's just. Well, you were so upset today."

Ruth laughed. "Don't worry. It's stupid."

Heddy exhaled, trying to blow smoke rings, her tongue getting in the way and making a mess of them. They smoked in silence, night overtaking the clouds.

"You realize Jean-Rose needs you more than you need her," Heddy said.

"Well, I need that envelope of cash every week, but this isn't about her anyway." Ruth loosened her bun, letting her hair fall around her shoulders. It softened her long nose, making her pretty. "To think, I was all set to go to cosmetology school." Ruth stubbed out her cigarette. "Did I tell you I was going to be a stylist?"

"That's amazing, Ruth." Heddy pressed her heel to her cigarette. A firefly flickered.

"Well, it's not happening now." Ruth sighed. "I just wonder how different my life would be if I hadn't been born on this island."

"Less simple, I suppose. The city is harried." Heddy was drawing in the gravel with a twig.

Ruth hunched, her back curving into a C. "That's what people think, sure. They come here, and they see a wonderland. You know what I see when I look at all this water? A fence, one tall fence. Everyone gets to leave. You'll leave. But I'm not sure I ever will."

Heddy stopped drawing. She didn't realize this was the conversation they were going to have.

"I could give up, too, Ruth. But I know what I need to do, and I do it."

"Easy for you to say, college girl. You'll have a degree."

Heddy shifted positions, moving onto her knees. How could she explain? Where would she begin? "There's a letter—"

Ruth cut her off. "He just makes it so hard." She leaned back against the mailbox post. "He takes all of it. . . ."

Heddy put her arm around her friend, squeezing her. "You'll make more."

"But not enough," she said, resting her head on Heddy's shoulder. "There will never be enough."

"Sleep over tonight, will you? You can stay in my room." *Don't go home to that sad place*, Heddy wanted to say.

Ruth shook her head. "I can't. Mother."

"Please, Ruth. I won't sleep tonight knowing you're upset." She sensed a nod, and while Ruth didn't say yes, they both knew one night wouldn't hurt anyone.

"C'mon," Heddy begged. "It will be like when we were little and had sleepover parties."

"You're a goofball." But Ruth was smiling, and Heddy knew she'd done good.

That night, after they practiced applying blue eye shadow to each other's lids, Heddy and Ruth climbed into bed, Ruth falling asleep while Heddy wrote in her journal.

June 30, 1962

Jean-Rose told me today that someday my social cache will be built upon how few wrinkles I have on my face. She gave me a bar of Pears glycerin soap to wash my face with, prescribed ice-water plunges to keep my skin firm, and handed me a jar of Pond's Cold Cream to apply before bed each night. She's even gone and set me up on a date, although I'm terrified that I won't like the guy but I'll have to pretend to, just to please her.

I am under pressure to please her always, or I get the sense that she'll turn on me. It sounds harsh, but I know it's true. While Jean-Rose is exceedingly friendly and quite likable, she's also studied. She's extra aware of what her words and behaviors reveal about her, and she acts as though shaping the family's public face is of highest priority. Even if she's friendly, I must remind myself that we are not friends. . . .

Closing her journal after midnight, Heddy went downstairs to warm some milk since she was having trouble sleeping. Ted sat at the kitchen table hunched over a sheet of notepaper and holding a pen, several crumpled papers gathering like snowballs at his elbow. She saw he was wearing a ribbed tank top and chambray boxer shorts, which meant she was standing there with Ted in his underwear.

"Sorry, I thought I was the only one awake," she whispered, wrapping her robe tighter, wishing now she'd never come down.

He jumped at the sound of her voice, grabbing at the papers, even the ones he'd balled up. With an irritated grunt, he disappeared into the darkness of the living room. A light in his study went on, and the door clicked shut.

She didn't bother heating the milk, and as she trudged up the stairs to her room, she wondered: *What kind of letter needed to be written in the dead of night?*

FIVE

The following Monday camp started, and Heddy went for a long swim after dropping the children off, pushing her body to the limit. After a leisurely shower, she holed up in the quiet of the attic and read. She and Ruth ate egg salad for lunch, gossiping at the kitchen table about the latest developments in *As the World Turns*, and at 2:00 p.m., she fetched the children. Jean-Rose had given her full use of their extra car, the Buick, but after pickup, they decided to ride bikes.

It was after three when the trio parked under a towering syca-more tree at the park across from town hall. Heddy spread the woven camp blanket she'd packed in her basket and unscrewed the red cap of the tartan thermos, turning it over to use as a cup and pouring water for the children to sip.

"I should have flipped that kid the bird." Teddy scratched at a scabbed mosquito bite on his knee. It started to bleed, causing Anna to examine a scrape on her elbow.

"One day you're going to get clocked in the face, you know that?" Heddy used a corner of her handkerchief to dab his knee. "Your dad isn't going to tell you that, but I will. You gotta stop making kids mad, or they're going to beat on you."

Teddy pushed her hand away. "No one will hurt a six-year-old."

"I've seen five-year-olds with black eyes." Heddy stuffed the hankie in her pocket. She was exaggerating but maybe it would keep him from holding up his middle finger to random kids zooming past him on their bikes. In the distance, Heddy saw a man walking with his dog across the field. She couldn't believe the animal wasn't on a leash, roaming wherever it wanted, lifting its leg. "I've seen little boys left in a heap, bruises and broken arms."

Teddy fell dramatically backward on the blanket, arranging his Yankees hat so it covered his face. "I'm so bored. When will Daddy take me camping? He and Mr. Mule go."

"Ask him. The only way to get what you want is to try." Heddy braided Anna's hair to get it out of her face, the girl seeming to relish the feeling. The man with the dog was coming down the hill now, and she wondered if she should worry about the children getting too close to the animal.

Teddy stomped his sandaled feet on the blanket. He had moods like this, where he'd swing into sadness or anger. "Mama *did* ask him; I heard her. But he told her that was his time. She had her time, and he had his." His arms outstretched, the boy grabbed at grass clumps with his fingers, sprinkling them on his chest.

Her heart ached. How did you explain to a child that parents could disappoint you? That parents had secrets? Her mother always wore a modest pearl engagement ring, telling Heddy that her father had given it to her. As the story went, they'd conceived before he left for the war, and he'd died overseas. To think Heddy believed that story until she was fourteen and found a stack of letters in her mother's closet from her father, love letters that became goodbye letters, the last one curt, typed on an otherwise blank sheet of paper: *DO NOT CONTACT ME AGAIN.*

Discovering her mother's dishonesty had soured her and her mother's relationship. Every disagreement they got in after that—and there were many in her teenage years—led back to the betrayal she felt when she discovered the truth about her father. *He was alive! Living on Long Island!* Her life suddenly felt like a laughable plot twist on *As the World Turns*. But when Heddy's grandmother died of lung cancer, which they blamed on her affinity for Lucky Strikes, she'd written Heddy a short letter: *Forgive your mother. She only wanted to protect you. That's what mothers do. Use your energy to discover something wonderful.*

It succeeded in setting Heddy's mind straight, and she stopped asking her mother about her father. Well, until a month ago, when she decided to contact him.

Heddy laid down next to Teddy, so her arm touched his shoulder. "I have an idea. Let's go camping. Me, you, and Anna. Wouldn't that be grand?"

He turned on his side, popped up on his elbow. "But where?" One-on-one attention could always break the boy's foul mood.

"The backyard. Then we can always go inside if we get cold or need to do our business." Heddy chortled at her own idea, sitting up, noting the dog was fetching a stick nearby. Teddy was on his knees now, forgetting about the bleeding, while Anna, lost in her imagination, bundled dandelions.

"And we can make a campfire," he said.

Heddy touched her finger to his nose. "A blazing one."

Now that she had his attention, she packed the picnic blanket and thermos into her bike basket, pulling out the simple diamond-shaped Hi-Flier kite she'd found in the garage, looking for the dog to make sure it wasn't edging closer. She dusted off the kite, walking a few paces away from the children. "Watch me, then you can try." Heddy took off running in the grass, tossing the kite to catch the wind, which was blowing through the treetops. Anna chased after her, while Teddy watched from afar. But Heddy couldn't get the kite far enough off the ground to fly. Every time she tossed it, it plunged straight down.

"I'll get it," Anna said, a dandelion tucked behind her ear. But just as she picked it up, the dog galloped straight toward her, all one hundred pounds of his tan, fluffy body barreling at the child. Heddy turned to hunt for its owner, who was approaching with a tennis ball, a bit too leisurely for Heddy's taste, so she put her arm around Anna's back. The man looked about her age, and judging from his faded rumpled tomato-red T-shirt, a small bleach stain on the neckline, he'd just rolled out of bed.

"Barkley, come," he yelled. "You don't have to worry. He's friendly."

Biting down playfully, the dog pulled at the kite, pushing it deeper into his jaws before running off with it, his tail wagging. Heddy let go of the kite's yellow spindle, afraid the thread might snap if she held on to it.

"Barkley, drop it!"

The dog took off in the other direction, and the children began screaming, like they were watching a horror film, crowding behind Heddy's legs.

"Barkley!"

The dog stopped, dropping the kite at his paws, cocking his head to the side and panting at his owner. The man ran his hand along his closely shaved crop of hair, striding toward the golden retriever.

He held up his hand. "Stay, Barkley. Staaaay."

Heddy rolled her eyes. Of course the dog wouldn't heel, the man's voice was hardly authoritative, coming out like a suggestion. When the stranger was a few steps away, the dog grabbed the kite with his mouth and bolted again.

She'd seen the man before, but where? She wracked her brain, considering the boys she'd met at school, but no one had those tortoise-rimmed glasses, not that she could remember.

"Tell them he's just playing," he said.

"Maybe if you kept your dog on a leash I wouldn't have to tell them anything." Who walked a dog without leashing it? The dog pranced by the man—a college boy, she decided, spying his boat shoes—but when he dove at him, Barkley ran in a circle. Then, taking a different tact, the stranger sat cross-legged in the grass, placing the tennis ball at his feet. The dog ran right over, dropping the kite and lapping his wet, pink tongue around the fuzzy ball.

"Good boy." The man attached the leash to the dog's black collar, decorated with musical notes.

"Sorry about that." He looked over the kite, which was dripping with saliva, and smiled. "Should still work—no tears." He handed it to Heddy, forcing her to wipe a long glop of saliva against her pocket.

"Lovely." She knew the sarcasm was snotty, but she didn't care. The man wasn't holding the dog tight—and he licked Anna's cheek, a whiff of rancid breath in her face, which sent Anna clawing at Heddy's legs. "You need to leave now," Heddy said.

"This is a public park." The man yanked the dog backward, awkwardly spitting his words. "And he's just a dog."

"Well, then we'll leave." The wind lifted her bangs off her face as the kids followed her to the other side of the field, where dense swaths of beach reeds lined the space. Heddy threw up the kite and ran into the wide-open lawn, but it plummeted. She tried again at the top of the hill, hoping if she ran down, she'd get it in the air. It fluttered in a wind gust for a few seconds, then dove back into the grass. Her heart thudded.

"That dumb dog ruined everything," said Teddy, barefoot and sulking. He was the quitting type; Heddy was always trying to keep him interested, keep him focused.

"We barely tried. Have some patience, Teddy."

"Let's play tag instead." Anna took off running toward the pond.

There was a tall sycamore tree near the park's ornate wrought iron entrance, and she noticed the man tied his dog there and was coming toward them. *What now?* When he was close, he pointed to the kite, saying rather nicely, almost like he was apologizing, "You may have more luck if you have the kid hold it."

Now that he wasn't acting annoying, he looked handsome but not too handsome, tall but not too tall, his features angular and strong but not overpowering.

"I'm sorry?"

He picked up the kite, holding it with two hands up to the sky. "It's just, if the wind is behind the kite, it can't push it up."

"What are you, the kite police?"

What made him attractive, she thought, was how inconspicuous he was—that nothing on his face stood out, well, except perhaps, the laugh lines at the corners of his eyes and that mellow smile he'd just plastered on his face.

The man pushed his round tortoiseshell glasses up on his nose. "I have an idea." He looked down at the grass as he walked, and she followed, since he was the only one offering any help. "Okay, now let out your line, a real lot, and walk backward." She unraveled the wiry string, the kids watching the scene with interest. "I'm going to hold it up. You're gonna run when I say go," he said, taking a baseball cap out of his back pocket and putting it on.

She recognized him then. He was the man at the ferry in the "H" sweater. A bachelor. The bachelor everyone was angling for.

He was staring at the smooth length of line, and when it started to pull slightly from the force of the wind, he sputtered: "*Go!*" Heddy took off running, tugging at the spindle as the kite pulled away from her. The line went slack, and once again, she felt the thud of the kite against the ground. She sighed.

He scratched at his head. "You have to, well, you have to hold the spindle up as you run." He pulled up the neck of his tomato-red

T-shirt and wiped at his mouth. He was sweating, his cheeks an exasperated crimson. He seemed different from the guy throwing the football on the ferry dock. Around his friends, he'd been bolstered with self-assurance and seemed like he could talk to anyone, but here in this empty field, he didn't seem very confident at all.

"Can you two please make yourself useful?"

Teddy's hands were on his hips and he was shaking his head in disbelief, something his mother did all the time.

The man gave Teddy a double take. "Don't be like that, kid."

Anna had given up watching and was rolling down the hill on her back.

"Then get the kite in the air," Teddy demanded.

The man looked at Heddy with something close to pity, at least that's how it felt, or maybe it was just her realizing she would have to take the abuse of this snot-nosed kid for the rest of the summer.

"Try one more time," the man blurted at her. "But hold the spindle higher." She took off running again, right on cue, her hair coming loose from her ponytail. The line seemed to unravel from the spindle, and the wind tugged at it, carrying the kite up into the sky with a whoosh. She watched it climb over them, unraveling the taut thread in whatever direction the kite pulled, airborne and sailing with the wind.

"You actually got it up, mister." Teddy ran under the kite, chasing its nimble twists and turns, and Anna jumped up.

"Higher, higher," Anna called.

Heddy grinned, thankful the man helped rescue them from disappointment. "Thanks. I couldn't have done it without you."

He mumbled something—she assumed "you're welcome"—as he continued to watch the kite dance in the cloudless blue sky.

"I'm Heddy." She stepped closer, careful to keep the kite steady in one hand as she outstretched the other.

"Sullivan." He shook her hand quickly, then pushed his hands in his pockets. "It should stay up now."

"I didn't think it would be so hard to fly."

"You always take this much abuse from Team Williams?" His five o'clock shadow gave him the look of a man on holiday.

"Some days are better than others," she laughed. "So you know them? Teddy, come take a turn." She carefully handed him the spool, and the child smirked with satisfaction, feeling like a big boy.

"The kid. He doesn't mean to be so rude." Sullivan stared at Teddy, the way a parent did when they saw themselves in a child.

Heddy raised an eyebrow. "And how would you know?"

He blushed. "Just remember that at some point he'll be a grown man embarrassed by all the things he said to his babysitters over the years. Like I am." Sullivan averted his eyes, like the sight of her might set off something unexpected. He hadn't looked at her on the ferry that day, either, at least not directly.

"I'm sure you weren't that bad. So, what, are you on the kite team at school or something?" She knew it was ridiculous, and still, she'd said it.

"Nah, I like to play with gravity." He pushed his glasses up higher on the bridge of his nose and shrugged. "Physics major."

Well, that explains it, she thought. The guys in her science classes in high school were just like him: slight and jittery, terrible at making conversation, their pocketed plaid shirts and glasses a reminder of how much time they spent thinking about theorems and experiments Heddy didn't care to understand. She wondered about those boys sometimes, how they'd look if they took off their glasses, stopped looking so square.

"Is babysitting your intended career?" he asked.

"Gosh, no. Lit major."

"Lit, huh? Well, you have a nice way with them." He rubbed his palms together, perhaps a nervous tic, and when their eyes met, she smiled at him, and he finally smiled back before looking away.

"Well, thank goodness for physics," she said. "These two were ready to ditch me."

The dog tangled himself in the sycamore and barked. Behind him, a white pickup pulled up to the post office across the field, a surfboard popping out over the tailgate. Even from there, Heddy could see Ash Porter open his door, and since she had on the Dior sunglasses Jean-Rose had lent her, she didn't have to hide her glances at Ash. He was standing next to his truck in loose white shorts, a collared short-sleeve shirt with a thick vertical black stripe on either side of the buttons, a straw fedora on his head. He was sifting through a few letters.

"You don't want to date a guy like him." Sullivan rubbed the palm of his hand with the other.

Heddy thought it curious he even noticed the truck. She cleared her throat. This guy had something to say about everything. "What do you know of him?"

"I told you already: a fool's paradise," he said. So he remembered her, too. But when she glanced at him, to confirm he was toying with her, his expression turned up blank.

There was someone else in Ash Porter's passenger seat. She had squinted to see who, but the blonde sat low in the seat. The truck zoomed away, leaving Heddy standing there, sucker punched. Of course Ash had a girlfriend. He probably had several.

The dog barked again, louder this time, pulling on his leash in the direction of the kite. "Heddy, I can't keep the kite up!" Teddy yelled, as it plunged down.

She went to him, placing the kite back in Teddy's hands, but labored to remember how to get it back in the air. "Sullivan, wait. How do I know where the wind is?"

Sullivan, who had started toward his dog, turned, seeming to like that she was asking. "Watch the line. It will jiggle. Hey, there's a carnival on Friday. Maybe I'll see you there."

"I'll be sure to say hello," she said. He shaded his eyes from the sun, like he was debating saying something else, but then he turned and continued to his dog, still barking from the tree.

* * *

Ted grilled flounder over charcoal that evening, and for the first time since she arrived, they ate dinner on the porch all together, the picnic table covered with a white linen tablecloth. Crickets chirped a chorus from the bushes, while citronella candles burned their unmistakable scent. The dinner started with small talk, but the children wouldn't stay in their seats, particularly Teddy, and both parents grew so aggravated that they yelled more than talked.

"*Anna!*" Jean-Rose got up from the table, grabbing the child's hand away from her ketchup. She had painted her white sundress with red circles. "Heddy, do something about this. Oh, Anna."

Heddy's fork clattered when she dropped it on her plate, and she wiped clean the child's fingers with a cloth napkin. Ted took a swig of his beer, slamming it on the table, which made her jump. His jaw was tense with anger, and she thought of her priest, how when he was particularly rapt, his veins bulged with fury.

"Eww, you're bleeding," Teddy chanted. Then Anna threatened to wipe a ketchup-soaked finger on Teddy, and someone spilled milk, Heddy couldn't remember who, and it soaked Ted's lap, making him push backward out of his seat.

"God dammit." He wiped away a sheet of milk with his hand.

Jean-Rose put her hand over his. "Ted, they're children." But her voice was abrupt, and the outburst was unexpected, like a balloon pop. Heddy saw fear in Jean-Rose's narrowed eyes.

"Jesus Christ, Jeannie. You need to see to it that they behave." He threw his napkin and it landed at his feet, a man-child having his own kind of fit. "If you weren't too busy playing tennis to teach them some manners—"

"If you could teach your son how to be a man." Jean-Rose dabbed at her mouth.

Heddy watched Ted's eyes bulge, like a squeeze toy. He gripped his hands behind his back, holding his wrist so tight he must be hurting himself. Heddy wondered why he wouldn't let his hand go, what he might do. She went back through the conversation looking for clues to explain his anger, but there were none. Perhaps something was going on at work.

Heddy wiped up the milk, while Ruth cleared the table of dishes. The air was charged, the way it got when an accusation was lobbed and no one knew where it would land next. The children hid under the table, Anna plugging her ears and humming.

"You're paranoid." Ted stormed into the house, Jean-Rose downing her gin and tonic. She stood and swayed, Ruth grabbing an elbow to steady her.

"Put them straight in the bath," Jean-Rose's mascara was going runny in the corners of her eyes, "but not together. Teddy is too old for that."

"I don't want her to give me a bath." Teddy crawled out from the tablecloth, stepping into a cloud of smoke from his mother's newly lit cigarette. Anna hummed louder.

"Nonsense." Jean-Rose pushed his back toward the door. Harder than Heddy would have liked.

"I won't do it."

"Teddy, not now. Go upstairs." The boy inched closer to his mother, like he wanted her to cradle him—Heddy knew, even big kids needed hugging—but Jean-Rose shooed him off.

Anna ran inside like she was running from a monster, darting up the stairs past her father, who was coming down in fresh white slacks. Heddy felt like she was witnessing something private, something that should be playing out behind closed doors. No one had raised a voice since she'd arrived, and now the landscape seemed to shift all at once, and she thought maybe that's what happened in a marriage. A couple could be happy sometimes, and miserable others, but something greater kept them together, although she'd yet to figure out what.

Outside, Ted's voice was muffled: "I'm going out."

Heddy's step quickened up the stairs when she heard a glass shatter against something, the side of the house, the car, she wasn't sure. She rushed the kids into the bathroom and turned on the tub faucet, thankful for its thunderous rush of water; it was what she did back in Brooklyn when her mother and grandmother fought about money. But when she turned, neither child was with her.

"Teddy, come in here," she called to the boy from Anna's room. Heddy checked under the bed for them, finally finding Anna sitting in a laundry basket in her dark closet. "What are you doing?" She lifted the child out, rubbing her small back.

Teddy appeared in the room. "She always hides in her closet when they fight."

Heddy lowered the girl into the clawfoot tub, kneeling at its side. "You don't have to do that. I'm here with you."

Teddy was twirling his finger through the yellow curls of that ragged doll he slept with. "One night, she fell asleep in there, and we didn't find her until the next morning. Mama was frantic."

Anna giggled at the memory, but Heddy wiped at her eyes before massaging shampoo into her hair. "Your mom and dad love you the most of anyone in the world. You know that, right?"

He snorted, then inhaled into the doll's ragged plaid dress; it was curious to see a boy so devoted to a doll.

"Is Mommy going to be okay?" Anna sucked her finger, and Heddy plucked it out.

"That's a dumb question," Teddy snapped.

"No, it's not, Teddy. Listen, all parents have disagreements some-times, but they still love each other." Disagreements, yes, but angry brawls and broken glass—even she wasn't so sure.

"Do your parents love each other?" Anna asked. She was genu-inely curious, and for that, Heddy was touched.

"I don't have . . . Well, you see, I . . ." Heddy sighed, wiping her eyes. A white lie was worth telling in this case. "Yes, they do. My parents still love each other." She'd never uttered the words before—"my parents"—and doing so now made her heart ache for Jean-Rose and Ted. A marriage had secrets, sometimes dark ones, just like she and her mother had secrets. And those secrets, happy or unhappy, could bubble up and make a mess out of things.

Later, once the children were tucked into bed and she had changed into her nightgown, Heddy heard a racket downstairs. She checked the driveway to see if Ted had returned, but the driveway was empty, the only movement a tire swing gently swaying in the breeze. She tiptoed down to the kitchen, uncertain of what she'd find. Even so, she'd startled at the sight of Jean-Rose sitting with Ruth at the Formica table; the older woman slumped over, her cheek pressed against the tabletop, snoring. An empty highball glass at her shoulder.

"I was trying to help her upstairs, and we fell." Ruth was wearing her maid's dress, but she'd taken off her apron, laying it across the back of the chair. Heddy smelled the vomit before she saw it. "She's not a drinker."

"Have you been with her this whole time?" Heddy asked.

"She was watching *The Ed Sullivan Show*. I figured I'd read in here until it got ugly." One of Jean-Rose's *Life* magazines was on the table, the one with Jackie Kennedy in a pillbox hat on the cover. Ruth must have pulled it from the stack on the bookshelf in the living room, where there were dozens of the red-spine readers.

"We can't leave her here." Heddy slid into the seat across from Ruth.

"If we prop her up, we might be able to help her onto the couch." Heddy softly shook her boss's shoulder. "Jean-Rose?"

Drool dripped from her mouth. Ruth wedged her slim shoulder under Jean-Rose's armpit, and Heddy followed suit. "On the count of three: one, two, three." The two strained to lift their boss up, and the push made Jean-Rose's head bob awake. A sweet smile drew across her lips.

"Heddy?"

She could smell the booze on her breath. "Jean-Rose, we're going to get you upstairs." Heddy buckled under the weight of her boss; Jean-Rose was slight, but so was Heddy, and she found herself growing breathless.

"Such lovely girls. Good girls, but don't let him see you weak. No, no."

"Do you think you can walk up the stairs?" Ruth's voice was slow, like she was talking to someone whose first language wasn't English.

"Of course, I can—" Jean-Rose let go of them, marching like a soldier, but she stumbled forward. She made it into the living room and crawled onto the couch like a cat, her long, filmy nightdress falling to the floor.

"This will do." Ruth grabbed a throw off the wingback chair and spread it over Jean-Rose.

Their boss's eyes fluttered open. "I'm going to find you nice boys. Very nice boys like my Nelson. And handsome!"

Ruth caught Heddy's eye at the name, a brow raised. Heddy ran for a tissue, cleaning up her boss's runny eye makeup, and rubbed Jean-Rose's back until she began to softly snore. She and Ruth returned to the kitchen, cleaning up and then pulling out a package of strawberry wafer cookies.

Heddy whispered: "They seemed so . . . without problems compared to the people back home."

"Guess it depends on how you define problems." Freckles ran across Ruth's nose like an open fan. She poured Heddy a tumbler of something. "Here, this will cheer you up."

"Do you think it's okay?" But Heddy gulped it back without waiting for the answer, repelled instantly by the flavor, stinging where it mixed with the sugary wafer on her tongue. Gin?

Ruth chuckled. "First rule of service: don't get mixed up in their life."

"How can we help it? I live here, and you practically do, too."

Ruth looked in on Jean-Rose, then came back. "I feel sorry for her," she whispered.

Strange, Heddy thought, to pity a wealthy steel magnate's wife. "Where does he go? You know, when he leaves."

Ruth took another sip, then rinsed the glass in the sink. "Somewhere he's not supposed to." She gathered her tote bag, flinging it over her shoulder. There was a sloshing in the bag, the sound of liquid splashing up against glass, and as the bag settled against Ruth's slight frame, some of what was inside pushed out of the top. Heddy recognized a box of Frosted Flakes, a short-necked bottle of rust-colored liquor. She could make out the shapes of something else, too: bananas, perhaps? Ruth sensed Heddy staring, so she shifted. The box, and the liquor, slipped down into the bag.

Ruth looked at her guilty but defiant. "They have so much," Ruth continued to the door.

Heddy popped the last of the strawberry wafers into her mouth. She was a bit surprised by how brazen the girl was. Heddy felt funny helping herself to food in their fridge, and she slept there. Still, it wasn't like Ruth was taking diamond earrings.

Heddy pretended to zip her lips. "I didn't see a thing."

Ruth visibly relaxed. "It's going to be a busy week, but our date is this Friday. I'll pick you up at six forty-five."

"I'm nervous. I've never been on a blind date."

Ruth smiled. "It will be great."

"Tell me what you know about him." Heddy followed Ruth out into the humid night, fireflies illuminating the rose bushes.

"Stop worrying and let yourself be surprised." Ruth walked one of the extra bikes out of the garage. The bike chain caught with a pop and a click, the squeak of a seat and the spin of the pedals as Ruth pushed through the pebbly drive. Heddy leaned into the screen door and watched wet air blowing in from the ocean as Ruth took off pedaling into the night.

{ SIX }

$\mathcal{N}$o one could say Gigi McCabe didn't have curves. Her hour-glass figure oozed so much sex appeal she stoked fires in men's hearts in just a pair of black pedal pushers and a white blouse, though, now that Heddy thought about it, the blouse did always seem unbuttoned a twee too far.

It wasn't just her cleavage that got people's attention, though, Heddy could see that now. Stretched out on a lounger beside Gigi's crystalline limestone pool, the children splashing in the shallow end, she realized Gigi was what her mother would have called a "substantial woman." Her legs were longer than Heddy's, and she had meaty shoulders with smooth rounded edges, yet a tummy so flat you could set a plate on it. Even her arms looked strong, and Heddy imagined Gigi sword fighting in an epic film set in ancient Rome.

Earlier, when Gigi answered the front door, Heddy had been starstruck all over again. Seeing a movie star in real life was surreal—the actress looked funny to Heddy, like a puppet talking, rather than a real-life person. Gigi was holding her purse and keys, clearly she'd altogether forgotten their meeting. Heddy couldn't stop apologizing and delivered an awkward hug, and then, if she remembered correctly, and she had to admit details were a bit fuzzy due to her dizzying state, Gigi had smacked her on the back. Smacked her hard, too.

"I'm just a hot-blooded woman, sugar pie. Now calm yourself, and come in." They'd gone straight out to the pool, where Gigi told them to wait while she changed. When she came out, her housekeeper followed holding a gold-trimmed telephone and dragging a long snaking cord, so Gigi could make a phone call. "I just need to rearrange some things," she'd said.

Now, as Heddy sipped the citrusy cocktail Gigi handed her, she thought it silly she'd been intimidated at all. Gigi was down-to-earth and easy to talk to—not at all what she expected.

The smell of coconut oil hung in the air, since Gigi had spent ten minutes lathering herself with it. "I'll tell you whatever you want to know about her. I know you're curious. Shoot."

Heddy didn't want to gossip about her boss. That morning, Jean-Rose didn't come out of her room for breakfast, while Ted, well, she wasn't sure he'd ever come home. She had questions about Jean-Rose's marriage, but she couldn't ask Gigi those. "I don't know. Was she popular?"

"Of course. All the mean ones are."

Gigi slapped Heddy on the leg with a tabloid magazine. "Don't be shy. Jean-Rose and I went to the same Catholic school in Darien. I was happy if my mother rifled around in the fridge each morning to scrape me together a lunch sack. Ms. Perfect? She has no idea what it means to make a dollar."

Heddy stared at Gigi's toes, painted fire-engine red. She was more curious about the actress, but it seemed Gigi wanted to talk about Jean-Rose. "What was Jean-Rose like back then?"

"The same as now. Self-absorbed, and oh, her family wasn't used to having money when we were little, and then they came into some, so they liked to flaunt it. New money. Of course, I didn't know that back then. I only knew my best friend was suddenly too good for me. You know Susanne, her friend here—the one who thinks she's the mayor of Martha's Vineyard. They've spent their whole life trying to keep up with each other."

Heddy knew Susanne. She'd sat next to Ash at the luncheon. She was tall, angular, a long, patrician nose. She and Jean-Rose had been gossiping about Gigi the day before on the phone. "Posing like that got her the most coveted roles in Hollywood," Jean-Rose had said, then wickedly, "I'm sorry, but I can't pretend I don't know."

Heddy smelled the salt air blowing in from the sea, nodding. "I think they're in the same bridge group."

"Bridge. Ha! As if I would go spend an afternoon playing bridge with those women. It's like they want to be as boring as their mothers."

"Have you ever played?"

"I don't play anyone's games, especially hers. She's the kind of person who will come see your first show on Broadway, only to be so jealous she leaves at intermission because, and this is a good one, she 'tripped on ice on the way there and bruised her elbow.'" Gigi hissed. "It's utter nonsense. She's never been able to handle anyone being better at anything."

"Maybe there is a story here," Heddy joked, clawing to sound natural in Gigi's orbit.

"Oh, there's a story here." Gigi closed her eyes to the sun. "Anyway, it must have been hard on her, too, since my career took off. What can I say? They opened doors for me." Gigi pointed to the oversize bosom stuffed into a black bikini top, so snug Heddy worried the closure might give. She didn't mention what Heddy already knew: every inch of Gigi's form had been featured in a *Playboy* a few summers before. Rumor had it that the "unauthorized" sale of the photos bought the actress's Vineyard home.

The kids played Marco Polo in the pool, neither one begging Heddy to come in. A miracle.

"It must be fun to have people want to photograph you all the time."

Gigi smiled. "Well, sometimes you just want to run to the store in slippers."

"Did you grow up coming here as a child?"

"Not really—it's a long story," Gigi said. Ted and Jean-Rose had purchased Elysian Fields as newlyweds from one of the Rockefellers. (Heddy had looked up the name—it meant "final resting place of the souls of those who are virtuous.") When Gigi built her estate a few years later in the off-season so as not to disrupt everyone's summer on the island, she had no idea they owned the house next door. One day Gigi got a call from her builder—she was on the set of *Egyptian Affair* at a studio in Los Angeles—that one of her neighbors had a problem with them paving the driveway. Someone named Jean-Rose Williams was complaining. He listed off the woman's phone number in New York.

"Imagine the surprise when she picked up and heard my voice— it was quite the conversation." Gigi sipped her Tom Collins, then put down the glass and lit a cigarette, blowing rings into the cloudless sky. "Of course, she acted thrilled to hear from me. But that's not why she bugs me. It's because Jean-Rose is like every other useless woman on this island. She spends someone else's money for a living."

Gigi ashed, then handed Heddy the bottle of coconut oil. "Would you mind rubbing some on my back? I need to flip." Heddy massaged the slick lotion onto the movie star's curvy back, and when she was done, Gigi squeezed a drop into Heddy's hand.

"I don't know—I burn," Heddy said.

"Sugar pie, this is the only thing that will give you a little color."

Heddy's shoulders were already pink, but there was glamour in Gigi's glossy skin, so she rubbed it on her too-skinny arms, her willowy thighs. She stretched her shiny legs out, pointing her unpainted toes and crossing her ankles seductively.

"What's your story, anyway?" Gigi asked.

"I'm afraid I don't have much of a story, Ms. McCabe." Heddy pulled her knees to her chest, keeping her eyes on the children. Anna was in a pink tube kicking her legs, Teddy diving under.

Gigi pushed herself up onto her elbows, her sunglasses falling down her nose. "Everyone has a story. That's why I asked you here. Something's up with you."

Heddy touched her grandmother's pearls. "Is it that obvious?"

Gigi cackled, pointing to a script on the table. "I'm studying for a role. Girl-meets-boy kind of thing. They date in London, get married, and when they get home to New York, it's clear she grew up, well, without the finer things. But she's sassy and smart. My kind of character."

The script lay on the table. *An Afternoon in Central Park*. Heddy wondered who else had held those pages. Had Cary Grant thumbed through the script? "Who is costarring?"

"Marlon Brando. You've heard of him, right?" A sly look passed over Gigi's face. "But you. I saw the safety pin in your sandal. Takes a certain kind of girl to walk around with a safety pin holding her shoe together."

"An industrious one." Heddy glanced at the ballet flats she'd worn that morning, the ones Jean-Rose left her a few days ago, along with a blue halter bathing suit, smooth and stretchy Lycra like all the new bathing costumes were.

Gigi's eyes crinkled. "For those who must be."

Heddy reached for the floppy woven sunhat she'd brought, positioning it squarely on her head to block Gigi's view of her face. She wanted to die. The actress had seen her for what she was: a bunny trying to run with the foxes. Gigi's invitation today had been inspired by pity. All because of her shoe. Imagine if she knew the real details of her life? That Heddy's mother had fallen for a man in a suit and fedora who would call her for a walk in the park, then a romp, then get on the train and go back to see his real family in their four-bedroom suburban house on Long Island.

Heddy reached for the silver cigarette case on the table, Gigi's initials engraved on it. "May I?"

"Of course." She felt Gigi watching her, and it was nerve-racking having a celebrity taking her in the way she'd taken Gigi in on the screen countless times.

Heddy blew the smoke out hard, fanning it away from her face. She hated cigarettes. "If you know girls like me, then you'll know how badly I want to go to your party." Heddy wanted to prove, maybe even just to herself, she belonged at a party like that.

Gigi giggled like she did in her films, like a man was watching her. "It's why I offered a dress."

"Why are you being so nice to me?" Heddy said. "Please, don't pity me."

"It's not pity. You make me remember." Gigi furrowed her well-shaped brows. "I was just like you once. Fighting for a place. On this island, I'm still doing that." She lay back down on her stomach, her right cheek resting on the lounger.

Heddy gave her a double take. "I hardly think that. . . ."

"Don't be fooled by all this polite bullshit. They treat me like a tramp."

Heddy bit at her nails. "But you're—"

"I don't play bridge. To hell with them. But look at you. You have something they love: credentials."

Heddy gulped back her drink. All this pretending. When everyone found out about her scholarship, they'd see she was an imposter. Gigi might snatch the invitation to her party back. Heddy picked at the cushion on the red-striped lounger. She had an idea, maybe it was dumb, but she would blurt it out anyway. "Men. I want to know how to attract a man."

Gigi burst out laughing. "What on earth does this have to do with men?"

Heddy closed her eyes, wishing she was not saying the words that were coming out of her mouth, and yet out they tumbled. "Not for a romp, either. For life. I need to know how to catch a husband."

"You're serious, aren't you, sugar?" Gigi sat up, spun her legs around so her feet were on the pool deck. She pushed her glasses on top of her head.

Thirty seconds passed, maybe a minute. Heddy felt like she was naked in Yankee Stadium. Then Gigi's tone softened. "You don't need to trap a man, sugar pie. Why would you want to be married anyway?"

Heddy thought it an odd question. Didn't everyone want to be married? It wasn't the *why* that confounded Heddy—it was the *how*. She needed to make it happen, especially if she wasn't going to be able to finish her degree next year. She needed security. But she didn't know where to begin, she had so many questions she was embarrassed to ask, and Gigi had the answers.

Heddy stared at the kids in the pool. "You've had so many men fall in love with you."

"I can attract a man, yes, but can I keep him? I'm not married, if you hadn't noticed," Gigi dismissed her. The actress closed her eyes, and Heddy grabbed the cocktail napkin under Gigi's glass. As a keepsake.

"You must know *something*." Heddy pleaded. "You're dating Cary Grant! He's only the most gorgeous man in Hollywood."

Standing up, slipping on a sheer, white cover-up, Gigi slithered past. "Do you see Cary here right now?" She twisted her hair to one side and laid it softly across her right shoulder. "Okay, Heddy the babysitter. I'll teach you about men."

The corners of Heddy's mouth twitched—she bit her cheeks to keep from smiling. When she thought back on this summer someday, she'd be able to pinpoint it with precision: this was the moment when her summer really started.

Gigi turned around to see if Heddy and the children were following behind her into the house. "Do you still want a dress?"

Heddy nodded. "Of course. I mean, sure."

"Good. Come back next Tuesday. Tell Jean-Rose I've invited the children here for high tea or some other nonsense she won't be able to resist. Then I'll tell you what I need from you."

That night, Heddy called home right after she put the children to bed. Jean-Rose and Ted were on the porch arguing about something, about what Heddy didn't know. Her mother picked up on the first ring.

"It's been two weeks. I've been worried sick. You told me every Sunday."

Heddy twisted the thick coiled cord around her finger, tucked herself into a corner of the front hall, her nose pushed against the fabric wallpaper seam. "I'm sorry, Mama—I've been busy. The children—I sent you two letters."

"The post is useless. Remember: you're never too busy for your mother."

She bit at her cheeks to keep from smiling, feeling a pang of homesickness. "You're right."

Her mother turned on the faucet; dishes clanged. "So does she wipe her own arse?" While Heddy was born in America, her mother had immigrated from Ireland when she was a teenager and still had an accent.

Heddy peered through the porch doors to make sure Jean-Rose and Ted weren't listening. "They're nice. She wants to help me."

"Get a job after school, I hope."

"Something like that."

"The damn lights are out—the electric bill—I'm trying to take on some extra hours, but . . ."

"There's something in the letter. To help." They went quiet on the line, the static crackling louder. Finally, her mother spoke.

"You didn't have to do that." Her mother always said that, but they both knew she needed the money.

"Mama, I met Gigi McCabe, the movie star. I went to her enormous house, and it was over-the-top gorgeous, just as you'd expect." Heddy felt herself blush. "And she invited me to a party. She said Hollywood people will be there."

"My daughter. Rubbing elbows with movie stars. Tell your father that, then maybe he'll think you're worth knowing."

Heddy banged her forehead against the wall. She and her mother had had a fight before she left, since Heddy had made clear she was going to contact her estranged father, much to her mother's dismay.

"He didn't deserve you, Mama."

"Well, you deserve that party."

Heddy grinned. "I drove a convertible. And Mrs. Williams gave me a bag like Princess Grace's." A white lie, Ruth had pulled Jean-Rose's old one from the trash, cleaned it, and dropped it on Heddy's bed. If she held it backward, no one would even see the water stain. She suspected the bag cost a quarter of her college tuition. Maybe she could sell it.

Over the sounds of silverware in a sink, rinsing, her mother said, "The lady's got money, eh."

Heddy wanted to tell her everything, but she didn't want to say too much and make her mother think she was becoming so grown-up that she didn't need her anymore. "They don't think much of it."

She was glad her mother didn't sound angry about the argument they'd had. The simple act of dialing her father's law office the week before she left for the Vineyard had sent her mother into a rage. Her mother had grabbed the phone, slammed it on the cradle, yelling into Heddy's face.

"You think I wanted to raise my daughter alone in this shit apartment with this shit life? He's not interested."

"He didn't want you," Heddy had yelled back, "but maybe he wants me."

As a girl, Heddy knew asking about her father inspired grief in her mother, but she was itchy with curiosity and she'd ask anyway, scratching at the floor when her mother's crying started. Sometimes she'd stare at her mother's tears, imagining them as bubbles popping against her face. Her thoughts would wander to what this mysterious father looked like—maybe like Gregory Peck, with his studious glasses. Maybe he was why she was at Wellesley; she'd inherited his book smarts *and* her mother's creativity and ingenuity. Her mother could paint a precise still life and fix a motor, if she had to, which is why when she worked nights at the laundry after leaving her daytime job at Tiffany's, she didn't just wash and fold, she sometimes fixed the machines.

Heddy had tapped her foot against her grandmother's chair. "You can't make this decision for me—I can do what I want."

Her mother had put her hands on the kitchen table. "Think about how your words hurt people, Hibernia."

"He's my father." Heddy had pulled out the junk drawer, reaching for a pen and a piece of paper. "Fine. I'll write him a letter."

"Hibernia Winsome, do as you wish. A bold, headstrong girl like you. But don't come crying to me when he doesn't want you." Her mother's voice cracked, causing Heddy to put down her pen.

Heddy had laced her arms around her mother's waist. "I just want to try, Mama."

Ted's voice drifted in from the living room; living here had only intensified her desire to meet her father, every interaction with Ted reminded her just how much she'd missed out on.

On the other end of the line, her mother sighed. "What are the kids like?" her mother asked.

Heddy whispered: "The girl is sweet as sugar. The boy's a brat."

"Well, you have your own family, and don't you forget it." A siren went by, and her mother waited until it was quiet to speak. "I got a call from your school, someone saying you needed to cancel your housing next year, since you're not returning. They said it was your scholarship."

Heddy swallowed, staring at a chip in her pale pink nail polish. What would her mother think of her now? What a waste it had all been, all those nights of study when she could have worked a part-time job and contributed. "I was going to tell you," Heddy said. "I'm sorry."

Her mother didn't yell, her tone quiet and forlorn. "What happened, Hibernia? You never got a bad grade in your life."

"I'm going to fix it, Mama. Really, I will." She was squeezing the cord of the phone so tight her fingertips hurt. She'd disappointed her mother, and she began to cry.

"I went to Dora at the bank. They won't give me a loan," her mother said.

"I'll find my way back, I promise." If she'd had a different response from her father, if he hadn't had his secretary write that rude response.

When Heddy put the receiver back on the cradle, she heard a creak in the floorboards, startling her, and whipped around to find Teddy sprinting through the doorway, pretending to be asleep as she passed by his room.

Now, with her face covered in Pond's Cold Cream, Heddy balanced her journal against her bare legs. On one page, she taped a magazine ad showing a photograph of the Bonneville convertible, and on another, the wrinkled napkin from Gigi's, a simple gold "G" at its center. Using a fine-tipped black marker from the kitchen, she wrote:

July 3, 1962

    Gigi smells of coconuts and even her lounge chairs were out of Vogue, *but we hung out like girlfriends. She seems to get me, or at least get a kick out of me, but I kept staring at her lips and wondering what it would be like to be so desired by every man in sight. How might my life be different if I'd been born buxom or long-legged and curvy—does playing fast and hard give you a hand up when it comes to dating? To finding a husband who won't leave you? What did my mother get wrong when it came to seducing (or loving) my father—what did she lack and is that why he didn't choose her? It got me thinking: How can I be everything to a man so that never happens to me?*

{ SEVEN }

Heddy took a moment to catch her breath, treading water several feet deep. She faced the shingled houses, distant and far apart onshore, giving her a clear view of Ash Porter's fishing cottage in the early-morning light. It was the Fourth of July, and even with her date with the waiter the following day, she couldn't get the surfer out of her head.

The outside of his cottage was different than she remembered, ramshackle even, since the old, weathered shingles were a deep, dark gray, and the newer ones, the color of honey. His house was closer to the water than the other houses, which she hadn't realized the day she lost the children; it seemed like they'd walked deep into the marsh, but the sandy path ran parallel to the beach. The high-tide mark hit near his deck.

A small sports car made a three-point turn out of the dusty driveway, but billowing beach grass blocked Heddy's view of the driver. *Someone was leaving Ash's house extra early*, she thought. The screen door slammed, and Ash padded out of the cottage sipping from a mug. She lowered her head deeper into the water, the sea tickling her chin. The unmistakable banter of sports radio crackled.

Ash hadn't seen her yet. He was focused on what he was holding. Bills. Were they dollars, twenties? Her eyes strained to see. He slid them from one hand to the other, and by the way his lips were moving, she knew he was counting. Over and over, the same stacks of money, in between sips of coffee. Something told her to duck her head under the cool water and swim away. But she'd be lying if she said she hadn't thought about him after the luncheon, wondered why he'd engaged with her, and even though he'd been in the car with someone else the other day, she had to see him anyway. She went back under the water and arrowed toward shore, pressure building in her chest as she swam, her lungs growing tight.

She popped her head up like a seal, scanning the shore for his deck, where he sat in the same director's chair he'd been in the first time they'd met. Ash must have caught sight of the ripples in the water because he waved at her, smiling. He strutted toward her, his denim shirt open, his feet bare, coffee mug in hand.

Heddy held her hand up in hello. She would never be so forward that she'd risk developing a reputation, of course, but she couldn't wait for the universe to lob a man at her, either. She bobbed her head out of the shallow water, floating on her belly, where small gentle waves were breaking. "Morning," she said.

Water pooled around Ash's ankles. "The Williamses got themselves a water rat. It's barely seven."

"I swim. At school." Oh God. She needed to say something else. She let a wave push her closer to him and propped herself up on her elbows. "I slipped out before anyone was awake."

He sipped his coffee. "Are you going to Oak Bluffs for fireworks tonight?"

"Jean-Rose said the noise scares the children, so we'll be in the yard with sparklers. Do you think I'll see the fireworks from the attic?"

He shook his head. "You're too far up island. It's a shame, though—it's quite a display. How is the job?"

"Interesting."

"I bet." He grinned. There was that smile, the one she couldn't get out of her head. "She's a feisty one."

Heddy ran her fingers along the sea bottom, pulling up an orangey rock and pretending to examine it. "I'm enjoying her."

Ash ran his hands through his tousled hair, shaking something off. "Well, the old bird puts up with a lot."

"She does." Heddy wasn't sure how to steer the conversation away from Jean-Rose now. "How old are you, anyway?"

"Twenty-four." Exactly three years difference.

"I'd say you're an old man then."

Ash laughed, revealing a row of perfect teeth, then raised his mug, covered in red sailboats, to his lips. "If by old man, you mean young and dashing."

She brushed her fingers along her clavicle, smiling. "I think you mean young and darling, like myself?" A silly feeling lolled inside her, and she pointed at her face, saying—"Eh? Right?"—and then she burst into giggles.

"Well, that's a given." The corners of his mouth turned up into a grin, and he went to sit on the sand. Heddy felt a small victory then. She knew he was charmed by her, just by the way he kept smiling and sipping coffee, even if he wasn't saying anything. She could tell already he'd mastered the pregnant pause—her psychology professor once said staying quiet was how you got people to reveal themselves, but Heddy couldn't do it. She always filled blank spaces in conversations erratically, patching the silence.

A flock of birds squawked overhead. "You know the people who own this place?" she asked.

He turned to look at the house, then back at her. Had she imagined that quick glance at her bosom?

"You always so nosy?"

She dunked her chin back into the water, stretched her legs behind her. "Someone told me you were watching the place, so it made me wonder whose house it was."

Ash picked up a rock, thumbed its surface. "So you've been talking about me." She was embarrassed he'd pointed that out, and yet she loved it. She wasn't worried about the gun anymore. It probably wasn't even his.

She rose out of the water dripping, wrapping her arms around her chest to warm herself. "'I have no special talent. I'm only passionately curious.'"

She sat next to him, and he leaned toward her, elbowing her playfully. "That's Albert Einstein."

Her mouth fell open. "How did you know?" She'd doodled the quote, written on her high school science teacher's blackboard, during many of his most boring lectures.

"It's on an index card on my fridge." He offered her the mug, and she sipped, thankful for the warmth it offered her fingertips. "You know, you stay up every night—I see your light. Then I see you swimming at dawn. I asked Jean-Rose: don't you ever sleep?"

"So you've been talking about me, too," she said, matching his *gotcha* tone from earlier.

"You got me too," he said, grinning.

For once, she stayed quiet, enjoying the possibilities of what it meant that he'd noticed her habits, spoken of her to someone else. They stared at a distant ferry.

Ash checked his watch. "Well, you have some kids to attend to. And I've got some business."

Heddy smiled at him like she would a professor, distant and mannered. She was being dismissed, but he was right. She had to get home. They would be up by now.

"We have to meet like this again," he said, on his feet, padding to his cottage.

"Ash, wait," she said. She ran toward him. The sight of him made her feel electric, like there was an invisible wire connecting them, and the closer she got, the brighter it got, illuminating her inside and out.

"Your coffee." Breathless, she handed him the sailboat mug, imagining his fingers sparking as he took it.

His shoulders relaxed, and he gave her a goofy military salute. "Another time, then."

She sprinted to the water, deflated and elated all at once. Heddy couldn't get into the sea fast enough, diving as far away as she could, kicking her feet wildly and pulling at the water to propel her forward. She wasn't sure what to make of him, but she knew this: there was something about Ash Porter. As she stepped out of the water by the Williamses' house, she stared into the woods where his cottage was, spying only lush trees. She had to find a way to see him again.

When she walked into the kitchen, dry and changed into linen shorts, Ruth was tucking a small pink envelope and a pair of pantyhose into her apron pocket. Their boss left their pay on the table every Wednesday. Heddy checked for the four twenties, plus a ten—holding the crisp bills to her nose and inhaling their inky scent. By the end of the summer, she'd have close to $700.

Ruth had pulled milk and cheese and eggs out, a pie pan already crusted beside her, and Heddy leaned over the counter: "Quiche?"

"Jean-Rose wants to try it." The magazine at Ruth's feet was open to a recipe depicting a perfectly set asparagus egg pie. Ruth checked to make sure Jean-Rose and Ted weren't nearby, then flicked a lock of hair over her shoulder, mimicking Jean-Rose. "The bridge ladies swear by it."

Heddy jabbed her middle. "You sound just like her."

Ruth positioned a mixing bowl on the counter, cracked open the eggs. "What's with you and swimming?"

Heddy stretched her arms up overhead, then shook the water out of her ears. "It helps me think."

Ruth retrieved the hand mixer from the pantry and plugged it in, centering it in the egg mixture, and Heddy stood beside her, leaning against the countertop. "What do you know about the bachelor next door?"

Ruth dumped a tablespoon of flour into the batter. "The surfer?"

Heddy smiled. "There's something about him." She pulled out a loaf of white bread, peanut butter and jelly to start the children's camp lunches. In honor of the Fourth, their camp was holding a field day with an egg toss and potato sack races.

Ruth poured the eggs into the pie shell. "I get the feeling he's big-time. You know, Ivy League degree. Slick job, fancy city apartment." She placed the quiche onto the oven's wire rack.

"But he's different from someone like Ted . . ." While spreading the peanut butter—the bread crusts cut off—Heddy struggled to make sense of his rundown cottage, his beat-up truck, that he was a surf instructor. He wasn't a typical businessman, hardly relying on his money to feel important.

Ruth dabbed at a stain on her apron, returned the flour to the pantry. "I bet it was the ramshackle house that fooled you. Here's a secret about this island. You can't judge a person on their summer place. Sometimes the older the money, the more dilapidated the house. It humbles them."

"Huh," Heddy said, packing two brown bags with the sandwiches, a few saltine crackers, and bananas. She used black magic marker to write on the bags: *Happy 4th! Sparklers tonight. xo Heddy.*

She heard the pitter-patter of little feet coming down the stairs, and Jean-Rose's voice: "Teddy, slow down." Heddy and Ruth stood with their hands folded, preparing for the family to enter.

Ted, who had been in the garage, came inside, hoisting a Styrofoam ice chest onto the counter, a cigarette balanced between his lips.

"I hear you visited the island's most famous resident yesterday," he said to Heddy. Then, "Pack this with ice for me, will you?"

Heddy opened the freezer. "I can't believe you grew up with a true-to-life movie star, Jean-Rose. What was she like in high school?"

Ruth kicked Heddy's ankle. "You didn't tell me," she whispered, the sun shining through the kitchen window.

"I meant to," Heddy whispered back, but she hadn't, because she didn't want to brag.

Jean-Rose settled the children into their seats at the table—she liked to choose their clothes every morning, and it was Heddy's job to brush their hair and teeth. Ruth had cereal waiting in bowls with spoons balanced along the rims. Jean-Rose poured the milk. "Not as pretty as she is now."

"Jeannie!" Ted was opening drawers, sifting through, not finding what he was looking for.

"Why can't we go to the fireworks?" Teddy pouted. "All of my friends are going."

"No!" Anna held her hands over her ears, like the fireworks were already going off.

When Teddy insisted they go, she screeched: "I'm scared, Teddy," tears coming fast.

Jean-Rose made a sad face at Anna. "Maybe next year, baby."

"I'm not a baby," Teddy hollered.

Heddy lifted Anna onto her lap, kissing her smooth forehead and rocking her, while Teddy began to follow his father, pestering him.

Jean-Rose pretended not to hear, continuing about Gigi. "It wasn't surprising she became an actress. She was always trying to be someone else. But she was popular with the boys. Right, Ted?"

He looked annoyed, shooing the boy away. "Why are you asking me?"

"Gigi's father had a thing for cards. Lost that lopsided little house of theirs overnight."

Heddy never heard that part of Gigi's story; she'd seen a photograph of Gigi's mother on a movie set, and she'd seemed as glamorous as her daughter.

"This will be full of fish tonight." Ted was staring at the ice on the bottom of the chest, and she could almost see it: rows of fish, mouths agape, their vacant eyes staring up.

"Mr. Mule says I can go fishing with them," Teddy told his mother.

"Edison?" Jean-Rose said, turning to look at Ted.

"We ran into him the other day at the dock," Ted said, patting the boy's back. "And good thing," said Ted, "because I'd forgotten my wallet."

"Well, good thing." Jean-Rose clapped her hands together, a sarcastic edge in her voice.

Ted went on with his hunt through kitchen drawers: "Where is that filet knife?" Ruth started to look for it, too.

"Can I come fishing this morning? I don't want to go to some dumb camp," Teddy said.

Jean-Rose sucked in a sharp breath, smiling pretty. "Kids aren't welcome where Daddy is going. I'm not sure I am, either."

"Jeannie, stop. You hate fishing at Menemsha. You hate fishing, period." Ted crouched down by Teddy's chair, kindness in his voice. "I'll take you out after camp next week. This is our annual Fourth of July fishing derby."

Teddy started to wail, a high-pitched yelping that made Anna hold her hands over her ears again. "You like Mr. Mule better than me," he hollered.

"Jesus Christ, can one of you women get him to calm down?" Ted said, shooting up to stand. "He needs a spanking."

Jean-Rose spooned another bite of cereal. "My parents didn't lay a hand on me, and I won't let you lay a hand on them."

Teddy wiped spittle off his cheek. "You never take me. Never, ever. Heddy said if I asked, you'd say yes."

"No, I never said that. What I meant was—" Heddy realized her voice was trembling.

The boy fumed at her. "You said to get what I want, I had to ask."

Ted raised his hand, his voice deep and angry. "I don't care what she said. I said we can go after camp next week."

Jean-Rose dropped her spoon, rising from her seat and resting her palm on the small of Ted's back. "I'll take care of this, honey," she said. "What else do you need for fishing?"

Ted slumped into the chair, rubbing his hands roughly on his face and mumbling something to himself. It sounded like he'd said, "Stupid bitch," but Heddy was certain she'd heard wrong. He was a member of the revered Island Club, an application that was so grueling, the *New York Times* had once written about it.

Jean-Rose didn't seem to note anything improper, and she turned to Teddy, clapping her hands. "Stop right now, young man. You need to go to camp, and you can't go to camp with swollen, red eyes. You'll fish with Daddy next week. Now stop the tears." Heddy, still scooping ice, waited for Jean-Rose to hold the boy in her arms and nuzzle him. Instead, she crossed her arms and narrowed her gaze. "I didn't hear you say okay. *Okay?*" Her voice went vibrato.

To Heddy's shock, the child nodded, working to muffle his cries, his tears slipping into his mouth as he ate. Anna disappeared under the table.

"Ted's filet knife is on the shelf by the potting soil in the garage. Heddy, would you fetch it for him? Anna, get back in your seat."

It felt good to be out of that kitchen, away from Ted's outburst. With the garage door open, she stepped into the cool, musty air. Standing on tiptoe, she leaned against a few cardboard boxes for support to reach for the knife but wobbled, and the highest box tipped. There was the shatter of porcelain, and after the shock of it, she realized what had fallen, a pile of gold-rimmed plate shards around her feet. One of the plates, upside down on the cold cement floor, had a stamp on the back: "Wedgwood." She knew those plates from her mother's job at Tiffany's. "Damn it!" she exclaimed.

"What was all that racket?" Jean-Rose looked toward the garage as Heddy handed her the knife.

What if Jean-Rose docked her paycheck? What if those plates were worth more than her entire week's pay? "I'm so sorry, but I may have broken your china." She waited for her boss's lecture on her carelessness.

Instead, Jean-Rose handed the knife to Ted. "Please gut them on the dock this time." Then she faced Heddy, looking at her like she was naive and unknowing of how the world worked, a look of pity spreading across the woman's face. "Anyone can see that pattern is dated, dear. My fashionable china is in the house."

When Heddy went into the pantry to grab the broom, Ruth was already in the doorway, holding it out to her. Ruth whispered: "Don't feel too bad. She loves when things break. It gives her an excuse to buy something new."

Heddy swatted her, a smile of relief on her face.

Now that she was in the musty garage sweeping up the pieces, the straw broom dragging along the concrete floor, Heddy laughed to herself. Ruth had something clever to say about everything.

"Who cares if he has it? It makes him happy, Jeannie." Loud voices, Ted's voice, coming from the porch. Dismissive and angry. *Now what?* So much for Beryl's idyllic description of these two— Jean-Rose and Ted pounded each other like boxers.

"I care. He's six years old," said Jean-Rose.

"We had a nice morning, Jeannie. Don't spoil it."

"A nice morning? Is that what you call freaking out on all of us? You're more like your father than you like to admit." Heddy looked to see if Ted was going to lose his temper again, but he stared at his crying son with remove, his expression distant.

"Give it to me, Theodore James Williams Junior," said Jean-Rose. "No bringing it to camp. No hiding it under the table at breakfast. I *told* you: only at night."

Teddy clutched that odd doll, Miss Pinkie, to his chest, and Jean-Rose ripped it from him, tearing the bonnet off its head. Anna tried to grab the doll, but Jean-Rose held it up high.

Ted slammed his cigarette onto the ground and stomped on it. "Jesus Christ, give it back to him." Jean-Rose narrowed her eyes at Ted, not seeming to notice Teddy, who had collapsed to his knees, heaving.

How strange that Teddy could be so attached to a baby doll, its hair a sickly butter yellow and pulled into pigtails. Without the bonnet, you could see how matted its hair was, frizzy and fake, the kind that reeked of plastic. Heddy thought of the little boys she babysat at her Brooklyn tenement with their metal trucks, the way they propelled them along the sidewalk, spitting their vroom-vrooms out as they went. Teddy had those toys, too—he just didn't seem too interested in them.

"He didn't soil her when he took her out, Mama. I made sure," Anna whispered, looking down at her feet.

"I don't need my son traipsing around town with a . . . *doll*." Jean-Rose looked like she might spit on it. She held the doll overhead, which made its eyes flutter open, and tossed it across the yard like a football. Miss Pinkie's skirt filled with air like a parachute, landing in the center of the lawn near a jar of bubbles they'd left there the day before.

Teddy took off running, his chubby hands frantically cradling Miss Pinkie when he got to her. He whipped around to see if his mother was coming after him, but she'd already disappeared inside.

Heddy, her heart racing, looked to Ted for some direction. Should she go after the child, or did his father want to talk to him? She got her answer when Ted walked away. Heddy fetched the pink bonnet,

then took Anna's hand and followed Teddy, who had stolen off to a
canopy of long weeping willow branches, hunched over his doll.

"It's okay, Teddy." She sat down in the grass beside him.

The boy flinched, his eyes bloodshot, his cheeks wet. He clutched
the doll closer to him. "I won't let you take her," he yelled.

"I just want you to put her in your room."

"Mommy gets mad when Teddy plays with my dolls, but we love
the dollhouse." Anna climbed onto Heddy's lap. "We put on lipstick
and we wear Mama's clothes. Teddy was punished for a week, but I
wasn't." Anna had her mother's blond hair, deep blue eyes and high
cheekbones; she was a child whose face people could imagine mor-
phing into its adult self, knowing she would one day be beautiful.

Teddy lifted the doll to his mouth, running her plastic forehead
along his lips. "It's not fair," he said.

"You have so many other toys. What about that robot I saw on
your bookshelf?"

"Mr. Mercury," Anna whispered. "See if he'll play with Yogi Bear."

"Let's get Yogi. We can make Jellystone Park out of sand." Her
voice was full of exaggerated glee, the voice she heard parents take on
when they didn't want their kids to sour a good time.

"You don't want other boys to laugh at you for playing with a
doll, do you?" She rubbed the boy's rumpled hair, but touching him
only made him scoot farther away.

"I don't care." He pressed the doll's blond curl flat, stroking it
over and over against her forehead.

"But someday you will. Have you ever seen Anna play with your
trucks? Boy toys are for boys. Girl toys are for girls."

Heddy looked to make sure Ted wasn't watching. She couldn't
yell at the boy or demand he march inside and pick another toy,
which is what her mother would have done. She wasn't a parent. That
he loved a doll was inappropriate, but with a child this upset, she had
to try a different tack.

"Here, I have her bonnet." Heddy dangled the ruffled hat from her fingertips, letting it wave near his face. It got his attention, so she kept on. "Can I put it on her?"

Teddy squeezed the doll to his chest when Heddy reached for its white patent leather Mary Janes.

"I promise I'll give her back."

Teddy must have loved the bonnet because he relented, handing her the doll.

"At bedtime tonight, maybe we can wet her hair to make her curl flatter." Heddy ran her finger against the curl. "She'll look pretty."

He stared at Heddy with something close to awe, like she'd said something revolutionary, so she repeated it.

"We'll do her hair."

"We can do that?" A smile peeked out of his hangdog look.

"Sure we can."

Anna jumped up. "Can you do that to Barbie, too? You shouldn't tell Mommy, though. . . ."

Heddy nodded, watching Ted emerge from the garage holding his tackle box; she knew he was waiting to see if she'd appeased the child. "But we'll have to put Miss Pinkie down for a nap so she'll be ready for her big night."

She led him up to the house, her arm around Teddy's back, the boy's head down. They passed Ted, who grinned at her, his eyes sparkling like sun on water: "I'd say it's time for camp." Ted patted Teddy on the back. "We're still on for fishing next week, right?"

Teddy sniffled.

How hard would it be to cancel his plans to spend a day alone with his son? She wished Ted could see how happy it would make Teddy, that it was obvious even to Heddy that Ted avoided spending time with him. She assumed he saw something of himself in the child, something he didn't like.

❧ EIGHT ❧

As soon as they'd gotten out in the dirt parking lot at Katama Beach, Heddy heard the hypnotic sound of the ocean, the big waves seemingly slicing the sky away from the sea, leaving behind a sheet of foam in their wake. The ocean always made Heddy want to run to it, feel the force of it wash up her ankles and chill her legs, and she always laughed, because of the playful nature of something so explosive.

Anna tugged at Heddy's denim shorts, holding a charred-over remnant of a Roman candle firework she found on the ground. "Will you carry me?"

"Let's put that in the trash first." Heddy plucked it from the child's grip.

Three surfers bobbed just beyond the breaking waves. Several beach blankets were spread out on the beach, many shaded with colorful umbrellas, a necessary reprieve from the blasting sun. She leaned down to balance Anna on one hip, switching the beach bag to the other, while trailing behind Jean-Rose, who was clutching her pink espadrilles in one hand, a streak of plum eye shadow softening her thick black mascara, and waving.

"Ash!" she said. Teddy ran to him, too, slamming his hand with a high five.

A thrill built in Heddy's chest, the slow climb of a roller coaster up the tracks. She'd been anticipating Teddy's surf lesson all week for this reason, and there was Ash rising from his aluminum beach chair, a long-pointed surfboard at his feet. He sipped a can of Narragansett beer.

Ash leaned in to kiss Jean-Rose's cheek. "I like what you've done with your hair, Mrs. Williams."

Jean-Rose's eyes grew wide. "Ted never notices these things. But I suppose he'll notice the bill next month." She touched the bejeweled topaz comb she'd used to part her hair in place; she was trying to preserve the cascade of ringlets from the hairdresser the day before. "And please, it's Jean-Rose. You make me sound ancient."

Heddy unpacked the beach bag, laying out a striped blanket near Ash's chair, handing Anna her bucket and shovel.

Ash leaned down, helping her pull the blanket taut. "Did you have fun with the sparklers last night?"

"We went through them fast—thank goodness Ted brought home an extra box," Heddy said, letting her cheeks dimple. She helped Teddy pull off his T-shirt, folding it neatly. Boys her age were tossing a football around, and Heddy took a minute to size them up; one was handsome, a head of caramel curls.

"That's right, the two of you have already met." Jean-Rose spoke to Ash, as if Heddy wasn't even there.

"A few times now," Ash said.

"Right." Jean-Rose motioned to the aluminum cooler. "Do you mind if I grab a soda?"

"There's plenty." Ash handed her a can of ginger ale, and Jean-Rose snapped it open and sipped, scanning the men in the water.

"Surfers on the Vineyard! I have to say, I didn't get it. Seemed like a sport for Florida boys."

"I'm trying to change that." Ash put his hands to his hips, and Heddy, pretending to be concentrating on building castles with Anna, noticed his biceps, the flex of his muscles. "If there are waves," he said, "you can surf. Doesn't matter if you're in Miami or New England."

"Everyone on the island is talking about it. Ash Porter, the mysterious South Florida boy who can ride on waves. When I say you're teaching Teddy, everyone—"

"Yes, thank you for the referrals. Got a full schedule now." He held his beer up to toast her ginger ale.

Jean-Rose presented herself like she was onstage, letting people look at her, immensely comfortable in her own skin. It was a talent, Heddy thought. "I know a lot of the women are dying to try," said Jean-Rose.

"We'll have to get you out there then," he said.

Jean-Rose grinned.

He pointed to several surfboards he'd lined up along the dunes. "You can pick up a smaller board for about fifty dollars. Name the day."

Teddy jumped up and down. "Can we buy one? Fifty is a good price, Mama."

Ash and Jean-Rose laughed, like they were tickled by his remark, and Heddy didn't let them see the roll of her eyes. *Why is it funny to raise kids that thought fifty dollars was a bargain?*

"Let's see how you do," Jean-Rose told Teddy. "Maybe we can make this a weekly thing. Would you mind dropping them home? I have a few things to pick up."

Ash tossed a red plastic shovel at Heddy's foot to get her attention. "We'll throw the kids in the back of the truck with the surfboards."

"Seriously, Ash."

Did Jean-Rose just giggle?

Ash got up, pulling his board to its side. "I'm sure Heddy won't mind if we all squeeze into the cab."

"Not at all," she said.

As Jean-Rose turned to go, Ash carried his surfboard to the foamy water. "Ready to get in the water, Ace? The waves are a ten." The ocean was rough but calmer beyond the break. Heddy watched Teddy sit on the board, digging her hands in the sand alongside Anna, making drip castles. But the child liked knocking them down more than building them up. Since it was too rough for Teddy to stand on the board, Ash beached it. Instead, he instructed Teddy to keep his balance every time a wave broke. They held hands, and if the wave was looming, Ash would pick him up and help him jump it.

A football landed next to her, and she reached for it, throwing it back to the guy with the curls as he ran toward her. He thanked her, and she'd leaned back into her hands, smiling.

"Heddy." Ash called from the water. "Come in with us."

"In a minute," she said. "I'm with Anna."

Teddy came running out of the ocean sometime later. The water from his bathing trunks plopped cold drops on Heddy's legs. "Did you see me? He's going to take me out next time." He hugged her thighs tight. It was the sweetest he'd ever been to her, and she patted his back, thinking maybe they were turning a corner.

Ash dragged the tip of his board up the sand to where Heddy and Anna were digging. "It's a little too rough for a first lesson." He wiped the water from his eyes, sand clumping to the undersides of his trunks.

"Have you been out yet?" Heddy asked.

"All morning. On a typical day here, you're paddling around, waiting for a few good waves. Today, it's like Christmas."

"Lucky you." She stretched her legs out, reclined in a pose. "I'd love to take a dip. Do you mind watching them for a second?" Heddy didn't think Jean-Rose would mind. She'd be quick.

Heddy pushed off her straps, wiggling out of the yellow terry-cloth dress, and strolled toward the sea. She dove into the wave, feeling it rush over her, enjoying it wholly before emerging. At the children's side again, she wrapped her towel around her, like she'd just gotten out of the bath.

"You didn't give yourself barely a minute." Ash held a tiny sand crab in his palm, the children begging to hold it. "We think you should try it."

She squeezed the water out of her hair. "Try what?"

His voice took on the tone of a dare. "Wave riding."

Heddy threw up her arms, shaking her head with laughter. "Told you, city girl."

"That's not a reason, Miss Heddy. It's an excuse. You may never get another chance to try," Ash said.

"Now why would I want to?" She met his eyes with a charge.

"Someone forced me out on a board once. You'll never see the ocean the same way."

"I couldn't possibly leave the children—"

"I'm telling you, the waves are plentiful. We'll be back in minutes," he said. "Besides, Susanne's nanny, Rhoda, is right here." Ash called her over. "Rhoda, will you keep an eye on Jean-Rose's kids while Heddy goes for a swim?" Heddy knew Rhoda from a playdate. She was on break from the University of Massachusetts, and she and Heddy had laughed when the kids put on a play about their parents, mimicking them sipping cocktails and smoking cigarettes.

"Do it. Do it," Anna chanted.

"When opportunities come your way, you've got to jump on them. The simplest rule of business." Ash stood, retying the roped belt of his red board shorts.

"Lucky I'm not in business school. I've had enough firsts for one summer already."

Ash raised his eyebrows, causing Heddy to explain. "Jean-Rose taught me how to drive a car last week." Heddy realized then that she'd wanted to tell him, and it had come out in a burst.

He shook his head, a smart grin on his face. "That woman can get anyone to do anything. How am I losing to her right now?"

Heddy had to laugh. He touched her arm right above her elbow, just for a moment, and nothing about it felt inappropriate, just tender. "Promise me you won't leave this summer without trying it."

Something about his backing off, giving her the choice, made her want to say yes.

"Okay, I'll do it."

Teddy wrinkled his nose. "You'll never stand up."

Ash snapped his fingers. "Yes! Now, don't worry, you'll see the kids the entire time."

He carried the long board out to the sea. She dove in after him and swam beyond the break, turning around when the water was chest-deep to check on the children. Teddy was staring, willing her to fail; Anna was digging.

Ash paddled the board to her. "Get on. Let's line up." Heddy pushed herself onto the board, water pouring off her sides. She scooted her bottom back, straddling it. "Lay down on your stomach," Ash instructed.

Heddy eased herself down on her elbows, pushing back her legs into an A to help balance the surfboard, pressing her belly against the smooth planed surface. Ash propped himself up in between her calves, pulling his body forward, inching closer to her while dangling his legs in the water. She could feel his breath on the backs of her knees and she needed to say something, anything to break the tension balling up inside her.

"You really think we can ride a wave like this?"

"Of course we can," he said. They rocked in the water, waiting, and Heddy saw the kids pointing at something in the hole they were digging. Teddy picked it up and Anna tried to grab it. Then she'd sunk down in tears. Rhoda consoled Anna, pointing at the water where she and Ash were.

"My time is running out." The water splashed up on the board, sending a burst of the sea onto Heddy's back.

"Don't move an inch," he told her. She'd pointed her toes then, and they'd momentarily grazed the side of his body. She couldn't see his face, but his voice felt close, enveloping her like a warm blanket. "On the count of three, pull your legs in, and I'll jump up. One, two, *three*."

She squeezed her legs shut, and all at once, Heddy felt the push of the water against the board. It was a force so strong, it pushed them downhill, and for a moment, it felt like they'd be crushed by the roar of the wave. They shot out just under the crest, and she felt the board propelling them forward like a jet plane. They were racing the water itself. She was still laying down, while Ash had popped up to stand, his feet planted on either side of her hips, and he steadied the board as the white water chased them. Heddy pressed up so she could see, then squeezed her eyes shut to protect them from the spray. The rush of the water made her scream out with glee, and Ash hollered back at her. "We did it, kitty kit," which made her belly laugh.

They sped toward shore, but Ash turned the board sideways to slow it down. In seconds, they were floating in the foam. Ash hopped off the board, the thunder of an impending wave rolling just beyond the break. "You better get off or you're toast."

Her body pumping with adrenaline, Heddy slid into the ocean, sprinting to the shoreline and picking up Anna, spinning her in circles. She grabbed for Teddy, spinning some more, until she was dizzy, collapsing on the sand with laughter.

Ash sat next to her and guffawed. "Bet you've never felt anything like it."

Heddy tried to catch her breath. "No one could tell you what that feels like—you wouldn't believe it." Their shoulders kissed for a moment, and they both readjusted their position, scooting farther apart.

"Will you describe it? I want to see it through your eyes," he said.

"Why?" She brushed at the sand on her legs, rubbing it away with her fingers.

"Because you can't stop the waves, so everyone reacts a little differently to surfing. Some people are threatened; others are inspired." He looked like a little boy to her then, curious about the world in a way she didn't know grown men could be.

Heddy shielded her eyes from the sun, feeling him next to her. "How would I describe it? I suppose it's like staring down the ocean, ready to take a punch, but then you figure out how to escape, and you outrun it. Faster than you've ever outrun anything in your life." When she'd been on the surfboard, she'd wanted to show the ocean she was mightier, that she could overpower it.

Ash punched her lightly in the arm, like she was his buddy. "So for you, it's all about the escape. I could see that."

Perhaps, she thought. Her lips turned up in a half smile. Or maybe there wasn't a deeper explanation. Maybe she just liked the rush of the water.

"I didn't think you could do it." Teddy smirked. He ran off to join Anna, crushing a sand castle with her foot.

Back at the beach blanket, Ash pulled a cold Narragansett from his cooler, reaching for something else. "I have one more ginger ale." He cupped it in his hand like a baseball, ready to toss it to Heddy, propped on her elbows.

"Sure." Heddy failed to catch it, and when she picked it up, it was coated in sand.

"You're such a girl." Ash said, resting his head on the back of his chair.

"Guilty," she said, brushing the sand off the can.

He gazed out at the ocean, so she did, too, her mind wandering to her mother, what she was doing right now. What she'd think of what Heddy was doing.

"Penny for your thoughts," he said.

Heddy smiled shyly, crossing her feet at the ankles and uncrossing them. It was too early to share anything about her mother.

"Walk with me." He reached for her hand, but once she was next to him, he tapped Anna and Teddy on the back. "Let's race. Whoever makes it to Dead Man's Rock wins."

And he was off. Ash, his back smooth, running in his red bathing trunks, the children chasing him, Teddy putting power into his little legs to stay ahead of Anna. She assumed Dead Man's Rock was the boulder ahead, and Heddy sprinted down the beach after him. She laughed, tripping on a thick nest of seaweed, then regained her balance and held her hand in front of her mouth. The salt air pumped hard in her chest, and she felt alive. Fully alive.

"Gotcha." Heddy tackled Teddy and Anna. "You're mine now."

Ash was already at the rock, leaning his hand along the tallest edge. "C'mon, kitty kit. I know you're faster than that."

Heddy folded her arms "You got a head start."

"Yeah, that wasn't fair," said Anna.

"Well, Anna Banana, that is true. You and Teddy can get a running start on the way back."

"What is it with you and nicknames anyway?" Running had left Heddy's hair disheveled, and she was pulling it into a tight, high ponytail. "I've only had one nickname in my whole life: my grandmother called me little owl."

"Of course she did—you've got those great big, round eyes."

Heddy scrunched up her nose. "I hated it. You can just call me Heddy, none of this 'kitty kit' stuff."

"You won't get off that easy with me. If we're going to be friends, you've got to have a nickname."

Friends. The children had taken off down the beach, determined to win the race. Heddy started to run, too.

"Well, then what do we call you?" she yelled back. Ash was running again, and he zipped right past her.

"Just call me handsome."

She shaded her eyes, taking him in as he ran. She heard her mother, the day she left for Wellesley: *Some people play the slots. Others put their money into a house. Well, I don't have any money at all, so I'm investing in you.*

It was improbable, of course, but perhaps, just maybe, Ash was the return on her mother's investment.

{ NINE }

*T*ed tapped at the steering wheel, the car idling in the drive-way, as Heddy arranged the last of the beach bags into the trunk. He turned around to see what was taking Jean-Rose so long, the kids playing tag in the grass. "Could we get there sometime this century?"

It was Heddy's day off, tonight was her date with the waiter, and she wanted—no, needed—to talk to Ted. She'd rehearsed her speech while lying next to Anna as the sun rose. The child had woken her early after having a bad dream and fallen asleep beside her, and as she watched Anna's little back rising and falling, the hot tangle of hair stuck to the nape of her neck, she decided today was the day to ask Ted for a loan. If she didn't return to school and earn her degree, she wouldn't just disappoint herself, she'd crush her mother. Plus, there were so many things she still wanted to do on campus, and leaving early meant missing out on opportunities, like writing for the *Welles-ley News*. She couldn't stomach it.

Unfortunately, now that he was before her, mussing up his hair and adjusting his aviator glasses, she stared at the orange stripes of his golf shirt, her mind coming up blank.

"This probably isn't the best time, but . . ." She paused.

Ted leaned out the window. "Yes, Heddy." He tapped the slit where the window rolled down, waiting for her to say something, and still she couldn't make the words come out. *Can I have a loan? I'll pay you back, with interest, of course.*

"I was wondering if— Well, if you might give me a . . . um, well it's complicated . . ." She paused, sucked in her breath. "It's Teddy. Can you get him his own fishing pole?"

He motioned to the garage. "You can use one in there."

"No, a child's pole."

"I'll check the hardware store." The children climbed into the car, Jean-Rose slammed her door shut, and Ted backed the Bonneville out of the driveway. Heddy closed her eyes, even as the children waved goodbye. Asking him for money had felt wrong, like a breach of contract. She didn't want to ask anybody for anything.

With the family gone, she stepped into the kitchen. Ruth padded around upstairs, Heddy leaned against the sink and sipped from the triangular opening of a large can of pineapple juice. It felt good to be alone, even if the house sagged without the children's voices echoing through the well-decorated rooms. In the silent living room, she noticed small cracks in the plaster shooting off like veins from the ceiling medallion. The tapestry ottoman's leg had a spot where the mahogany finish had rubbed off. Heddy let her eyes follow the crown molding, the bookshelves that flanked the fireplace. There were model ships of all sizes, some tucked into clear glass bottles with necks so narrow Heddy wondered how they got inside. On another shelf was a thick stack of records. Music. That would quell the loneliness gathering like Ted's cigar smoke.

Heddy sat with her legs crossed on the plush oriental carpet and flipped through the album covers. Ella Fitzgerald, Fabian, Elvis Pre-

sley. She slid Little Eva's "The Loco-Motion" out of the cover, balancing the smooth edges of the vinyl in her fingertips, and placed it
on the turntable. She lowered the needle down with a steady hand,
careful not to make any scratches. The singer's perky voice sounded
out, and Heddy turned up the dial on the record player so it filled
the vacant rooms.

Ruth bounded down the stairs. "I love this song."

"There you are! It's creepy in here when it's quiet."

Ruth rolled her eyes. "Making my way through the bedrooms."

"You want help?"

"Really? Would you make the bed in the master?" Ruth grabbed
a cleaning spray from the kitchen.

Heddy had never been in Jean-Rose's bedroom. The room
smelled stale, a musky mix of Chanel N°5, Old Spice, and a night of
sleep. She set her sights on the mahogany four-poster bed. Pulling
taut the white cotton sheets, Heddy noticed the sheet was kicked
down on one side and only one pillow indented, like a thumbprint
cookie. The trash can overflowed with crumpled tissues.

In the adjoining sunroom, several pieces of stained glass hung in
a bay window. She'd seen the room from the back lawn—it jutted out
from the rest of the house like a jewel, ornate spindles carved into
the outside trim—and inside, a plush chaise was positioned in front
of the windows, offering a glimpse of the sea. Someone had crudely
folded a set of sheets, tossed two pillows on the chaise. "What should
I do with the stuff on the settee?"

Ruth yelled from the hall. "Stack it in Ted's closet."

On her way to the closet, a sharp pain seared through Heddy's
toe. "Shit, shit, shit," she yelled. She grabbed at her big toe, a punc-
ture where an earring had stabbed her. In the bathroom, she dabbed
her cut with toilet paper, sitting down at Jean-Rose's ornate wooden
vanity, an oversize mirror carved with a decorative fleur-de-lis. A
large jewelry box sat on the vanity, a pale blue rectangle with three

drawers and painted snowflakes on the lid. Spindly letters, written in the hand of a child, spelled out: "Jeannie." Heddy unlatched the clasp. The top sprung open, the notes of "Someday My Prince Will Come" chiming, and a tiny figurine, an ice skater, began to spin on a single blade, her movement reflected in a tiny oval mirror.

Tiny interior compartments lined in pale blue satin each held a pair of sparkly earrings. She'd seen jewelry like this behind glass when visiting her mother at Tiffany's, but she'd never tried any on. She picked up a large emerald earring shaped like a rounded square, a frame of tiny diamonds around it. A clip-on, it pinched Heddy's earlobe when she closed the back. Heddy dug her finger under the feathery-light chain of a diamond pendant, fastening it around her neck. She slid a diamond eternity bracelet around her wrist, admiring the delicate circle of linked jewels.

"You little fox." Ruth stood behind her in the bathroom, pressing a broom to her chest. "You have to see her drawer of hair accessories."

Heddy pulled one of the tiny glass knobs, revealing a row of jeweled hair combs, and Ruth opened the next to show rows of glittering rings tucked into fabric slits. She looked at her reflection and thought how plain her headbands and ponytails seemed, how unremarkable her features. The upside was her Kelly-green tank top and short-sleeve knit matching cardigan. She'd paid less than ten cents for both pieces at the Salvation Army, but she knew they could pass muster with the girls accustomed to buying short sets at Bloomingdale's on Fifty-Ninth Street.

She turned to Ruth. "I want to change my hair. Will you help me?"

Ruth set the broom against the wall. "Sure. Now?" When Heddy nodded, Ruth ran her fingers through Heddy's shoulder-length mane, the way hairdressers do when they take stock of a woman's tresses. "A trim?" Ruth opened the medicine cabinet in the bathroom and pulled out a pair of Ted's haircutting scissors and a comb.

"Chop it. I want it short." *The shorter the hair, the harder they'll stare*, she'd overheard someone say once.

Ruth put a towel around Heddy's shoulders. She sprayed her hair, soaking it, combing her wet hair flat against her head. "Never make a rash decision about your hair. Let's trim it."

"No, I want it, short. *Roman Holiday* short."

Ruth grimaced. "But you'll look like a boy."

"I'll look like Audrey Hepburn. Like I'm planning a trip to London, just because."

Ruth held the scissors to the first lock. "Are you sure?"

Heddy tugged on her hair. "Come on. Before I change my mind."

With the first snip, Heddy gasped, a long chunk of hair drifting into her lap. Ruth paused, resting her hands on Heddy's shoulders.

"Sorry, keep going," Heddy said.

She watched each lock fall into her lap—*snip, snip, snip*—clumping it in her fingers. Without all that hair, her cheekbones seemed higher, and her lips were soft and pink. Kissable. She looked kissable. When Ruth was done, she stepped back to admire her work. "It suits you. You need more eye makeup, though."

Heddy felt the back of her neck where her hair used to hang. It was bare. The cut was girlish, framing her face perfectly, just like she'd imagined.

"I love it. Really, I do."

Ruth put her hand on her hip. "Then why are you crying?"

Heddy wiped at her eyes, laughing. "Because it's perfect. I belong in one of those Pepsi-Cola advertisements. 'The sociables prefer Pepsi.'"

Heddy loved the spangly earrings with her short haircut, how the shape hung from her ear like a swing. "Maybe you don't need to go to school, Ruth. Why don't you just open a salon?"

Then everything seemed to stop. A car traveled up the gravel driveway, the unmistakable popping of rocks under tires. The truth rushed at them: They were in Jean-Rose's bathroom, wearing her jewelry, Heddy's hair in a pile on the tiled floor. Ruth ripped the towel off Heddy's shoulders.

"Put those things away. I'll sweep," Ruth barked. They worked quickly, Heddy frantically pulling the earrings off her ears, returning them to their satin square. She unclasped the necklace, spiraling the chain back into place.

Outside, the engine turned off. "Stall them," Ruth said, broom in hand.

Heddy closed the top of the jewelry box as beads of sweat gathered at her temples. She needed to turn down the record player, still playing the album she'd put on earlier. She didn't think Jean-Rose would mind her putting on music, but she didn't want to seem unhinged to her boss, who always kept the music low. Heddy took the steps two at a time, a nagging feeling that she'd forgotten something, but what?

"Morning."

Heddy whipped around to see Ash standing on the porch. He was freshly showered, the smell of soap and aftershave wafting through the screen. "Wow. You look different."

"Hi," she said stupidly. She exhaled, her hands clasped behind her back; she felt Jean-Rose's tennis bracelet slide on her wrist. She'd never returned it to the jewelry box.

"You changed your hair?"

She nodded, hoping he would say something else, while stuffing the bracelet into her shorts pocket.

"I like it," he said.

"Thanks," she smiled, unable to meet his eyes for a moment.

He peered behind her into the house. "I'm looking for Ted. Is he here?"

"They're at the club." Upstairs, Ruth was shaking out the bathroom mats, her arms out the window, slamming them against the house.

"Do you think you could leave this in his office?" Ash handed her a sealed yellow envelope. "Came to me by accident." A postmark from Worcester, Massachusetts, Ted's name written in messy black pen on the front.

Tucking the envelope under her arm, Heddy stepped outside the porch doors as he descended the steps. Watching him go was like watching egg white slip away from yolk, a slow unraveling, and she was determined to stop it. She sat in a pretty recline on the steps, stretching her legs the length of them. "I had fun on the surfboard," she said.

Halfway to his car on the slate walkway, he turned. "You want to try again?"

She fluttered her eyes. "Is that an invitation?"

"You'll be with Teddy at Katama Beach on Wednesday, right? Come back on the board. I'll teach you." He crouched down, reaching his hand to her cheek. She held her breath, staring at his wet hair, golden at the tips. She imagined them sitting at the high-tide mark at sunset, how his face would look serious just before he kissed her. How he'd smell like vanilla, and the salt air would nudge them closer.

"There's some hair, from your haircut," he said, brushing her cheek with the back of his hand. He turned to leave, and she watched his truck disappear around the bend, hollow with longing.

Ruth came out on the porch and sat beside her, a dirt-streaked rag in hand. "You're so red you look like you've been rubbed with Indian rocks."

Heddy buried her eyes in her fists. "He thinks I'm nothing but ordinary."

Ruth leaned her head on Heddy's shoulder. "I asked around about him, you know, and I heard some things. You know, rumors."

Heddy lowered her fists. "Like?"

"Like he needs to roll it up in Saran Wrap."

Heddy pushed Ruth away, erupting into belly laughter. "You're disgusting."

Ruth played innocent. "And old Mary at the boatyard told my cousin's friend that he has a thing for the wives."

"Why would he waste his time?"

Ruth grabbed the cleaner. "I dunno, to convince them to buy into his development."

"That's outrageous. Many of them could be his mother."

"Just telling you what I heard," she said.

Heddy bit at the skin around her thumbnail. Her short hair. It had been for him. But what if the rumors were true?

She climbed the stairs to her room, diving headfirst onto her made bed, propping herself up by the window and staring out at the choppy water and the mainland beyond. She glanced at Ash's cottage, feeling her bare neck; she was spending too much time thinking about this surfer who was nothing more than a flirt. In her journal, she turned to a blank page and wrote: *school, school, school.* She tapped the pen's tip to the page, creating a burst of dots. Her conversation with Ted was pathetic, and she was certain she wouldn't try again. What could she do? An image of Gigi popped into her head. Gigi, with the slick legs and big ego, digging her gaze into Heddy.

"You will fight, little girl. That's what. Now *do* something."

Heddy sat up, words coursing through her, forming an argument that she had to get on paper. She *would* fight. She would do exactly what the women on this island would do: Act entitled. Blame others for anything standing in her way. Before she lost her train of thought, she sat at her desk, pulling a sheet of paper from the top drawer.

Dear Members of the Financial Committee:

I am a third-year student in Wellesley College's Department of English, and I was informed that my scholarship was revoked. It is devastating to my future, but it's also a detriment to Wellesley.

Sometimes it feels like I'm the only student who didn't grow up in a place like Darien or Scarsdale. I ask the committee how many students at the college come from a less affluent background? How many of your students work at the diner after school and send most of their earnings to a single mother in Brooklyn?

Here's why you need students like me at Wellesley: I lend a different perspective to your rarefied air. Many of the women I've met at college are there because their parents force them through the wrought iron gates. I'm not at Wellesley to earn a "Mrs. degree," I'm there to graduate and earn an advanced degree. I want to be a writer. Or a teacher. I'm not certain, and I think that's okay. But what I am sure of is how much I want to learn. I want to slide into a desk chair every morning and be given the chance to dream my way out of the Brooklyn tenement where I grew up.

I ask you, respectfully, to review my transcripts one final time. You'll see that my failing grade in biology was an anomaly. I will never make the same mistake.

She signed her name, folded the letter into thirds, and slid it into an envelope. The committee would change their minds about her. They had to.

TEN

"Why do you drive so slow?" Ruth gulped down something she'd brought in a red thermos, handing it to Heddy.

"I like to take my time." Heddy sniffed the rim, repelled by the strong smell of rum. She took a sip anyway, the liquor stinging her chest.

"We might not get there before midnight, but okay. Sorry I couldn't drive—I didn't know my dad needed the car." Ruth rolled her eyes.

Heddy took a sarcastic tone. "Cards again? Well, it's good to have a passion."

Ruth sipped her thermos. "Not if it's messing everyone's life up."

While Ruth hunted for a station on the radio, Heddy wondered about Ruth's father. Heddy, having longed for a dad all her life, imagined that her father would have anchored her, bringing with him a whiff of cologne and a wallet of cash, a warm kiss on the cheek before bed. Ted wasn't a perfect dad, but he didn't have any threatening vices, like alcohol, and he provided his children with a lovely summer house, the best cuts of steak, a steady roster of activities. Sure, he disappeared sometimes, and maybe she'd thought a father would be more present, but still, Ted was there when Jean-Rose needed him. That a father could cause pain, that someone could curse their father's existence, interested her the way algebra did. A strange equation adding up to an unexpected outcome.

"You don't have to stay on the island." Heddy could see the fairgrounds up ahead. A large Ferris wheel rotated over the treetops. It took twenty minutes to drive up island, which is what Ruth called this part of Martha's Vineyard. It was more rural, farther away from the ports with their crowds and charming commercial strips.

"Where would I go?"

"You could come to Brooklyn." Heddy clicked on her blinker, turning into the parking lot where people emerged in groups from cars, doors slamming. "There's a cosmetology school there, or you could get a job."

"But you're going back to Boston! I don't know a soul in New York."

Heddy put the car in park. "We could be roommates in the city after I graduate." She still hadn't told Ruth about her scholarship.

Ruth checked her lipstick. It was the first time Heddy saw her wearing makeup. "Me? In New York? What a daydream."

They wandered the rows of games, colorful stuffed animals hanging from tented walls of the booths. "Step right up, miss. Three balls for a quarter, three balls for a quarter," called a hunchbacked man with thick stubble on his beard.

"Don't waste your money." Ruth took Heddy's arm, leading her away. "No one ever wins."

The grass was muddy from being trampled, and with the sun setting, the breeze turned chilly. Heddy zipped the "KATAMA BEACH" sweatshirt she'd grabbed in the mudroom. They stopped to watch people slamming a sledgehammer on a silver discus, hoping to win a stuffed pink puppy if the "Strong-o-Meter" announced them a "Master." But no one, no matter how muscled, seemed to get beyond "Bulging." Ruth kept an eye out for someone named Jerome, who was bringing the boy Jean-Rose had arranged for her.

"We have to ride the Tilt-A-Whirl." Ruth pointed to the flamingo-pink capsules shaped like hamburger buns, spinning around while zipping along a track.

Heddy put her hand to her stomach. Rides made her queasy, but she didn't want to be a spoilsport. "Let's get some popcorn. My treat," she said, stopping at a cart manned by a teenager in a striped hat. Heddy reached into her satin clutch for a dollar, realizing now how light the bag was. She'd taken five dollars out of her sock drawer and put it in her wallet, but then the children had distracted her and she left her wallet on her dresser. Her heart sank. "Oh, Ruth, this is so embarrassing. I must have left my wallet—"

"Cheapskate." Ruth smiled, and Heddy felt a tight line form in her lips and a blush in her cheeks. When Heddy was twelve, she and her mother were paying at the grocery store and they hadn't had enough. They'd put back crackers, a hunk of cheddar, shampoo, just so they could pay, while the clerk rolled her eyes. "As if you've never had a hard week," her mother had snapped at the cashier.

The carousel's music played on, and the popcorn clerk sighed, tapping his metal scooper, while Ruth dug coins from her change purse: "Lady, do you have enough or what?" the clerk said.

"Maybe we should get to the back of the line," Heddy said, tugging on Ruth's arm.

"No, I have it." Ruth gave him the dimes and nickels.

A man behind them cleared his throat, reaching his hand between her and Ruth's shoulders, dangling three dollars at the zitty kid behind the stand. "We'll take three large tubs," a baritone voice rang out.

"No, please. It's fine, we're . . ." When Heddy turned around to apologize—she was so mortified at not having her wallet and for slow-

ing the line down—she came face-to-face with Ash, his eyes glistening, looking quite pleased with himself. Had he been behind them the
entire time? She tried to remember what they'd been saying.

"It's okay, really. I just left my wallet, and Ruth, she wants to pay
with . . ."

"Get me next time," he said, handing Heddy one tub of popcorn
and Ruth the other. He stuffed a handful of buttered popcorn in his
mouth. "Enjoy."

And he was gone, his broad shoulders disappearing into the
crowd. Her instinct was to follow him, to find out who he was with.
Who *was* he with? A rickety roller coaster zipped by, the screams of
riders shrieking as they flew past. Still stunned, she followed Ruth
to a small circus tent where she bought three tickets a piece from a
man with stubby hands—Ruth counting change again to pay—then
to the spinning ride they'd seen earlier.

"Jerome, over here!" Ruth was standing on tiptoe, waving to a boy
holding a bag of cotton candy. The boy had tight red curls, narrow
eyes, and a face full of freckles. He grinned when he saw Ruth in line
at the Tilt-A-Whirl, revealing two gapped front teeth.

"Hi, pretty lady. You just get here?"

Ruth nodded. "Heddy, this is my friend, Jerome."

"We're more than friends. I'd say we're very close friends." He
put his arm around Ruth.

"It's true—our mothers have known each other since they were
both in service at the Harbor View Hotel and we were both in dia-
pers." Ruth didn't pull away, she nuzzled him.

Heddy avoided looking at them, glancing at a clown on six-foot
stilts waving to the crowd. She thought it odd Ruth didn't mention
she had a boyfriend.

"Excuse me, I need to use the bathroom," Heddy said.

Jerome blocked her. "Wait, I want to introduce you to my buddy."
He turned around, pulling at the shoulder of someone Heddy thought

looked familiar. He was wearing the same round tortoiseshell glasses, his hair the same tidy buzz of closely cropped hair.

"Sullivan?"

"Oh, hey, Heddy. I didn't recognize you for a second—your hair. How's the kite? I mean, the kids?" She was impressed he remembered her name, smiling at him when he pushed his glasses up the bridge of his nose.

"It hasn't been windy enough"—then, flustered, she managed— "did you know this was happening, when I saw you at the park?"

"You two know each other?" Ruth faced them, her hand on her hips.

Jerome patted Sullivan on the back, like he was congratulating him. "You're always one step ahead, paper boy. But you couldn't have planned this one, even you aren't that good."

"Paper boy?" Heddy looked at Sullivan for an explanation, but Sullivan shot her a look, like Jerome was a bit of an idiot whose behavior needn't be explained.

"Can we hop on with you?" Jerome cut into the line beside them, panting like an excited puppy. Nearby, a man in a candy-striped suit was spinning cotton candy onto paper cones, sending the sickly sweet scent of spun sugar all around them.

"Sullivan is the guy that helped me with the kite."

"The one with the annoying dog?" Ruth blurted out. Heddy kicked her.

"He did bark a lot," Heddy told Sullivan.

"That's what dogs do." Sullivan stuffed his hands in his pockets. The roller coaster whizzed by again, the shrieks of riders fading into the distance.

"We're waiters down at the Clamshell," Jerome bellowed. "Paper boy is my rowing pal. He rows; I watch." He held up his hand to high-five Sullivan, but when Sullivan went to slap it, Jerome pulled his away. "Too slow, man." Jerome snickered, looking at Ruth and

Heddy for a laugh but getting nothing. Sullivan opened his mouth to say something, then wrinkled his blond eyebrows; his hair dirty blond.

"I row at school." Sullivan tapped his thigh with his fingers, a fast-ticking clock, until he noticed Heddy glance down. His hand stilled.

There goes Mr. Fidgety, Heddy thought. She couldn't believe this was "the catch" Jean-Rose rounded up, Sullivan the waiter. She willed herself to find her manners.

"Where's school?" asked Heddy.

"Boston."

Jerome pushed Sullivan's shoulder, like he couldn't believe him. "Listen to you. Boston."

Heddy remembered his Harvard sweater from the ferry. "I attend Wellesley."

"Oh yeah?" Sullivan smiled, revealing deep dimples, and for a moment, she saw him differently: baby-faced and sweet, a shy boy trying to talk to a girl.

"Heddy is a swimmer." Ruth pretended not to notice Jerome's arm was around her waist, and he was tickling her ear with his tongue.

"What's your race?" Sullivan asked her.

"The butterfly."

"You ever win?"

"Sometimes."

Heddy handed a ticket to a man standing at the entrance to the Tilt-A-Whirl. They climbed into the pod, the seating becoming a bit political as Heddy stepped over Sullivan, who was originally between her and Ruth, so the two girls could be sandwiched between the boys. As the ride began to spin, Heddy felt her stomach lurch, and she closed her eyes, trying to keep the dizziness at bay.

She heard Sullivan say: "Lean against my shoulder, it will feel better." And she did, and it did feel better, anchoring her until the pod twirled the other way, and then she slammed into Ruth, who was hysterical with laughter, especially since Jerome was pushing his weight in the direction the cart was spinning, making it spin faster.

When the ride came to a stop, and she got still-footed enough to get off, the ground was undulating.

"I think I'm done for the night," Heddy said, cupping her hand over her mouth.

Ruth pulled away from Jerome and pulled Heddy to a bench. "Are you going to be sick?"

"I'm okay. Just dizzy." She gagged, willing her stomach to calm.

"You know what she needs? A ride on the Sea of Love." Jerome pointed to a ride with red illuminated hearts blinking on the outside. His gapped front teeth made him look like a beaver. Heddy wanted to sock him.

"I'm happy watching all of you. Someone can have these." Heddy held up her remaining tickets, dropping her clutch at her side. Sullivan sat next to her, handing her a cup of ice water he'd fetched.

"This will help. Drink it." He bounced his leg up and down, like it was itchy, then took some ice, wrapped it in a napkin and pressed it to her forehead. "If I'd known you got sick easily, I would have told you to skip the Tilt-A-Whirl. We study that ride in physics."

Heddy downed the ice water, feeling a bit better. "Why?"

His leg went still. "Because a Tilt car behaves differently depending on the speed it's moving. It never spins the same way. The motion is truly chaotic." He gestured at her belly. "Of course, it's also why your stomach got so churned up." His leg began bouncing again, vibrating, like he couldn't keep it still if he tried. Heddy released the grip on her stomach.

"How interesting." She only half understood what he was talking about. How did Ash manage to be so captivating, no matter what he said, while this boy was making conversation with her about a subject she despised most, something dreadful, like science. Who cares why the ride was spinning—all that mattered was that she nearly lost her lunch.

Ruth and Jerome were kissing now, and Heddy pretended not to see. She looked in the direction of the Ferris wheel, but the lights— or maybe all the lights at the carnival—made her feel queasy all over again. She put her hand to her temple and closed her eyes. She sensed Sullivan leaning over, his elbow on his knees, picking up something in the grass. And when she opened her eyes, he held up a tiny bunch of clovers.

"It's okay if you don't want to go on any more rides. We can just sit here. I like to people watch," he said.

Heddy reached for the clippings, finding herself smiling, despite the strangeness of it all. "Thank you." She touched the tiny stems, the bottoms damp from where he'd torn them off, raising them to her nose.

"What do they smell like?" Sullivan pressed his fingertips together into a pyramid.

"Grass." She smiled.

"I'll get you real flowers next time." He didn't lift his head to look at her, and she found herself wondering if he was grinning—she liked his dimples.

Next time? That was presumptuous, wasn't it? Yet, it loosened the tight knot in her chest. He was already thinking about another date, so he must like her. Even if she wasn't sure she liked him, it was a relief someone thought her tolerable. She glanced over at Ruth, who was leaning her hip against the bench, her mouth open and probing into Jerome's. *Ruth!* She wanted to yell, *Stop making such a fool of yourself.*

"I'd love to take a walk," she said, her head no longer spinning.

Sullivan jumped to his feet. "Where to?"

"The Ferris wheel?" The carnival was getting more crowded—it seemed like every teenager on the island was there now. Heddy and

Sullivan walked behind the hordes of people until he stopped short, deciding he wanted cotton candy, and an older woman, walking too close, crashed into his back. He bent down to help her to her feet.

"Sorry, ma'am." When he saw the lady's face, his deflated. He stood straighter, cleared his throat. "Hello, Mrs. Nickens."

The old woman looked delighted, pulled a handkerchief out of her pocket and dabbed her drawn-on brow, careful not to wipe any away. "Dear me, Sullivan. Thank you. How are you? Is your mother still sailing?" She turned to Heddy. "One of the smartest ladies I know, Mrs. Abigail Rhodes."

"Father says she can do anything." Sullivan folded his hands in front of his waist in the formal way Heddy remembered doing when she met the president of her college at a luncheon.

"You know, Sullivan, I need another board member—"

Sullivan coughed. "Excuse me, Mrs. Nickens, I'll tell Mother to call you." Sullivan steered Heddy away, so fast that Heddy nearly tripped.

"Sorry about that. I just don't feel like running into anybody," he said. They fell back into the crowd, cotton candy in hand, Sullivan pulling a large swirl of the sticky pink candy and handing her the rest in the paper cone.

"That's sweet, thank you." She took a mouselike nibble, not wanting to upset her stomach any further. Someone shoved Heddy from behind, her nose smashing into the tip of the cotton candy.

"Heddy!" It was Ruth, breathless, like she'd been running. "We found you. Why didn't you tell us you were leaving?"

When Heddy turned around to face her; she didn't try to hide her irritation. "I didn't think you'd notice I left."

Ruth ignored her. "Let's all go on the Sea of Love. Jerome is saving us a place in line."

"I don't know." Heddy glanced at Sullivan.

"It's fine, Heddy. Really." He pulled a strand of cotton candy.

"You're sure you don't study this one in physics, too?"

"Never."

It was pitch-black inside the Sea of Love. Heddy and Sullivan sat in the first boat in the chain, gliding through the dark. Every few feet a dim light bulb illuminated their faces, just long enough to glimpse each other.

"Jerome and I aren't really friends, you know." Sullivan's voice was quiet, and being in the dark seemed to calm him—at least his leg was still. "He's a bit of an ass, isn't he?"

Heddy beamed in the dark. "I'm not sure what Ruth sees in him."

"Tell your friend she could do better."

"Have you known him long? I didn't know you grew up here." They passed under a light, and Heddy saw him lifting his arm slowly around her back, but she never felt it press against her. Then it was dark again.

"Me? God, no. Mother wouldn't tolerate me staying in New York, no matter how hard I try, so I'm forced to come every summer."

The boat chugged upward, and Heddy slid closer to him, squeezing her own thigh, wondering if she'd been tricked into a roller coaster. He put his hand over hers, pressing down, and saying: "Don't worry. I promise you, it's nothing."

At the top of the incline, the boat went in a circle before plunging downward, just for a second, before splashing into a pool at the bottom. He lifted his hand, and Heddy relaxed.

"That wasn't so bad," she said. When they passed under the light this time, he was gazing at her.

"You should come for lunch at the Clamshell," he said.

They slipped back into darkness. "Is the food any good?" she said.

"The company's better," he said.

The boat came to a halt, and everyone got out, stepping into the bright lights of the fair. The Gravitron's shiny capsule spun like a top. Ruth and Jerome emerged holding hands.

"Ruth, I think we should be going. Ted wants the car back by ten thirty."

"But it's quarter after nine."

Sullivan held up his wristwatch. "She's right."

"Well, I suppose we could stay a bit longer," Heddy said. She didn't know why she was in a rush. Sullivan was nice enough. There was pressure, though, in being set up, in Ruth and Jerome necking nearby.

Ruth pulled Heddy aside toward a concession stand, the sizzle and pop of frozen hamburger patties hitting the grill, the smoky smell of meat everywhere. "You want to ditch the boys? I'm tired of hanging out with Jerome anyway."

"I didn't even know you had a boyfriend!"

"Jerome? Gosh, no. I'm just bored."

Heddy sighed.

"I told you—I've gotta get off this island."

They returned to the boys, who had paid a quarter to throw darts at a clown's face, winning a prize if they landed one square in the nose.

"We're going on the Ferris wheel—see you boys later." Ruth slid her arm back into Heddy's.

"Don't be like that." Jerome put down his darts. "Let's go together."

Ruth shrugged. "Maybe later."

Heddy shouted bye to Sullivan, watching as he stuffed one hand in his pocket, his mouth turning down in disappointment as he waved. Jerome punched Sullivan on the back, holding his stomach and laughing about something Heddy couldn't make out.

"Well, he recovered quickly."

Ruth looked over her shoulder. "Don't ever let me date him. I can't stoop that low, Heddy. Please."

Heddy squeezed her arm. "We gotta get you out of here."

"Like I said, what a daydream."

"Heddy?" Sullivan tapped her on the back. He'd run after them, and now facing her, he'd gone mute. He darted his eyes from Heddy to Ruth, then back again. "Um . . ." He faked a laugh, his lip curling up just a little, like Elvis. "Forget the Clamshell. Do you want to go out for breakfast? You're free, right, when the kids go to camp?"

Ruth grinned at Heddy, whose eyes wrinkled with delight. "That sounds nice."

He stuffed his hands in his pockets. "Okay."

"Okay."

He seemed like he might keep standing there, saying nothing, so Ruth steered Heddy away. They were arm in arm, laughing like schoolgirls.

"He could have asked you to a proper dinner," Ruth snorted.

"Nah. Breakfast is shorter—what are we going to talk about for more than an hour?"

"His parents."

Heddy raised an eyebrow. "No one wants to talk about their parents on a date."

"They do, if said boy's parents own the *New York Post-Courier*."

Heddy stopped short, two teenagers walking right into her from behind. "Sorry. What are you talking about?"

Ruth laughed slyly. "My mother cooked for the Rhodes one summer; biggest house on the island." His last name was Rhodes. But what had that meant to Heddy?

"He told me he's a physics major. And a waiter. You were standing right there!"

"Step right up, miss. Three throws for a nickel." A man with a feather in his cap called to them.

Ruth pulled Heddy to walk again. "Well, that science nerd goes to the same club as Jean-Rose. He's a Harvard man. His family is grooming him to be the publisher."

Heddy felt her cheeks flush. "But he's awkward. Didn't you see how he doesn't stop fidgeting?"

"So?"

"So, how could he come from a family like that?"

Ruth put her arm back in Heddy's, looked up at the stars, like they were finally aligning in her favor. "Who cares? Imagine the life you'd have."

Heddy was so stunned that she followed Ruth onto the Ferris wheel feeling dazed. It was admirable that even with that background, he understood the value of a hard day's work. It made him seem strong, although for all she knew his parents forced him into the job at the Clamshell.

And as the Ferris wheel took them higher into the sky, she was trying to figure out: Why would someone like him ask her out on a date?

She and Ruth hadn't been alone much on Saturday, and Ruth had Sundays off, so they hadn't been able to talk the entire weekend. Heddy wondered if Sullivan would call for a second date. By Sunday afternoon, she was tired of analyzing it, and she called her mother early in the afternoon as a distraction. Jean-Rose and Ted were gone; Heddy and the children had spent the afternoon making robots out of shoeboxes, and now they were happily watching cartoons.

Her mother picked up on the first ring. "You shouldn't call this early. You know the rates go down at night."

No one was home, so Heddy placed the black rotary phone on the floor, sitting down cross-legged on the oriental carpet, her back against the telephone table. "Mama, it's okay. They don't mind."

"Well, we should only stay on for a minute or two. On principle."

Heddy smiled into the receiver; her mother was tight-fisted, even with someone else's purse strings. "All right."

"So how are you—your letter makes work sound like play."

"Yes, it is. I love it. It's just . . ." She ran her fingers over the circle of the rotary dial.

"Oh, shit on a potato, I hear stars in your voice. You better not be running around the island making a fool of yourself with one of these guys she set you up with. I told you Ken McKinney is waiting. He's a college boy, too. Got that degree from . . ."

"CUNY, I know."

Heddy covered the receiver with her hand, pinched her eyes shut and opened her mouth in a silent scream. *Ken McKinney. KEN McKINNEY?* Back home he was the most eligible bachelor, since he was manager at the shipbuilding factory. He had taken Heddy on a picnic at Prospect Park before she left for the island. But in between bites of sandwiches, they'd struggled to make conversation, mostly because he did all the talking: how he graduated with honors; how great he was at managing employees; how he and his future wife could live upstairs from his mother (there was already an empty apartment!). The odd thing was that he expected Heddy to be as fascinated with the minutiae of his life as he was, and it dawned on her then that if she ever had a son, she wouldn't treat him godlike the way Ken McKinney's mother had. It made for a grown man with zero self-awareness.

"Are you there, Hibernia? Who has your attention? The waiter?"

Heddy cleared her throat. "No." She wanted to tell her mother about Sullivan, about the finer points that made him a catch, but then she imagined her mother coming to the island in her scuffed patent leather shoes, having to stand next to the perfectly coiffed, well-dressed Mrs. Rhodes, and she changed her mind.

"Did you figure out your tuition, Hibernia?"

Heddy sucked in a deep breath, feeling the clamminess gathering under her palm against the receiver. "Mama, what if I don't want to go back to school next semester?"

"Don't dare talk like that," her mother snapped. "I'll call another bank."

"No, no. I worked it out with school. It's more a feeling of dread."

"Must I remind you, Hibernia, that the girls at Tiffany's would die for an opportunity like yours." Her mother sighed. "Joe says his pop wants to raise the rent twenty-five dollars."

"I'll call him," Heddy said. Joe was the landlord's son, and he'd always been sweet on Heddy. She even flirted back sometimes, just so he'd be nicer to them.

"Don't. And don't you dare say you're not going back to school. Some people play the slots. Others put their money in a house. Well, I don't have any money at all, so . . ."

Heddy finished her mother's sentence; she'd heard her say it a million times. "So you're investing in me." Heddy wiped at the corners of her eyes. "I know, Mama. You're right. Of course, I'm going back."

She promised to call again next Sunday, then trudged up to her room, curling up in bed. That she was getting good at lying only made her feel worse. A house of cards could stand only so long.

ELEVEN

*H*eddy, who was in too much of a daze on her first visit to Gigi's to get a good look around, had imagined the inside of the actress's house as a cacophony of animal-print linens, faux fur rugs, and sultry photographs taken of the actress. But standing in her entryway, a candle burning the smell of sandalwood, there wasn't a leopard-print pillow in sight. Instead, the estate was all understated glamour, and most certainly, pulled together with the help of a decorator. The expansive living room had a bricked fireplace so large a child could step into it, and an enormous royal-blue velour couch that was horseshoe-shaped and featured throw pillows patterned with navy anchors and yellow stripes. On the glass coffee table, a stack of books: *Hollywood in the 1920s* and *Fashion Girls*.

Gigi glanced over her bare, tanned shoulder. "Your hair is fabulous."

Heddy scrunched the back with her hands. Jean-Rose hadn't been as complimentary, giving her a double take and saying, "Quite a change."

"I think I like it, too."

Gigi turned to face her and poked her shoulder for emphasis. "You don't *think* you like your hair—you love it. And so do I." Gigi winked at her, then walked on. "Children," she called, "careful up the stairs."

She followed Gigi to a grand double staircase, bronze railings climbing up both sides. The walls were wallpapered with turquoise palm fronds, and once upstairs, a long corridor of doors stood to the left and right. The carpet was cotton-ball white, so clean Heddy checked the bottoms of her feet.

Gigi shrugged. "Don't worry. It's just a rug." But it wasn't just a rug. It was pure opulence, soft and plush underfoot, like walking on clouds. She imagined how warm a rug like this would feel in winter, when stepping out of bed onto chilled wooden floors made her want to climb right back under her covers.

"Is this really your . . ." Heddy didn't know where to look first. *And this is what money can buy you*, she thought. *A better life*.

The walls of Gigi's bedroom were a muted ballerina pink, and the carpet was pink, too. But nearly everything else in the room was white except her nightstands and dresser, which were glass and mirrored, reflecting the bright morning light around the room. A sitting area featured two tufted white leather couches, a white oval coffee table between them. And the white curtains parted at either end of the long row of floor-to-ceiling windows looked as though a theatrical performance was about to begin, this one starring the ocean, since the room overlooked a large expanse of open sea.

The children began bouncing up and down on Gigi's enormous bed. "Jump with us!" they beckoned. Gigi hopped onto the bed, holding their hands and springing them up and down. Heddy slunk down to sit on the carpet and clapped to be a good sport. Teddy was holding Miss Pinkie, throwing her up and catching her.

"Heddy let me bring her, even though Mommy says I'm not allowed to leave the house with her. Right, Heddy?"

Heddy nodded, lifting her finger to her lips to shush him: "Our little secret." Their relationship was improving now that she was allowing him to smuggle Miss Pinkie in a backpack wherever they went.

Gigi sprung up, getting air. "What's the problem with the doll?"

"It worries Jean-Rose."

"Meaning?" Her motions made the kids fall backward, laughing.

Heddy shifted. "I guess she worries it means something. I mean, it could."

Gigi landed on her feet, jumped again. "And so what if it did? Some of my best friends in the business are light in the loafers. He is who he is." Gigi turned to Teddy. "You can always bring Miss Pinkie here." Teddy's happiness sprung him higher.

"Is that Mama?" Anna, who had tired of jumping, was holding a small framed photograph she'd found on Gigi's dresser. The picture was small, yellowed with time, but it showed two little girls with braided pigtails posing in bathing suits next to an in-ground pool, a refined woman in a sophisticated knee-length dress held a martini behind them, her arms around both children.

"We were so sweet, weren't we? Like sisters," Gigi said, and Heddy realized then that it was Jean-Rose in the picture.

She saw two other framed photographs: one of Gigi accepting her Academy Award and a formal black-and-white wedding portrait. "Those are my parents," Gigi said.

"You look just like your father." It was their shared expression, a clarity in their eyes.

"But I have my mother's bleeding heart." Gigi emitted a throaty laugh, scanning the listings of that week's *TV Guide*. "Oh, right. Dick Clark's *Bandstand* is on." She called to her housekeeper to make the kids popcorn, then carried the portable television to her bed, propping it up against the pillows; it looked like a small grass cloth suitcase.

Teddy spun the metal dial, clicking on *Bonanza*, the blue skies and green hills of the Wild West on the screen. "You have a portable—*color*—TV?"

"Yes, but you'll have to watch Dick Clark in black and white." She fiddled with the antennae until *American Bandstand* zapped to clarity. "The network is too cheap to switch *Bandstand* to color." The theme song exploded from the television's small speaker, and the kids tried to imitate the dance moves of the show's regulars.

Gigi mixed herself and Heddy each a Tom Collins at a bar cart in her bedroom, smirking at the children's tiny gyrations, and led Heddy down the hall to her changing room, where a large bedroom had been transformed into a dressing room with a raised step and surround mirrors, so she could pivot 360 degrees and see every inch of herself.

"Let's get to it." Gigi ducked into her closet, connected to her changing room by a door. "This is where I keep summer cocktail dresses." She pressed a button, which made the dresses in her closet motor around in circles. She pulled a navy-blue strapless dress and walked over to Heddy.

"Gigi, can I talk to you about something?" The hanger bumped Heddy's chin when Gigi held the dress up to her small frame.

"You are a scrawny little thing, aren't you, sugar pie?" Gigi returned the dress to the closet, pressing the button to send a new set toward her.

"Gigi, I know you don't really know me, but you're being so nice to me, and I . . . Well, I have a big favor to ask of you."

Gigi didn't take her eyes off the dresses circling around. "You like to keep things interesting, don't you? What is it now?"

Heddy took out the letter she'd written. Typed and properly formatted, addressed to the scholarship committee. It spoke of Hibernia Winsome as a promising young woman who had surprised everyone who knew her with her tenacity and smarts, and whose script was currently being reviewed by Hollywood directors. Heddy gulped for air as Gigi read it, the actress laughing at parts, and still Heddy didn't lose her nerve. She needed this recommendation to accompany her appeal.

Heddy pointed to the blank spot at the letter's end, just under "Sincerely Yours."

"All you have to do is sign it. Please, I know it's a lot to ask, and I'll explain everything, if you want to know, but really, it would help me tremendously."

Gigi dropped the letter on her dresser. "Wow, you make me sound so articulate, like a producer."

Heddy scrunched her toes, gripping the rug pile. "I know it's odd and . . ."

"Parts of the letter are untrue." Gigi folded her arms.

"Yes, I know." It was nervy—worse than nervy, possibly atrocious, that she was stooping this low—making up the contents of an entire letter. But what other option did she have? "But I didn't have anyone else to ask, and I thought I'd make it easy and write the letter. Then you only needed a pen. To sign." Heddy handed her a black fountain pen, but Gigi turned back to the closet, pulling another dress.

"Strip. I'm going to start handing you stuff to try on."

Heddy placed the pen on the dresser, reassuring herself that Gigi hadn't said no—yet. She reluctantly pulled off her shirt, revealing her bra, which was frayed and gray, and not at all white, even though she washed it in the sink every other night. Gigi handed her a dress that was like a nightgown, spaghetti straps and a panel of black satin to the ankle. Then she gave her a yellow strapless mini, big white polka dots covering the bust. Heddy liked a powder-blue A-line dress with a matching bolero jacket. She tried each one, parading around for Gigi.

Gigi wrinkled her nose at the bolero jacket. "It's so matronly. If you always blend in and never stand out, who is going to notice you?"

Heddy nodded. "That's why I cut my hair."

Gigi remembered something then, her face turning brilliant. "I have just the dress for you." She hit the button again. "I wore this in *The It Girl*, but the scene was cut, so no one ever saw it. It was always too tight on me, but it may be perfect for your figure. It's an Oleg Cassini—one hundred percent silk."

As soon as Heddy zipped up the back, she fell in love. It was a simple strapless dress made of shiny red fabric that wrapped snug around her bust and waist until it popped out in an A-line, falling right above her knee; a matching silk-satin belt wrapped her midriff in a row of rhinestones. Heddy wasn't sure if it was the color or the way it curved her hips, but she seemed taller.

Heddy giggled. "I feel like Grace Kelly."

"Why does every woman want to look like Grace?" She sighed. "I guess before I was me, I wanted to look like Grace, too."

"Is Mr. Grant coming to the party?"

Gigi's tone grew peevish. "Oh, I don't know. Cary's out promoting *That Touch of Mink*." The movie was a box office smash, with tickets selling out in Vineyard Haven every Saturday night since it opened.

Gigi slipped off back into her closet, digging through a cupboard marked GLOVES, bringing Heddy back a pair of long, red satin ones. She tossed them at Heddy, who obediently slipped them on.

"Your hair changes everything—we can see you now," Gigi agreed. The actress gazed at her. "You can pull off the pixie with that darling face." Gigi turned to look at herself in the mirror and started doing something funny with her eyes. Heddy watched as the actress's light eyes turned into pools of sorrow. Then they changed again, as a deep feeling of happiness pushed to the surface, making the blue of her eyes twinkle.

Gigi sensed Heddy staring. "Your expression is so real. I'm copying it. I want to use it someday."

Heddy looked at her in the mirror. "I'm confused."

"You help me, I help you, right?"

"Sure, but—"

"But what? That's what actresses do. We step into someone else's shoes for a bit. I want to step into yours."

Heddy picked at her cuticles. "Do I seem pathetic?"

Gigi shook her head. "No. You look like a girl who wants the world to know she's there but isn't sure how to do it. I can't remember what that feels like anymore, and this role in . . ."

Heddy remembered the script, her curiosity about the pages. "*An Afternoon in Central Park.*"

"You're a quick study, aren't you? The character—how do I say this gently—has similar roadblocks."

Heddy turned back to herself in the mirror, ashamed that Gigi could see through her. She liked to think she could protect any painful parts that lurked inside her. But she'd let her guard down enough for Gigi to see beyond those walls.

Heddy pointed her left toes and twirled around, stopping to take a good look at her reflection. She needed shoes. She had only her mended sandals or these flats, and neither matched. "I'm a six. Do you have any shoes I could borrow?"

Gigi ran her hands down her curves. "You think all of this could balance on a size six? Definitely not. But I'll find you a pair somewhere."

Back in her bedroom, Gigi picked up a copy of *Style Me* magazine off her nightstand, flouncing on the bed, and Heddy sat beside her. Gigi opened to an article called "Be a Lady on Your Big Night," depicting several women dressed in formal wear, each with a different tip. "'If your date doesn't like to dance, don't go to the dance floor without him. Stay beside him, so he knows he's important to you,'" Heddy read aloud.

"Forget the article! It's drivel. Look at the eyes." Gigi ran her fingers along a model's smoky eye makeup, thick with black liner. "It's all the rage in Los Angeles. You'll look so thoroughly modern."

Heddy didn't own eyeliner, let alone liquid eyeliner, which is what Gigi said the model had used. "I couldn't possibly, Ms. McCabe."

"Do you want to catch a husband, Heddy the babysitter?"

Heddy nodded.

Gigi ran her fingers through her long locks. "Then trust me on this."

The idea was thrilling, of course—going to a Hollywood starlet's party dressed as a Hollywood starlet. But she didn't know if she had the guts to do it.

"Since you don't have much down there," Gigi motioned to Heddy's small bust, "let's bring the eye up here."

Smiling though she felt a little defensive of her modest bust, Heddy stepped out of the dress, hanging it up. "Thank you for letting me come to the party, and for today. It means a lot to a girl like me."

"Oh brother, Heddy. 'A girl like me'? You need to stop apologizing for doing nothing more than existing. You don't feel entitled to a goddamn sunny day." Gigi scribbled something down in a notepad on her dressing table. "Cary may surprise you, you know. He's skinnier than he looks on screen. And do you know his real name is Archibald?" Gigi laughed. "Really. We all do a little self-reinvention, don't we?"

"But that smile! Those eyes." Heddy blushed, getting dressed. "Sorry, I know he's your boyfriend."

"A damn lousy one." Gigi parted her hair, twisting it and laying it on her shoulder. The click of a lighter, the sizzle of tobacco.

Brushing her hand along the velvety pedestal where she sat, Heddy wondered if Gigi would sign her bogus letter. She rested her chin in her hands, and when Gigi sat beside her, she asked for a drag of her cigarette.

"I was the same way as you once. You need to believe in yourself more." Gigi stood, reaching for the paper on the dresser. She scribbled on it, and for a moment Heddy thought she was crossing portions of it out, but then she handed it to her—Gigi McCabe signed at the bottom. "I told you, I got my mother's bleeding heart."

"Thank you, thank you." Heddy lunged at Gigi, nearly knocking her over with an embrace.

"Come here Monday morning," Gigi said, "when the kids are at camp. Ten a.m. We'll start."

"Start what?" Heddy was so happy, she'd forgotten why she was there.

"Lessons. We have less than two weeks before my party, and a dress is just a dress if you don't know how to inhabit it. We're going to get you noticed, sugar pie."

July 10, 1962

Beryl wrote to say that she and Phillip are engaged. Rats. Of course, I'm happy for her, but I wish I were one of the lucky ones. I'm trying so hard to be appealing, but I wonder if it's a waste, all this face washing and hair styling. I think I want the husband and two kids, the four-bedroom brick colonial with a housekeeper, afternoons spent playing bridge. But what if it's not enough for me? Gigi makes her own rules, and even though the thought of living that way is terrifying, it also electrifies me.

{ TWELVE }

There was the sound of sewing machines rattling, hundreds of stitches being punched into fabric, and Heddy's high heels pressing down on a metal pedal, the smell of starched cotton burning her nostrils. She was sewing business shirts, neat lines of seams attaching collars and sleeves. Ruth was frantically sewing, her mother, too— and all the workers on the factory floor were wearing evening gowns. When Heddy heard the shrill cry of an infant at her feet, her mother took it: "This is where unwed mothers work," she said. *But I don't have a baby*, Heddy said.

Heddy bolted upright in bed, her temples throbbing—the sun a thin sliver on the horizon. *Go back to sleep*, she told herself. But it was no use. She tossed and turned, until finally giving up and easing out of bed. She slipped on her bathing suit, tiptoeing downstairs past Jean-Rose's door.

Outside, the air already warm, she followed the path to the beach, and once there, she dove into the sea, plunging into the sting of the cold. The shock of it sent a jolt from her fingertips to her navel, and as her body glided through the water, she let herself slow, loving how weightless she felt, how nothing could touch her here.

A factory job. Never. A baby. Not without a husband. She sliced through the water with her forearms, her thighs burning with fatigue. *I'm better than that.* By the time she emerged, she'd swam away her anxiety, and she ambled to the house, determined to mail the letters to the scholarship committee straight away.

"Heddy, have you seen Miss Pinkie?" In the backyard, Teddy's hair was sticking up in different directions, and he licked the crumbs off his fingers while spinning, dropping his muffin in the grass. He brushed it off and took another bite, spinning some more. She suspected he'd throw up at any moment.

"Where did you last see her?"

Teddy stopped, grabbing for a ball. "In bed last night." He gave her his best puppy-dog eyes. "Will you find her?"

"He's been looking for it since you creaked down the steps at that ungodly hour," Jean-Rose said. She was in a knit dress, fitted with a belt, her blond hair in a flip.

Heddy bit at her lip. "I hope I didn't wake you."

"Well, you did."

Heddy apologized, feeling blindsided. She'd said it was okay for Heddy to go for early-morning swims, yet she seemed perturbed whenever she did. She wished Jean-Rose prepared her a handbook, like the one she received on her first day at Wellesley, something that spelled out the rules.

There was a patch of dirt by the back fence, and Jean-Rose pointed to it. "We're going to plant a garden today."

Anna began to scream, a red splotch on her forehead where she'd been hit with Teddy's ball. She ran to her mother, Jean-Rose burying her nose in Anna's hair. Heddy knew that scent: Johnson's Baby Shampoo. "I'm sorry, honey," she cooed to Anna's wet cheeks. "Teddy, you're just like your father, you love to torture the women in your life."

Heddy wished Jean-Rose wouldn't say things like that to him. Besides, if that was true, then Anna was just like her mother, quick to the drama, throwing herself down to the floor and crying for her way.

"It's Wednesday," Heddy said. "Doesn't Teddy have his surf lesson?"

"Ash had something come up, and better for it. Now we can get these tomatoes in the ground."

A cloud of disappointment blew over her. Jean-Rose settled in an Adirondack chair near the proposed garden and began to paint Anna's nails, while Heddy pulled at the overgrown tangle of vines. "When are you going to see Sullivan again?" Jean-Rose asked.

"Not sure," Heddy said. She wanted to see him, but he hadn't called. It was strange since he'd made the effort to run back, asking if they could have breakfast.

"I thought you said the date was fantastic."

"Surprisingly good" were the words she'd used, but still.

On her knees, Heddy dug her hands into the soil, pulling at a stubborn vine. "He said he'd call."

Jean-Rose blew on Anna's nails. "They always say that. Maybe I can do something, to move things along."

Heddy dropped the vine, her hand muddied. "You would do that?"

"You know that Susanne is his aunt, and she's my best friend," Jean-Rose said.

"Isn't Ted your best friend?" Heddy was genuinely curious. Their marriage confounded her. Last night, Ted got home from sailing, and Jean-Rose returned from Lobster Night at the club, and they sat together in the living room without much conversation between them while Heddy chased the kids about before wrestling them into bed. Is that what marriage added up to—a string of plans that rarely involved each other?

"God no. Ted's my husband, dear. We have expectations of each other, and there are, well, finances to deal with because we must tend the nest and give each other what we need. But I wouldn't call him my best friend; I have no idea what goes on inside his head."

"But you must know him best." Heddy imagined men to be as emotional as women, just more guarded, like if you knocked at the walls a bit, they'd come crumbling down.

Jean-Rose twisted the cap on the nail polish. "I've given up on him when it comes to matters of the heart. I'm lucky if he asks me how my day was. A word to the wise: a man may be benign or he may be sinister, but don't expect him to be interesting." Anna ran off.

"It can't be true." Heddy didn't mean to say it aloud, and Jean-Rose didn't like it when someone disagreed with her, the woman's forehead wrinkling in a frown. Heddy hurried to change the subject. "So you met Ted at your father's office?"

Jean-Rose's expression broke into a cunning smile. "Wherever did you get that?"

"You mentioned it."

Anna joined Teddy in his search for earthworms; polish never lasted on a child's fingers for long.

"I don't think so," Jean-Rose clicked her tongue. "Talking about me with someone?"

Heddy kept her head down, so Jean-Rose wouldn't see her cheeks. "Maybe it was Gigi. She said you made a fabulous pair."

"Did she? I'd really prefer you stop spending time with her."

Heddy pressed back onto her knees, looking up. Jean-Rose couldn't take Gigi away. "Gigi also said she wishes she was as fashionable as you."

"Imitation is the sincerest form of flattery, dear, but I'm pretty sure I don't share fashion sense with a Hollywood tramp."

That stung, and Heddy, digging at a spot that didn't need digging, found herself wanting to make a case for Gigi, how she had a photograph of Jean-Rose on her dresser. How that had to mean something. "Sorry, it's just . . . well, she's been so kind to me."

Heddy couldn't admit the truth, that they had an agreement, especially now that Jean-Rose promised to move things along with Sullivan.

Jean-Rose put her hand to her neck, pained. "I love Gigi, and she's sweet inviting you over, dear, but . . ."

The garden was clear of weeds now, and Heddy wondered why she was doing this; they had gardeners. "What is it?"

Jean-Rose tapped her long acrylic nail against the Adirondack chair's arm. "Well, I hate to . . . but, well, while Gigi seems glamorous, she's incredibly selfish. She uses men, has no respect for other people's husbands, and she hated that I chose Ted over her years ago. Like it was some sort of competition." Heddy stayed quiet, considering what Jean-Rose had said about men earlier, that they were rarely interesting. So why marry one at all? Isn't that what Gigi had asked?

At that, a car pulled into the driveway. A fancy-looking station wagon, puttering. Susanne. Tall, statuesque, with short blond hair. She was all legs and golden-faced, due to an abundance of face bronzer. Jean-Rose sauntered to the car, embracing her. "We were just talking about you." Jean-Rose whispered something in Susanne's ear. The pair glanced at Heddy, trading more whispers. Heddy waved, feeling them studying her.

"Hi." Susanne waved.

They settled on to the porch, Ruth greeting them with fresh glasses of lemonade.

Susanne's voice sounded like she was perpetually stuffed up. "It's in the gossip columns. You didn't see it?"

Jean-Rose rocked in the rocker. "Why would the president pass off a whore like Marilyn Monroe to his brother? It's disgusting."

"Because he's gorgeous. He can do what he wants."

"He can do what he wants with me." Jean-Rose cackled.

They toasted.

"And there's something else," Susanne's voice lowered, but Heddy could still hear. "It's about Edison Mule. He was seen kissing someone by the boathouse, and not his wife." Susanne looked alight, like she knew the words about to tumble off her tongue were electric. "And from what's going around, it seems it was a man."

Jean-Rose coughed out her lemonade. "Stoppit."

Susanne shook her head with pride, pleased she'd gotten such a rise. "No one at the luncheon knew who the other guy was. Only Edison came back into the club. But poor Julia. She must be beside herself."

Jean-Rose cleared her throat. "What luncheon?"

Susanne looked apologetic. "It was nothing. Just a few girls eating tea sandwiches at Gigi's house."

Jean-Rose rocked in the chair, ticking back and forth, with the steady beat of a metronome. "What girls?"

"Me, Alice, Sabrina, and Katherine."

"That sounds like my closest friends."

"I thought you hated Katherine. Anyway, Gigi is ridiculous. I went out of curiosity."

Later, after darkness spread through the island, Sullivan called—he'd clearly been nudged along, but that didn't matter to Heddy. He asked if he could pick her up for breakfast at ten the following morning. She agreed, and as she searched for something else to say to him on the line, she knew she'd wear the shift dress with the daisies that Jean-Rose had given her.

"I guess I'll see you tomorrow."

"I promise I won't take you on any spinning rides." He cleared his throat.

A nervous laugh slipped out of her. "You better not drive fast, either, especially around the bends."

His voice turned playful. "Then I better go cancel the boat rental."

"And you can forget the carousel." She smiled. *This is going to be interesting.*

❧ THIRTEEN ❧

*D*eep into an indigo night, Heddy startled awake. A loud crash, a rattle of a lamp, then moaning. She sat up in bed, rubbed her eyes. From the downstairs landing came Ted's voice. It was sharp.

"Where were you?"

"What do you care?" It was Jean-Rose's two-drinks voice: a little slurred, but pulled together enough she couldn't be called drunk.

"I was ready to call the police," Ted said.

"Who else are you going to call? Your man friend?"

Heddy heard a struggle, a thud—a body falling against a wall on the landing outside their bedroom door. She swung her feet over the side of the bed, ready to jump down.

"Don't touch me, you pervert." Another smash, a picture frame perhaps, and then the agonizing sound of Jean-Rose's tears. Heddy tiptoed out of her room.

"You smell like cologne," Ted growled. He must have heard Heddy's footsteps because he yelled up to her: "Go back to bed. I've got her under control."

It was an order, and Heddy returned to her room, laying her head down. *Is he going to hurt her?* But the noises quieted, and at some point, she drifted off to sleep.

Jean-Rose wasn't at breakfast. Heddy wondered how long she should wait before she went to check on her. Teddy stabbed his eggs with a fork. They still hadn't uncovered Miss Pinkie.

She drove the kids to camp, staring at Jean-Rose's bedroom windows as they pulled out of the driveway, glimpsing a twitch in the curtain. Upon her return, she gave Ted, who was in the garage, a cursory wave and tiptoed past her boss's door, listening for any sign that she was okay. After a few minutes, there was a slight creak of the bed, just enough that Heddy knew the woman was alive. Then the door opened. Startled, Heddy rushed into Anna's bedroom. But it was Ruth who emerged.

"What went on here last night?" Ruth whispered.

"She was out late, and Ted got angry. They woke me up."

Ruth curdled her lip. "It stinks like vodka in there."

Heddy hesitated, uncertain if she should tell Ruth what happened. She stared at a painting of a sailboat gliding in calm seas. "There was a scuffle. It got physical."

Ruth shushed her, taking Heddy's hand and pulling her downstairs to the kitchen, smelling of the morning's eggs. "He's not the kind of man who would hurt a woman."

"Did Jean-Rose look okay?" She hoped Ted hadn't left a mark. A black eye.

"Mouth open, drool coming out, snoring. I've seen worse." Ruth patted Heddy on the back. "She's fine. Why are you so pretty?"

"Sullivan's on his way." Heddy glanced out the window to see a small blue Aston Martin pull up the drive. "Actually, he's early."

"Well, Sleeping Beauty will be just fine."

Outside, Heddy slipped past the open garage door, avoiding Ted. She couldn't face him, not after last night; even if he hadn't hit Jean-

Rose, he'd been rough with her. She'd heard a body slam into the wall.

The sky was overcast as she ducked into Sullivan's car, grinning hello and nervously running her hand along the supple tan leather seats. His cheeks dimpled.

"Where are we going?" she said, trying not to look at the bundled bunch of carnations on the seat. She thought of the wilted wrist corsage her prom date had gotten her for the dance, how all she'd wanted was a crisp white carnation.

He backed out of the driveway, lifting a hand to Ted. "It's a bit of a dive."

All that money, and he's taking me to a dive? "As long as they have Bloody Marys, I'm good." She'd need a virgin today, though, since she had to fetch the kids.

He smiled sideways, tapping his fingers on the wheel. "Those are for you."

She reached for the flowers, inhaled. "They're beautiful. Thank you."

They were quiet for a moment, and Heddy laid the flowers on her lap. She supposed Jean-Rose and Ted went out on a first, then a second date; her mother must have gone out with her father on a couple, too. The first few dates were always ripe with possibility. But at what point did cracks emerge in these men who seemed so good on paper?

That morning, Heddy had scribbled in her journal: *Jean-Rose is powerful among the women she knows because of her link to Ted, but if Ted is this cruel, and if this has happened before, and she endures this cruelty to hold on to her social standing, then she may be the weakest person I know. It's incredibly sad, and I judge her for staying, but I also understand. Maybe she's scared? The cynic in me believes she puts up with it because Ted makes her feel strong on the outside, even if he's shattering her on the inside.*

Sullivan broke the quiet. "We're going to a place called Navy Sea. It's at an airfield hangar near Katama Beach," he said.

With airplanes? She turned on the radio, fiddling with the dial. "Never heard of it."

"Don't worry—we're not flying anywhere. But there are some cool cats down here—you got to hear the voice of this summer girl, Carly Simon. Man, this girl can sing, and she's only seventeen. We'll come back for folk night."

"Folk night?"

"You know, folk music. Pete Seeger, Joan Baez . . ."

"Protest songs?"

"Some of it is, but Carly's isn't."

He parked the sports car along a dirt road, a hand-painted wooden sign with an arrow pointed toward the horizon, reading NAVY SEA. Sullivan ran his hand along his hair. "I always leave my shoes in the car."

Heddy, surprised, kicked off her flats; they didn't match her clutch anyway. "I'm game." She was intrigued, more than intrigued. "What is this place?"

"It's neat. Come on."

Sunglasses pushed atop their heads, they walked along a field with biplanes parked in rows. One of the small planes sputtered to life, spitting out fumes, a propeller spinning, and Sullivan waved to the pilot in the open-air two-seater.

"A buddy opened this place last summer, on the property of a friend. It's far-out in a way nothing else on the island is. Your boss wouldn't be caught dead here."

"She's not that bad," Heddy said.

"They're all that bad." He cleared his throat. "Sorry, that was rude."

"Are you talking about your parents?"

The plane taxied to the runway, nothing but a stretch of dry, yellow grass. The pilot positioned goggles on his eyes.

"Them and everyone else I've ever known," he hollered.

"My mom told me you should never forget your people—you take care of them. They take care of you. It's who you are."

He swatted away a mosquito. "Well, it's not who I want to be." The plane bumped over the meadow, soaring into the sky in the direction of the ocean.

She wanted to say tough luck; it must be so hard to be filthy rich and have a plum job waiting for him after college. She wanted to tell him he shouldn't blow off his people when said people could pay your college tuition ten times over. When said family gave him options. Instead, she rubbed his arm.

"I think every person you meet has something they can teach you, whether it's good or bad."

He nodded. "Well, people don't inspire me, but jazz does."

She remembered the musical notes on his dog's collar. "I thought you were a scientist."

"I am. But I play sax a bit, too. My uncle taught me. My mother hates it when I play, so I play all the time."

Seemed childish to Heddy. "Where do you play?"

"Here."

"On the beach?"

"No, at Navy Sea," he said.

He turned to face a barn with two large sliding doors and chipping paint, open to the grassy meadow. The wood trim had been painted a jewel-like aquamarine, and on the patio stood a crowd of mirrored tables, mismatching turquoise chairs around them. It was early, but still, clusters of people had gathered for breakfast, all young, barefoot, since their shoes were tossed in a basket at the front door. A girl with long hair pulled in a loose ponytail waved, the guy next to her calling out to them, but Sullivan pulled Heddy to a quiet table.

"I want us to be able to talk." He put his hands on the tabletop, then on his lap, then back on the table. "So what do you think?"

Heddy glanced around. "I'm impressed. Why did you call it a dive?"

His dimpled cheeks flushing when he looked at her. "Some girls might see it that way."

She glanced at the menu. "Eggs with goat's cheese? How did they get a kitchen in there?"

"My friend went to cooking school, but he turned down a gig at the Plaza to open this place. He's so real."

Again, Heddy had to hold her tongue. She wanted to say that his friend could turn down a gig at the Plaza because he had a father who could write him a check to open this restaurant. That he could afford to fail. But she couldn't say that without sounding bitter, so she glanced at the swinging kitchen door. "He sounds well set up."

Sullivan's leg started to bounce. "Mother would flip if I pulled a stunt like that."

"I can't imagine not wanting to work at the paper." She wouldn't pretend not to know.

But he shook his head, like she didn't get it. A seagull glided overhead, and it made her feel something closer to tenderness for him: freedom was all he wanted, right? She was being harsh.

"She'd take away your dreams like that?"

He tilted his chin up, smiling again. "I want to work at NASA. Help get rockets in the air. It's the future, Heddy. Someday we'll all take weekend trips to the moon. It seems out of reach, but it's not." She put her hand on top of his, steadying his tapping fingers against the table. He flipped up his palm and squeezed hers; she hadn't expected his boldness and darted her eyes away.

"Sorry," he said, letting go.

"No, I liked it," she said, offering him her hand.

He blushed, taking it. She wondered then what it would be like to kiss him.

A waiter came over, slapping Sullivan on the back. "Your set the other night, man. Like silk."

Sullivan's lip curled up.

"That song your own?"

Sullivan's eyes twinkled. "I merely play other people's brilliance."

The waiter hummed, closed his eyes. "That moody number, where the notes went up and down. Couldn't get it out of my head."

Sullivan was a surprise, this boy with the tortoise-rimmed glasses. When the waiter left, Heddy leaned toward him.

"'Like silk'? Who are you?" She was laughing.

"Did you think I only knew how to fly a kite?"

"You're surprising me, that's all."

The owners had hung rectangular chalkboards on the walls, and Heddy's eyes were drawn to the aluminum can filled with chalk at the center of their table—at the center of every table. Someone had written: "Free Dr. King!" Another had drawn a large dragon blowing fire at the White House.

Heddy handed him a piece of chalk. "Draw with me?"

He held the chalk to the board. "I have a dreadful hand."

"What does it matter? Draw a saxophone."

She found a bare patch of wall and leaned down. Her hand began sketching rows of books in a library, a girl sitting at the center on the floor, reading. She wrote titles on a few of the bindings: Jane Austen, Doris Lessing. She couldn't see what Sullivan was drawing, he seemed to be hiding it, but he turned when he heard her stop.

"What is it?" he asked.

"It's me, reading. I'm a bookworm." She watched his eyes take in the titles.

"Doris Lessing? You one of those man-hating types?"

She gave him a double take. "No, I—"

The color must have drained from her face because he laughed.

"I'm joking. I believe in that stuff, too. My mother made me read that report, the one about how badly women are treated at work. She forced Dad to put in paid maternity leave at the paper. We're one of the first."

Heddy blinked. "Some boys don't think like you."

He shrugged. "Mother is friends with a columnist at the paper—she's working on something, a book about the misery of women, housewives. Keep an eye out for it. Mother says she's the next Lessing."

She caught herself staring at him, her thoughts full of wonder. She wanted to share something then, something from home, so she circled her drawing with the chalk. "This is my favorite bookshop. It's in New York. Rodman's."

"Just over the Williamsburg Bridge."

She dropped the chalk. "Yes, I'm always there. You've been to Brooklyn?"

"What, do you think I grew up under a rock?"

"I just don't know many people like you that . . ."

He adjusted his glasses square on his nose. "If the Bird is there, I'll travel. My uncle lives in Brooklyn." He was more down-to-earth than she imagined him.

"What did you draw?"

"It's dumb," he said. She nudged him aside so she could see. On the wall, he'd sketched the Tilt-A-Whirl from the carnival, a sweet girl's face leaning against a boy's shoulder. He was no Edward Hopper, but she knew what she was seeing. She leaned up against him. "I thought you couldn't draw."

He started to erase it. "I can't."

She stopped him, tenderly wrapping her fingers around his wrist. "It's good."

He took her hand again, and she felt giddy as they walked back to the table.

The waiter brought out breakfast, pouring them fresh coffee as they took their seats.

"You play anything?" Sullivan spooned a dainty square of egg. After every bite, he raised his napkin to dab at the corners of his mouth.

"My grandmother had a piano. The lady she worked for left it to her, and she had it crammed in this tiny living room. I can play 'Chopsticks.'"

"You like it?" He pointed at her plate. "The goat cheese?"

It was saltier than she preferred, but she wouldn't complain. She nodded.

"You know there's a piano inside," he said.

Heddy winced. "Please don't make me."

He poured her more water from the carafe. "I don't make anyone do something they don't want to. Mother gave me too much practice at that." He sipped his water. "No, I meant that I could play for you."

The sun had popped out, and it was high above them now—a quick glance at her wrist told her it was close to noon. Heddy had to pick up the children an hour earlier today. "Raincheck? We better be getting back."

Sullivan waved for the waiter, taking care of the bill, and they walked back down the field, a few inches closer this time. A family loaded their suitcases into a tiny plane and she wondered how they'd all fit inside.

"I'm playing next Friday night. I go on late, ten o'clock, but will you come?"

She slid into the passenger seat, feeling glowy and happy. "I'll bring Ruth."

He closed the door, and in the moment it took him to walk to the driver's side, she exhaled. He wasn't snobbish or entitled. He was sweet, and he'd surprised her with his unconventional sensibilities. He was a true bohemian.

❧ FOURTEEN ❧

After pedaling over a steep hill to the unmistakable scent of manure wafting from the wire fence running along the roadside and the sound of her panting, Heddy crested over the top, rewarded with a wide-open view of the sea, choppy waves storming the shore. The bike ride into Vineyard Haven was longer than Heddy remembered, but she was coasting now. State Road roamed the countryside, running along stone walls with few houses in sight. So many shades of green: the distant grasses of the salt ponds, lush lawns, soaring pine trees, the leaves of oak and maple trees glowing chartreuse in the sunlight.

She relished the warm sun on her face, remembering a unit on astronomy in her general sciences class when she'd learned the sun was a star. When the professor with the tight suit and skinny mustache wrote it on the blackboard, Heddy thought back to when she was a young girl and she'd strain to see a star out her living room window, so she could wish on it. The city was too bright with cars and streetlights to see anything, and back then, she thought that luck eluded her, that only special people could see the stars. But the greatest, most powerful star—the sun—followed her all day long, watching over her like a protective parent. Its power, the way it lit her up inside, had always been right there.

The sun had propelled her out of bed early that morning, with Teddy up before she was since he wasn't sleeping well with Miss Pinkie missing. It was her fourth Sunday on the island, and Heddy had decided she'd spend her morning off on a bike ride. Earlier, she'd checked on the children at the breakfast table, who were mopping up the last of their yolks with buttered toast. Then Heddy had excused herself to find Jean-Rose on the porch.

The night before, Heddy had been having trouble sleeping, so she popped downstairs after midnight for a glass of milk. On the second-floor landing, she'd heard sniffling from Jean-Rose's room. She supposed she and Ted had had another row. At dinner parties with their friends, they would finish each other's sentences, lavish compliments on each other, emit a magnetism few couples could emulate. And yet, in private, they seemed to cause only pain.

She'd found her boss in an Adirondack chair, slices of cucumbers on her eyes. "Excuse me, Jean-Rose. Do you mind if take a bike ride into town?"

Jean-Rose didn't say anything, and Heddy waited a few awkward moments before saying, "Jean-Rose?"

"If you must," Jean-Rose told her. Jean-Rose would never protest spending time with her children, but she had seemed perturbed by Heddy's request, even if technically Heddy had off Sunday mornings before noon—and even if Heddy had never actually taken a Sunday morning off at all. Jean-Rose preferred to keep the children at a distance, waltzing in and out of their day like a beloved aunt, generous with her attention when it was convenient but slipping off the moment she grew bored of them. It was Heddy who wiped their bottoms and tied their shoes. She cleaned smudges from their cheeks and knew when they'd last taken a bath.

"I hooked up the sprinkler yesterday," Heddy had said. "Perhaps set them in the grass for a bit. Oh, and I left their sidewalk chalk on the porch."

Jean-Rose lifted the cucumber slices from her puffy eyes. "I know how to care for my kids."

Heddy had searched Jean-Rose's face to understand what she did wrong, but she didn't see anything but the navy head scarf Jean-Rose had tied at her temples. "I try to have a plan, and I just thought it would be helpful—"

"Lots of plans. Lots of things to do here on the island, hmm." Jean-Rose yawned, lowering the green slices onto her eyelids. "We'll be fine, thank you."

Things got worse when, feeling dismissed, Heddy had gone to the garage to fetch the creamy yellow Schwinn cruiser she favored out from behind some boxes. Poking from the top of one box, she'd noticed a familiar Mary Jane shoe. A doll, her legs bent sideways, carelessly stuffed in. Heddy pulled Miss Pinkie out, clutching her like Teddy would have.

"Teddy!" she'd called, gleeful, running her finger along the doll's peculiar blond curl, but as the boy's footsteps approached, she realized someone had taken the doll and hidden it. No doubt his mother. She stuffed the doll back into the box.

A car beeped at her, and Heddy swerved the bike into the grass before realizing it was Susanne, her eyes glued to the road.

Heddy's mind drifted to Sullivan, how awkward he'd been until the airfield, how he'd drawn them at the carnival, how he tried to erase it. She remembered the carnations still in a vase on her nightstand. That he came from money was intoxicating, she could admit that. Still, even though she wanted to improve her lot, she would never be one of those women who hung around fancy hotel bars hoping to meet a man with deep pockets. So many men opened their wallets only if women opened their legs. The last thing she needed was a problem she'd have to drive across state lines to fix.

Heddy leaned the Schwinn up against the white-painted clapboard of the drugstore. It was easy to locate the makeup aisle, a small display in the front near the racks of nail polish, and she picked up the cheapest liquid liner. She examined the lipsticks, suddenly wanting to buy Jean-Rose a gift, as a thank-you for everything she'd done with Sullivan, even if she'd been moody that morning. Then she found a small bottle of perfume smelling of honeysuckles: perfect. She bought one for herself, too, and had the shopkeeper wrap one in pretty pink paper and ribbon. She'd go to Martin's Shoes next. She shouldn't spend money on a pair of heels she'd wear once, but she couldn't go to the party in her boss's flats, either.

Someone laid on a car horn as soon as she stepped outside, the piercing honk cutting through Heddy's quiet thoughts. She jumped backward on the sidewalk.

"What a relief! We've been looking everywhere for you." Jean-Rose pulled the convertible to a screech alongside the curb. She opened the car door, shooing Anna and Teddy onto the sidewalk, her hair held back with a cheetah-print headband.

"I planned to be back on time," Heddy muttered, hiding the bag behind her.

"I forgot Susanne is having a luncheon, and I told her I'd help her set up. I couldn't possibly bring the children."

Heddy knew Susanne's babysitter, Rhoda, and from what she'd been told, Susanne had a live-in staff that rivaled the White House. She doubted she *needed* Jean-Rose's help. "Susanne just passed me on the road."

"She had a last-minute errand." Jean-Rose pressed a crisp five-dollar bill into her palm as the children climbed out. "Take them for hot dogs at the clam bar."

"But Jean-Rose, the bike. How will—"

She blew Teddy and Anna kisses. "Mommy will see you later, lovies."

Anna began to cry: "Mama, mama. I want Mama."

Heddy picked her up, watching the tourists stepping all around them. Strangers in shorts and tank tops, others in sleeveless dresses or gauzy cover-ups, some with sunburned shoulders, others so white they blinded the eye. She grabbed Teddy's hand, exasperated. "Let's get bubbles."

It took Anna nearly an hour to calm from her tantrum, but now she ran around chasing bubbles on a rectangle of grass with a small beach and dock. They walked back to Main Street to a clam bar near the ferry, where picnic tables lined the docks in rows near a take-out window. They ordered hot dogs and french fries, a trio of lemonades. Heddy stared across the street at Anchor Grill, a white-tablecloth brasserie where the well-heeled lunched. A woman in a large-brimmed straw hat got up, and Heddy could see deeper into the restaurant, where she recognized Lane Hutchinson—"Lainey," as Jean-Rose called her—and her husband, Max. Ash was between them, the top few buttons of his white collared shirt undone, talking with his hands. He laughed, then leaned in conspiratorially.

"I need more ketchup." Teddy liked to dip his hot dog in it, and she got up to pump more into a small paper cup. When she slid back into the picnic table, she glanced across the street. Lainey and Max were standing, grinning, shaking Ash's hand. Max put a few bills down on the table, then handed Ash what Heddy assumed was a check. Ash watched the couple walk off, sitting back down in his seat for a moment and sipping at his drink. He pulled a small notebook and pen from his chest pocket and made a few notes.

"Are you guys done?" Heddy reached into the drugstore paper bag, spritzing her neck with her new honeysuckle perfume. But she sprayed more than she intended, and now she smelled like she'd bathed in it.

"Here, hold this." Heddy handed Anna the last of her hot dog. "You can eat while we walk. I see Ash."

Anna wrinkled her nose. "But I need ketchup."

Heddy gathered the trash onto the tray, heading to the can to toss it, and Anna followed, tears welling up in her eyes again. "I need ketchup, Heddy."

Heddy rushed to pump a neat smear of red down the top of the hot dog. She handed the hot dog back to Anna, who threw it on the ground at Heddy's feet. She could see Ash leaving the restaurant. "I want to dip it. Like Teddy." With fury in her eyes, Anna wailed, loud enough that people started to look. Teddy yanked Anna's ponytail, making her bawl even louder.

Heddy scooped a flailing Anna into her arms, grabbed Teddy's hand, and moved onto the sidewalk. When she lowered the child, there were still tears streaming down her cheeks. Heddy saw that Ash, farther down the sidewalk, was about to turn the corner. They were going to miss him altogether.

"Ice cream," Heddy blurted out. "We'll get ice cream. And we'll ride the carousel." She wiped at the girl's tears.

The child folded her arms—instantly quieting. "Any ice cream I want?"

"Yes, any flavor!" Heddy tugged her down the sidewalk.

Anna stopped fighting her. "In a cone?"

"Yes, yes." As they approached him, Heddy slowed her step, pushing her bangs to the side. From there, she let the children do all the work.

"Ash! Ash!" Anna yelled. "Heddy said we can get ice cream." He turned around, spotting them.

"What are you all doing in town today?" he asked, grazing his elbow against Heddy's.

Looking for you. "A little shopping, a little bubbles," she said.

Ash grabbed gently at her fingertips, then stepped back, a pitter-patter of nothing that sent Heddy aglow.

"Did you spend a little too much time at the perfume counter today?" he asked.

"It was Anna. She sprayed too much—"

"No, I didn't—" Anna protested, but Heddy pressed her hands down on the girl's shoulders and steered her toward the ice-cream parlor.

Teddy pouted. "How are we getting to the carousel? Heddy doesn't have a car."

"Ash has a car," Anna demanded, eyebrows cross.

"Do you need a ride?" Ash said. "We'll get ice cream there." They climbed into the gray velour cab of his truck.

They parked at a gas station in Oak Bluffs that doubled as a homemade ice-cream parlor, since Ash swore it was the best on the island. He insisted on paying for their soft-serve ice-cream cones, pulling a folded set of twenty-dollar bills from his wallet. A business card fell out, with something scribbled in pencil on the back: *10 Meeting Lane, 2 pm* she saw as she handed it to him.

"Anna, remember to tell Mommy the best key lime pie is in West Florida." Ash called to her as she ran by. "Teddy, you, too. If your mommy and daddy get a place near me, you can eat ice cream every day."

They walked the dock, with its fishing boats and large trawlers smelling of fish. Anna and Teddy pretended their ice creams were people, making them kiss, and giggling as they pressed the ice cream together, then pulled them apart.

"Thanks for the treat." Heddy licked her cone. "How is business?"

Ash cleaned up the edges of his cone, where it was melting. "Things are looking up, kitty kit. I got another couple to sign on. That makes two this week. There's a floor plan I wanted you to pass on to Jean-Rose. Would you do that?"

She nodded. He patted his shirt pocket.

"All of this is bringing me closer to what I'm here to do."

"Developing an entirely new town?" Heddy wondered if it had its own post office, or zip code.

"Ultimately, I'm trying to buy my mother her house back in Montclair."

Heddy watched the children running zigzags in front of them and felt a prickle of excitement as Ash touched his soft fingertips to hers once more. Would this be their special thing? Their one unique touch that marked them as two people truly in harmony, like in the movies. She wondered what her mother would think of Ash. Certainly, he was handsome. But he also had this way about him, like when they were together, they were always on a fabulous adventure.

"We've had a tough go of it, the Porters. But we're on the upswing," he said.

"But I thought your great-grandfather . . ." Her cone crumbled when she bit into it. "I thought you were a Florida boy."

"I spent my childhood in New Jersey." A seagull perched on a wooden post tracked them, pivoting its head in pace with them. "Something happened to my dad, something terrible, and Mom couldn't pay for the house, and by the time I got there, she'd been evicted . . . our stuff was in boxes on the sidewalk." He paused. A motorbike zipped by, beeping them out of the way. "I've actually never said that to anyone before."

"I don't understand." Heddy turned to face him. Why would his family be so worried about money? "Couldn't someone help?"

"My grandfather left more of his money to charity than he did family. And without Dad around, I need to take care of my mom. I need to get her the house back." He cocked his head. "What is it about you that makes me want to tell you the truth?"

She leaned closer to him. "People say I've got an honest face."

Ash held up his hands like he was holding a camera and sucked his cheek to make a clicking sound.

"What was that?"

"Just taking a picture." He grinned in that sun-kissed way hand-some men did. "I want to remember you as you are right now."

She stuck out her tongue and rolled up her eyes, making a ridicu-lous face that would have sent the kids into fits of giggles. "Remem-ber this instead." Relief washed over her when Ash laughed.

The distant sounds of the Flying Horses Carousel's organ music grew louder as they approached the gabled-roofed building. Teddy ran inside, and Anna followed. Hand-painted seahorses adorned with real horsehair traveled up and down on poles. At the ding of a bell, the attendant pushed out a long metal arm holding dozens of small silver rings, but only one brass one, which won a free ride.

The kids were choosy with their horses, settling on two on oppo-site sides of the ride. Even with the windows popped open, it was stuffy inside; so hot a rider could overheat like a car.

"I'll go with Teddy." Ash followed the boy to his preferred stal-lion.

Heddy gave Anna a boost to help her up onto her creamy-white horse, the bridle painted sky blue. As the ride started to rotate, the notes of the organ music sounded a familiar tune, and Heddy held Anna's waist secure as the girl squealed.

On the other side of the carousel, Ash held the horse's reins, pretending to gallop, while Teddy kicked the horse's hinds in their imaginary race. The little black notebook was slipping out of Ash's back pocket, and she wondered if it was a ledger, tracking the invest-ments in his development, or more of a diary. Learning that he was working for his mother's benefit made Heddy want to run the back of her hand along his cheek, and tell him that she was falling for him, even if she wasn't sure he was ready to catch her.

The carousel slowed to a stop. As Anna and Heddy met Ash and Teddy at the exit gate, across the street, she saw Sullivan closing his car door, and she spun around so her back was to the street. She didn't want to run into him. How would she introduce Ash and Sullivan to each other? She turned to see if he was coming toward them, but he was quarreling with a pert redhead she didn't recognize.

"My horse was faster than yours," Teddy teased Anna, who stuck out her tongue, then screamed at him to stop.

"Quiet, children," Heddy said, separating them.

Over the din of voices, Ash pulled at his shirt, wiped his brow with a handkerchief. "Hot as Hades in here. I need to get home and change. Are you looking for somebody?"

Heddy whipped her head back to Ash.

"I thought I saw Ted," she lied. Ash pulled a second handkerchief out of his pocket, dabbing it at her temples, and she'd wanted to close her eyes, feel the pads of his fingertips through the fabric on her face.

Then Ash said: "Let's get out of here." She snuck a glance at Sullivan, who was back in his car. She couldn't exit, not now, too risky.

"I just want to see something," she said, pretending to read the nursery rhymes on the walls. Once Sullivan drove off, she took Anna's hand.

"How are you getting back?" Ash asked.

"I left my bike in Vineyard Haven. Could we pick it up and ask you to drive us home?"

Ash positioned his fedora on his head, little wisps of hair sticking out the sides. "Only if you come over for a bit. I'd say Jean-Rose's luncheon should keep her gossiping for a few more hours."

They squeezed into the cab of his truck, the children sandwiched between them, and when they pulled up, his cottage looked the same as the last time she was there. The sink piled with dishes, a few gnawed drumsticks on a plate. On the counter, a stack of hardcover library books: *New York's Great Buildings*; *Gustave Eiffel: The Man*; James Michener's *Hawaii*. The kids shuffled through the living room, scanning it for toys, settling on the chess game on the kitchen table.

"Don't worry—I'm not that smart. I rarely finish a book." Ash noticed she was looking at the titles and came to stand next to her. "I'm a grazer. I flip through, take what I need."

Heddy devoured books like others did chocolate. It was her way of escaping into another place whenever hers was too much to bear. "My favorite book is *Jane Eyre*."

"Pretty depressing, kitty kit. Heathcliff could drive anyone to an insane asylum."

"That was *Wuthering Heights*, silly." She opened the book with the Empire State Building on the cover.

"English is my second language. Maybe my third or fourth." He was in his sunny bedroom, the door half-closed, and he walked past the doorway shirtless, making her look away.

"I don't believe that. You have a way with words—it's like you always know just what to say, no matter who you're talking to. I would have taken you for debate. Like you trained for law."

"Close—I doubled in psychology and criminal justice." A drawer slammed shut; he chuckled. "Not using either one now. All I really want to do is help put up interesting buildings in cities like New Delhi. Skyscrapers in San Francisco. Palaces in Marrakech."

"So why aren't you?"

"Because I'm building houses in Florida. We all gotta start somewhere." Ash emerged barefoot and wearing rose-colored shorts, a clean white T-shirt with a chest pocket. He pulled two glasses out of the kitchen cabinet. Ice cubes cracked onto the counter, the sound of the faucet filling up a glass. He handed her water, and she sipped before putting it down. She thought people like him propelled to the top instead of starting at the bottom. Didn't family connections do that for someone?

She turned the pages: one photograph showed the Chrysler Building being built, another was of a brownstone with a bright blue door.

Heddy looked out at the dunes, the smooth arc they made to the sea. "I've always thought that different doors are ways into different lives. Like, what would it be like to walk out one door and into another? I like to imagine the characters who would live in a penthouse, a Cape Cod, a sprawling beach house."

He stood beside her, looking at the book. His eyes crinkled. "But what goes on inside those houses, the lives of these characters, is all the same—love, betrayal, sadness, and joy."

She looked up at him. "You say it like you know something of it."

"I do." He passed her another book: *Great Estates of New England.* "Houses are symbols, kitty kit. They mean something to us because we build lives inside them. My childhood home is the keeper of so many of my best memories: the doorway where dad marked the date every time I grew an inch, the banister I'd slide my hand down as I ran to the living room on Christmas morning. I mourn that house like I would a relative; it was a part of me."

She took in his boyish profile, his clear eyes, the way his fingers rested on the counter, like he was the most relaxed person in the world. "I don't need a big house," she said. "Just a cozy one. A fireplace in the living room, those two little square windows on either side."

He laughed. "But that might change. Houses make us feel things they didn't at first, whether it's purpose or restlessness, success or failure. A man writes a million-dollar check for an estate because it makes him feel like he has a reason to get up in the morning. A woman may love her house, then begin to resent her husband's inability to fix it up, resenting him as well. People are always thinking about houses, like a better one will make them happier. But people believe in houses too much, actually—they think the exterior offers some outward picture of what goes on inside. Beautiful house, beautiful family."

She closed the book. "But you don't think that's true?"

"Not always."

It certainly wasn't true of Jean-Rose, Heddy thought, and yet the perfectly trimmed hedges implied otherwise. "And yet, you're letting your parents' house consume you. Why not just let go?"

"Because it was taken from us," he sighed. "It wasn't right."

"I'm sorry." She nodded, turning the page to a pristine Tudor. "You know, I hate when people say money doesn't mean anything. Money is survival. Pure survival."

"You're right," he turned to her, surprised. "Money is everything. Look what happened to my mother's house."

"And my mother, too. She's struggled to make money, enough of it, her whole life."

They stared at each other knowingly, until Teddy, bored with their exchange, kicked Anna, and Anna kicked back harder. Heddy separated the children.

"Anyway, that's not why I want to build skyscrapers," Ash said. She and the kids followed him onto the patio, Teddy clutching the chess set. "That's more about ego and wanting to make a mark. I can't draw them, but I can raise funds, hire the architect, pore over the plans until that glittery piece of art is added to the city skyline."

She could see him already: a smart suit, pushing through the revolving door, strangers thanking him for the stunning structure. He wasn't a dreamer, she thought. No, that was Sullivan. Ash was practical, a man who knew what had to get done and did it. She liked that he knew what it meant to struggle.

He relaxed into his director's chair and put his hands behind his head. "What are you majoring in?"

"English. I want to write a screenplay."

"Kids, your babysitter is one of the most ambitious women I've ever met." Anna smiled, while Teddy ignored him. "Have you written one yet?"

"I have some pages, but it's mostly plot notes." Heddy shrugged. "I study strangers, like I do doors"—she laughed—"and I make up stories about their lives, like where they're going, what they're worried about, their dreams. Then I turn them upside down looking for the story."

"I do that with airplanes. When you see one flying overhead, don't you wish you knew where it was going? Are they on their way to a Cubs game, or heading to the Galápagos to photograph sea turtles?"

"Or to reunite with family."

"Or to see someone they're falling for," he said.

She felt her breath catch in her throat, keeping her eyes on the kids, the chessboard. They knocked all the pieces over, and Anna threw one at Teddy. "I want to travel like that," she said, reprimanding Anna.

"If you could go anywhere, where would it be?" His eyes twinkled.

She considered it. "Top three: Los Angeles, Los Angeles, Los Angeles."

"We could sip Bellinis at the pool at the Beverly Hills Hotel." He laughed.

She rested her chin in her hand, grinning. "And I'd cast actors for my movie."

"When do you finish school?" he asked. He was pretending to write down the details in a notebook on the table, like they were planning a trip.

"One year left."

Ash scratched his head. "We have a problem."

She looked at him.

"You need to write a screenplay," he said.

"Yes, that would help." They smiled at each other.

Teddy begged Ash to show him how to play chess. "Teach me, teach me," Heddy teased.

"If you love people," he told Heddy, "you'll love chess. It's about reading motives."

She sat with the children and listened to him explain the significance of a rook, a pawn, a bishop, a queen. Every piece had a purpose, every move was a decision that led a player to loss or victory. She watched him use the bishop to take Teddy's queen on a diagonal, then the rook, who swept a forgotten pawn.

Ash tapped his rook on the square. "Don't get trapped in zugzwang. It's when you get stuck in a position where any move you make is a bad one."

"How does that happen?" It sounded a lot like life.

"Mostly in the end, when you've got fewer pieces, and fewer options," he said.

"I bet you know all the right moves." She cupped her chin in her hands, smiled broadly, and Ash chuckled. Heddy instructed Teddy to use his king to take one of Ash's rooks, but then Ash cornered their king.

"Checkmate." He winked at her, and she punched his arm playfully.

"Sorry, kitty kit. You made it too easy."

Heddy could see her whole summer on that chessboard. Jean-Rose and Ted might think her a pawn, but she was a rook. She wasn't as powerful as the queen, but a rook could jump over anything standing in its way. A rook didn't have to capture anyone to win. It could simply leap.

Heddy was ready to leap.

{ FIFTEEN }

Heddy hadn't even knocked on the door when it opened. Five days before the party, and she'd been waiting for this: a chance to hear how a true-to-life movie star got the guy.

"You're late." Gigi was wearing her big Italian sunglasses and a slouchy, striped sweatshirt that hung off one shoulder, revealing the ties of a black bikini about her neck. Several silver bangles on her wrist jingled as she pushed by her.

Heddy checked her watch: "Barely a minute." She'd dropped the kids at camp, and stopped at the grocer and post office for Jean-Rose.

Heddy followed Gigi under an arbor with bunches of wisteria twisting through it, the purple flowers dangling like grapes, coming to a stone path to the beach. The actress moved like a gazelle, swiftly stepping one bare foot in front of the other, her toenails painted the color of beach roses.

Heddy struggled to keep up with her, quickening her pace. "Ms. McCabe, why are we rushing?"

Gigi swung around. "Call me Gigi! And if you must know, I'm having a bit of a day. Brando dropped out of the movie, so the studio is hemming and hawing about the start date, and I've had it up to here." She held her hand up to her neck, like a guillotine ready to slice into her. They crossed the large expanse of lawn in bare feet, having left their shoes at the arbor, and the grass was wet from the sprinklers. "Anyway, I'm sorry. You arrived just as I was hanging up."

Heddy sped up. "We can do this another day."

"Don't be silly. There's a lot to cover. And my party is Saturday. I want you ready." Gigi pulled her by the arm to a pier, really a private dock, long enough one could pull a boat up to it.

The dock creaked with their footsteps, the gentle slap of waves rippling under them. At the end were two fishing poles, each one with a colorful feather lure at the end of the line. Gigi bent down to sit, taking off her sweatshirt and dangling her feet off the side—the jingle of her bracelets announcing her every move. Heddy scooted next to her, dipping her toes into the cool water.

"Your posture. It's all wrong." Gigi accused. The movie star was leaning backward on the palms of her hands, shoulders back, bosom forward, the pose of a pinup girl.

"Excuse me?" Hyperaware now of her own stance, Heddy pushed her spine up like a broom pole.

"That didn't come out right." Gigi patted Heddy on the back like an obedient puppy. "What I mean to say is, I used to stand against a wall with my shoulders back for fifteen minutes a day, a requirement of Miss Lilliana's Manners School. I think you'd benefit from the same. Your posture is the only unattractive thing about you."

Heddy took off her shirt so she was sitting in her bathing suit. "Is that all you got?"

"Well, you're a cute girl. That doe look. A softness in your manner that disarms people. The boys I knew in high school would want to bring home a girl like you. So what's bugging you, pussycat? Are you sad? You know, men can sniff out sadness as easily as they can seduction."

"I'm not sad." Heddy pulled her feet out of the water and sat cross-legged on the dock. A ball caught in her throat as she tried to figure out how to explain how she was feeling. But Gigi made her so nervous—she felt nauseated, like she did on the Tilt ride—because she couldn't think of what to say.

"You realize marriage is a bit of a drag."

Gigi might be right; it certainly didn't seem easy for Jean-Rose and Ted. She seemed to fear him more than she loved him, and yet, even without a perfect union, Heddy believed they were better together than they would be apart. "That's for me to decide."

A flock of seagulls flew overhead, squawking to the scattered clouds. Gigi followed them with her glittery eyes. "Here's the truth: no one is going to love you if you don't love yourself. I know, it's dime-store phooey. But a therapist in the Hollywood Hills told me that years ago, and you know what? He was right."

Heddy followed the curve of Gigi's back. "I'm just, well, finding my way. Do you remember what it was like to be twenty-one?"

"I was in a picture at twenty, my breakout role in *Streets of San Francisco*. I was right where I wanted to be." Gigi lay back on her elbows, pleased at the memory. "You don't feel the same, I gather?"

Heddy covered her face with folded arms. "Not so much."

"So what's with all this husband-snagging stuff? I thought you were a Wellesley girl trying to pave your way with your own gold."

"I'm the first in my family to go to college." Heddy thought back to the day she got her acceptance letter, how she'd sat at the kitchen table turning the thick cream envelope over in her hands before getting the courage to open it.

"Well, I was the tenth in my family who didn't go to college." A throaty laugh. "So what if you're the first? Be proud. Move on."

Heddy scratched at a mosquito bite on her arm. "I just need some insurance."

"What kind of insurance?" Gigi shot back. "Does this have to do with that letter you had me sign?"

"Maybe. Look, I just need a guarantee I'll be okay, even if I don't get my degree."

Without replying, or even indicating she'd heard, Gigi climbed down the ladder at the end of the dock and dove into the sea. Then she was back on the dock, water dripping off her curves, her red lipstick unchanged.

"Didn't you say you grew up in the city?"

A vigorous nod. "Brooklyn."

"Mother?"

Heddy nodded some more.

"Father?"

Knees to her chest, and a whisper. "Not really."

"Oh God, so that's why you like Ted Williams. Classic daddy issues." Gigi gave her a knowing look, like she'd heard it all before. "Anyway, you and your mother struggled to make ends meet. You bury your nose in school. You fight hard to get out. But it feels like you'll never win the battle, unless you marry the right man."

"Something like that." Heddy was stunned at how easily Gigi summed her up, how it caused all those layers of muscle around her heart to ache.

"And you think this works against you because . . ." A Boston whaler sped by, the driver waving. Heddy and Gigi watched him pass.

"Because my mother wants me to marry someone back home. 'My people,' she says. You know, the ones who work in the shipyards." Heddy didn't want to cry. It was silly to cry at a detail like that—it was love that mattered, right? And maybe she could fall in love with a neighborhood boy, regardless.

"First off, don't listen to your mother. You have nothing in common with those men." Gigi pointed her toes like a dancer. "They're not looking for a wife who can argue the virtues of Lady Macbeth in Act Three. School changed you, and that's okay. Hollywood changed me."

Heddy felt the lifting of a weight, the leather book bag she shuttled her textbooks to and from class, suddenly lighter. Being at Wellesley showed her that there was more to life than Atlantic Avenue. She left home with one identity, but while away, she dared to step into another one. But it left her feeling lost, since she wasn't firmly planted in the upper-crust circles at school or the working-class neighborhood back home. She was somehow both, teetering between the two worlds, lost in a way no one else she knew was.

Gigi stretched her slender arms up overhead in that elegant way gorgeous women do. "Not having a father made you hungry, and that's what sets you apart. It doesn't matter that you grew up with nothing." She fished around in her bag, pulling out a green leather notebook and tossing it to Heddy. "Write that one down."

Heddy jotted it on the first page, while Gigi twisted a lock of hair around her finger.

"No one ever tells you this when you're a kid, pussycat, but I'm telling you now. The best part about growing up is that you get to write your own story. Don't worry who grew up where, or who went to what school. Just write the part, then play it. You want to be a writer, don't you?"

"Yeah."

Gigi grew exasperated. "Well, start writing."

Heddy considered her life until this point. The sequence of events that led to her birth had nothing to do with her. The day her grandmother died was arbitrary. Going to college had been her counselor's idea, and her mother, shocked that it was within reach, helped pay for Heddy's applications, working overtime to cover the initial fees.

Those things happened to her; it wasn't a destiny she had any part in controlling, and whatever was meant to happen to her from now on, simply would.

"I'm not sure you're right, that I can write my way into a different life," she told Gigi.

"And why not? I did it." Gigi squeezed Heddy's shoulder. "Look, not having a father, not having the kind of family you wanted, is one thing that happened to you. But it's not the *only* thing that happened to you. You shouldn't let it define you that way. I never did."

Heddy wrote it slowly in her best cursive, liking the sound of it. *It's one thing that happened, not the only thing.*

"If I let every little shit thing that's happened to me bring me down, I'd be living in a goddamn sewer."

Heddy chuckled.

"You should see the arrogant asses I've dealt with in Hollywood. I've had to bow to them, worship the temples of their egos. I had one guy, a director, tell me he'd give me the part if I was committed. Committed? What did marrying someone have to do with winning the lead?"

"Did you ask him?"

"Bet your bottom I did. He told me he was afraid he'd cheat on his wife with me, giving me this slick look that turned my stomach."

Heddy pretended to vomit.

"I politely told him he was bold to assume I'd even want to see his hairy back." A buzzer rang out, and Gigi reset a kitchen timer for fifteen minutes. Then she rolled over.

Heddy held her hand over her gaping mouth. "Did you say that?"

"Of course not. I needed the role. Anyway, I had the last laugh. This was before *The It Girl.* Now I tell those monkeys what movies I'll be in, and they worship the temple of *my* ego."

Gigi picked up a fishing pole, casting the line into the sea, and handed it to Heddy. Then she picked up the other pole, cast out the line similarly, using the spindle to reel her line taut. "And we wait," she said, humming the tune from *Singin' in the Rain*. "You see, a lot of people go fishing, and they wait for a fish to bite. But we could sit here all day with these poles and nothing may come of it. The same is true for love." Something tugged her line, and Gigi reeled it in, revealing nothing but a clump of seaweed. "Don't let these women, these Mrs. Perfects, make you think a man falls into your lap."

"Certainly not a well-connected one." Heddy smiled, but what she'd said seemed to agitate Gigi. The actress narrowed her eyes to slits.

"You can marry a Vanderbilt, but if it's not for love, even a little bit, it'll be empty. These are different times, and you can make your own way. You don't need a husband to define you. You can define yourself."

Heddy looked around at footsteps on the dock. A woman in a tight bun and white apron carried a tray with two drinks, each a Tom Collins, a wedge of lime on the rim of the glass. The woman gave one to Heddy, the gin stinging her tongue.

"It's strong."

Gigi drank hers down like water. "Hardly. Karina makes them like lemonade." On a small table, Karina arranged a water pitcher, a bowl of lemon wedges, and two glasses filled halfway with ice cubes.

Her glass empty, Gigi asked for another. "Much better. Now where were we?"

Heddy gulped, liking the sting this time, and picked up the small notebook to look back through her notes. "I shouldn't wait for a fish to bite."

"Right, exactly. So first, you must decide which man is worth your time. Let's call him the mark. And don't go by attraction alone to find the mark. You're not looking for a sordid affair." Gigi dangled one foot off the dock, lifting the other so she could pick at her toe polish. "I tend to look at watches. They tell a lot about a man."

This surprised Heddy, and she scribbled *watch?*, amused. "But it's just a timepiece."

Gigi batted her long eyelashes. There was a whole lot of sultry in those lashes. "Oh no, sugar pie. A man's watch is a powerful piece of information. It tells you everything you need to know. Is he practical, wearing one of those department store Timexes? Is his choice gauche, a gold Rolex shipped on a boat from Switzerland? Maybe he's new money, and desperate to announce his financial standing. Cartier? A sense of style, classic taste, old money. Stay away from a man with a pocket time piece—too old-fashioned." Gigi crossed her legs at the knees. "Personally, I like men with a pilot's watch, something with multiple dials. Says they like a good adventure, to do a little exploring on you. Cary's got my attention right away: a handsome dark face with white numbers, a few little dials. Gives me goose bumps just looking at it."

Heddy used to stare at the watches in the case at Tiffany's when she'd visit her mother at work. There was one, a woman's watch with a skinny, slinky gold band, that had tiny diamonds at every hour. She wondered what it'd be like to own a watch like that.

"And those pilot watches," Gigi purred. "They usually mean he's good in bed."

"Gigi!" Heddy swallowed another gulp of Tom Collins, blushing. "So I found him, the mark. Now what?"

Gigi stood, so Heddy rose up, but she listed, the sun making her woozy. Gigi took her hand. "Pretend I'm, I don't know, Rock Hudson. No, no. I'm the mark, and I walk up to you," Gigi said. Heddy peered down at her feet as Gigi approached, seeing lines of water through the dock slats.

Gigi did her best baritone voice. "Can I get you a drink?"

Feeling the pull of a shy smile, Heddy averted her eyes to the horizon. "That would be nice."

"Oh brother," Gigi sighed. "I need to start at the beginning. It's more like this . . ." She rested her hand on her hip, her opposing shoulder pushed down in a sexy stance, her head angled to the side. "I'd love a sidecar. . . . I'm from the city. You too—wow! Have you ever been to the Village Vanguard? Great jazz. Maybe we should meet some time."

Heddy buried her face in her hands. "I can't do that."

Gigi frowned. "Well, it doesn't have to be exact. Let's start with the eyes. You need to make eye contact—no one trusts someone who doesn't make eye contact."

Gigi pretended to scan a crowded room. She stopped at Heddy, held her gaze. It was like a spotlight shining on her. Nothing else but Heddy. It made Heddy feel funny; she had to look away.

"No, no, no," Gigi scolded. "Think of it as a pause. When a guy catches your eye, don't look away. Then you look nervous, like you're waiting for the commuter train to whisk you out of there. His eye will move right over you." Gigi kissed her chin to her shoulder, let the soft smile pass back over her face. "But if you pause, return his stare for an extra-long moment, that tells a man 'come get in my taxi.'"

Heddy lost herself in a fit of giggles, trying to stop. "My turn." Heddy walked through an imaginary door, settling her gaze on Gigi, who was standing at the end of the dock.

"Count to five in your head," Gigi encouraged. "Let the mark know you're there. That's it." She matched Heddy's gaze, perfectly serious, and Heddy bit her cheeks to keep from laughing again.

"Think of it as your signal," Gigi said. "And it's okay if you're shy. That's sexy, too. Because when a shy girl goes for it, guys go bananas."

Heddy set down her Tom Collins. She was feeling on top of the world from her buzz, but she had to pick up the kids later. "I can do this. I'm going to stare at him until he sees me." She went to hug Gigi, but the actress just patted her on the back.

"There, there," she said. "Let's get you some water." Heddy guzzled down the water, then poured another and drank that, too. She burped.

Gigi took a fresh cocktail from Karina, the ice cubes already melting. "So once he comes to you, chat him up, let him buy you a drink, laugh at all the right places. But then, do the boob rub."

Heddy crossed her arms over her chest, like she needed to protect her breasts from incoming nuclear missiles. "The boob rub?"

The sun disappeared behind a cloud, then shot its rays back down on them. "It's my little trick. Men love to feel strong, even little boys do; they're born that way. So at some point, maybe after the first drink, find a reason to squeeze his arm, right up between here." She pointed at her cleavage.

"Gigi!" Heddy yelped. "I couldn't!"

"Oh, but you can, sugar pie—it's nothing." Gigi acted out the scene. "Grab hold of him like you just saw something scary, or maybe like you're extra excited about something. Use your hand to squeeze his bicep—what is it with men and their bicep muscles? Then hug his arm against your chest." She held her hands up like she was squeezing two big muscular arms, and getting tremendous pleasure from it.

"But what if Jean-Rose saw me do that? What would she think?"

"I'm sure Jean-Rose boob-rubbed her way across Darien in her day. She found her own mark, then reeled him in. Trust me when I tell you: Ted was not her first choice."

The alcohol made Heddy feel like she'd been rocking on the rough seas, and now this. What was Gigi saying?

She hiccupped.

"You've convinced yourself that these society ladies exist on some holier-than-thou plane. Well, hardly." Gigi lit a Chesterfield. A cloud of smoke plumed overhead as she blew O's. "Look, sugar pie, everyone leaves parts of their past behind as they grow up, even Jean-Rose. You don't have to carry yours around like a backpack weighing you down with bricks. All anyone cares about is who you are right now."

She wasn't telling Heddy to be someone else. She was telling her to edit. To omit. To figure out the parts of herself she was proud of and let go of the parts that she wasn't. It was like revising a story; she was always cutting details to shape the plot. Perhaps Heddy *could* revise her own story. She was doing that already at luncheons at Wellesley or even when she talked to Jean-Rose—she simply left things out. And what Gigi was saying is that it didn't matter; everyone edited. Maybe it's how we all survived, how we all emerged out of childhood in one piece. We figured out who we wanted to be and called ourselves that, despite what anyone else said we were.

"That's why this nonsense about her blocking my application at the Island Club is ridiculous," Gigi went on. "Her scrappy little self can't stand how far I've come, how she'd never be able to support herself the way I can. But she made her own bed, marrying for money. She could have married for love. Anyway, I digress. I'm sorry. Sometimes I get the stage, and I can't stop. Enough about this old nonsense."

Heddy imagined a youthful Jean-Rose bonkers for someone other than Ted. When Jean-Rose was drunk on the couch that night, she said something about a man named Nelson; was that him?

"What do you know about Ash Porter?" Heddy asked.

Gigi fiddled with her bracelets. "I know he likes to surf—I ran into him on the beach once, a golden boy. Not my type. You have something for him?"

"Maybe." Heddy peeled back a splinter of wood on the dock.

"Oh yeah, what part of him?" The actress lifted her eyebrows suggestively.

They burst out laughing for a second, and when Heddy recovered, she said, "But I have a chance with someone else, and I like him, too. Quite a bit, actually."

The actress purred. "Haven't you seen *The Trio in Tuscany*?" When Heddy shook her head, Gigi waved her off. "It's okay. No one saw it, but the point is, my character was in love with two men, and it makes for an impossible ending."

Heddy leaned forward. "What happens?"

Gigi bit her lip. "I don't want to confuse you."

"I could just ask someone." Heddy laughed. "It was in the theaters."

"Okay, I'll tell you. She chooses the good boy, the one who her mother wants her to be with. But the night before her wedding, the bad boy sneaks into her dressing room and convinces her she's making a terrible mistake, and they run off together."

Heddy grinned. "Why was that movie such a flop?"

Gigi smacked her. "Because my costar stunk." Gigi creased her eyes, like a tired cat. "Look, with Ash, you can get away most of the time with just smiling pretty. He seems like a flirt, and men like him want women to flirt back." Gigi's lips parted into a soft grin. "Like this, no gums. Don't smile so big that your eyes wrinkle. Let the muscles in your face relax."

Heddy mimicked the downy-soft look on Gigi's face.

"That's it! You got it." Gigi applauded. "But who's the other boy?"

"Sullivan Rhodes."

"The one with the paper? I had lunch with his mother the other day. She's incredibly sophisticated. I kept watching how she raised her fork to her mouth, parting her lips just so and tilting her fancy hair. With every bite. That's some high-class stuff, little girl. You sure you're ready for that?"

Heddy stared at the ripples in the sea. "You mean, is his family ready for me?"

"No, I'm talking about you. Marrying someone like him comes with responsibility. Endless social engagements, then those ridiculous conversations where you're forced to nod along to whatever anyone says. You've got to be sure, that's all."

Heddy imagined a jeweled comb in her hair, a spangly dress, hanging on to Sullivan's every word—it didn't fit. "But Sullivan is different from that."

"That's what *he* says, but they all get trapped in it. Money like that, it's like velvet handcuffs."

"I suppose," Heddy said.

Gigi ran her long fingers up the smooth plane of her legs, squinting. "Sullivan. I bet he wants to talk books and history. Pretend you're a professor with him. Not literally, but channel your intelligence. He's used to his mother, who is cold but whip-smart. Snuggle him up, since his mother probably never did, then list what's on your nightstand. Men like girls who are passionate."

"But aren't most men looking for a girl to tend house?"

"A man doesn't want to marry a maid. He wants to marry a woman who screws like a one-night stand but still gets up to make breakfast. Show him what a good time you are."

Heddy burst out laughing. Perhaps it's why Gigi got the guys. Because she was free in a way that other women weren't. She thought of Ash, how he'd taken her on his surfboard. How she'd been able to see the force of the ocean, how much it seemed to open him up to her.

"Don't laugh, it's true." Gigi ran her fingers through her hair, combing the tangles from her swim. "It's not all sex, of course. There is something to the glow. Happy girls always get the guy. Be light. It's infectious."

"How am I going to do this?" Heddy buried her face in her hands.

"Don't think you have to be so mature around a boy. Unbutton."

"Well, not until the third date." In the distance, Heddy saw a 4WD truck bumping its way down the beach.

"Is that what girls have declared acceptable these days? In my day, it was marriage."

"I mean, it still is, but if you're not going to hold out, I mean."

Gigi sat up, cross-legged, facing Heddy. "You think I care when you're going to make it with a boy? C'mon. Half the men on this island have seen me naked."

Heddy stared dumbly, like she didn't know what she was talking about.

Gigi smacked her. "Don't be one of those people who pretends not to know!"

That made Heddy laugh. "Sorry."

A light bulb went on in Gigi's eyes then. "One more thing, pussycat. You'll need this to land the mark. Copy his body language. If he runs his hand through his hair, wait a moment and do the same. If he's looking out at a passing ship, lean forward and look, too. It's this unconscious thing, but it turns men on. We always do it in movies to let the audience know that a girl is into a guy."

"Really?"

"You can practice at my party. I'll help you." There was a guy with a camera inside the 4x4, and he started snapping. "This is private property, asshole." She put on her sweater, her wet bikini top soaked through two circles on her shirt. It was unfortunate or extremely fortunate, depending on who was looking. "I have to run."

Gigi flashed her a megawatt smile before striding away, swaying her hips for the photographer. "Can't wait to see you in that dress."

"But don't you need to ask me questions, about stuff?" Heddy realized then that she'd been looking forward to Gigi prying into her past. It might feel good to come clean about everything.

Gigi blew her a kiss. "I got everything I need."

That night, she wrote Beryl:

July 16, 1962

Dear Beryl,

First off: Congratulations!

Now, sit down because you may faint: Gigi McCabe has become my confidante. I'm going to her party, she lent me a dress from The It Girl, *and this guy I can't stop thinking about will be there. I could get you an invitation—Hollywood people are com-*

ing! It's July 21. You could stay here, and we could gossip about the sorry old lots trying to be chic.

How is Phillip? You'll be happy to hear that I'm dating more than I ever have, and I'm considering making it with one of them. And why not? Gigi said to go after what I want.

The bad news is that there's been a bit of a housing mix-up at school, and I lost my place in the dorm. You may need to find another roomie. . . .

Love,
Heddy

❧ SIXTEEN ❧

"Why does everyone look the same?" Ruth smirked, tilting her head toward the women at the next table. Navy Sea was thick with tanned slender wrists, the women long-haired and glossy, wearing either collared shirts in various colors tied above the navel, or black sleeveless sundresses with thick liner rimming their eyes.

They'd waited all week for their Friday night off, and now that it was finally here, Heddy felt anxious about seeing Sullivan. Heddy yelled over the voices, "It makes me want to get a short, black dress." In her sweater set, she was feeling square, but, thank God, her hair was chic.

Onstage, the guitarist broke down his set. "Is he next?" Ruth asked.

Heddy glanced at her watch. Timex. From the five-and-dime. "He said ten. It's about that."

Closer to the stage, Heddy caught the eye of a redhead, her prim hair falling at her shoulders, parted to the side with a barrette. Someone patted the microphone, and for a second, Heddy thought it was

Sullivan. Scanning the crowd for a sign of him, she caught eyes with the redheaded girl, who erupted into laughter with her girlfriends, all of them looking at Heddy.

"Ruth, do you know them?" Heddy hollered. "The ones up front at the corner table?"

"The girl with the headband?"

"The one next to her, with the red hair."

Ruth shrugged. "The carrottop Sandra Dee? Nope."

"They keep looking at me, and I don't think kindly."

A man's voice blared into the microphone. Sullivan had walked onstage, sitting on a stool, his Yankees cap pulled low so the audience could barely see his eyes, stubble where he hadn't shaved. He tapped his foot against the footrest, his chin tilted downward, his hands gripping the bottom of his saxophone, shiny in the overhead lights. He wouldn't look at the crowd. Heddy felt a rush of excitement; she glanced back at the redheaded girl and smiled when their eyes met, but the girl glowered, her lip curling in disgust. Heddy's smile dropped.

"We're thrilled he's back tonight. The Vineyard's own Sullivan Rhodes. Take it away, Sully."

As Sullivan raised the reed to his lips, he caught sight of Heddy. She shot her hand up to wave, beaming, and he let the corners of his mouth turn up around the instrument. He inhaled, and when the sound came out, it was bluesy and smooth, a butter knife spreading frosting across a cake, her hand running along a satin sheet.

"He's dark," Ruth whispered.

It was true. You could feel the sorrow in his song, the soulfulness, too. She imagined him as a child, sitting in his uncle's cramped Brooklyn apartment, learning to play the sax. How it filled him with something that Heddy would never understand. How he'd get home to Manhattan and find his mother, hands on hips, forbidding him to play that nonsense. Who could ban music this penetrating?

Then came the *rat-a-tat-tat* of a drumstick tapping on cymbals, and Sullivan's sax picked up tempo, spinning around the drumming, gleefully, like she was back on the Tilt with him, the sound out of control. Heddy fluttered her eyes open, and Ruth tapped her hand on her highball glass. A few people cheered.

"That's it, Sully," someone yelled.

Sullivan knocked off his hat, his hair damp with sweat. He tapped his foot, his horn frantic and possessed, a quickened beat that made everyone want to move.

"We have one Charlie Parker record, and I play it on repeat for my mom." Ruth began dancing. Soon Heddy was on her feet, the other patrons, too. Heddy slithered her hips, a desire to get all her excitement from the inside out.

"He's good," Ruth said when they collapsed back into their seats, lighting a cigarette, her cheeks flush. But they were up again dancing with the next song. When he finished the set, Sullivan left the sax onstage.

Heddy lunged at the stage, wanting to give him a hug. "How did you learn to play that way?" The waiter brought Sullivan a glass of water. He reached for it and dumped it over his head, then took off his glasses, grinning.

"The lights are so hot up there," he said.

Heddy pointed to Ruth, who reached out her hand. "You remember Ruth." Sullivan shook his hand dry, then shook hers.

"That was Charlie Parker, right?" Ruth asked.

"Started that way. Then I went somewhere else." He dried his glasses with his shirt, pushed them on.

"You have to tour the country," Heddy said. "Make an album."

He looked drunk on adrenaline. "You think?"

"I should be listening to that on the radio. Didn't you see me dancing?"

Sullivan brushed back his wet hair, slicking it. "I wish everyone heard me like you do."

Heddy wondered if he was going to make the rounds, chatting and thanking his friends for coming. "If you have other people you need to talk to . . ."

But he sat down at their table, his eyes intent on her. "What have you been up to?"

"I looked for you at the Clamshell yesterday," she said. "I was picking up oysters."

"I was at the ballfield," he said. He looked around the club, waving to someone in the distance. "Can you believe how many people came?"

A couple of guys smacked Sullivan on the back, and he introduced the one holding a guitar as a Shaw, one of the long-time families on the island. He was opening a coffee shop in Oak Bluffs next summer, the Mooncusser, after a thief who lures boats into the rocks to steal its booty. "We need a home for folk music on the island. There's this singer, Bob Dylan, playing in Greenwich Village. I'm trying to book him. Hey, Ruth Jennings, is that you?"

Ruth smiled politely, saying hello, but the guy continued to rattle on, and when the conversation turned, Ruth whispered to Heddy. "He and I went to high school together," she said. "I had a mad crush—he used to call me Red Butler."

"What happened?" Heddy said.

"He's in a different league: the father is this out-there artist with a big inheritance, driving his Mercedes around the island barefoot even in winter." Ruth crossed her arms and went back to chatting about the set, asking what Sullivan would play next. He bought them a second round of drinks.

They'd settled into a quiet conversation, just Sullivan and Heddy, when he pushed back out of his woven chair, the back banging into someone else's. "Peg, hi."

It was the girl with the shoulder-length red hair, her barrette sparkling with a row of tiny diamonds. "Your mother told me you were playing." She glanced at Heddy. "Are you going to introduce me?"

"This is He-He-Heddy," he stuttered.

Peg pointed at Heddy's hair. "Did you cut it while studying in Paris?"

Ruth guffawed, a little too loud.

Heddy ran her fingers by her neck, swelling with pride. "A friend did it."

Peg covered her mouth, laughing, her tone turning condescending. "Well, obviously. It's shorter on one side." Heddy felt the tiniest muscles in her lips spasm.

"You're being rude." Sullivan kicked the table leg, and Heddy caught her drink to keep it from spilling.

"And you're being ridiculous." Peg leaned into Sullivan, fingering his collar and folding it into place. "Stop slumming with the babysitter, Sully. I'm not going to wait forever." Sullivan pulled away, turning her eyes to coal, dark with anger.

Ruth put her hands on her hips. "I suggest you apologize for calling her hair crooked."

"I think we know who cut it," Peg said, looking to get a laugh from Sullivan, but he struck a match, lighting a cigarette and glaring at her.

"I'm sorry," Sullivan said to Heddy. "You need to go, Peg. I didn't ask you here tonight."

Peg looked Ruth up and down, settling her gaze on her scuffed flats. "Everything will be set right soon enough."

Sullivan faced Heddy as Peg strode off. "It's not what it seems. She's . . . It's Mother." Heddy sat and folded her hands in her lap, or she might have smacked him.

"She said you were slumming. Is that what I am to you? A second-rate girl?"

Sullivan's eyes were all over the place; he puffed on his cigarette. "She's a spoiled brat, that's all. I invited you here, not her."

Peg stood in the opposite corner of Navy Sea, cast in amber light, a trio of girls with shiny hair and pressed blouses gossiping. Peg lit a cigarette and mouthed to Heddy: "Slumming."

When the announcer called Sullivan back onto the stage, Heddy stomped toward the exit. She couldn't stay a moment longer. She'd been trying to fake her way into Sullivan's world, and look where it got her: utterly humiliated.

Ruth chased her through the airfield, grabbed her by the shoulders by a red airplane. "Stop. I can't run anymore."

Heddy stumbled. She could hear applause from the club, the blaring of the horn as Sullivan took the stage.

"What the hell was that about?" Ruth asked.

"These people. I don't get them. They act so classy but say such cruel things." Heddy folded her arms around her knees, dropped her head in the space between.

"I know it." Ruth tried to catch her breath. "Anyway, you're going back to school, and you'll never see them again."

Heddy buried her head deeper into her knees. "Ruth?"

"What is it?"

The heat of her breath was suffocating, burning her nostrils, and still, Heddy kept her head down. "I'm not going back to school."

"Of course you are."

Heddy lifted her eyes. "No, I . . . I lost my scholarship. Sullivan is, in fact, slumming."

"Cripes." Ruth dropped down beside her.

The saxophone was moody and sad, a loneliness pervading every note as it drifted over the parked, unmoving airplanes, silhouetted in the darkness. Heddy thought of Peg, her prim hair and wicked laugh.

"I thought this would be a perfect summer, you know," Heddy wiped her eyes. "That feeling, like I was running for a train that I couldn't catch, would go away. But . . ."

"But the train pulled away from the station without you." Ruth put an arm around Heddy's back. "Hey, listen. There's always another train."

"I know, but . . . I don't think I'm getting a do-over." Heddy wiped her nose.

Ruth laughed, then laughed some more, cackling so hard she couldn't breathe, waving her hand about her face. Heddy didn't think it was too funny.

"Sorry, but she's right."

"Who?" Heddy said.

"The redhead. I see it. There's one spot by your ear that's longer."

Heddy felt for it, and there it was, one lock that she'd never noticed. "She was really staring, like I'm some threat." Heddy's chest seized, and she hiccupped with laughter.

Ruth slapped her thigh. "That crazy girl probably hired a detective to snuff you out. Did you see how she talked to him like a baby?"

Heddy imitated Peg's childish-sounding voice. "I wear Jean Naté perfume. Does that count for getting a haircut in Paris?"

"If she knew we bought our body spray at the five-and-dime. Oh, the shame!" Ruth put the back of her wrist to her forehead, like she might faint.

That put Heddy over the edge and made everything seem funny the rest of the way home.

The moon was full when she and Ruth, who was sleeping over, pulled up to the house. The two women climbed onto the porch, closing the side door in silence, careful not to step on the squeaky floorboards near the kitchen sink. They were whispering in the dark about ice cream, how they'd take a tub of vanilla and two spoons upstairs. One of them tripped on the rubber mat, making the other muffle her laughter.

The light flicked on, and they stared at the doorway, where Ted stood. His eyes looked black and opaque, unsettling. "Isn't it a little late?"

"It's before curfew," Heddy said. First, Peg. Now, Ted. It was maddening.

Ruth stood straight, attempting to hide her anxiety. "Can we get you anything?"

Ted ran his fingers through his hair, his lip turning down with irritation. "Don't wait up," he said, grabbing the car keys off the hook. He pushed past Ruth, gripping his small black camera bag.

The screen door slammed shut, and Heddy released her back from the refrigerator, where the cold metal handle had been jamming into her vertebrae.

"Do you hear something?" Ruth asked. She wandered into the living room, her ear cocked to the second floor.

They climbed the steps, and there she was: Jean-Rose in a sleeveless satin nightgown, lying in the fetal position on the thick green rug.

Ruth ran to her. "Let us help you to bed."

Heddy scanned her boss's body for blood, contusions, anything that might show Ted had hurt her—like the small cut on her temple. "I'll make you chamomile tea and get you some biscuits."

"Put it on her favorite cabbage-flower saucer," Ruth instructed.

Jean-Rose's blank face contorted, her eye makeup mudsliding. "You think this can be fixed with a cup of tea? That I can undo this night—this life—with a plate of cookies? You stupid girls." She crawled into her bedroom, her nightgown clinging to the rug with static, using her bare foot to kick the door shut.

If the children were awake, they didn't get out of bed. Heddy pulled at the loops in the carpet, staring at Jean-Rose's white-painted door, the bronze doorplate with its jagged keyhole. On the other side, fists banged on the floor, and Heddy started to cry. *Bang-bang-bang*, like a wild animal in pain; she was certain Jean-Rose's hand was bruised.

"Did you see the cut on her head?" Ruth whispered.

"Should we call the police?"

Ruth shook her head, a deer in headlights. "And say what, that our boss had a fight with her husband?"

"Well, no, but . . ." *Bang–bang–bang.*

Finally, it stopped. Ruth pulled Heddy up.

"I hate him," Heddy said. "I don't think I've hated anyone more."

{ SEVENTEEN }

Jean-Rose got up early on Saturday morning to play in a tennis tournament at the club—she'd come downstairs in a white tennis shirt with a matching headband positioned over her temple. She sipped her coffee at the back door in silence, watching the children poke at a spider. Heddy held up the pink-wrapped present she'd gotten Jean-Rose.

"I got you a little something for being so good to me," she said. It wasn't expensive, but she hoped it would bring some cheer.

Jean-Rose smiled miles of sadness as she opened it. "How nice, thank you, Heddy," she said, tossing the perfume on the counter. "The clambake is in three weeks, Ruth. We should start preparing. The Clamshell will do the clams, but we'll need to make a list for . . ."

Ruth nodded. "Of course, Jean-Rose."

The small perfume vial had cracked, the scent pooling on the Formica, and Heddy ended up throwing it out. She felt Ruth's hand on her back by the trash can and heard her whisper: "She's still upset from last night."

Ted shuffled into the kitchen for coffee, his hair disheveled and his skin reeking of stale cigarettes, and Jean-Rose breezed out. "Morning," he said, and when she didn't answer, he shook his head.

"What has her knickers in a twist?" He took his coffee from Ruth, adding an extra spoonful of sugar. "Must be her time." He snorted, and Heddy and Ruth chuckled, as good domestic help did. Heddy hoped he'd go straight to his office. But when she turned back from the fridge, he was still at the table.

"Were you taking night photographs?" she asked. Addressing him felt confrontational, even if what she said was benign.

He stared at the spot between her eyebrows. "Photographs?"

"The bag you brought with you last night. Your camera?"

"Oh, I was returning it to a friend."

Nearby, Ruth chopped strawberries for a pie on the counter, exchanging a wary glance at Heddy. Ted opened the paper to Sports, and Heddy stared at his hands: smooth around the knuckles, his fingernails neatly trimmed, a gold band positioned on his ring finger. No scratches. Not a bruise.

"Can I help you with something, Heddy?" He glowered. "Jesus, I need a shower."

Heddy rushed outside, calling to the children, wanting to get as far from the house as possible. She'd take them to Katama Beach and she'd make up a story about Teddy begging for more lessons if Ash were there.

Even as they walked from the parking lot, she spied Ash, carrying his surfboard, a woman in a skimpy bikini emerging from the waves beside him. As she got closer, she realized the scantily clad woman was Jean-Rose's friend Susanne. Heddy wondered if she knew about Ted's tendencies toward violence, but she must not or she'd surely be comforting Jean-Rose this morning.

The beach was wide-open, less crowded thanks to the cloudy skies; still, she arranged her blanket near Ash's.

"Nice to see you, kitty kit," he said, drying his face with a towel.

Susanne cocked her head with interest, and Heddy felt herself being studied. "You here for a lesson, too—*kitty kit?*" She twisted her hair to wring it out.

Heddy's words came out warbled, like she had a mouth full of marbles. "The kids were begging to come to the ocean. Teddy wants another chance on the board."

Susanne folded her arms. "I thought Jean-Rose decided it was too dangerous."

Heddy's lip twitched; she *had* said that, not that it was Susanne's business. "Not in the water, on the sand."

"Hmph." Susanne wrapped herself in a terry cover-up, looking Heddy up and down, settling her eyes on the black bathing suit she was wearing; the spaghetti straps lined with tiny delicate pearls. "I remember when Jean-Rose wore that bathing suit. Gosh, four or five years ago now. How time flies!"

"She was kind to lend it to me." Heddy glanced at Ash, who pretended not to hear. She'd rather he didn't know that her bathing suit was borrowed. Heddy popped a piece of gum from the beach bag, fussing with the blanket to wriggle out of the humiliation.

Susanne tossed her wet towel at Heddy, who caught it and found herself folding it. "She takes good care of her help, wouldn't you say, Ash?"

Heddy handed her back the towel, worrying how the story would be told to Jean-Rose; Susanne had a flare for exaggeration. Not to mention Sullivan—this was his aunt. What would he think of her being seen with Ash?

Ash folded his arms, grinning. "Susanne is just cranky that big wave knocked her down."

Heddy lifted her eyes to the two of them, a smile creeping away from her lips.

Susanne affectionately patted Ash on the back. "If I had half a decent surf instructor, then maybe I'd have more luck. Thanks for the wild ride. I'll see you at Gigi's tonight, right?"

Ash put his hands to hips, the soft blond hair running up his arms reminding Heddy of velvet. "Is the whole island going?"

"Pretty much." Susanne slung a straw bag over her slender shoulder. "Ciao."

When she was gone, Ash sat on Heddy's beach blanket, and even though they weren't touching, she could feel him along her edges. A red propeller plane offering rides flew overhead, doing air rolls, and the children cheered. "I can't believe people pay for that sort of torture," she laughed.

Ash grinned. "You get paid for a certain kind of torture, too. I hope you don't let Jean-Rose speak to you the way Susanne did. You have better manners than most of these chicks."

Heddy laughed; it was true. "No one makes you spend time with them." She took in his back, the beauty marks arranged haphazardly down his shoulder blades; if she connected them, they'd make something close to a "W."

"It's business. Susanne has a place in Palm Beach. I've been trying to convince her to buy a plot with me instead."

She imagined kissing those beauty marks, what his skin would feel like under her probing lips. "Is she going to?"

"Probably not," he laughed.

The kids were fighting about a shovel, screaming about what this one did and the other one didn't, and Heddy knew she should attend to them. Instead, she fell backward on the blanket, the sun beaming across her cheeks. She closed her eyes, trying to make sense of him. He was always grazing against her, finding a reason to touch her. Was it just lust?

"Give it back," Anna yelled.

She tuned them out, feeling his shadow pass across her face. She fluttered open her eyes and saw a goofy grin on Ash's face. "What's gotten into you?"

Ash noodled her, tickling her in the belly, and she laughed, scurrying her hands down his stomach. When he didn't squirm or smile, she tried tickling his sides.

"I'm not ticklish," he said, flexing his abdomen tight with muscle. But he broke into a grin, and she laughed, but soon they were just gazing at each other, the silence broken only by their breathing.

"*Heddy! Make him stop.*"

She wiggled away from him and marched over to the kids. "Teddy, don't you dare steal Anna's shovel," she attempted to scold but erupted with giggles, looking over her shoulder at Ash. She tried to compose herself, but being near him made her giddy. She couldn't wait to surprise him at Gigi's party.

A plastic sand shovel in hand, Heddy helped the kids build a castle as Ash came over to set up a chair.

Heddy flipped the bucket, revealing a clean-lined sand castle. "Tell me more about Montclair."

"You remembered." Ash turned up a Ray Charles song on his handheld transistor radio. "Our house was the loveliest on the street, a Queen Anne. My mother planted rows of red tulips, and in the spring, our yard had hundreds. They practically covered our lawn."

Heddy smiled at his memory. "Seems idyllic."

Ash rubbed at the back of his neck. "It was, until it wasn't anymore."

"You'll get it back." She thought of Gigi, of everything she'd said about men. She rubbed at the back of her neck to mimic him.

"Enough of my sad story. I have a game. Think of a number from one to ten."

Two, she thought.

His eyes danced. "Okay, multiply it by nine."

Eighteen.

"Does the resulting number have two digits?"

She nodded. "Then add them."

Nine.

He told her to subtract five, and then think of the corresponding letter in the alphabet. The trick got Teddy's attention, and he was listening, too. He looked at Heddy, who whispered in the child's ear: "D."

Ash pretended to look perplexed, his lips pressed together like he was trying to figure something out. "Is your letter 'D'?"

Teddy's eyes lit up, and he and Heddy exchanged amazed glances. "How did you do that?"

Ash laughed. "My psychology degree finally coming to use. People are predictable, that's all."

She pressed on her skin to check if she was getting sunburned, but it sprang back pink. She swore she'd gotten more freckles this summer than in her entire life. "No, this was random. How did you know my number?"

"It only seemed random. Say I'm selling a bottle of wine: One is two dollars, one is five dollars, and one is eight dollars. Most often, people choose the middle one. They won't want to appear cheap or extravagant."

"Huh." She would have picked the $2 one, but she kept quiet.

"I'm trying to get people to buy what I'm selling, but I barely talk about the house. I talk about who else is buying, what size that person's house is, etcetera."

"Who knew you were into mind games?" She smiled.

"Which is why if I could get Jean-Rose and Ted, I'd get others. People look up to them. Their perfect marriage, beautiful home."

Heddy waved back Anna, who had gotten too close to the surf.

"Do you think Jean-Rose convinced Ted to buy in?" Ash wondered.

They'd spoken about the Coconut Coast, and Ted had shut down the conversation. She didn't have the heart to tell him the truth, or the truth about what Ted was really like in private.

Heddy spoke quietly, so the children didn't hear. "Last night they were guessing what movie stars had signed on. Jean-Rose wondered if Gigi McCabe had." It wasn't a total lie; she'd heard Jean-Rose ask Susanne the question.

His pupils seemed to expand. "Would that seal the deal?"

Heddy rolled her eyes, whispered. "Probably. Those two have a row going."

"Is that so?" He rose out of his beach chair, pacing in front of her.

"So if Gigi bought one of my houses, Jean-Rose would insist on getting a bigger one."

Heddy smelled hot dogs, then spotted a man with a hot box on his chest walking toward them. "Ted's opinion doesn't even matter."

Ash scratched his head. "But I thought he was the money."

"Sure, but like I said, Ted is barely there, which is for the best, and he'll do whatever Jean-Rose wants if it stops her from getting on his case. He nods along with her about running for state senate—and she's hosted a couple of meetings with donors at the house—but I don't think he even cares. I heard him say as much. Anyway, hint to Jean-Rose about Gigi, and you'll get her, and she'll get Ted."

"That's my girl—you're right." Ash grinned. On the radio, a man announced Bobby Darin's "Dream Lover." Ash reached his hand down to her, pulling Heddy onto her feet. "Dance with me."

She glanced at the other beachgoers; she didn't know any of them, but still. That almost made it worse. "Here?"

He nodded. "It's just a dance, kitty kit."

He spun her out, twirling her around, meeting her eyes with a soft smile. Then he let go, dancing a slow cha-cha, snapping his fingers, and when Heddy matched his footing, he threw his head back with glee: "That's it, you got it." A large wave crashed onshore.

Heddy swayed to the beat. "All those nights catering cha-cha parties have finally paid off." Beaming, Heddy took Anna's hands, twirling her.

They tried to get Teddy to join, but he grimaced. "You guys are weird," he said.

"It feels good to break the rules sometimes, kiddo. You should try it," Ash said.

Heddy snapped to the beat, adoring the way that Anna was trying to copy her in her purple-ruffled swimsuit. "You're a terrible influence. Besides, Teddy breaks enough rules."

When the song ended, Heddy and Anna applauded. Ash reached into his cooler for a cola, handing one to Heddy, and she sat cross-legged on the blanket.

Ash stretched out in his chair. "I could go for a lobster roll."

"What's that?"

She and her mother had lobster specials once on the boardwalk at Coney Island—and she'd loved wearing the plastic bib, picking at the stringy meat.

His face puckered with disbelief. "You've never been to Surf Shack?" Surf Shack was a take-out seafood restaurant in Oak Bluffs. She'd noticed its kitschy light-up sign on her first day.

"I've seen it."

"Chunks of lobster stuffed in a hot dog bun. It's about the best thing you'll ever eat. They started making them a few summers ago. Let's go, right now, for lunch." He folded his chair. "Kids, we have to take Heddy to town. She's never had a lobster roll."

She waited to see Teddy's reaction; his mood dictated what they did and didn't do. He planted his feet in the sand. "I hate lobster rolls."

Heddy eyed the red-and-white stripes of the hot dog man's shirt. "What did I tell you about using the word 'hate'?"

"Teddy, they're only the most delicious thing on the island." Ash was looking over his wayfarer sunglasses, which he'd pushed down his nose.

"But we just got here," the boy whined.

"I'll go," Anna said, "if you get us ice cream." Heddy thought she sounded just like Jean-Rose.

"We should stay," Heddy said, waving over the hot dog man. "Three dogs, please."

Heddy begged Anna to sit still. The girl's hair was tangled, and every time Heddy went to run the plastic comb through, the child ran away. Heddy threw the comb onto the bed. "I give up."

She stood in front of Anna's oval dresser mirror, tugging her shirt off one shoulder and arching the bare slope of her upper arm, trying to re-create the sexy pose Gigi had demonstrated. With her hair gone, she could see the supple skin of her neck, and it electrified her to imagine Ash brushing his mouth there. She pouted her lips, tilting her head to the side, and batted her eyelashes, testing her look in the mirror.

"What are you doing?" Jean-Rose, her hair sculpted into glamorous Grecian curls atop her head, a sparkly headband hiding her bruise, dropped a package onto Anna's floor.

Heddy jumped back, so startled that she tripped on Anna, who was lying on the floor with Teddy. "I was just . . . looking at my freckles."

"Mommy!" Anna threw her arms around her mother's legs. "Where is your dress?"

"The party isn't until eight. Anna, your hair is beastly," she said to the girl.

Heddy grabbed the brush off the bed. "I was trying. Anna, come here." But the girl spun away.

Jean-Rose tapped her navy flat against Anna's plush pink rug. "What made you take the children to Katama?"

Heddy hoped her face didn't betray her. "Teddy was begging to play on the surfboards."

"No, I wasn't," Teddy said. Heddy opened the girl's top drawer, taking out white folded camisoles and refolding them. She hoped Jean-Rose didn't notice her burning cheeks.

"Mm-hmm. I see." In the mirror, she could see Jean-Rose's reflection, arms folded tight below her emerald necklace. "Don't make this the summer of your rebellion, dear girl. What happened with Sullivan?"

Heddy shrugged; she was still working it all out. But it was starting to feel like Jean-Rose didn't want Heddy to see Ash. Was it because Sullivan, at least on the surface, was like Ted, bringing money and a good name to the courtship? Did dating him reinforce Jean-Rose's ideas about who was husband material and who wasn't?

Jean-Rose used her foot to slide a brown-paper package, like a hockey puck, toward Heddy. "This has your name on it. Someone dropped it off." Then she handed her a letter, from Wellesley.

"Maybe it's from Sullivan?" Heddy pretended to be delighted, playing to Jean-Rose's desires, even though she wanted to tear open the letter. She set it on the bed.

"Well, go ahead. I'm as curious as you are."

Heddy turned the package over, fiddling with the red-and-white twine. Inside was a shoebox made of thick black parchment, COCO CHANEL spelled out in shiny white lettering on the lid. A scripted note read: *I didn't forget. xo Gigi*

Inside, layers of black tissue paper separated, opening to reveal shoes, but not just any shoes. Stilettos. Fire-engine red, slip-on mules with a peep toe, stacked on a skinny, four-inch heel. She took one out, running her fingertips along the glossy finish of the patent leather, the double C's engraved on the arch.

Jean-Rose's lip twitched. "Good luck walking in those."

Heddy let the heel fall in the box. "She's helping me. With that project."

"I think we know who has a project." Jean-Rose rolled her eyes, marching off with Anna at her heels. Heddy grabbed the letter from Wellesley off the bed, clawing it open and racing to read it. The first line, then the second. Her eyes grew misty, and she sniffled, then tore at the words manically until it was confetti, stuffing the pieces in her back pocket.

Teddy, lining up Anna's stuffed animals on the floor, looked up. "Don't you like your present?"

"These are happy tears," Heddy lied, blowing her nose. She supposed she hadn't really expected Wellesley to reverse their decision, but at least she'd had hope.

She slipped on the heels, if only to distract herself, and the soft seams hugged her slender feet. *As indulgent as a slice of red velvet cake*, she thought—like the ones they served on china plates at the Waldorf Astoria. She slid on the other and bit her cheeks to keep from crying, since these heels were powerful and victorious and representative of everything her life was suddenly not.

And yet, while staring at her stilted expression in Anna's floor mirror, she knew that no matter how her fortunes dipped, she would never go back to Brooklyn. She would be the dutiful daughter and help her mother with the rent. Oh, she would be the good girl. But her resolve would also propel her forward. She'd get her own apartment. She'd get a job. Any job. And all those old classmates who gossiped about her when she didn't return to school, who pitied her for not being able to pay her way, she'd prove them wrong. Because Hibernia Winsome wasn't the type to give up.

{ EIGHTEEN }

A fierce rapping on the bathroom door made Heddy drop Emily Post's *Etiquette* onto the floor. She was on the toilet reading about "Balls and Dances," her stomach in knots, her red dress still hanging from the towel rack beside her. She wanted to see what Ms. Post would say about attending Gigi's party without an escort.

"Go ahead without me, Jean-Rose," she said, embarrassed to speak through the bathroom wall.

"We'll wait five more minutes, Heddy, but that's it."

Heddy had decided that she'd purposely run late, just so she didn't have to arrive on the arm of her employers. She wanted to walk into Gigi's party like an invited guest, not a third wheel. "It's okay. I'll meet you there. I'm not even dressed yet."

Jean-Rose sighed. "You'd think you were going to your own wedding." Small, careful steps down the creaky stairwell. Minutes later, she was back: "Ted will leave keys in the Buick."

Heddy pulled her lace underwear—the only pair she owned that her mother *wouldn't* approve of—over her hips and checked her makeup in the gilded vanity mirror. She looked bewitching. Long false lashes fanned out from her eyelids, outlined with thick black liner. She'd used the pencil to draw a small diagonal line up from the corners, so her eyes looked winged, just like Gigi showed her. Rather than a thick matte of red on her lips, she applied a simple, clear gloss.

She clasped her grandmother's triple strand of pearls around her neck and zipped her dress—the silk hugging her hips. In the mirror, she blew herself a kiss. "Go get 'em, Brooklyn."

Ruth wolf-whistled when she came into the kitchen.

Heddy fidgeted with the rhinestone belt. "You like it?"

"Oh, shut up. You know you look incredible." Ruth licked a finger, wiped at a smudge on Heddy's cheek.

Heddy hugged her close, not letting go when Ruth did, holding her for an extra second. "You're sleeping here again tonight, right?"

"Jean-Rose asked me to stay, with you being out and all." Jean-Rose had said she expected Heddy up with the children Sunday morning. Rightly so. But Heddy was so grateful for Ruth's standing in she almost hated to leave.

The sky was streaked with pink and orange as a line of waiting automobiles pulled around Gigi's circular driveway. Two gas lanterns flickered on either side of the glass-paned double doors, and a young man dressed in a top hat and coattails ran out to each car, offering a gloved hand for the keys. A statuesque blonde in a strapless sky-blue evening gown emerged from a black sports car. Out of a sedan came a couple with coordinating outfits; his powder-pink bow tie the color of her floor-length taffeta dress. Heddy took out her compact and brushed on a little more powder, her cheeks tingling with anticipation.

No one knows about Wellesley, she reminded herself.

Before she knew it, Heddy was out of the car, feeling unsteady in the Chanel heels. She faced the house's grand double doors, and an usher led her through Gigi's lobby, the living room with the horseshoe-shaped couch, and out the sliding doors, where throngs of people clustered in groups around the pool. To one side, a wooden dance floor lit with tiki torches stood before a rock-and-roll band. Japanese lanterns flickered in the pool like fireflies.

Heddy gulped in the salty breeze, aware of the click of her stilettos on the patio, scanning the crowd frantically for a familiar face. In the cacophony of conversations, the clink of glasses, she noticed a few of Jean-Rose's friends. A woman rammed into her on accident while dragging a friend up the patio, nearly knocking Heddy over, the notes of their conversation traveling to her ears: "I think he's messing around." Heddy shifted to the side, dropping her eyes to her heels. She adjusted her belt, even though it wasn't out of place.

She began examining her polished fingernails. Should she get a drink? She wished she'd asked Ruth for a cigarette. Maybe she could ask a passerby for one, perhaps strike up a debate about which brand was best. She crossed her arms over her chest, then forced them to her sides in a charade of confidence. Maybe she should turn around and drive home, get in her pajamas. At the pop of a flash bulb, she looked up. And when she did, she saw Ash.

He was on the lower patio, near the bar, a black bow tie fitted about his neck. His blond hair, which was often windswept and loose, was styled to one side, a gloss of pomade holding his wave in place. Perhaps he sensed her staring because he looked up, and while he didn't stop talking to the group of men surrounding him, he didn't take his eyes off her, either.

Heddy tilted her chin down, looking up toward the first stars of night, letting her winged eyes find him again, and when he smiled at her, she grinned broadly. She had a desire to run to him, to tell him how often she thought of him, how she hunted for his truck on the road and searched for the back of his head in town. That when she lay in bed at night she stared at his cottage, daydreaming about what he was doing, what they could be doing together. She wanted to say that she didn't know what it was, but he made her happy, that when she was with him the sticky things lost their stickiness.

Out of the corner of her eye, she spotted Gigi trying to get her attention, nudging her head toward the crowd, meaning something like: *Get your butt down here.* She remembered the lesson then, the mark.

Count, she thought. Heddy inhaled the smell of cigars and cigarettes, citronella and salt air, and exhaled, calming the fluttering sensation in her chest. She willed herself to find him once more, waiting until he was fixed on her. *One Mississippi, two Mississippi.* He looked effervescent, exuberant, talking animatedly, like he believed every word he was saying with all his being. That's how he spoke to her at Katama Beach, like she was the only one there, a genuine smile topping off whatever he said.

She gazed at him, willing him to come to her, counting *three Mississippi, four Mississippi*. Heddy felt for her hair, making sure it wasn't sticking up, the anxiety of the situation turning to panic, since he wasn't moving, not one step, like Gigi promised he would. She considered something she hadn't before: *Maybe none of it would work.* Maybe Ash wouldn't be impressed with the movie star's red dress, maybe he wouldn't fall for these tricks. Maybe despite all of this, he would tell her what a sweet girl she was and seek out a more sophisticated woman. *Five Mississippi.*

He wasn't coming. She imagined a metal discus barreling down a pole, a wheelbarrow dumping bricks at her feet. She hunted for Gigi in the crowd, wanting her company desperately, but the actress was busy with her own friends. Her eyes roamed, burning with the threat of tears. Was that one of the nannies serving canapés? Heddy saw the back of Jean-Rose's head. Perhaps she should stand beside her? No, the bathroom. She'd reapply gloss.

When Heddy returned to the patio, she forced herself to take the stairs down to the party. Ash was nearby, and when he saw her standing there, he motioned to the dapper men circling him to wait a moment. He began pushing toward her through the other guests, using his broad shoulders to break up conversations. She imagined placing her palms on his shoulders, squeezing the muscles there, standing on tiptoe to meet his lips. Her eyes didn't leave his as he edged closer.

Heddy laced her fingers behind her back to keep her arms from hanging awkwardly at her sides. When he was in front of her, she could see the specks of green in his eyes. He looked wonderstruck, surprised at the girl standing before him. She shied away from him, swaying in her heels, and this time, the corners of her mouth turned up.

"Look at you," he said, and for a moment he couldn't look at her, and she knew then that he was smitten. "You didn't tell me you'd be here."

She straightened his bow tie, feeling emboldened, and elation coursed down her arms. "I thought it would be fun to surprise you."

Ash grinned, placing his hand just above the red silk bow on her back. He led her into the thicket below, snippets of small talk circling like cigarette smoke. Jean-Rose watched hawklike as they breezed by her and the pool, aglow in aquamarine.

"Glad you finally made it," Jean-Rose said, her eyes running up and down Heddy's figure, red shoes to winged eyeliner.

Ash's grip on her was confident and full of direction, and he told Jean-Rose: "Can I have her for a minute?" But he didn't wait for an answer. He led her to the bar, the crowd seeming to part for them, even if the chatter around them carried on without pause. Everyone was looking at them— No, at her.

He handed her a glass of punch, the rim coated in brown sugar. "You looked like you needed saving."

"Was it that obvious? I don't know anyone here."

He held up a shot of whiskey in a toast. "Well, you know me."

"Cheers." She swigged her drink, waiting for that tingling feeling that came with it, the one that made her feel like she could do anything.

The band was finishing an up-tempo doo-wop song people a generation older preferred. Ash leaned up against the bar sideways to face her. Smelling his aftershave—citrus and vanilla, she guessed—and gazing up at him, she nearly forgot she was at Gigi's party, or that they weren't the only two people there. Ash flattened the back of his hair with his hand.

"You're different tonight," he said.

Heddy matted her hair down in the back, too, mimicking him. "Possibly because I'm not chasing two little kids in a bathing suit." She laughed. "And anyway, we didn't stumble upon each other; I came looking for you."

She watched a look of understanding flash across his face. His eyes were shiny then, a boy who was told he could ride the carousel a second time around, and she smiled softly.

"When I saw you, I thought, *That dress.* But it's not the dress, it's you. You're so . . ." That he couldn't find the right words made her blush, and she stood regally, for perhaps the first time in her life.

Heddy did her best pirouette: "I love this dress."

"You're having fun tonight, aren't you?" His eyes twinkled; she swore it.

Nearby, she spotted Gigi on an outdoor wicker sectional, men hawking her on all sides. Heddy searched for Cary Grant's pretty-boy looks but didn't see him. Gigi caught her eye, waving seductively. She cupped her hands around her full red lips and mouthed: "Boob rub."

Heddy worked to block Ash's view of Gigi. "It's a party, isn't it? Besides, only four weeks until I leave the island."

"Summer is flying by." Ash tapped his hand to Chubby Checker's "Let's Twist Again."

Heddy took another swig of punch, then tapped her hand, too, while sneaking a look at his watch: Peugeot. Gold-toned rectangular face, weathered brown leather strap, two dials (one for the hour hand, one to count seconds). Ash leaned his elbow on the bar, gazing at her.

"Every so often you get a summer you don't want to let go of."

"This is one of them," she said. Heddy's eyes followed a girl in a tailored lavender sheath as she sauntered by. Then she copied Ash's position, leaning against the bar with her elbow resting on the bar top.

He looked at her like she was up to something. "Why are you doing that?"

She pooled her eyes with innocence. "What?" She turned her head, grinning.

He hooked his thumb in his trouser pocket, the muscles in his eyes pulling back a smile. "Nothing."

"Maybe I'm just a little starstruck."

"Bartender, another whiskey, please." Ash stared into the shot glass for a moment, shaking his head. A whiff of pineapple chicken drifted by, and she moistened her lips, the reassuring flavor of strawberry gloss on her tongue.

"You took my breath away tonight. Did I say that? I don't want the night to end without you knowing that," he said. The liquor sloshed in her stomach, giving her courage, too.

"I think about you . . ." The bartender dropped a martini glass, the shatter pausing conversations.

Ash pushed off the bar with his fists. "There's something I need to do. But . . . will you dance with me, first?"

Hypnotized, she let him lead her to the dance floor, where a few other couples held each other at arm's length, slow dancing to "Can't Help Falling in Love."

Heddy locked her arms around his neck, his hands resting on her back, his warmth enveloping her. Theirs would be a Cape Cod house, sweet yellow shutters with a paved drive. He would do the yardwork and she would bake the cookies. At night, they'd snuggle on a couch they picked from the Montgomery Ward catalog. They'd watch *I Love Lucy* and have two children, a boy and a girl, and she'd dress them in coordinating outfits on Christmas, and they'd drink a little too much spiked eggnog and make love after putting out the children's presents. She would kiss him goodbye in the morning and again when he got home. He'd never cheat on her, and they'd never be pressed for money.

The song drifted to an end, and he pulled away. "I need to go now, but I'll find you."

She looked away from him, her cheeks hot. "Oh, of course." Did Ash see the beautiful blonde standing near them, the woman she'd seen get out of the car earlier? She seemed to be watching them. Heddy ran her tongue along her lips, tilting her head to the side, like Gigi had the other day.

"I'll be right where you left me," she said, as sultry as her voice would go. Once he disappeared into the party, she tried to hide her disappointment that he'd gone off. She inched her way closer to where Gigi was, thankful when the actress noticed.

"Ohhhh, Miss Heddy." Gigi hollered from the outdoor sectional. The actress swatted away the harem of men who surrounded her and reached her hands out to Heddy's. "Look at you."

Heddy put her arms up, posing like she'd won an Academy Award of her own. "I feel like a million bucks."

"Because of the dress—or because of the boy?" Gigi gestured to the spot where she and Ash had danced.

Heddy shrugged. "He had to talk to other people."

Gigi's eyes were luminous. "And so did you." She planted her hands on her thighs, twisting her hips ever so slightly. "You look stunning. If I wasn't here, no one would be able to take their eyes off you." Gigi twirled a tousled lock of auburn hair around her finger.

For a moment, Heddy was lost in a daze staring at the movie star. She snapped back. *I'm supposed to compliment her.*

"That dress is unlike anything I've ever seen—what material is that?" said Heddy, pinching at the knit.

"A designer in LA specializes in crochet. Isn't it incredible?" The dress clung to Gigi, an elaborate white crocheted mini that fell to the mid-thigh, and lacked lining in parts, giving guests small peeks at the skin on her hips, her cleavage, even her thighs. "These ladies won't wear anything like this in their lives—I feel sexy as hell in it."

"You look sexy as hell in it."

Gigi laughed wickedly, then kicked at Heddy's stilettos.

Heddy nearly forgot her manners. "Thank you for these!" She pointed her foot like a ballerina to show off the heels, and Gigi's grin spread from ear to ear. "They're so gorgeous I may display them as art after this."

"Her face must have been priceless." Gigi smirked.

Heddy searched for Jean-Rose; she was talking to Ash, and he held a drink at his chest, his stance triumphant. *That's who he had to talk to?*

"I'm sure Jean-Rose could afford them, if she wanted them," Heddy said. Ash and Jean-Rose toasted, then he began chatting with a few well-dressed men.

Gigi jutted out her chin, sarcasm in her snicker. "The Williamses have money, sugar pie, but these heels are limited edition from Paris, something you get only if Coco Chanel is your dear friend." Gigi cackled, like she and Heddy were in on the same joke.

Time stopped. The cacophony quieted, the dancers slowed their footwork, the music trailed off. Of course. That's why Gigi was being so nice to her. Heddy was a pawn in a drama that had nothing to do with her. Gigi wasn't interested in studying Heddy's mannerisms for a role. The actress wanted to drive Jean-Rose to the brink of madness, showing her that even her own babysitter, who she paid to respect her, would rather emulate Gigi. That getting an invite to a party wasn't so special if the babysitter got one, too.

"Heddy." Gigi snapped her fingers in her face, but she stared at Gigi's face, like she was seeing it for the first time. Gigi in her skimpy dress, her face flushed with liquor, drunk with ambition and ego. Even with all her beauty and the bloated bank accounts, she was just another girl trying to prove she was worth something. Maybe Heddy had known that all along. Maybe it's why she asked her for help. However different they were, they had that in common. Two girls from the wrong side of the tracks working to right their ships.

Ted rested his hand on Gigi's shoulder, and she turned to Heddy first, secretly rolling her eyes, then facing him with a phony smile.

"Nice job, Gigi. You turned our Heddy into a swan," Ted said, sitting beside the actress.

But even as she considered Gigi's intentions, she didn't care if the actress had used her. Because in the end they'd helped each other. Heddy was here, wasn't she? She knew Gigi wouldn't forget her, and she had a feeling they'd remain friends, as unlikely as that seemed.

Gigi bent toward Ted, allowing the tops of her breasts to fall out of the ornately crocheted bosom. "I heard you're running for state senate?"

"Oh, sit up." He chuckled, but they couldn't miss his stern tone. He sipped his champagne. "I've decided not to run."

Gigi threw a crumpled napkin toward Edison Mule, his arm around his wife, a petite woman in a plum-colored sleeveless shift dress. "Too many skeletons in the closet?"

A waiter came by to refill Ted's champagne glass, tiny bubbles popping at the surface. "Where is your date, Gigi?"

Gigi blew a kiss to the men gathering nearby, waiting for a turn to meet her. "I have enough to keep me busy. Where is that opportunist you call a wife?"

"Even after all this, she gets to you. Do what I do: pleasant ignoring." Ted snorted, and Heddy stared at her hands. She didn't like Jean-Rose, either, but still, she wanted to clock him.

Gigi pushed the barrel of his chest. "You always were a little cruel." She wondered then if Gigi knew what he did to Jean-Rose sometimes.

When he was gone, Gigi put her arm around Heddy's shoulders. "Did you see his wristwatch? Audemars Piguet. Stainless steel. One of the finest men's watches—extremely expensive. He's always trying to prove something, probably to make up for those awful eyebrows."

Heddy spit her olive back in her martini. She dabbed at her mouth with a napkin, composing herself, then breaking into laughter. "What do you know about Peugeot watches?"

Gigi found Ash, deep in the same conversation. "Is that what he wears?"

Heddy nodded.

"Affordable luxury. Moneyed, but practical. Waiter, I want one of those chicken thingies." A man in a red jacket swooped in, handing her a plateful.

"So he's not going to blow his savings on diamonds," Heddy said. "Good, I don't need diamonds."

Gigi blew the stink of liquor into Heddy's face. "Oh, Heddy the babysitter. Didn't I teach you anything?"

"I thought he wasn't going to come. I kept staring, and he wasn't, and then."

"I saw it. A perfect scene. You did good, little girl." Gigi sipped the last of her martini, slamming the glass on the table, something else clearly on her mind. "Do you know that you're the only one on this island I can trust? You and my agent. But you're the only one I don't pay. Everyone else just wants bragging rights. You like me, don't you?"

Heddy pressed her hand over the actress's slender fingers. "I love you, in fact."

Gigi squeezed Heddy's hand, smiling seductively, like the cameras were on her. They were. "Cary broke my heart not showing up tonight. We're done."

"He must have good reason." Heddy ogled a plate of shrimp cocktail whizzing by, and Gigi whistled to the waiter, handing her a tower of them.

"He didn't even call." Gigi pushed a cascade of hair across her shoulder, posing for a clicking camera. How often did Gigi smile for the wrong reasons? "See, sugar pie, you can't make assumptions about people. On-screen, I get to control the ending. Real life is so much more disappointing."

Heddy tugged a shrimp off a skewer. "Maybe that's why I want to be a writer. Then things can only be as bad as I make them."

Gigi slapped her on the back. Rough, the shrimp cocktail sauce splattering her face. Heddy wiped her cheek with a cocktail napkin. "Why are you smacking me?"

Gigi pushed Heddy's shoulders back. "Because you're fretting. Look how wrinkled your brows are!"

Heddy put down the plate of shrimp. "What if he doesn't like me?"

"Easy. Then you move on." Gigi scooted closer, pointing at the partygoers. "These people come here. They don't care about me. They don't care about you. You know who they care about?" She held up one finger, wagged it in Heddy's face. "Numero uno."

Heddy fiddled with her gold-post earring.

"That's our problem, me and you. We don't put ourselves first. We think that finding love is about making someone else happy."

Heddy stared at the couples on the dance floor. If she didn't find someone to love her, what future could she have, except one like her mother's? A life full of lonely. "With all due respect, I'm not sure you and I play by the same rules. You could spend your life unmarried. But me. I'm out of options."

"All I'm saying is don't squander your degree." Gigi tilted her head toward a group of men in dinner jackets talking to Ash. "He's just the first. Give yourself time."

"I don't have that kind of time." Heddy cleared her throat. "Sorry. There are some things I haven't said. Important things."

Gigi reached for Heddy's cheeks, cradling them in her palms, looking deep into her eyes, like she might kiss her. "I've been playing along with you, sugar pie, about this husband stuff. But listen to me: Discovering who you are isn't about finding love. That's about the only real truth I know in this wretched world, and I'm still trying to learn it."

The rims of Heddy's eyes began to burn, and all she could imagine was her eyeliner. That it might run down her face, staining her cheeks with thick streaks of black. "But what if I . . ."

Gigi used her hands to push Heddy's bangs into place. "There, there, dear. All I'm saying is: Why not figure out what you want first? You don't want to become one of these vacant-eyed housewives slow dancing with your vacuum every afternoon." She motioned her hands around, disgusted with the sight of everyone before her, a queen shooing away peasants. "You could be more than this. You want to be a writer? Start writing, send me a script."

A song picked up, a fast-tempo jazz number, which made Heddy think of Sullivan. She fidgeted with the hem of her dress, wondering if he was here, worrying that he was. "Can we talk about something else, please?"

Gigi kissed her cheek, and Heddy stood. "If only I had someone like me at your age," Gigi said, swatting her away. "Go find him. And don't forget our little trick." Gigi shook her breasts, which seemed to excite the men waiting for her on the sidelines. They swooped in, angling for a spot next to the movie star. Gigi eased into them, gushing in their admiration.

With sunset, the sky turned indigo, and all at once a dozen chandeliers illuminated over the patio, casting the party in an amber glow.

Men in tuxedoes balancing shiny silver trays zigzagged through the guests while the swimming pool glowed with underwater lights. Heddy found Ash near the bar, arm in arm with Susanne, her husband holding a drink for a toast, all of them laughing.

A freckled waiter sidestepped to face her, a large, pleasing smile on his face. "Triscuit with cream cheese, salmon, and pimento?" The waiter bowed, like the food was something prepared especially for her to consume. *I'm being mistaken for someone with money.* She'd approached the women at the country club when she used to cater like this, like they were a species that needed special attention. Heddy reached for a cocktail napkin and took one of the hors d'oeuvres.

She made her way through the crowd to look for Jean-Rose, who was near a gazebo strung with lights, talking to two women.

"There you are! Everyone has been asking about the mysterious woman in the red dress." Jean-Rose opened her arms in an embrace. "Have you all met our superstar babysitter?"

A woman with long dark waves pushed to one side with jeweled combs, offered a slender hand: "Abigail Rhodes."

Sullivan's mother. The other, holding a notepad and pencil, looked Heddy up and down: "I'm Estelle Pintard. I write the Around the Town column for Abigail's paper." Then: "A babysitter wearing Oleg Cassini? Impressive." She scribbled something. "Do you mind if I take a photo for the paper?"

"That's Jackie's favorite designer." Jean-Rose scoffed, running her hand along Heddy's skirt, looking seduced by the feel of it. She put her arm around Heddy for the photograph.

Estelle, whose nose was as pointed as her tone, dropped her gaze to Heddy's shoes. "Where on earth did you get special-edition Chanel? Jean-Rose, you treat your help *very* well."

Heddy looked at Jean-Rose for assistance—should she say that it was all Gigi's? No: *Fake it till you make it,* as Grandma said when she left for Wellesley.

"Thank you, ma'am. I borrowed it all from a friend."

"I'm not sure I'd call her a friend." Jean-Rose looked toward Gigi, and Estelle wrote something else in her notebook. Her wrinkled lips had flecks of dried mauve lipstick in the creases.

The music stopped, and Gigi took the microphone. Her husky voice welcomed "the Vineyard's most beautiful people to the season's most beautiful party."

"She always sounds like there's a frog in her throat," Jean-Rose whispered to Abigail, who snickered.

Abigail, a triple strand of diamonds hugging her neck, shared Sullivan's baby face and turned to Heddy when Gigi's speech was over. "Jean-Rose says you're a Wellesley girl. I graduated in 'forty-one."

Heddy looked around the glowing pool for Sullivan—she hoped he wasn't there tonight, that he hadn't seen her with Ash.

"I begin my senior year in the fall." A blatant lie. What if she knew? What if she was on the Wellesley board and had a list of students who'd lost their scholarships?

"Are you studying for a Mrs. degree?" Abigail snorted. The waves in her hair were a cascade of coiffed hills and valleys. "Peter and I married my junior year, and I was pregnant by graduation."

Heddy smiled. "I'm just trying to keep my nose in the books."

"I'm sure you are." The woman grimaced, glancing at Estelle, but the reporter was impatient, tapping her foot.

Estelle rolled the pencil between her fingers. "I thought you said Cary Grant was coming."

Jean-Rose pretended to look for him. "He'll be here. Gigi said he was running late."

Heddy took in Jean-Rose's blush-colored evening gown, a stunning, fanned bosom casting an accordion of delicate silk against her chest. Hanging from her wrist was a shimmering golden cuff.

"You always manage to look perfect," she told her boss, sad that she had to stand here and pretend the night before didn't happen.

Jean-Rose feigned modesty, pushing a bobby pin deeper into her braided bun. "Why thank you, Heddy. You look lovely yourself. I love your pearls."

"They were my grandmother's." Her buzz made her want to tell Jean-Rose more, like how her grandmother gave them to her on her sixteenth birthday, that they were the finest thing she owned, and how she'd put them on the day of her high school graduation and wouldn't take them off until she graduated from Wellesley, a symbol of her perseverance. Even after reading her rejection letter earlier tonight, she'd left them on.

The drummer used his sticks to bang out a finale, finishing big with a slam on the cymbals. Everyone clapped.

"I hope I got the right drink, Mother." It was a man's voice, and Heddy recognized his uncertain tone straightaway. She raised her punch to her lips, hand trembling. Sullivan, underdressed in khakis and a navy sports coat, stepped beside her in the circle, so close their elbows grazed. She felt him notice her, his eyes lingering on her profile, but he didn't say hello. She gave him a sideways smile, not sure if he was angry with her. Her breath quickened, heat gathering up the nape of her neck.

Jean-Rose nudged Heddy, wrinkling her nose. "I think you two know each other."

Sullivan shifted from one foot to the other, holding up his drink in toast. He sputtered. "Mother, this is the girl I told you about."

Heddy grinned. Here she was chasing Ash, and Sullivan had told his mother about her.

Abigail tilted her head forward, blue shadow coloring her eyes, pasty with foundation. "We were getting acquainted. Sullivan didn't want to come tonight—he's always late, this one. I'm starting to suspect on purpose. But he cleans up well, doesn't he? My handsome boy." She reached for his face, but he smacked his mother's hand away. She turned to Heddy. "Who was your friend at the bar?"

"Mother, please."

Heddy filled with dread, realizing Abigail was addressing her, asking about Ash. "A friend from the beach. He's teaching Teddy to surf."

"You seem to have many friends, Heddy," Abigail said, causing the muscles in Heddy's cheeks to twitch.

Jean-Rose cleared her throat. "What are you doing this summer, Sullivan?"

"Waiting at the the Clamshell. But I'm also teaching baseball at the town camp." His voice brightened, and he glanced at Heddy. His mother was right: without his glasses, Heddy could see how handsome he really was—full, round lips; hazel eyes.

"You didn't tell me you did that, too," Heddy said, and he smiled at her.

His mother clicked her tongue. "So curious, this one. Curious about everything but the paper. We're going to have to give him the science pages." Everyone laughed, except for Sullivan, who mouthed to Heddy: "See?"

His mother winced. "Where is Peg? I'm sure she'd love a dance."

Heddy's lip twitched. Was Peg here?

"Mother, Peg and I are over. Long over." He gave Heddy a cursory glance. She stared into her martini.

Abigail shoved him in the chest. "Oh, Sully, go find your future bride. She doesn't have complications, like some girls do." Her eyes narrowed on Heddy.

"Piss off, Mother." Sullivan stormed off, his head low, and Heddy dashed after him. He ran up the steps into Gigi's house, and she followed him until she felt a tap on her back. The smell of vanilla and citrus. She spun to find Ash, the crest of his chest leaning into her. The last few minutes washed away like the receding tide. She felt something close to awe. He'd come for her.

A tickle of warm breath in her ear. "You're a hard woman to track down. You think you'd be easy to spot in that red dress."

"Ash." She wanted to hug him, to follow him to the dance floor and do the twist. Watch the fireworks from the gazebo on Gigi's lawn. But Sullivan's mother. She'd said those things, about Heddy being "complicated," and Peg was here somewhere—his future bride—and Heddy felt ridiculous. "I have to go. This night. It's been . . ."

She wasn't going to be someone's punching bag. She didn't need to take this assault on her character. She knew she didn't belong here. Why did everyone else seem so intent on reminding her?

Ash whispered in her ear: "I have to hang around for a half hour. I'll meet you on the beach, near the path to my cottage."

A part of her wondered why he couldn't leave now, why he wasn't as lost in her as she was in him. But she supposed she was willing to wait thirty minutes if it meant spending more time with him, especially since the eye makeup, fancy red dress, and studied sex appeal had been for him. Sullivan was nowhere to be found, and she certainly wasn't driving the island to hunt him down.

"Okay," she said, watching him disappear into a circle of tuxedoed men.

Heddy sat on a large piece of driftwood under a near full moon, listening for his footsteps down the beach for close to an hour. Had she misunderstood? Perhaps he meant they'd meet at his cottage—or maybe he changed his mind. The party was still going, the music sounding distant and faraway from here. She stared across a smooth plane of dark sea, watching lights flickering on the mainland.

She heard footsteps and saw his form ambling toward her.

"That took longer than expected," Ash said, dropping his dress shoes in the sand; she'd already kicked off her heels.

"I almost gave up on you," she said. *More than once.*

Ash skipped a stone into the sea. "The party took a turn. Susanne changed into her bikini and nearly lost it in a dive. Sally and Judy jumped in in their evening gowns, and Gigi made them do handstands for prizes. 'Utter trash,' one lady told me." Ash was laughing. "They haven't a care, these people, do they?"

He put his arm around her shoulders, pulling her close.

"You were busy," Heddy said. The truth was she was disappointed. No, she was mad. Why was he always with women like Jean-Rose and Susanne? She found a flat gray rock, throwing it like a discus, so it would skip over the surface of the sea, but it dropped into the deep after one bounce.

"I'm sorry, kitty kit. I had to close a few deals. And it's happening. Jean-Rose is signing on. She handed me the contract tonight. We got them, Heddy. That means we'll get more."

We? Was she part of this?

She hugged him, her frustration waning. Perhaps, someday they could be a team. "Congratulations. You did it."

"I'm going to get the money I need." He picked up a flat rock and handed it to her. "This is how you skip a rock." With Heddy gripping the stone, he pulled back her wrist and let her fling it. The press of his chest on her back made her breath slip. Her feet pivoted, and she spun in his embrace to face him, tilting her head up to meet his gaze. She noticed a small scar just above his lip, the tiny pores where he'd shaved.

"What I need is a lesson in money," she said, covering her eyes with her fingers. Ash gently moved her hands away, and she batted her lashes just once, a coy invitation that beckoned him to come closer. She imagined that her winged eye makeup was as sexy as Elizabeth Taylor's in *Cleopatra.* That he might see her that way.

"How can I help?" He ran his fingertip along the edges of her lips, parting her mouth. A buoy bell rocked with the waves. His nose brushed against the bridge of hers. She desperately wanted to kiss him. "People do crazy things to get money," he said.

She wondered what he'd say if he knew she needed more of it. But then she felt his lips press into hers, and she yielded, melting into him, tasting peppermint and molasses, perhaps from the whiskey. He dug his fingers into her hair, pulling her deeper toward him, and she shivered, from the inside out.

When he pulled back, his lips were swollen and red. He took her hands, pressing his thumbs softly into her palms. "You're quivering." He kissed her again, satin spreading across her mouth, then drank in the sight of her.

"I better get back," she said, because she knew she didn't want to get back at all.

"You won't get away that easy." Ash jumped in front of her, walking backward while she walked toward home. "Are you free one night next week?"

"It depends," she flirted.

"On what?"

She listened to their footsteps kicking up sand. "On whether Jean-Rose and Ted have plans. I have off Fridays, sometimes I can get Monday nights off."

"Then try for Monday. I want to take you out on the water."

"I thought we were having lobster rolls," she laughed. If she began spending more time with him, she'd have to stop calling Sullivan.

"That will be our next date." Ash turned to face her, using his finger to trace a line down her neck, stopping at her clavicle and letting it linger. At night, the sweet lines of the Williams house's gingerbread lattice looked ominous, haunted.

"This is you," he said.

She pulled on the pocket square in his suit. "This is me."

Ash reached for her hand, and she held it up to him. He leaned down and kissed the top of it, just below her bent knuckles, leaving behind an imprint that felt as definitive as a signature.

"Can I have this?" She pulled out the pocket square, dangling it in front of his face.

"What for?"

"To keep a piece of you." She knew that all of this—tonight—
was a fantasy, that someone like Ash Porter would feel faraway from
her life next year.

"If it means something to you."

"Good night, Mr. Porter."

"Good night, kitty kit."

He chuckled, a bit giddy himself, and walked off in bare feet, the
moon reflecting in the shiny dress shoes he carried in his hand.

{ NINETEEN }

Heddy woke the following morning to Ruth standing over her, already in her apron. "So?"

Heddy reached for the alarm clock on her nightstand, knocking off a book. "Ruth, it's six in the morning." She rubbed sleep out of her eyes.

"Sorry, I promised Jean-Rose I'd make the sand muffins." Sand muffins, as the kids called them, were Ruth's specialty, banana nut.

Heddy rolled over, slamming a feather pillow over her head.

"Come on. Spill," Ruth said. "I zonked yesterday."

When Heddy peeled back the pillow, she saw the dark circles under Ruth's eyes, the anxious way she licked her lips. She worried if things were getting worse at home.

"It was a disaster. Actually, it was amazing. There were endless platters of shrimp cocktail, colorful drinks with little umbrellas floating in them, and at least three Hollywood directors wearing those thick black glasses. But the best part, the only part that matters really, is that Ash asked me to dance, and he walked me home, but . . ."

Ruth got back in bed next to her, her eyes crinkling. "But what?"

"Sullivan was there."

"Oh cripes."

Heddy sat up, propping her elbows up against the pillows. "And so was Peg. But I didn't see her."

"Little Miss Stuck-up," Ruth huffed.

"And his mother made plain I'm not good enough." Heddy cringed thinking of how Abigail had referred to her *many friends* on the island.

"Sullivan's mother doesn't decide who he dates."

"Or does she?" Heddy glanced out the window at Ash's fishing cottage; the gleam of the rising sun reflected in the windows. She pushed the feelings of shame away. "Anyway, I'm not sure it matters."

Ruth thumped her with a pillow.

Heddy giggled. "But Ash. He's just so . . ."

Ruth nodded. "He's a man, not a boy."

She studied Ruth's profile; her nose was small and buttonlike, a nose so cute Heddy wanted to pinch it. "It's not that. He just makes me feel like we could read the dictionary together, and it would be fun."

"So that's what falling in love feels like." Ruth grimaced.

Heddy had been in love once, although she wasn't sure now that she would call it love. She walked the Brooklyn Bridge arm in arm with Mikey O'Shauney after school sometimes, liking his company more than she expected, particularly because he cracked jokes about everything—imagining ridiculous conversations between squirrels or saying his dad, an elevator repairman, was going nowhere but up. He made so many jokes it was hard to know what he was ever really thinking, but one day, on the Manhattan side of the bridge, he kissed her, and she told him she loved him, and he got all fidgety. After that, she didn't hear from him.

"Oh, Hibernia, maybe we're more alike than I thought," her mother had laughed, drying Heddy's tears.

After that, she'd promised herself she'd never make a fool of herself with a man. She'd be levelheaded, but keeping that promise was proving difficult.

"You know you're going to meet someone, Ruth. And it probably won't work out for me anyway."

Ruth pushed the blanket back, standing and smoothing the pleats of her apron. "I'm sorry. That was lousy of me." She stopped at the door, like there was something serious to say. "I have to stop sleeping here. My mom . . . I can't keep pretending this is my life."

"Do you think he'll ever get help? Your dad. There are meetings, on this island, at the church. You could make him go." She'd seen a flyer for Alcoholics Anonymous in town one day.

Ruth's cheeks flushed as she tied her apron tighter around her waist. "I can take care of myself."

"I just . . . I care about you is all." Heddy felt like she could cry.

Ruth nodded, wiping at her eyes. "Let's drop it. Okay?" Before Ruth turned to go, she said: "I hope it works out for you, I do."

Minutes later, there was the pitter-patter of little feet, Teddy's slight frame barreling into her bed, his chest heaving.

"What's wrong?"

"I-I-I—" He was spitting, tears rolling like rain down windows. "I had a dream, and Miss Pinkie . . ."

She smoothed his sweaty hair. "There, there."

"Is she coming back?"

"I don't know." To think that the doll was tucked in a box in the garage. Why was Jean-Rose keeping it from him?

The boy nuzzled her, and she wondered how she'd leave him and Anna; she'd grown to care for them.

"But I love her."

"I know you do." She could take away his pain, if only she went to the garage. "Stay here."

Heddy wrapped herself in a blanket and padded down the stairs, sprinting past Ruth in the kitchen, going straight to the side door of the garage. After grabbing the doll and stuffing it in her robe, she took the steps two at a time until she was back in her room, holding Miss Pinkie behind her back.

The boy rubbed his eyes.

Heddy was out of breath. "You have to make me a promise that you'll never tell your mother." The child wrinkled his forehead, trying to see what she had.

"I found her." When she held the doll up, he snatched it, clutching her tight, the doll's legs curling up. Then he threw his arms around Heddy.

"Keep her hidden," she warned.

He pulled back. "Can I sleep with her?"

Heddy bit her lip. "Put her to bed in your closet."

"Okay." He spun around with the doll, lifting her puckered lips for a kiss. Strange, thought Heddy, a boy comforted by a doll—and yet, how was it different from a teddy bear or a beloved pillow? It was simply what he loved. She wished Ruth were here now so she could point to the child and say: "No, Ruth. That's what love feels like."

Instead, Heddy leaned her head against her pillow and stared out at the wavy lines of the sea. Teddy climbed in next to her, tucking Miss Pinkie under the sheets and giving Heddy an innocent smile.

"When I die, I want to be buried with her," the boy said. The comment made her frown.

"Don't think like that."

"Do you have something you want with you?" he asked, and she cringed. She hated thinking about dying.

Her journal? Gigi's dress? Tempting. Definitely her grandmother's pearls. "My books. Just my favorites."

He wrinkled his nose. "That's weird."

"Maybe I'm a bit strange then."

Teddy turned on his side to face her. "Do I have to go to the library again today?"

"No, you and Anna have a birthday party at your friend Matthew's, remember? Besides everything will be better now that Miss Pinkie is back."

"Can we pick blueberries first?"

She'd forgotten about the blueberries; she couldn't wait to get out of bed then, and in the bathroom, she pulled on shorts, washing the last of her eye makeup off. "Let's see if Anna is up."

She and the children crunched on Frosted Flakes in the kitchen, the morning gloomy and gray with cloud cover. Heddy opened the newspaper to the comics, reading the new *Dick Tracy* aloud while Ruth wiped counters.

Jean-Rose appeared in the doorway, her hair pulled back in a patterned satin scarf and her arms crossed over her robe. They stopped laughing.

"Cinderella returned from the ball?"

"Mama!" The children ran to her, hugging her legs, but Jean-Rose didn't budge. The kids slunk back to the table.

It was clear by the way Jean-Rose was staring at her that Heddy had done something wrong, so she put down her comic. "Did you have fun last night?"

Jean-Rose padded to the cabinet, removing a juice glass. "I did, but I wasn't out of my league. The question is: Did you have fun?" Jean-Rose poured a cup of the tomato and lemon concoction Ruth made for hangovers, gulping it back.

Heddy considered running up to her room and hiding, like a child—she was terrible at confrontation, being the first to give in or make concessions if someone was angry at her, even when it wasn't in her best interests. "A girl like me at a party like that? I'll never forget it."

Jean-Rose put her elbows on the table, resting her chin in her hands, her mouth so close Heddy could smell the tangy tomato juice on her breath. "You think he likes you, don't you?"

"Heddy, are you in love?" Anna asked, coming to her mother's side, one eyebrow cocked.

Heddy shifted in her chair, smiling at Anna, while searching for the right answer.

Jean-Rose kept herself close. "You realize you'll never fit into his life, right? He's certainly not taking you to Florida."

Sourness balled in Heddy's throat. "Of course not."

"Who, Mama?" Anna said. Heddy rubbed the child's hand, holding her fingers to her lips to shush her, while Ruth scrubbed harder at a cutting board, her back to them.

Jean-Rose stood, her eyes half shuttered with a sneer. "To think I stuck my neck out setting you up with Sullivan Rhodes."

Heddy folded her hands in her lap, turning down her gaze. "I appreciate that. And I like Sullivan. But his mother. You heard her." She wanted to scream: *What did I do wrong?*

Jean-Rose pulled Ruth, still holding a sponge, to the table next to Heddy.

"Children, finish your breakfast. We'll be in the living room." Heddy and Ruth exchanged anxious glances, then followed Jean-Rose, who sat down on the velvet couch while retying her turban.

"Sit," she said.

Heddy didn't know what to do with her hands, and they went from her pockets to flat against her thighs to folded in front of her navel.

"What is it?" Heddy stammered. She could see why Jean-Rose would be disappointed if it didn't work out with Sullivan, since she had set them up. But why did she care if Heddy liked Ash? Or if Ash liked her?

Jean-Rose held up her wrist. "This is a bracelet I wear every day. It was a gift from my godmother, and it's special to me. But it's nothing compared to my diamond eternity bracelet. Ted gave it to me on our first anniversary."

Heddy examined her bitten fingernails, then met Jean-Rose's eyes. "I love that bracelet," Heddy said.

Jean-Rose looked pleased, like it was the answer she'd expected. "Well, it's missing."

Ruth stood. "I'm not sure what you're implying."

"Sit down. There's no ill will, dear—it's not like Heddy was wearing it at the party last night, although she borrowed everything else," Jean-Rose scoffed, making Heddy swallow hard. "I just want my bracelet back. It means something to me, and you are the only two people here who have access to my bedroom."

"I don't even take oyster crackers for my clam chowder." Heddy glanced at Ruth, whose face had turned beet red.

"Perhaps you lost it?" Ruth said, her back arched like a scared cat.

"I'll check my locker at the club. But I'd like it to show up in my jewelry box." Jean-Rose didn't take her eyes off Heddy. "Understood?"

"But I don't have it, Jean-Rose. I would never . . ." Heddy, legs crossed on the wingback chair, balled her hands into fists.

Jean-Rose talked right over her. "And when you take the children to the birthday party today, no unnecessary stops, miss. You can go to the beach here from now on."

Heddy was aghast. "I've never done anything improper . . ."

Jean-Rose slammed her hand on the coffee table. "May I remind you that this is a job, and I need you to work. I heard all sorts of whispers last night about people seeing you and Ash together. All a surprise to me. I just hope you had the sense not to take the children to his house."

Heddy massaged her forehead. "He gave us a ride the day you dropped us at the beach. You told him to."

"You need to use your head."

Heddy stood abruptly; she wanted out of this conversation. "I plan to go out on Monday night," Heddy said. It would be ridiculous to hold back; this *was* a job.

Jean-Rose waved Ruth back into the kitchen. "And with who?"

Heddy creased her lips together in an uneven smile, croaking: "Ash."

Jean-Rose drummed her fingers, and Heddy folded her arms tightly, her heart racing: This felt like war. "I would prefer a different night."

"Wednesday?"

Jean-Rose mocked her, repeating "Wednesday" with disgust. She paused, then said: "Fine."

Heddy stormed out the front screen doors, nearly letting them slam. She heard Anna calling her, and then the child was next to her, holding her hand and begging her not to leave. Heddy picked her up and pressed the back of her head against the porch column. *What was she doing?* There were four weeks left of summer, and she needed this money. At the least, a solid reference.

"I need to apologize to your mom," she kissed Anna's plump rosy cheek.

"You better kiss her feet," Ruth quipped when Heddy returned to the kitchen. She found Jean-Rose in her bedroom, smoking a cigarette.

Heddy coughed, causing Jean-Rose to glance up. "I'm sorry about my temper," Heddy said, looking at Jean-Rose's eyebrows. "Thank you for watching out for me. I was just upset."

"Love is complicated." Jean-Rose puffed, closing her eyes, like the inhale relaxed her. "Remember, you're still in my charge. I don't want your mother calling me to ask what happened to her daughter at the end of the summer."

Heddy's blood boiled, but she silently backed out of the room.

"And please, help me find my bracelet," Jean-Rose called after her.

When they heard Jean-Rose's door click shut, Heddy and Ruth huddled in a corner on the porch, while the children carried toys outside.

"I swear I put it back," Heddy said. "That afternoon. After I got back, I remembered it was in my shorts."

Ruth buried her face in her hands. "Are you sure?"

"*Yes!*" She yelled it, and Ruth gave her the eye, holding her finger to her lips.

"Okay, I believe you," Ruth whispered. "So either she lost it or you lost it, and let's hope it's not the latter. Then we'll both be out of a job."

With panic swirling her stomach into knots, she and the children carried their pint baskets to the silvery blueberry bushes lining the yard. Jean-Rose charged them to pick as many berries as they could so Ruth had enough for preserves and a pie. Heddy found herself popping the juicy berries into her mouth one after the next, trying to distract from her anxiety.

Still, she couldn't distract her thoughts from the eternity bracelet. Earlier, she'd ran up the steps to her room, digging her hands through the pockets of her shorts. But they'd all cycled through the laundry at least once, since the incident with the bracelet was weeks ago. She looked under the bed, under the desk, in case it had fallen. Nothing.

After stuffing a handful of berries into her mouth, someone jumped out from behind the bushes yelling, "Boo!"

Heddy startled, coughing on a blueberry. "You shouldn't scare people like that, Sullivan."

"Sorry." He grinned. "I didn't want you to see me and run the other way."

Heddy bristled. "Aren't you looking for Peg?"

"Where's your dog?" Teddy asked as he dove behind Heddy.

"At home." Sullivan looked toward the gloomy horizon, then back at her. "Forget Peg. I wasn't expecting to see you there last night—"

"Oh. Why not?" She came to face him, her hand on her hip. A rogue raindrop fell to Heddy's arm, even if the sky hadn't committed to pouring.

"Because I didn't think you knew those people." Sullivan edged closer. "I liked that you didn't. I would do just about anything to escape a party like that."

"Well, it would be pretty hard to keep a fiancée a secret if I knew them."

Heddy wasn't sure why she was giving him a hard time—after all, Ash was in her thoughts, as was, of course, the missing bracelet—yet she couldn't stop. She'd believed he liked her, and that he had been promised to someone else made her feel foolish.

"She's not my fiancée. Mother has ideas, terrible ones. I'm sorry she was so rude." In the distance, a boat zipped across Vineyard Sound.

Heddy frowned. "What Mama says, Sullivan does, because Sullivan doesn't have a backbone."

She was being cruel, and she knew it. She wanted him to smack her clear across the cheek, but he only sighed. He removed his glasses, cleaning them with a corner of his chambray shirt.

"I guess I deserve that. But if you knew her, you'd understand. She just has this way. Father calls her the Little Engine That Could."

Heddy loosened her fists. She knew a little something about parental expectations, how crushing it felt to stand in the disapproving scowl of your mother. "We don't choose our parents, do we?" she said.

In high school, Heddy had boarded the Long Island Rail Road bound for Cold Spring Harbor, walking a few miles from the station to the address she'd memorized from an envelope in her mother's top drawer; the letter, dated ten years earlier, read simply: *It was special, but now it's over. Stop calling. Good luck. Jack. Jack Devlin, 22 Maplewood Drive.* It was dusk by the time she stood on the sidewalk across from his handsome Long Island colonial, hoping no one would notice her spying into the living room window. And there he was, sipping milk beside a young girl in her pajamas. A girl who might have been her.

"I never even knew my father," she said.

"Oh." Sullivan let his glasses fall down the bridge of his nose, his eyes peering over the tops. She supposed he felt guilty, complaining about parents that were too present.

He asked if he could help pick berries, and they did so for an hour or so, comparing notes about restaurants and dance clubs in Boston, until Heddy announced they needed to pick up the car at Gigi's.

Sullivan looked at his Cartier watch. "You want a ride?" His Aston Martin, a two-seater with a soft top, sat in the driveway. God, she wanted to ride in that car again.

She sucked on her pearls. "I guess." She ran inside to tell Ruth they were leaving for the party, grabbing the birthday present and bounding back out to the car.

The kids climbed onto Heddy's lap, while Sullivan grabbed a small black camera bag from the console, putting it in the trunk. "You take photographs?" she asked.

"Learning." Sullivan pulled on a Yankees baseball cap, steering the car out of the drive. "Don't tell me you like the Red Sox."

Heddy kissed the back of Anna's head. "I've never been to a baseball game."

He gave her a double take; his hazel eyes flickering. "That's very un-American of you."

"The time has never been right."

He leaned over to position his baseball hat on her, beaming, which made her smile. Sullivan tried to be bohemian, and she supposed he was, but she bet he could spend hours playing catch or throwing a football around, too. Most guys would say they're athletic, science-minded, or creative, while Sullivan was truly all three. "We have the best seats, right behind home plate. Maybe we can go sometime?"

"Heddy already has a boyfriend." Anna removed his hat, tossing it in Sullivan's lap.

Heddy stared hard at the dirt road. It was sort of, maybe true, so why was she having so much trouble admitting it.

Sullivan pushed his glasses up on his nose. "I meant, as friends."

"Heddy is a tart." Teddy bounced up and down on Heddy's leg, chanting.

She smacked his knee, and he turned around, sticking his tongue out at her. "Teddy! How do you know that word?" Where was the boy thankful she'd given him his doll back?

"That's terrible, Teddy. You could go to jail for saying it." That got his attention.

Teddy pouted: "Mommy called you that."

Sullivan pulled the car into the field where she'd left the Buick, meeting Heddy's eye with a smirk. She knew what he was picturing—Heddy roaming the island as a streetwalker—and, despite the insult, they burst into laughter.

"What's so funny?" asked Anna.

Heddy patted her back.

"Why are you laughing?" Teddy snapped.

Sullivan hiccupped.

"Can we get out of the car now?" Teddy, irritated that he wasn't in on the joke, jiggled the door. Heddy pushed her weight into it and lifted both kids out, turning to Sullivan. He drummed his fingers against the tan leather steering wheel.

"I'm playing again this Friday. Will you come?"

Heddy hesitated. She and Ash weren't going steady, hardly, and a girl had to keep her options open. She ducked into the passenger window; it *was* her day off. "Only if you keep that ridiculous girl away."

That night, her mother called. Jean-Rose and Ted were at the club for dinner, and she'd already read to the children and tucked them into bed. Her mother sounded odd, her tone guarded, and Heddy knew like she did about rain: something was wrong.

"Is everything okay, Mama?"

"I just needed to hear your voice," her mother said with phony optimism.

Heddy, like all children do when talking to their parents, took it as an opening to talk about herself. "Mama, I've been thinking about what I want to do. After graduation."

Her mother must be listening to the radio; she could hear strange voices. "Teach at PS Thirty-Nine. You've always loved kids, and Eileen says her daughter Mary Kate makes seventy-five dollars a week."

Heddy knew all about perfect Mary Kate. She shuddered, standing at the double screen doors. Being a teacher seemed boring now, like having to sit through a movie she didn't want to see. "My future isn't that clear to me."

"A job is just a way to pay bills, Hibernia. Don't think so hard on it."

Heddy rested her cheek against the screen, the mesh scratching her face. "I've just been thinking. What if I wanted to work in the movies? Be a writer."

"A writer? Women aren't writers." Her mother's voice was exasperated. "Are these people getting to your head?"

Heddy kicked at the screen. "I suppose."

"Hibernia, I'm not saying don't have dreams but be realistic, please. We all have hobbies. My paintings never paid the rent."

Her mother was right. She was getting swept away.

"I need to tell you something," her mother said.

A strange woman's voice yelled: "I need the phone, lady."

"Mom, where *are* you?" This whole time, her mother's voice had been reticent, on edge, like someone was about to push her off a cliff.

"They raised the rent, more than I could pay. I'm at a rooming house on Pineapple Street. I'm sorry, I tried to keep as many of your things as I could."

Heddy tried to imagine the rundown brownstone, a public bath in the hall, her mother crammed into a single room, strange voices slipping through the thin walls. "What about the furniture?" She felt childish and sick saying that, but it was all they had.

"I have Grandma's chair. And the quilt she knit you. Listen, honey, I'm fine. Focus on getting back to school, graduating, and then Ken McKinney . . ."

Heddy rubbed her forehead, feeling the creases. "But, Mom, I'm falling for somebody, someone here." It slipped out, and now she regretted it. She was being selfish, and how would it help her mother?

Her mother exhaled, bored. She imagined her mother's tight bun, the two pieces of hair that fell by her puffy eyes. "So fall for him. Have your summer fling, but don't let it sidetrack you."

"But I like him." Heddy wouldn't mention that she was actually interested in two men.

In the background, someone grumbled: "You're on ten minutes, lady."

"I need to go, Hibernia. But listen, I'll get us a new apartment."

"I'll give you the deposit, Mama."

"Stoppit, I'll be okay. It's you I'm worried about. Hibernia, I love you." Her mother hesitated, then sighed. "But these boys, boys like the ones on that island, they don't take girls like us seriously. Okay?"

"Mm-hmm." Heddy dabbed her eyes with the back of her wrist, choking out a goodbye. She pushed her finger down on the cradle until the line went silent, the steady hum of the dial tone returning. "You're wrong, Mama," she whispered.

In bed, she crawled under the cool sheets, the tears sending mascara down her cheeks. She lay in the fetal position, staring at the moon, low over the water. Outside in the darkness, a light flashed—not the lighthouse—making Heddy sit up. Then it flashed again, and she realized it was coming from Ash's cottage. Two more blinks through the trees. A pause. Two more.

His living room light, maybe his outdoor spotlight, she couldn't tell. Each time the light flashed twice, then paused.

Heddy switched off her lamp, letting her room fall into darkness, then turning it back on. She paused, before flashing her lights on and off four times straight. She pressed her nose against the screen, waiting.

Sure enough, the lights in Ash's house did the same, flashing four times. She giggled despite her tears, smiling into the dark night sky. He was saying good night.

"Good night, Ash," she whispered.

❧ TWENTY ❧

"Heddy, telephone," Ruth hollered from the foyer.

She'd been cutting out Teddy's drawing of an octopus so he could make a mask to play with. Heddy excused herself, and whispered to Ruth, hand holding the receiver. "I took off the sheets, looked under the bed, in the closet. I don't have the bracelet, Ruth."

Ruth bent to pick up dust bunnies with her hand. "Jean-Rose said she didn't find it at the club."

"We can't make it appear—we don't have it." Heddy was tired of feeling a thief; she hadn't taken anything. "What are we going to do?"

Ruth didn't answer, disappearing into the living room, so Heddy pressed the phone to her ear, hearing jazz music blasting. "Hello," she said.

"Heddy, it's Sullivan." Through the static, she heard loud voices, laughing girls.

"Where are you? It's nine in the morning." She looked at her watch. "Not even."

"It's been a late night. We didn't sleep. I watched the sunrise at Navy Sea." She wondered who "we" was, then remembered the crowd at his show, the boys in gingham button-downs with the sun-kissed hair. How the girls watched him, keenly aware of Sullivan Rhodes.

"You must be exhausted," she said.

"I'm calling because. Well, I'm calling because . . ."

Someone yelled: "Let's go skinny-dipping."

And Sullivan must have moved away because she heard a door click shut, and the noise quieted.

"Is Peg there?" Heddy could see a rich girl like her taking off her clothes, running into the water, and loving that everyone was staring at her perfect behind.

"No, Heddy. Listen, I'm calling because as I watched the sun come up, I wanted you to know that I wished you were here. Everyone had someone, and I could have asked one of the girls to sit with me, but I sat alone, because I wanted you. My buddy was like, 'What is it about this girl, man?' And I know what it is: I can be myself with you. You know about my family, but you don't care about all that. And it makes me want you. It makes me want to just talk to you. God, I love talking to you."

"Sullivan." She imagined them sitting together at sunrise, his friends asking her for her opinion, calling her Sully's girl. Peg would see them, and her prim smile would turn into a scowl, and how Heddy would sink deeper into Sullivan's embrace, pretending to be apologetic but feeling nothing but pride.

"Sullivan, I like you, too."

"When can I see you again?"

Heddy kissed the mouthpiece, wishing then that they could keep talking and she could be forever distracted from her mother's predicament and the missing eternity bracelet. But he needed to sleep. She didn't want him to say something he didn't mean in his delirium. "I'm not sure."

"Can you come over tomorrow?" he asked.

"I have the children."

"We have plans Friday, anyway. I guess I can wait. Let's have dinner after. Will you have dinner with me?"

"Sure, I will." She grinned as she hung up the phone, rushing to follow the kids into the sunroom. Jean-Rose popped her head in.

"Remember: A reward if it turns up." She leaned down to kiss each child on the cheek. "I'm off to the hair salon."

Heddy's chest tightened with anger, watching Jean-Rose drive off in the rain. "Ruth?" She was at a loss; what would they do?

Ruth balanced her hands atop the broom. "We might not have taken it, but we're going to find it."

Heddy took the children to a matinee of *The Music Man* that afternoon, and since it was raining, she convinced Ruth to avoid the storm and sleep over again, so they could talk. She was trying to be excited for her dates—first with Ash, then with Sullivan—but she was too distracted with the bracelet. Her headache centered between her eyebrows, a throbbing that wouldn't stop. She popped two aspirin.

Ruth came out of the bathroom, already in her nightgown. "Stop worrying. It will turn up."

Heddy's brow furrowed, and she worked to relax the creases. "Do you think she'll call the police on us?"

"Of course not. Ted probably gave it to his girlfriend."

"Ted has a girlfriend?"

"No, but probably." Ruth laughed. "You're a ball of nerves, aren't you? We're going to be okay."

Heddy inched her way under the sheets, not even bothering to change her clothes. She curled up, making a fist with her hand and biting her fingernails.

"Ruth?"

Her friend wiped the drool gathering in the corners of her mouth. "Hmm?"

"Why do you think she blamed us? I mean, it could have been anyone." She imagined the gardener sneaking upstairs or the lady with the fabric swatches. There were the bridge ladies, sometimes with distant relatives in tow.

"She told us why: because we go in her room." Ruth said.

"But she thinks we're capable. And why? Because we're not society girls."

"If I lose this job, Mom won't get her medicine. I never told you that. Jean-Rose gives me extra, just for that."

"She does?" Heddy put her hand on Ruth's. "Ugh. I'm sorry."

Ruth closed her eyes, pulling the sheet over her small frame. "I need this job, Heddy."

As Ruth's breathing grew steady, turning into a low snore, she realized that her friend was just as scared, she was simply putting on a brave face. That they were in this position at all angered her. Heddy knew that Jean-Rose lost the bracelet—the woman was cavalier about everything she owned—and of course, she'd blame others for her own shortcomings. Heddy tossed and turned, thinking every shift in position might bring clarity. But her thoughts kept drifting back to the bracelet. If she didn't find it, Jean-Rose would label her a thief, and what if she told Susanne, and then Abigail Rhodes?

She opened her journal, writing in the moonlight about the possibility of Ruth losing her job, which reminded her about her mother losing her apartment. When she was done filling an entire page, she realized that only two lines mattered. She rewrote them, larger this time, on a blank page: *My plan B: Find the bracelet. Then ask Jean-Rose if she needs a nanny in the city.*

It was time to find a job for the fall.

{ TWENTY-ONE }

*I*t was dark when Heddy hung her pink shift dress on a hook on the back of Ash's bathroom door, fastening her bikini top. He'd told her they were going out on a boat, but she hadn't put on her bathing costume because she assumed they'd eat first. Instead, he'd packed a picnic basket to bring along, which she found incredibly romantic. She apologized for arriving an hour late, since Jean-Rose insisted that Heddy bathe the children and tuck them into bed before she left.

Heddy finished changing, returning to the living room with Ash in his bedroom, and struggled to find a comfortable but seductive position on the couch. With her freshly shaven legs folded under her, she let her eyes explore the coffee table, where she saw a folder labeled MONTCLAIR, NJ. She unfolded her studied position, leaning forward to open the folder, spying a few yellowed clippings, each one neatly cut out, additional columns of text stapled to the back.

"Montclair Home of Suicide Financier on the Market." The article depicted a stately Victorian nestled into a manicured garden. A second clipping asked: "Is It Financial Suicide to Own This House?" Heddy recognized the gossip column from the *New York Sun* and read the first few lines:

> When Edward Green's splendid six-bedroom home came back on the market last week, real estate tycoons from 42nd to 14th Streets were abuzz. But buyer beware: The painted lady's $42,000 price tag— nearly triple the cost of the average home—may have helped drive Green to his 1955 suicide after Green's Madison Investments failed to secure bids at the eleventh hour.

Ash's door unlatched, and she snapped the folder shut. He whistled as he stuffed two towels in a beach bag and filled the cooler with ice. Neither one of them said anything for a second or two, and the quiet made her anxious until he put his hands on her bare shoulders, massaging them.

"I have a surprise for you," he said. "Do you have a sweatshirt?"

She smelled his aftershave and Colgate dental cream; he must have brushed his teeth. "Do I need one?"

"The water can be chilly—I'll get you something." He emerged with a flannel collared shirt with buttons down the front. "A little big, but it's warm."

The navy flannel reminded her of a blankie she'd had as a kid, and when he turned around to pack a thermos from the fridge, she raised it to her nose and inhaled, smelling Downy fabric softener.

"Can we stop with all this mystery? What are we doing exactly?" she said.

"We're going night crabbing off Menemsha." He handed Heddy a large metal flashlight, and she slid the red switch on. A thick yellow beam cast a circle of light on the wood floors.

"We're catching them?"

He stuffed a second flashlight into his bag. "Maybe. I'll bring a lobster pot."

"How did you know I'd be game?" She arranged her denim tote bag on her shoulder.

"I couldn't date a girl without a sense of adventure."

Menemsha, a tiny fishing village "up island," as they called it, was twenty minutes away from Jean-Rose and Ted's house, and the drive reminded Heddy just how large Martha's Vineyard actually was, even if it was as third as big as nearby Cape Cod. As soon as she and Ash parked along the sandy road lining Menemsha Pond, Heddy smelled the fetid stench of rotting fish. Rows of drag fishing boats backed up to the docks, and even after seven, men, their shirts stained with sweat, were sorting through their catch. One man's hands were bloodied from filleting a fish on the dock railing, others were hosing down their boats, washing away the seaweed and salt water, the slime and smell.

He tickled her waist. "Sorry, it's a bit grizzly down here."

"I like seeing it," she said, because she liked everything when she was with him. "I've never thought much about how it all happens: the fishing, that is."

They came upon a squat shack built of faded gray clapboard, the white paint chipping off the trim, a simple sign over the door: BAIT. Inside, an older woman with leathery skin and snow-white hair sat behind the counter. She didn't look up, and Heddy wondered how she took the smell, a commingle of salt air and the gaseous muck of low tide.

"The water is calm," the wizened woman said, reaching over to a row of keys hanging on tiny hooks behind her, picking the one with the purple toggle. "You shouldn't have a problem. The tide is low, perfect for crabbing. Take the *Kelly Anne*." She handed Ash the keys, and he bowed to her.

"Thank you, Mary girl," he said, which made the craggy woman snort.

Ash took the helm of the small boat, and she stood beside him. Heddy hadn't been on a pleasure boat yet this summer, or any summer for that matter, and she held on as the zippy vessel slammed against the surf. The boat climbed whatever crest it could find, coming down with a thud just after flying up, sending up a sprinkle of water across Heddy's skin. She was cold as soon as they started, grateful for Ash's shirt.

The island looked different from out there. She could see its edges, the way the forested hills and rocky cliffs tumbled down to the sea. The houses hidden down long drives in the countryside of Chilmark, where farmland gave way to large sprawling homes, were visible; many were cedar-shingled and neatly shuttered, lush green lawns rolling like carpet to the sea. As the tiny village of Menemsha disappeared into the distance, Heddy stopped looking back and only watched what was in front of them, a wide expanse of dark blue water with a dot of green land.

"We're heading to the Elizabeth Islands," Ash said over the rev of the engine, the rhythmic *bah-boom* of the boat making it hard to hear. "Most of them are owned by some wealthy family in Boston, but you can dock at Cuttyhunk. A few hardy year-rounders live there, although its mostly summer folk, but they don't have phones, and most of their TVs are so full of static it's like watching snow fall."

She sat in the passenger seat, sea spray chilling her legs. "What do people do there?"

"Enjoy the quiet. You can buy an ice cream, and, of course, there's oysters." He glanced at her for a moment, then fixed his eyes on the skinny spit of land.

Cuttyhunk Island's stone walls and tidy houses looked similar to the Vineyard's, although she couldn't see much with dusk closing in. The boat rounded a bend and was a few feet into an inlet when

Ash killed the engine. He handed her a small iron anchor. "Toss this down up front, will you?"

Heddy carried it to the tip of the boat and threw it overboard, feeling the weight of its fall. She stared into the water, a murky view of the sandy bottom. It took a moment to find her balance, the boat gently bobbing in the sea, and her footsteps echoed against the fiberglass floors as she went back to where Ash unpacked the cooler.

"I hope you're hungry." He opened a bucket of fried chicken from Cronig's, a container of potato salad. They settled onto the red leather bench at the back of the boat, eating the crispy chicken off paper plates. Sunset was an orangey glow in the sky, and the water shimmered, surrounding them with a circle of sparkling jewels.

"Is this where you bring all the girls?" She worked to sound flirty rather than jealous.

He laughed, scooting closer to her. "Nah, I normally come alone and cast a line, let my mind drift."

"I've never met a businessman who liked to daydream before." She giggled, then kicked herself for sounding too childish.

"Hey, I'm not some money-hungry Wall Street trader." He nudged her with his elbow. "Kitty kit, you're good at getting me to talk, but I want to know more about you, and not about your life here. Your life away from here."

She rested her plate on the side of the boat, calculating what she should share, how much. "Oh, I dunno. I suppose my details are boring. I grew up in Brooklyn. My dad wasn't around. Mom works at Tiffany's, and sometimes the laundry, and she paints, watercolors. My grandmother lost her husband young and she helped raise me. She died last year."

Ash sipped his wine. "That's some strong women in your lineage."

Heddy stared into her tumbler. "Yes, I'm grateful to them. I love Wellesley, though. Well, now I do. At first, I felt like I was in outer space."

Ash wiped his mouth, discarding his plate. "It makes sense to me now, why you're so tough. And empathetic, too. You were raised feeling different, and that's made you more accepting of people who are different from you." Every time he said something like that, she wanted to kiss him.

"Just what I need—an analyst for a boyfriend." Her cheeks were hot. Had she just called him her boyfriend?

"An analyst? No. But I know this much. You look for the good in people." He touched the tip of his finger to her nose. "You've certainly found the best in me. It's why I like being around you. There's no rain, even on a rainy day." A flutter tickled her chest; she liked that he saw something in her that she didn't see in herself.

Ash pressed his lips in her hair. Not quite a kiss, but the beginning of one. "What's one of your best childhood memories?"

Heddy stared off at the horizon, the sun sinking lower behind the distant lighthouse, flashing. "I was ten. My mother took me for high tea at the Plaza Hotel. She'd sold one of her paintings, a scene of Central Park in the rain. She wore a lilac dress and mascara, and she looked so happy when she ordered, like we were a pair of regulars." Heddy imitated her mother's accent: "'Someday I'll take you back to Ireland, where we drink our tea with milk. Here, we put a spot in the cup, of course, but it's nothing like brewing true Irish breakfast tea. The world over wishes they had tea as good as ours.'"

Heddy pretended to pout, one leg folded into a triangle underneath her, the memory evoking sudden insight. "Mother is quite proper for the servant class, you see. She seems more sophisticated than she is, and she gave me this way of being, of carrying myself, that has allowed me to be a chameleon. I think she got it from her father. He was a statesman in Galway, you know. Our family's shining star. But he died of influenza when he and my grandmother came to America in the 1920s. My mother was a child. They could have gone back, but they were determined to make it." She smiled.

Ash cupped the side of her shoulder, squeezing. "Like I said, you have some strong women in your lines."

The boat rocked with a wave. Perhaps she needed to remind herself of that sometimes: she was raised with a fighting spirit. "What about you? What's your favorite childhood memory?"

He squinted, struggling to settle on one. "Here's one," he laughed. "Dad used to call me Little Mickey, because I could throw a baseball clear to the neighbor's yard, like Mickey Mantle. One summer—I was eight years old, I think—he'd come in my room on weekends and wake me at dawn, saying, 'Want to work on that tree house, Little Mickey?' He gave me this toolbox he put together, and plank by plank, we built a tree house in an oak tree in our backyard. It had a roof, windows, a ladder up the trunk. I don't remember playing in it as much as I remember making it."

"You were close to him, then."

His mind seemed far away, until he spoke. "My mom tries to make up the difference, but she can't. Nothing's the same without him."

The inky sky pushed shadows across Ash's face. She ran her finger along a tiny scar she found near his hairline, wondering how he'd gotten it. A gash sewn up sloppily. He smiled at her.

"Funny the moments you remember as a kid," he said. "I have snapshots. My mom's red velvet dress on Christmas, or my sister's sneer when she called me stupid, or the time the dog threw up on my rug. But to be hugged by Mother or to have my dad's hand pat my back with pride, I wish I could remember that feeling."

"That's why I love writing; you remember everything," she said. They were quiet for a moment, listening to the gentle lap of the water against the boat. She tucked her hands under her thighs. "I had an idea for a movie—I've been developing it, in my head."

"Oh yeah? What is it?"

"It's about a woman who leaves her husband for another man, but the man murders her, so her husband is forced to solve her murder and he falls in love with the female detective who helps him track the killer."

He laughed, his eyebrows cocked. "That's what you want to write? I thought it would be a sappy love story or a tale of an underdog. You want to write about a nasty love triangle? A murder?"

She cast her eyes down to the silvery water, the rising moon changing the color again. Heddy loved to read a good whodunit, but she thought many of the mysteries out there were geared to men; hers would be written for women. But now, she was losing confidence. "I suppose it's silly."

"No, no," he said.

"Just some stupid idea . . ."

He stood, hollering. "Stupid? Heddy, it's brilliant. You've got to write it. I want to see that movie." He pulled her to her feet and spun her around the boat, chanting: "Brilliant, brilliant."

Heddy was against his chest now, staring up at him, their lips inching closer together. "What is it about you that makes me feel like anything is possible?" she whispered.

Heddy closed her eyes, waiting for him, and when he was finally there, his lips were soft and velvety. He cradled her face in his hands, giving her quick kisses on both of her cheeks, her chin, her forehead.

When he pulled away from her, she nearly yanked him back.

He kissed the top of her hand. "I liked you since you showed up on my doorstep this summer."

She was sheepish. "I thought I'd lost the children. You acted like you barely noticed me."

"Maybe it was when we got off the surfboard then." He positioned his finger at the spot where her shirt was unbuttoned, running it up and down her bare skin. "But I didn't think I had a chance with you." It was the other way around, she'd thought. Ash lifted her chin so she looked in his eyes. "It's rare to meet a girl like you. You think big, but you're honest. So very honest."

She grinned. "My grandmother used to say my nostrils flared if I tried to lie."

"You're so authentic, and true, and—"

"But I'm not, I need to tell you . . ." But he shushed her, taking her hands and squeezing them. "It's about Wellesley," she tried.

"Let me finish," he said. "Look, someday the world will try to ruin you, kitty kit. Chip away at your weak spots and make you hate yourself. But right now, you're good. You make me want to be." He looked guilty then. Of what, she wasn't sure, and she pulled him toward her. In his lips she felt a part of him she hadn't known before—a vulnerability—and that's what she hadn't expected. That kissing could do that. She thought about what it would feel like if he unbuttoned her shirt, his shirt, in the cool night air, arching her back to the sky. But he pulled away, and she slowed her breath.

"I want to show you something." Ash picked up the flashlight, and she wondered why he'd stopped. How he could wait.

She billowed her shirt. "You think it's dark enough?"

He waved her over to the side of the boat, where they shined their lights into the water. Heddy saw a rock, a few pebbles, rocking with the waves along the sand below. Dizzy with the smell of him, she pretended to be interested.

"We have to wait," Ash whispered.

In the quiet, the fiberglass bottom creaked with their weight as they moved to the other side, shining their flashlights on the bottom of the sea, green and brackish in the shining light. "There's one," Heddy yelled. A blue crab as big as a food-cart pretzel walked sideways underwater, moving straight across a cluster of slipper shells. It crept faster when it sensed the shadows looming above, and they lost it to the darkness of the sea.

Ash turned off his flashlight. "Crabs have a sixth sense about danger. When that light goes on, they probably think we're martians coming down to abduct them."

Heddy scanned the boat. "We are! You have a net, right?"

He turned his flashlight on again, and they spent some time hunting for others, plunging the nets in the water at the sight of one. The more crabs they found, the sillier they became. Heddy was the first to catch one, and when she pulled the spider crab up out of the water, she squealed at its long, spindly legs and threw the net on the boat, howling. The crab scurried down the floor of the boat, sending Heddy and Ash up on the padded bench. Ash managed to scoop it in his net and throw it overboard, unharmed, and they couldn't stop laughing.

Ash shined his flashlight on the nearby beach, dug in his pocket for matches. "Want to start a bonfire?"

She pretended to shiver. "I am getting chilly."

Ash hopped off the boat first, holding his swim trunks up, so the sea, which came up to the middle of his thighs, didn't soak his shorts. "I'll carry you in."

Heddy wiggled off her shorts so she was wearing his button-down shirt and nothing but her bathing suit bottom. She sat on the side of the boat, her legs dangling over, her toes grazing the water. She shined the flashlight to make sure there weren't any crabs and slid in. The sea was balmier than the air, and its heat closed around her like a warm bath. It wasn't until they walked toward shore, emerging from the tepid waters into the cool night air that she got cold. She wrapped a towel around her waist to cozy herself.

"I can help with that." He tossed the box of matches in the sand. Ash pressed her body to his, spreading his heat around her. He whispered to her: "I like seeing you in my shirt."

Heddy was terrified then, because she knew how easy it was to forget her mother's warnings with Ash. The reality was: she was standing on an abandoned island in the middle of Vineyard Sound kissing a man like she'd never kissed anyone before.

He brushed his lips against hers as they stood facing each other, and already her body felt loose. She must have spread out the towel because she was lying on it now, Ash on top of her, and he was kissing her neck. He moved up to her lips, tracing a path of sensation everywhere he went. She started to unbutton the top button of her shirt, but he continued the job, burying his face in the tops of her breasts as soon as he'd exposed them. With a firm grip on his shoulders, she pulled him back up to her face and imagined that somehow all her goose bumps from earlier had changed into something else, little pinpricks of longing. She pictured dominoes falling one by one, each one stacking on the last and building momentum as they went. What came after the kissing, she wasn't so sure. She only knew what happened last.

Her ears caught the sound of a motor, and it edged closer. She knew Ash heard it, too, because he went still. He sat up, and she pushed on to her elbows, cool pebbles digging into the backs of her arms. She buttoned her shirt back up, then remembered her shorts were on the boat.

The boat slowed, and Heddy heard voices. The distant echo of two men arguing over which way to go, the faraway laughter of both.

Ash rubbed at the back of his neck. "There's something I need to tell you." His voice sounded small, like a boy worried over spilled milk.

She gulped in the night air, steeling herself for whatever he was going to say.

"I haven't been truthful." He dropped his head between his knees, massaging his temples. "When I told you about the Coconut Coast, I left something out."

She took his hands in hers, squeezing them. "I did, too. You see, it's . . ."

"No, Heddy. You're perfect. There's nothing you could say that would change how I feel about you."

"I feel the same," she whispered, a feeling of satisfaction overcoming her.

"I wish we could stay like this until dawn," he said, running his lips along her forehead.

She wrapped her arms around his neck, hugging him fiercely. "I didn't know men could be like you, Ash Porter. It scares me how much I like it."

She unbuttoned the top buttons of her shirt again, and he watched with interest. When she finished, she brought her lips to his neck, trailing her mouth up to his ear, then finding his lips. He pulled his shirt over his head and returned her kiss. She felt his fingers slide under the straps of her bathing suit, sliding them off her shoulders and down her sides. He looked like he wanted to devour her.

She ran her fingers along the contour of his chest, kissing him right above his navel. The crinkle of a wrapper in Ash's hands, the necessary pause to slide it on. He lowered her down, coming down along with her, pressing all of him everywhere, their breath quickening, until there was nothing left to feel except zigzags of bliss coursing through her.

When it was over, they laughed at nothing in particular, and then everything, rolling on their sides and lying there. She felt like she'd experienced a small earthquake, like something unexpected had shaken everything up between them, and when it stopped, it left them different.

He drove her home around one, and with the Victorian dark except for the porch light, they kissed one more time, a sweet press of the lips.

"And there she goes," he whispered as she opened the car door.

Her steps up to the house were as light as her head, and she turned once, blowing him a kiss good night.

She'd made it with Ash Porter, and it was glorious and sweet and felt like love. She knew what her mother would say. She knew what Jean-Rose would say. But Heddy ignored their voices.

Moving to the island had tossed her cards in the air, and now, even she could see, she'd been dealt an entirely new hand.

❧ TWENTY-TWO ❧

*T*he next few days fell into a comfortable pattern with the children since Heddy, feeling light and happy, threw herself into keeping them busy and well tended. They went bug hunting and painted watercolors. They wrote and illustrated their own books, and Teddy made a comic book about a bumblebee, while Anna wrote about getting a cat.

She and Ash spoke by phone that week, and she'd chatted with Sullivan on Friday morning, after she canceled their date. She chose to stay in with the children that night to work her way back into Jean-Rose's good graces; she and Sullivan would go out the following Friday instead. But even as her mind was on the fall and finding Jean-Rose's bracelet, her head ping-ponged between these two men. And as the last few days of July blended into the first days of August, she vowed to break it off with Sullivan.

And yet, she couldn't. Something urged her to go on the date anyway—perhaps, fear that Ash wasn't being true—and before she knew it, she was meeting him at Navy Sea. She'd go, she'd decided, so she could be sure about not choosing him. With the kids at camp that morning, she ticked errands off for Jean-Rose, and then helped Ruth clean.

August 3, 1962

We turned the house upside down looking for the bracelet one last time—moving the couch out, edging out the grandfather clock, hunting the grass along the porch's edge. I even rifled through Jean-Rose's jewelry box, but to no avail. I fear I will pay the consequences of a crime I didn't commit. So much for asking for that job in the city. . . .

Sullivan went on promptly at six, playing to an older crowd, which was incredibly quiet and laidback compared to the raucous young people who'd cheered him when she and Ruth had come before. Cigar smoke wafted toward the sea, while one woman, a silver-haired, artist-type with huarache sandals, closed her eyes and tapped to the beat. By the time Sullivan finished his set, around eight, younger people were ambling down the beach.

"Where ya going, Sully?" said a young kid strumming a guitar. Sully was pulling Heddy past him.

"Sorry, Jimmy. I'm taking a girl to dinner." The kid, Sullivan explained, was a young musician named James Taylor.

The powder-blue Aston Martin pulled onto the main drag, driving through open fields until they passed the narrow streets and white picket fences of historic Edgartown, a former whaling port, where the finest French wines were paired with lobster dinners at a premium.

"Where are we going?" she asked, praying they didn't run into Ash.

"I have something planned." Sullivan smiled sideways at her, his cheeks dimpling. The wind smacked at the convertible's plastic cover as they parked on a two-automobile car ferry for a five-minute ride across Edgartown Harbor to Chappaquiddick Island, or "Chappy," which is what everyone called it. She'd heard that a relation of the Kennedys had a house there—there were rumors of wild parties with the president's younger brother Ted, who visited from Hyannis. She'd never been to the island, but she'd seen the colorful red-and-white cabanas of the members-only Chappaquiddick Beach Club from Edgartown.

Sullivan pulled the car down a gravel road marked with a white sign and black lettering: 10 MEETING LANE, and she labored to remember where she'd heard it before. A large sprawling gray-shingled house sporting three chimneys—twice the size of Gigi McCabe's estate.

She tried to hide her shock. "Is this where you live?"

"It's where my parents live—they prefer to be out of the social fray, when they're not socializing. There's a joke that if you're crazy enough to live on Chappy, town hall will say nothing of what you do over here. I stay in the garage. Ten Meeting Lane, Unit B." He laughed, but it was hardly a garage, more of a carriage house with three garage doors and a second floor lined with paned windows, tidy black shutters on the gray shingles.

"Come on." Barkley wagged his tail inside the front door.

Sullivan's living room had a neat arrangement of couches, and through a wall of windows, Heddy could see the ocean, the waves foamy and white, crashing along the vast shoreline. There was a pool table, textbooks stacked on top, and on the formal dining table, glass cases with insects on pins. A yellow highlighter illuminated constellations on a poster of the night sky on one wall, a storage rack on the other held three black cases, presumably his saxophones. He puttered around in the kitchen for a moment, pulling out two glasses, cracking an egg, and folding the white into a highball glass with gin, seltzer, and lime. "I think this is what girls like these days."

Heddy forgot how much she loved the creamy texture of a gin fizzy; she wondered why he'd brought her to his house. Is this where they were having dinner? "You were more subdued on stage tonight," she said.

He smiled sheepishly before slumping next to her on the couch. "You noticed," he said.

Barkley rested his head on her thigh, and she was about to push the dog away when Sullivan began to stroke his back.

"I'm feeling less churned up, ever since that morning I called you."

He gazed at her, then tilted his chin down to reach her waiting mouth. She kissed him back because it felt rude not to—she didn't want to embarrass him—but also, because she wanted to. She liked how tentative he was. They were such an unlikely pair—he had all the money in the world, the support of a traditional family and a trust fund—and yet they had the same problems. They were both searching for a way out of their pasts. She felt his hand go up the back of her blouse. He was more forward than she'd imagined; the shy Sullivan she'd met at the beginning of the summer nowhere to be found. When he fumbled with her bra, she wondered if he only wanted to sleep with her, and she pulled away from him.

Perhaps I am a tart.

Guilt washed over her. After the night with Ash, as fond as she was for Sullivan, it felt wrong to be necking with him. If she saw Ash with another woman, she'd be crushed and completely undone. And yet, here she was, like a little harlot, trying her darnedest to keep another man—one of the wealthiest, most well-connected men on the island—interested in her. Had she become so committed to landing a husband that she'd stopped considering other people's feelings? Then again, she was mad at Sullivan. All that nonsense on the phone with him saying how much he loved to talk to her, *that is what he'd said*, and he'd taken her to his house so he could unsnap her bra?

She wondered if he was trying to prove his feelings for her to himself, if he was using her to compare Peg against.

Heddy folded her arms, turning her head away from him. "You've barely asked me how I am."

He buried his face in his hands, then peeked at her, trying to be charming. "I'm sorry, you're right. You just look so *you* in that lilac blouse, and I haven't been able to stop thinking about you since I called you, and then you were here . . ."

She stared at the navy crew neck of his white sweater, how tight the Shetland weave was, how he shared the same moneyed Ivy League style of the president. Sullivan's baby face was sweet, and she liked him—she did—but he didn't live by the same conventions that she did, that Ash did. If he acted badly one night, he could forget it the next day, because his money could erase uncomfortable situations. And he'd grown up with that reassurance. But more than that, the way he dove at her, he didn't think, he simply acted. That he was so impulsive scared her. She preferred a boat with a steady course.

"I thought you just wanted to talk."

He brushed a piece of hair off her face. "I did. No, I do."

At the tinny ring of some sort, not a telephone, Heddy jumped.

"Sorry," he said. Sullivan stood, pressing a button on a silver wall box and speaking into a tiny speaker: "Come on up, Roy." Loud trudging footsteps sounded from the stairs, and three men in white coats, chef buttons across the front, carried in silver platters.

Heddy uncurled her legs, putting her bare feet on the floor, then crossing her legs in an effort at decorum.

"Mr. Rhodes, we'll set up on the dining table," the man said.

"I'd like it in here," Sullivan said, motioning to the pool table and moving textbooks out of the way.

"As you wish, sir." The men lifted the lids off the platters, fastidiously arranging two place settings, silverware wrapped in cloth napkins. She imagined medium filet mignon, perhaps sides of mashed

potatoes and creamed spinach, since that's what they served on special occasions at Wellesley. Sullivan thanked the staff.

"Let's eat." He handed her a plate, and from the weight of it, she
knew it was fine china. "There's a story here."

She'd never seen this kind of food: black beans and rice, chicken
thighs sprinkled with brown spices, whole chunks of garlic on top.

"What are those?" she asked.

"Cooked bananas. Plantains. And that's roast pork with oranges.
My favorite restaurant back home is this Cuban place run by two
brothers up near Harlem. They serve it on paper plates. I asked Roy
to learn how to cook it, and he did. Though, I told him to skip the
paper plates."

Heddy smiled as he spooned her a heaping of rice and beans. He
was going on about the food, but she'd stopped listening. Sullivan
said he didn't want to live this fancy. He resented the money and the
social stature it gave him; he hated the desires his parents had for
him. And yet, in his world, it was perfectly normal to ask a personal
chef to make him a recipe from his favorite restaurant.

Heddy told him a while ago that she understood why he wanted
to escape these golden handcuffs, but she didn't. She'd never understand. And the truth was, she wasn't sure he got the implications
of what he was doing, either. Once you lived this well, how did you
inhabit an apartment like her and her mother's, where the window
didn't close all the way and snow sometimes flurried in? Would you
crumble if you were too low on cash to afford your favorite Cuban
restaurant?

"I don't believe you could live without this," she blurted. The way
she saw him had shifted, emboldened her to challenge his notions.

"That's why I had them make it." He grinned, adding drips of
hot sauce.

"No, without money. The house and the pool table and the chefs
and the fancy car."

He stiffened. "But that stuff isn't me."

"Maybe you don't *need* all that, but it's harder to live without than you realize. Making it on your own—it's tough." She thought of how often the apartment lights had been turned off and she'd had to sit in the hallway to do her math homework by dim light bulbs. She thought of Wellesley and how she couldn't afford to return.

"I won't be on my own. I'll have you," he said.

She shifted on the pool table, looking out onto the ocean. Sullivan was a dreamer. People like him could be turned upside down in the real world, when the trappings of their upbringing faded away.

"You have to make peace with who you are, Sully. There's gotta be a way to live the life you want and still please your mother."

He rubbed her cheek with his hand. "You worry too much."

"You sound like Ruth," she laughed. She liked the sting of the chicken on her tongue, but she needed water, downing a glass.

"I have a plan." Sullivan refilled her glass from the faucet. "It's not like I'm going to be peddling for change. I'll have some money saved."

"Does your mom still want you to marry Peg?"

"Stop with all this. Let's talk about us." His voice was low.

"Just answer me." Perhaps there was a part of her that wondered if they could make it, if she could get lost in those daydreams of his.

"We don't need them, Heddy. We'll do what we want."

"But it matters to me."

He pushed beans around his plate. "Mother thinks she can set a date for an engagement, and that I'll simply show up, like a caterer or the band."

She gulped down her water. He liked her, she could tell, but he'd never win this battle with his mother. No matter what he said, she knew what he'd choose in the end: whatever his mother insisted on. And it wasn't going to be Heddy.

"It's a ridiculous plan," he said. "Her family owns the other New

York paper, another in Boston. Our parents want a merger. They want an empire."

"You should consider it." She hated Peg, and she wanted him to prove that he did, too.

"Are you crazy? Peg wouldn't touch this food or anything I care about. She's only interested in the Society Pages." He was next to her again, sitting cross-legged, their knees touching. "Besides, I'm hung up on someone else."

"I wonder who," Heddy said. Could she love him someday? He was intoxicating, and yet, something about how he lived, without strings, frightened her. She wiped a spot of sour cream off the corner of his mouth, and he kissed her on the cheek.

Later, when they finished, he led her into his bedroom. At first, she resisted; she imagined him throwing her down on the bed, trying to run his fingers under her bra, and she cringed.

"I promise, nothing funny," he said, pushing his glasses up his nose. He led her by the hand to an octagonal window in his bedroom. Her eye went to a shoebox on his dresser, piles of twenty-dollar bills lying flat inside. She was tempted to make a joke, ask him if he believed in using a bank, but she liked that he kept his savings in a shoebox.

"Look," he said, opening the window. He pointed up at the eaves, where a single baby bird poked its face out of a nest, two little eyes peering over the edge. "The mother abandoned it." Sullivan reached for a bowl on his dresser filled with tiny seeds. "I've been feeding it."

"Do you think it's going to make it?" she said.

Sullivan dropped a few specks of food into the nest, and the bird pecked.

His eyes crinkled. "We're all going to make it."

Just not together, she thought.

* * *

On Monday morning, after bringing the children to camp, she found another to-do list from Jean-Rose, each bullet point written in black magic marker. Even her handwriting felt abrasive: *SIFT THROUGH CLOTHES, SORT OUT SIZES. PACK UP TOYS THEY DON'T PLAY WITH.*

Heddy went upstairs to shower, jotting a few thoughts down first.

August 6, 1962

I get the feeling that I did something deeply wrong in Jean-Rose's eyes, something other than take a bracelet that I didn't take. I'm dating the guy she wanted me to, I care for her children like they're my own, and I've always been careful to respect her rules. It's unfathomable that she'd be jealous of me—who am I to her but a puny, uneducated girl from Brooklyn?—and yet, I think she's tiring of the sight of me.

In the hall bath, Ruth was wiping spittle out of the sink.

"Where'd they go?" Heddy asked.

Ruth sprayed more solution. "Jean-Rose left in a tennis skirt. He drove."

"The club."

Ruth nodded. "Did you hear Anna ask Ted why Mommy is always crying?"

She felt a pit in her stomach. "I'm starting to think them wretched people."

Ruth sprayed the wall tiles, the smell of ammonia burning her nose. "We all have our sad stories."

In Teddy's room, Heddy emptied his dresser, refolding each shirt after checking the sizes. Most of them still fit, but she took out a few anyway, just in case Jean-Rose thumbed through. A yank on the hanging cord in his walk-in closet switched on the light, illuminating rows of pressed and hanging pint-size clothes. Heddy tucked the shirts in a box labeled appropriately, noticing another box—a rather large one at the back. She leaned over the side of it, discovering four small throw pillows surrounding a stepstool. Miss Pinkie sat at the head of the makeshift table, and she had three guests—three of Anna's Barbies—each with a matching porcelain teacup and saucer.

"Oh, Teddy." Heddy put her hand on her chest. She had no idea when he even came in here. After she tucked him in at night, did he tiptoe inside his closet, turn on the light and play?

Her eyes traveled around the pretend table. There was Barbie, wearing a strand of pearls, the necklace enormous and twice her size, and another Barbie with a teardrop earring clipped to her bathing suit. Something around Miss Pinkie's head sparkled, and in the dim lighting, she'd assumed it was a crown until the beam of light found the gleam of jewels.

Heddy snatched the eternity bracelet from Miss Pinkie's head. The weight of the bracelet made her legs heavy. She was aware of every link, every diamond, pressing against her palm. She dangled it, examining it to make sure it was the one. It had to be. Just having the bracelet in hand felt illicit, like Jean-Rose was going to catch her.

"Ruuuuth," she screamed, causing Ruth to bound into the closet.

"Jesus Christ. What is it?"

Heddy dropped the bracelet in her hand. "I found it on the doll's head. What do we do?"

"Shit, shit, shit. This is not good." Ruth tried to hand her back the bracelet, like they were playing a game of hot potato, but Heddy wouldn't take it.

"We'll put it back on the doll," Ruth said. "You have to show her. All of this."

Heddy bit her palm and paced. "I can't do that to him."

"I won't lose my job because some little rich kid likes to play dolls with Mommy's jewelry." It was the first time Heddy heard Ruth yell.

"But she'll take the doll. It will crush him." Plus, she'd fire Heddy on the spot for giving him the doll back.

"If you don't tell her, I will." Ruth stormed out of the closet; from the bathroom, Heddy could hear the scrubbing. Faster, harder, bristles dragging on tile.

Heddy followed her. "Ruth, give me a few days to think of another way. I want to avoid hurting him."

Ruth rolled her eyes, scrubbing the urine ring out of the toilet with a brush. "You've got twenty-four hours before I rip the bracelet off that doll and give it to Jean-Rose myself."

❧ TWENTY-THREE ❧

_T_he afternoon newspaper arrived later that day, and Jean-Rose, who had been reading a novel on the porch, came inside and smacked the front page on the kitchen counter. Heddy and the kids looked up from their coloring. "Did you hear about Marilyn?"

"A new role?" Heddy craned her neck to scan the story: Found dead in her Los Angeles home, bottle of pills, apparent suicide.

"Messing around like that," said Jean-Rose, pleased and sounding vindicated. "She was nothing short of a prostitute."

"What's a pros-ta-toot, mommy?" Anna put down her crayon.

"Never mind," Heddy said, redirecting the child's attention back to her half-colored unicorn. _Marilyn Monroe. Dead?_ It wasn't possible. "She was a sad person, really. Arthur Miller once said she was the saddest person he ever met."

"Sad? Is that what they called her?" Jean-Rose rolled her eyes, adjusting the glossy belt on her linen shorts. "Why are _you_ crying?"

Ruth turned around from chopping carrots for her roast, her eyes pooling with tears, her nose blotchy and red. "It's just . . . she was so young. And so beautiful."

Heddy began crying, too, then, and the two of them embraced at the kitchen sink, which made Jean-Rose storm out with a disgusted sigh. "Get a grip, ladies," she hollered on her way back to the porch. "You didn't know her."

But it felt like they knew her. What woman didn't wish they were even a sliver as sexy as she was when she sang to the president? What woman couldn't relate to Marilyn's longing to be accepted, to be loved?

"I can't believe it," Heddy whispered, wiping her nose with her hand. "Why would anyone do that to themselves?"

"So much of her life ahead of her."

"I'm hungry," Teddy said without emotion, as if he had no idea that anyone was even upset. "Can I have some crackers?"

Heddy filled a bowl with saltines, then moved to the transistor radio on the kitchen window ledge, tuning it for the news. She suddenly remembered an old *Life* magazine: Marilyn, wrapped in a blue robe pool-side, grinned from the cover with the headline "A Skinny Dip You'll Never See on the Screen." Heddy remembered the actress radiating joy. How her pain must have crept up on her when she was alone; she must have felt like no one really knew her at all.

Heddy sighed, feeling a bit lonesome herself then, and that's when she remembered: There still was the question of the tennis bracelet.

Ash's crisp white shirt was tucked into linen trousers, a gelled wave in his hair. She'd called him that night, a Monday, in a panic, and he'd agreed to pick her up.

"Thank you for taking me out on such short notice." Once in his truck, she fiddled with her yellow skirt, prickling with nerves.

"You kidding me? I've been trying to take you out for this lobster roll for weeks." That he was being so nice made her more anxious.

"Ash, we need to talk."

With one hand on the wheel, he rested the other on hers, probably to stop her fingers from thrumming against the fabric. "Everything okay? Terrible news about Marilyn Monroe."

"I can't stop thinking about her. Ruth and I wonder if she really killed herself—what if someone framed her?" She frowned. "Someone in high places?"

"Maybe committing suicide was the only way for her to feel in control. She was . . ." Then he shook his head. "Let's not talk about this." A beat, and she knew this was her chance to change the subject.

"A piece of diamond jewelry went missing at the house," Heddy started. "Jean-Rose not so subtly accused Ruth and me, but of course we didn't take it."

For a second, he looked like he licked a lemon. "That's insulting."

"I know, but I found it. In Teddy's room. Problem is, it will get him in trouble if I tell."

"So how do you give it back without her knowing it's you?" The truck whipped around the curves of State Road, Ash honking at another car for going too fast.

"Exactly."

Ash ran his tongue over his teeth, thinking. "What if I bring it by? If you can get it out of the house and bring it to me, I'll tell her I found it in the driveway."

She scrunched up her face. It couldn't be that easy. "Do you think she'll believe you?"

"I'll be sure of it." He hummed, giving her a sideways glance, the greens of his eyes piercing her with brilliance. She let it sink in, that he was willing to help her this way, and she popped another kiss on his cheek.

"See? All better." He grinned, and she nearly jumped into his arms.

The Surf Shack's large marquee sign was a few buildings up on Main Street. The white clapboard had been painted with a giant blue wave. They found a spot near Ocean Park and walked up to the take-out window, where customers could order "the Maine, a quarter-pound cold lobster roll, with knuckle, claw, and tail chunks mixed in mayo" or "the Connecticut, a quarter-pound lobster roll, with warm, buttered knuckle, claw, and tail meat chunks."

"We'll take two Maine specials," Ash told the teenager working the counter. "And two lemonades."

He carried the tray with their food to one of the navy picnic tables, but the dinner rush was in full swing, so they had to squeeze in with a group of high school girls. Heddy heard one of them whisper: "Isn't she lucky?"

"Ready?" he said, holding the lobster roll to his mouth. They toasted the buns like champagne, then tore away enormous bites.

"It's the best thing I've eaten all summer," she said.

"And I know you'd tell me the truth if you didn't like it, that honest face of yours." He handed her a lemonade, and she sipped, looking out over the heads of the patrons to the street, where a barber shop pole spun red, white, and blue.

But she *wasn't* being truthful; she'd lied to him, like she was lying to everyone else, and she hated herself for it. Her shirt grew hot and stifling at the thought of telling him how deep her financial problems went. If he came to Brooklyn and met her mother and saw the rooming house, what would he think of her? Being around Jean-Rose and Ted all summer had tricked him into thinking she lived in the same glossy magazine spread simply by association. Here, he saw her drive a convertible, twirl in designer dresses, and chat up a movie star. At home, there would be a throw arranged to cover the large hole in the couch, and the requisite mouse running along the floorboards. She was pretending to be a Wellesley girl, an aspiring writer. What rubbish. And while she'd discarded her shame about the past, she realized she was still embarrassed by the present.

Heddy put her lobster roll on the plate. "I haven't been completely honest with you." The words trickled out like a slow leak.

He took another bite. "How so?"

"Well . . ." She cleared her throat, pushing her shoulders back in an act of pride. "I lost my scholarship at school, and I can't go back. My mother and I will get an apartment. Perhaps by Coney Island. Wouldn't that be fun? There's a shipbuilding factory nearby that is hiring, and I can work my way up. Maybe be secretary. Or, maybe a nice family will give me a job as a domestic."

Ash set his lobster roll back on his plate. "But you want to be a writer or a teacher. And you can find another way to go to school. You can always find a way to get money."

A jarring cackle slipped out. "See, that's the funny part, Ash. I'm not a magician, and I know I sound like my mother now, but money doesn't grow on trees. I'm out of options." The corners of her eyes grew moist, and her face crumpled. She was ruining their date. Ruining it. But a dam broke open inside of her, and the pain she'd held in over the past few weeks came flooding out.

She felt Ash hugging her, and she folded into him, because that's what she needed: to be held.

"Heddy, listen." He tried to lift her chin, but she kept her head down, embarrassed to be making a scene, hearing the teenage girls' whispers. "Heddy, I can help you. We'll find a way," he said.

"Stop saying, 'We,' like we're in this together. *We're* not in this together."

He crouched down below her, so he could peek at her face. "But maybe we are."

That she might marry someone her equal, who needed her as much as she needed him, was a different way to think about marriage. Was it even possible that someone else would join her life, that there could ever be a "we" other than her and her mother? She knew there'd be a day when she'd lose her mother, and that she'd be alone then. But imagine having someone else, a backup—a life partner.

"Let's start with the numbers," he said. He pulled out a small black notebook and pencil and flipped to a blank page. "What are your expenses?"

She supposed the telling of it wouldn't hurt. "Well, tuition and board is two thousand five hundred. A deposit for an apartment for my mother is around one hundred, then there's incidentals. Books are one hundred and necessities"—she didn't want to say maxi pads, toothpaste, long-distance calls home—"that's maybe fifty."

"For the year? You can get by on nothing." He ran his pen through the $100 for her mom's apartment. "Take this off your plate. She'd be upset if you didn't return to school for this." Heddy knew he was right, so she didn't object. "How much do you have?"

She bit her bottom lip. "About seven hundred dollars."

Ash tapped the pencil against his teeth: "I would sell Jean-Rose's eternity bracelet. The black market will fetch you a nice price."

Heddy smacked his shoulder, and he was pleased he'd made her laugh. "I told you, I'm not that kind of girl."

He took another bite of his lobster roll, then fed her a bite. His eyes were shiny. "When I was a kid, we had a nanny, but we were in school and didn't get home until three. You can put out an advertisement, in the *Boston Globe*—I'll help you—that offers your services: Afternoon and night nanny. Then you can take classes during the day and study when the children are asleep. It would save you expenses on paying for a dorm room. You'd have a salary."

She rested her head on his shoulder. "You make it sound so easy."

"That's just one idea," he said, thumbing her chin. "You could ask someone for a loan. Ted Williams, for instance. Or Gigi? Or me."

She kissed him deeply, right there, without even considering the people around her, feeling his kiss all the way down to her toes. She would never ask him for a loan; the thought of it mortified her. But a hardness in her chest softened when Ash said he'd help her, that he trusted her to pay him back, that he cared about her that much. The offer was kind, but more than that, it made her realize how true his intentions were. He wouldn't sleep with her, shove her problems in her face, and wish her well. He wanted to help.

The bonfire at the beach later that night kept them warm as they sipped wine out of a thermos. They watched the dance of the flames, for how long she didn't know, and they made it again, this time slower. Around 2:00 a.m., he walked her home, kissing her one last time by the kitchen door.

"Wait," she told him. She left him outside, silently opening the kitchen door and moving soundlessly through the living room and up the stairs to Teddy's room. The child's mouth was agape while he slept, the moonlight casting a ribbon of light across his bed. His closet door creaked as she felt her way to the back and grasped the slithery bracelet resting on Miss Pinkie's head. With it tucked in her palm, Heddy moved quietly down the steps and back into the cool night air.

Ash smiled at her, and she held a finger up to her lips while cupping his hands around the hidden bracelet. She kissed the top of his hand.

"It's as good as done," he whispered.

She watched him disappear into the beach path, and with Ruth asleep in her bed, she clicked on the light in the bathroom and opened her journal:

Dear Ash,

Do I love you because I feel protected by you—or do I love you because all the women on the island think you're the biggest catch and still you want me? Does it matter? I could see you trimming the turkey on Christmas and my mother asking you to fix a leaky sink. You could be the man who we never had around but desperately wished for. Is it crazy to think that you're already mine? Is it crazy to believe that we'll leave this island together?

❧ TWENTY-FOUR ❧

Anna pushed the beef Wellington around her plate with a fork. It was family day that Tuesday at the club, and the children, dressed in formal wear, were required to dine on grown-up fare.

"Please eat it, Anna," Heddy pleaded, but the girl turned up her nose.

For how much Jean-Rose spoke of it, the club wasn't all that fancy, nothing more than a simple, cedar-shingled rectangle set a few hundred feet back from the ocean. In the white-walled dining room, rows of black-and-white photographs featured group shots of members from every summer season since 1934. A mahogany wooden bar, running the back length of the room, was glossy and polished, framed with bright, colorful sailing flags.

Heddy and the children sat on wicker-style chairs in the stifling un-air-conditioned dining room, white cloth napkins in their laps. Little boys in navy ties teased little girls in poufs of satin, and whether the kids' manners matched their outfits was debatable. A little girl in stiff pink crinoline sat next to Anna, encouraging her to steal the olives from Heddy's martini to wedge into her eyes.

"You need to eat *something*," Heddy begged.

Anna covered her mouth with her hands, so Heddy buttered her another dinner roll.

A woman's voice came over the microphone, thanking everyone for coming. Heddy looked for Jean-Rose and found her sitting at a corner table, an empty seat where Ted should have been, clinking her gin and tonic against a friend's, laughing when their glasses hit too hard and splashed.

"Everyone, let's head outside for a swim," the announcer hollered. Chairs scooted back, the clang of silverware as it fell on dinner plates, as everyone rushed into the locker rooms to change.

A few steps down from the dining room there was a large slate patio with a built-in saltwater pool. White loungers outfitted with orange cushions surrounded it, each family with their own navy-and-white-striped cabana, their name displayed on a small sign. Jean-Rose waved to Heddy when she stepped outside with the children in tow. A cabana boy set a fresh towel on each of their chairs.

"Now where's Ted?" Jean-Rose stood on tiptoe, watching for him in the stream of people coming out of the dining room. He emerged with Edison, his hair slicked smooth from his forehead. Teddy ran to his father, who scooped him, nodding to Edison, who strode away to his own family.

Ted lowered Teddy and lit a cigar, the smell of maple and tobacco thick in the air.

Jean-Rose gritted her teeth. "Where were you?" Thirty seconds of silence passed. Then: "You promised me. People are *talking*."

Heddy pretended not to listen, helping the kids into the pool.

"I feel bad for the guy," Ted hissed, puffing on his cigar. He beamed at a woman walking toward them in a black halter one-piece bathing suit. "Susanne Kenner. Now where have you been?"

Jean-Rose whipped around.

"What's wrong, Jeannie? You look like you've seen a ghost," Susanne chirped.

Ted sat next to another man, this one in thick black glasses. "I'll leave the two of you to it."

Jean-Rose looked like she'd been slapped across the face. "A bit under the weather, I suppose."

They ducked into the cabana, and Heddy could hear them gossiping about people she didn't know. She listened, watching the kids swim.

Jean-Rose popped her head out. "Heddy, do you mind running to our locker to get my beach cover-up?"

She rose and went inside, coming face-to-face with Sullivan near the locker room doors. She tried to dodge him, feeling strange, but they'd locked eyes. He put his hand on her elbow, pulling her behind a payphone stall.

"Why haven't you called me back?" he asked, pushing his hands into his khakis. "I thought we had fun."

"We did. I just, I got distracted." She didn't want to say that she couldn't stop thinking about someone else.

"With him. I knew it." Sullivan folded his arms.

She stared at her flats. "I like you, Sullivan, you know that."

"But not as much as him, huh?" He looked out the window, where someone yelled "cannonball" and jumped into the pool. "What is it about him? He's not right for you—I know he's not."

"I dunno." *He's adventurous but not irresponsible; he's financially secure but not moneyed; he believes in me and wants to help me. He makes me feel . . .*

"I don't actually want an answer," he snapped. "There's things about him, things you don't know."

She felt like a python, ready to strike. "You don't think I'm good enough for him, do you? Well, then I'm not good enough for you, either."

She stormed to the locker room doors, but he met her there and spun her around. "You're better than he deserves, better than both of us deserve. But for the record, I believe in us. It's you who doesn't." The words sounded hollow and sad; he knew he couldn't win, yet he was trying.

"Well, you have your hands full with your engagement, Sully-love."

He parted his lips, about to speak, then stopped himself. He ducked out the front door, and she watched him go, wondering, not for the first time, if she should walk away from someone as rich and cultured as Sullivan Rhodes. But the heart couldn't be controlled or pressured, cajoled or pushed—it beat in the direction of whoever it loved most. She watched him speed off in his car, knowing he would hate her for a long time, and that anger would make it easier for him to forget her.

When she got into the locker room, she was so distracted that she forgot the locker combination. She returned to the Williamses' cabana, coming up behind the structure. Inside, she could see the dark outline of the two women, facing each other in loungers. She was surprised to hear her name.

"She's driving me nuts if you must know the truth, insisting on going to that party." Jean-Rose puffed on her cigarette. "And do you know Ash walked over with my eternity bracelet? Said he found it on the beach. What a cowinkiedink. If the kids didn't love her . . ."

"Sally said she strutted around like who-she-thought-she-was in that dress. Nothing more than a bored actress's pet project."

"The actress we won't let in the Island Club." Jean-Rose cackled. "Thank goodness I stopped Irv from signing off on that. Anyway, you should have seen her. The dress, the two-hundred-dollar shoes, and then her cheap pearls. She has no idea about Ash, either, staring at him all weepy-eyed like they're falling in love."

Susanne snickered. "Little does she know that he's got a little something for everyone on this island." They erupted in laughter. "I've warned my nephew. Steer clear."

"Can you believe she's been sneaking out to meet him?"

"Sullivan?"

Jean-Rose smacked Susanne's shoulder. "No, Ash. I haven't said anything because I could care less if she screws up her life. If she's up to watch the kids every morning, that little tart can roll around with whoever she wants." Jean-Rose howled, and Susanne hooted along. "Is she coming?"

They stopped talking, and Jean-Rose must have peeked out of the cabana.

Heddy hurried back into the locker room, barreling into an empty shower stall smelling of bleach, a lump balling in her throat. *He has a little something for everyone on this island.* She thought of Mount Vesuvius and how it blew its top, fire spewing out everywhere, sudden and violently. And she worried that she might do the same thing. But then the lump in her throat turned to a searing pain in her chest. She began to tremble, her eyes stinging, and then came the tears.

That little tart. Did he have something on the side? With Jean-Rose? With Susanne? Why would they even care about someone like Ash? Or worse, what if she was the side dish and one of them was the main course?

Heddy kicked the white-tiled wall of the shower stall, her mother's voice popping into her head: "Hibernia Rawley Winsome, what did you do?" The answer: exactly what she'd set out not to do. She fell for someone who wasn't serious in his intentions. She opened up to him, and she didn't even know him. She had no idea how he spent the rest of his week, how many women he brought back to his fishing cottage. Hadn't she known this in her heart of hearts when he tried to tell her something on the boat? The tears were streaming down her face now, and she smacked them away, pressing her cheek against the shower tiles for support. She had to pull herself together, get back to the cabana. She'd dive in the pool with the kids, finish her job for the day. But as soon as she got back home, she would go straight to Ash's house. She'd slam her fist into his cheek.

And Sullivan. She'd hurt Sullivan for him.

Heddy turned on the shower's cold water, splashed her face. She closed her eyes, drew in a deep breath, letting the air massage the pain in her chest.

That little tart.

She would not be made a fool of by Ash or Jean-Rose. Heddy looked at her puffy red eyes, smiling as big as she could and smacking her cheeks like Gigi would. "Go get 'em, Brooklyn," she said.

Heddy returned to the women in the cabana, her chest tight, like a subway car was sitting on her, and announced that she forgot the combination.

Jean-Rose sighed like she was waiting on a long line. "I asked you for the simplest of things . . . to go in my locker and fetch me my—"

"Maybe you'd rather I get you my cheap pearls instead?" Heddy barked, and Jean-Rose and Susanne exchanged shocked looks. "You said you liked my pearls, and I actually believed you."

The color in Jean-Rose's face drained, and she and Susanne became interested in looking around at everyone else at the pool except Heddy until Jean-Rose tapped Susanne on the shoulder.

"Let's get Bellinis at the bar," she said. The women were a couple of loungers away when they collapsed against each other with laughter.

Heddy dove into the deep end and swam with long strokes toward the shallow side, where Teddy and Anna were playing. They climbed on her back, begging her to give them rides. Every few minutes, she'd leave the kids and push off the pool wall, not coming up for air until she reached the other side. Someday, she would come up for air from all of this.

Jean-Rose avoided her the rest of the day, and by the time they had all showered, changed, and brushed their hair into neat side parts, it was late afternoon. The family piled into the Bonneville, the top up against the impending rain, and headed home. As the car meandered out of the scrub pine forest, Heddy listened to Jean-Rose chatting away to Ted, like she was the happiest girl in the world: a renovation on the Schwartz's house that went awry, how Angela's husband had to go back to the city because his mutual fund was failing. "I feel terrible for them," Jean-Rose said.

No, you don't, thought Heddy. Beyond her fancy clothes and high-brow taste, Jean-Rose was nothing but a tight ball of unfinished business. She was threatened by other people's happiness like some people are threatened by other people's money—it made her feel inadequate, a reminder of how unhappy she was. Having money couldn't fix that. Nothing could. Maybe that's why she'd hired Heddy in the first place. She liked seeing herself through the eyes of someone so young and inexperienced—it made her feel better to know someone, anyone, thought her sophisticated, gorgeous, a harbinger of fashion and elegance. Heddy had given her exactly what she needed, and now that she dared step out, get a little attention, Jean-Rose was done with her.

Ted leaned forward to turn up the radio.

"Are you even listening?" She folded her arms, and he nodded. "Well, then why don't you say something?"

He glanced at the back seat. "I wanted to hear what they were saying about the Yankees."

"You could at least *listen* to me after *embarrassing* me today," Jean-Rose snapped.

Ted and Jean-Rose: the couple she once thought the most perfect on the planet were potentially the most imperfect. They didn't even seem to like each other. They may even despise each other, and yet there they were, together, at social functions, faking their way through a life they'd decided was their own. She was done with all of them.

That little tart. She had to get to Ash's house. But she couldn't take the children. How could she talk to him if the children were there? Ruth. Maybe Ruth could help.

They ran onto the porch, shielding their faces from the rain, and Ruth came out to meet them with towels. The rain was coming sideways now, and they piled into the kitchen, kicking off heels and sandals, leaving muddy footprints and puddles on the floor. "Ruth, can you watch them?"

"Sure. Why?"

But Heddy already grabbed a bright yellow raincoat from the hooks by the back door, pulling the hood over her head. She ran through the yard, the rain splashing mud up onto the backs of her legs, until she was on the beach path.

"Heddy! Wait!" It was Teddy. He'd pulled on his galoshes and raincoat. "I want to go, too."

She stopped. "Ruth is going to play with you." The sound of rain pitter-pattered against her hood.

The child airplaned his arms out, flying them from side to side. He didn't seem to hear her, or care about his soaking-wet legs, so Heddy kept running, letting him follow. She couldn't move fast enough, and she felt the weight of every step, like that dream she'd had where her feet felt leaden by quicksand.

Ash's screen door was unlocked, and she bounded inside. Teddy tugged on her hand. "I don't think we're supposed to go in someone's house when they're not home."

Heddy leaned down on one knee, water sliding off her nose and dripping down to the wood floors. She dried her face. "Ash told me to come over."

"Can I play chess?" Teddy dropped his raincoat on a chair and sat in front of the chessboard, always set up on the rickety kitchen table.

She scanned the room for something damning, a glass with an imprint of lipstick on the rim, a compact left on the coffee table. In the bathroom, she checked the shower for women's shampoos. His bedroom. She hated to go in and yet she was driven by a love sick-ness she'd never experienced before. She had to know. The bed was unmade, a mess of sheets kicked to the bottom. A glass of water on one side of the nightstand. It smelled of him everywhere.

She slumped onto the couch, only then noticing a small wooden chest resting on a side table in the living room. It was the size of a large cigar box with the ornate carvings of an eagle with outstretched wings. She ambled toward it, thinking it the perfect hiding place, and opened the lid. It was empty.

"I hear Ash's truck." Teddy ran to the front door.

Resting on the tabletop, next to the wooden chest, was a large yellow envelope stuffed thick with papers. She peered inside, dump-ing the contents out on the table, all of it tumbling into a pile in front of her. Neat bundles of money, each one held together with a skinny rubber band. Thick wads stuffed with twenty-dollar bills, Andrew Jackson's face staring up at her again and again. She counted how many rolls; at least fifteen. She slipped a ticket out of a Pan Am Air-lines brochure dated for August 14, New York International to São Paulo, Brazil. A week away.

Quick footsteps of someone running into the house—Ash duck-ing in from the rain. She opened a leather wallet that had also fallen out. Inside, a driver's license listed a man by the name of John Green, a man who looked like Ash. Who clearly was Ash.

She wondered if all men had a dark side, then—Ted hit Jean-Rose, but when did it start, and how did Jean-Rose come back from the disappointment of knowing what he was truly made of? Heddy remembered her own father, how his wife knew nothing of Heddy, that his children would grow up without any idea that they had a half sister. She thought marriage was open and honest, but marriage, courtship, being in love . . . How long did it take a person to reveal their true nature?

"What a happy surprise." Ash opened his arms to hug her, dropping his eyes to the money piled on the table. "What are you doing?" He began to stuff the cash back into the envelope.

She felt scared then by what she'd found. It seemed worse than what she'd been looking for. "I came to find out if what they're saying about you is true." She squeezed her lips together, looked up at the ceiling, her eyes burning.

Ash rubbed at the back of his neck. He did it whenever he didn't know how to answer her—how had she not noticed that before?

"What who is saying? Why are you rifling through my things?" He moved closer, his jaw tight.

"They said that there are others." She sunk down to the floor then, her face scrunching up. Teddy was there, and she didn't want him to see her, so she hid her face behind her forearm. "Why is Jean-Rose saying there are other women?"

Ash picked Teddy up in his arms "C'mon, Ace, let's bring this outside."

"But it's raining."

"You won't get wet on the deck with the awning up." By the time he came back in, she'd had time to compose herself.

Ash looked pained. "I've never done anything with Jean-Rose or anyone else. She's a lonely housewife who likes to flirt, but I never took the bait. Can you imagine the row that would cause?"

Heddy couldn't stop the tears. "Why did you pretend you liked me? To steal from Jean-Rose, to get them to buy some stupid house?"

He reached out his hand to her, then dropped it back to his side. "I do like you."

"Then who are these women?" She clenched her fists.

"I don't know. Nothing but the gossip of bored women. Do tell me that's where you heard it? There was someone else early in the summer, but that ended. I never lied to you."

Maybe that was the woman she'd seen in his car.

She pointed to the money on the table. "Well, don't lie to me now." She slipped the license out of the wallet, held it up for him to see. "Who is John Green?"

His head turtled inward, like it was being swallowed by his shoulders, and her skin prickled with fear.

His voice came out in a whisper. "I can't tell you."

She threw the license at him, pinging him in the stomach. "Then I'm going to walk out this door, and you'll never see me again."

Ash reached for her. "I tried to tell you the other night." He looked her square in the eye then, his face ashen. "Losing a parent that young changes you, Heddy. It makes you do things you don't think yourself capable of."

Heddy watched his fingers thrum on his thigh, his eyes searching for a place to land. "That money you found—" he went on.

"Is for the Coconut Coast. It's the deposit for the houses." She wanted to be right.

Ash's head was in his hands now, making his voice warbled. "There is no development. I cashed their checks; I was going to take their money."

She looked for one of the Coconut Coast brochures. There was a stack on the coffee table. She grabbed it, held it in front of him. "What are you talking about? Then what is this?"

He kicked the table leg, moved into his salesman voice. "These people have so much. Seven thousand is a drop in the bucket for them. I didn't think they'd miss it. Ted's investments, everything you see . . . he takes people's money, Heddy. He takes it, and he ruins people's lives, all to make buckets more so he can be—what word would he use—'comfortable.'"

"Well, everyone on this island seems to think his business is peachy keen. Maybe you're just jealous. Maybe he's a better businessman."

He rubbed his face with his hands, leaving it splotchy and ugly. "People pretend they don't see, sure, but they know. Sky Top Steel and Financial is built on the backs of other people's financial ruin. He tells companies he's going to save them, bolster their profits, but at the last minute, with creditors breathing down their necks, he changes the terms of the deal—and pays some watered-down price. It's what he did to my father, and I lost him because of it." Ash wiped his nose; it was running now that his eyes were pooling.

"I don't care about Ted and his dumb company or some dumb deal. I care that you're a liar." Teddy must have heard her frantic yell because he looked up at them from outside. When she was certain he'd looked away, Heddy lifted her hand. She'd never hit anyone, but it had boiled up and out of her, and she couldn't have stopped herself if she'd tried.

"I lied to everyone, but never to you. Not about us," Ash grabbed her arm, gripping her elbow. "Look, I was a teenager—my mom lost the house. My childhood home, for Chrissakes. I wanted it back, and when it came up for sale, I thought of Ted. Of how I could get the money quickly. He's unethical, Heddy, and he's a crook, and I wanted revenge."

Heddy remembered the article clippings she'd seen in Ash's living room. What had it said? *Montclair Home of Suicide Financier on the Market.* How the company lost funding at the eleventh hour.

"You had me drop hints to push Jean-Rose to put down a deposit. And what about the others—the others who signed a contract for a house? You're stealing from them, too. What kind of person could do such a thing?"

He was staring at his wet flip-flops. "A despicable one. But Ted's the bad guy here. He's the monster. Not me."

She thought of the bruise on Jean-Rose's temple, what she heard at night. If anyone knew Ted was a monster, it was Heddy, but that didn't change what Ash had done. "And you were going to leave and go to some city in Brazil? I'm not sure what's worse: finding out you're a crook, or seeing how easily you could throw me away."

He gathered up the money, putting the bundles back into the envelope. "You're wrong about that."

She was afraid to look at him. "Correct me."

"It's money. Paper bills. Stop letting money mean goddamn everything."

"It is everything. And it ruins everything."

"Maybe it does, but . . ." He shook his head again, like she kept getting it all wrong. "I just needed it sooner rather than later. By the time anyone got wind of it, I'd mail them a check."

"How? By stealing from someone else? And here I was thinking I'd met someone who wouldn't disappoint me."

He took one step closer to her, cautious, like she was a bomb that would detonate if he came too close. "You were the surprise—I didn't expect to find you in all of this."

She threw the airline ticket at his feet. "Well, it wasn't going to stop you from stealing off and leaving me to wonder what *I* did wrong."

"Maybe I wanted you to go with me."

She laughed with exasperation. "And live the life of a thief? Leave my mother? I liked you, Ash Porter, or whoever you are, but I didn't like you that much. If you haven't noticed, I've got a bright future." She picked up a pack of the money, hurling it across the room. She picked up another and threw that one, too.

"Stop it, kitty kit." He left the bundles there. "This could pay for everything. For your senior year."

She'd let his alleged pedigree cloud her judgment. She'd trusted him. But she knew now: her mother had been right about the men on this island.

She ran out of the house, grabbing Teddy's hand on the porch and dragging him away with her out into the rain. The boy started to cry—"Heddy, stop!" and tears came out of her eyes, too. Ash's footsteps were behind them. The rain made it hard to hear him, the wind blowing wet clumps of hair onto her face.

"Listen. I'll give it all back if you want. Every last cent, but this could be good for you, too."

"Don't do it on my account. We're over." The wind blew a sheet of rain sideways, stinging her cheeks.

He ran after them. "After Gigi's party, I knew I had to tell you. I tried, but I was falling hard, and then . . ."

She thought of all the questions Ash had asked her about Jean-Rose and Ted, how he was always scooping the kids up in his arms, passing Heddy a brochure. It had all been part of an elaborate ploy. Ash had used her to perpetuate his lie, and now, ultimately, she had been an accomplice. Heddy stopped short, turned around and ran back to him, feeling like a child. The rain pelted Heddy's hood.

"I spent the summer feeling lucky that you picked me," she said. "Of all the other girls, it was me. But now I know why: I was just some dumb girl you thought would help you steal other people's money."

Ash reached for her fingertips, but she pulled away. "It wasn't like that. It seems like it was, but it wasn't."

She took off again. Her feet no longer leaden. Her heart was, and she felt it pulling her open, like a bowling ball exploding from her chest.

At the house, Heddy went straight to her room, slamming the door and locking it, refusing to emerge for the rest of the day, even to Ruth's quiet knocks and pleas. She packed everything she owned in Beryl's suitcase, folding all of it into neat rows and tucking her envelope of savings into the silken underwear pocket. She'd catch the first ferry out, meeting Ruth in the kitchen at dawn to explain. To say their goodbyes.

The next morning, Heddy dropped her suitcase at the bottom of the stairs, wearing her busted sandals—she hadn't been able to mend them, after all—dreading her goodbye with Ruth. Smoke wafted from the kitchen, and inside, Jean-Rose stood at the stove, burning French toast.

"Where's Ruth?" Heddy coughed, opening the back door to let the smell out; the children were still asleep.

"She called in sick. I couldn't fall back asleep." Jean-Rose fanned the smoke away from her face. "You're going to have to be two people today. Don't pull that nonsense you did yesterday locking yourself in your room. You're lucky I didn't—"

"Jean-Rose, I'm . . ." The first ferry left in thirty minutes. She planned to surprise her mother, launch into a speech about how she wanted to spend more time with her. How good it would feel to be back in New York, away from this dreadful island and the vile people she'd met here.

Jean-Rose handed her the spatula. "Can you please make something edible?"

Heddy hesitated. "But that's the thing . . ." She wondered if Ruth was sick, or if something happened with one of her parents. What if Heddy left on the morning that Ruth's mother passed away? She wasn't the kind of person to steal off without checking on a friend, to forgo a proper goodbye. It wouldn't be right; she'd come to care for Ruth like a sister. She couldn't just abandon her here on this dreadful island. She'd stay one more day, make sure Ruth was okay and get on the ferry the following morning.

"Give me a second," Heddy told her, dragging her suitcase up to her attic bedroom.

Back in the kitchen, Heddy turned the flame down on the stove and tied on an apron. "I'll take over from here." Jean-Rose disappeared with a mug of coffee while Heddy used the telephone by the front door to call Ruth.

"Is everything okay?" she whispered into the line.

Ruth didn't miss a beat. "I should be asking you the same thing. Why wouldn't you open the door?"

Heddy twirled the telephone cord, stalling. "Why aren't you coming to work? There's so much smoke in the house from Jean-Rose's attempt at breakfast."

"It's Mom. The doctor just left." Ruth got quiet.

"Is she okay?"

"We'll know more in the next day or two. Can you fill in for me?"

"Of course. Whatever you need." Heddy considered the rest of the week, how she could avoid Ash and Jean-Rose. She would stay busy with the children and stay out of town. Oh god, the children. She was about to leave them, too.

"Thank you, Heddy." Ruth's voice wavered, just once, right as she'd said her name.

She wanted to tell Ruth: *I'll come over right now. It's going to be okay.*

"Can I bring over a casserole?" Heddy said.

"You can cook?" They both laughed, said their goodbyes, and the line went dead.

{ TWENTY-FIVE }

The skies were bright blue, the air thick and warm, and Heddy busied the children indoors with a board game. They were making crafts out of Popsicle sticks, while she tidied up the toys they'd scattered about their bedrooms.

She heard the pad of Jean-Rose's footsteps before she saw her deep purple caftan flowing around her. Jean-Rose leaned against the doorframe, ice cubes floating in ginger ale. "I just got a call from Ash."

Heddy didn't look up: "Oh."

"Why won't you return his calls anymore?" In the last two days, Jean-Rose had left a stack of notes by the phone, Ash's name and number, an identical message: *Please call me.*

She shrugged. If only Jean-Rose read her journal . . . she'd written pages about how phony Ash was, how disappointing men could be.

"Well, his development is on hold. His backer fell through, but I'm sure you know this already." Jean-Rose slid her foot in a semi-circle. "He's giving our deposit back. Don't you think that's odd?"

Heddy gathered Anna's alphabet blocks into a bin. "Not especially." She hoped her voice sounded cool.

"And he can't come to my clambake on Saturday night. I'll admit I'm a bit bruised by the RSVP."

That was good of him to cancel, Heddy thought. Still, she'd stay inside and wash dishes, keeping her distance from the guests.

She wished Ruth would come back to work. There was no one to giggle with or snicker at how ludicrous their boss was, and Heddy just wanted to go. Once she made up her mind about something, it was hard going back, but she'd help Ruth however long she needed her. On the phone the day before, Ruth had been upbeat about her mother. But that was Ruth—always holding it together.

After cooking dinner, after baths and pajamas, after Heddy read the children several stories and they'd begged for more, after she washed and dried the dishes, folded and put away the clothes from the dryer, she had a minute to herself. She called her mother, like she'd promised.

"I've been thinking about the boys here—maybe you were right," Heddy said it quickly, quietly, since Jean-Rose and Ted were watching television nearby.

Her mother sighed. "What did he do to you?"

She tried to cover. "No, I just changed my mind, is all. I'm going to come home a little early. We can have some girl time."

A city bus roared through the other end of the line, perhaps the window was open, and she struggled to hear her mother's voice: "Don't come. Things aren't so good here, Hibernia. They laid me off."

"The laundry?"

Her mother sniffled. "Tiffany's. All the older girls were let go. I gave them ten years, but I guess I'm not pretty enough anymore."

Heddy pressed her eyelids together. "Mama, no. It's not possible."

"We'll be okay, though. I'll find other work." It wasn't much, but her mother loved that job. The little robin's-egg blue boxes brought her pride, the way she starched her blouses, how she loved helping men pick out gifts for their wives.

Heddy tasted blood on the inside of her cheek; she'd been biting it. "I have seven hundred dollars. I'll give you all of it. We'll figure this out together, like a team."

Later, Heddy collapsed into her bed with her journal. She wrote in big block letters: *You fight and you lose. Again and again and again.* Then she slammed the notebook shut and threw it against the wall.

A bang of thunder rumbled through the house, the humidity finally breaking open the sky. She checked her watch. It was a little after nine. She entered the living room, to a cloud of cigar smoke, the laugh track of *The Andy Griffith Show*.

"Do you mind if I go see Ruth?"

Jean-Rose glanced at Ted, who nodded. "Just be careful. You don't have much experience driving at night," Ted said.

She imagined sitting down and telling them the truth about Ash, that his name was John Green, that he'd stolen their money and never planned to give it back. She imagined that they'd applaud her, brag to their friends about how their babysitter took down a world-class criminal. The local papers would want to interview her, asking her when she'd known, if there had been clues. She'd say something smart, like she knew it all along, as soon as she saw the shine of his pistol in his closet, but she had to find the evidence, so she pretended to like him so she could snoop. Abigail Rhodes would be so impressed that she'd consider giving Heddy an investigative reporting job at the paper after she finished school and help her pay her way at school, too; it was the least she could do. She and her mother would laugh about that hard time they went through, with the distance of people who would never know a hard time again.

Ted guffawed so loud that Heddy startled, and Jean-Rose covered her mouth demurely, laughing at the TV. The sight of Ted's popped collar and shiny watch, the gold band on his left hand, reminded her that they'd find a way to be the heroes of the story. If she turned Ash in, Jean-Rose and Ted would take the credit. They would find a way.

As soon as she got in the car, she knew where she'd go. The Clamshell, housed in a weather-beaten cottage off Main Street, was beloved thanks to its large screened-in porch. Even with the rain, the picnic tables were full of people eating steamers and lobsters under the awning, the smell of melted butter wafting through the sticky air. Sullivan wiped at a table, pushing the damp rag into his back pocket.

"Sullivan!" Heddy roped her arms around his neck, burying her damp cheek against his chest. He hugged her back, although his arms were limper than she imagined they'd be. He shifted out of the embrace. "I'm sorry about the other day. I don't know why I was so cruel," she said.

"Is everything okay?" He pushed his glasses up his nose.

"Can you get a break?"

"I've got tables."

"Hey, lovebirds." It was Jerome, baring his gapped teeth. "Order up, paper boy."

She covered her face with her hands, so he wouldn't see the tears. Sullivan hollered to Jerome.

"Cover for me, will you?"

Jerome snickered. "As long as I get the tips."

Sullivan grabbed her hand, lightning flashing through the sky. They scurried along a row of parked cars until they found his and barreled inside.

"What happened?" he said.

She wiped at her eyes. "I don't know. Everything." With Ruth gone, she'd held it in for too long; she needed to tell somebody.

Sullivan clenched his fist. "Did he hurt you?"

"No, no. Not like that."

"Then what is it?" He tapped his finger against the steering wheel.

Heddy sent him puppy eyes, a half smile. "Can we take a drive?"

He looked at her over his glasses. "You realize I may lose my job over this?" He started the car, shoving it in reverse. "Fuck it. Why do I care?"

Once they were on the road, the windshield wipers punching out a rhythm in the muggy car, Heddy turned to him. "I'm sorry for how I treated you at the club."

Sullivan pushed his glasses up on his nose, smug and satisfied. "Unlucky in love?"

Outside, tourists in ponchos ducked in and out of the tidy shopfronts along Main Street.

"Okay, that's fair," she said.

He drove to the small lighthouse in town, the parking lot empty, the ice-cream stand shuttered. The ignition went quiet.

"Are you going to tell me what happened?" he said.

The surf pounded along the shoreline, splashing against a large piece of driftwood that washed ashore. A family in matching yellow rain jackets walked the beach. "It's not good. It's really, really bad actually."

He stared at her, waiting. "And?"

"And. I don't know." The family carried two buckets of shells, and Heddy wondered if she would ever have two kids toddling behind her, if she and her husband would ever wear a matching raincoat and walk the beach in the rain.

She turned toward him. "What would you do if someone you loved did something bad? Something unforgivable?"

Sullivan ran his fingertip along the odometer, dusting it. "Is it illegal?"

She nodded. Outside, the kids were singing a song about the

rain, and she thought of Teddy and Anna, how sad it was that after she left, she may never see them again. "Very illegal."

"Did this person harm anybody?" His glasses were fogging, and he rolled his window a crack.

She hedged. "Not physically, just financially."

"Did he have good reason?" he shot back.

"It may not be a 'he.'"

Sullivan shifted in his seat, then cleaned his glasses on his shirt. "I say let sleeping dogs lie. Don't bother with the police."

"Really?" She expected him to say the opposite, especially since he was the heir to a newspaper. Shouldn't he want to investigate? Then again, Sullivan hated the news; maybe he hated it so much he fought against its core tenets.

He shrugged. "The cops will swarm. They'll ask questions. If this person is your friend, you've got to consider if you were involved in what they did, even unknowingly. What if the blame is pinned on you? I say never involve the cops, unless you have to."

She had a vision of Jean-Rose standing before her holding her diamond bracelet. Heddy was an easy mark, wasn't she? The babysitter who was paid a modest salary, a girl who needed money to pay for her scholarship. Cops would find motive. She imagined strangers telling the cops that they'd seen Heddy in town in Ash's truck. If she turned Ash in, she might implicate herself.

"You're right," she said.

"Can I go back to work now?" Sullivan drove past the lighthouse, its light flashing the windshield, then turned back onto Main Street. His spot was still there, and he pulled into it. When the car was off, Heddy leaned across the center of the seat and kissed him on the cheek.

"You're such a good guy," she told him.

"That's why you picked me, right?" He slammed the door and ran into the Clamshell, not bothering to turn around.

And she knew then she'd lost him. She'd lost him forever.

{ TWENTY-SIX }

From the kitchen window, Heddy, who was soaping the second round of cocktail plates, could see guests mingling in the yard, the skies pink with sunset. The Williamses' unassuming backyard had been transformed into a gleaming party space, with twinkling lights, a dozen white picnic tables, and a gravel pit, where the makings of the clambake were tucked under the hot coals.

A bespectacled man in a shirt too small for his belly stuffed his mouth with a pastry puff. A slender woman laughed with Susanne, while Abigail Rhodes, smoking long skinny cigarettes, kept her eyes on Edison Mule and his wife, dark rings under her eyes. In all directions, clumps of guests pulled at meat on sticks, glasses of punch in hand, while a rectangular stereo speaker, the wire lowered down from the living room window, played Little Richard.

"Now aren't these darling?" A sultry voice carried over the others, and Heddy startled, dropping a plate into the suds. Gigi, dressed in a low-cut spangly tank and pedal pushers, examined one of the table centerpieces: white buckets with lobster bibs, a lobster cracker, and

decorative placemats of the island. "Ted, I just *know* you had something to do with this." A throaty laugh.

With Ted's back to Heddy, she watched his Hawaiian shirt jostle
in response, and how he wiped his hand on the back of his khakis
after shaking hands with the man on Gigi's arm.

That man, who was he? A stranger with dark skin and imposing
height, chiseled, but hardly an actor—no Cary Grant. Even from
here, she could see the dull energy of the party had heightened with
Gigi's arrival, a rise in the octave of everyone's voices, the darting of
eyes, partygoers shifting an inch or so forward or back or sideways,
trying to get a little closer to the actress, the intoxication of celebrity.

"Ted, what happened to my invitation?" Gigi pouted her lips, her
eyes sultry and full of dare. "Am I not on 'the list'? Your wife has been
keeping those lists since high school, you know."

A waitress rushed into the kitchen and slid another stack of
plates into the sink, splashing Heddy's apron with water. She dried
her hands on the front, untying the apron and throwing it over the
back of a chair.

Heddy hoped she didn't look positively homely as she approached
Gigi, who was nibbling on cheese with her date, but if she did, Gigi
didn't let on, pulling her into an embrace the moment she laid eyes
on her.

"Did you hear anything from school?"

"They said no." Heddy cast her eyes around until finding Jean-
Rose, standing with friends near the back door, pretending not to
notice Gigi.

"Oh, honey." Gigi rubbed Heddy's back. "We tried."

Heddy got on tiptoe to reach Gigi's swaying earring. "There's
something else . . . Ash Porter is a phony, and he was going to steal
everything, and I'm not sure I can forgive him." She'd whispered it,
and perhaps, Gigi hadn't heard or cared, because she pulled at her
date's hand.

"Heddy, this is Nelson Cruz, a friend from Darien." She thought of Jean-Rose drunk on the couch at the beginning of the summer, repeating that name: Nelson. *Was this him?*

The man puffed on his cigar. He raised Heddy's hand to his half-cocked smile, kissing it. "Pleasure."

"Nelson owns Havana Nights Supper Club in New York. Have you heard of it?" He tucked his thumbs into his belt loops, puffing out his chest, making apparent his healthy ego.

Of course, Heddy had heard of it, as notorious for its airtight guest list as it was for hosting celebrities.

"Imagine my surprise when my agent and I go for a drink, and it's Nelson who comes over. He and I grew up a few houses apart."

"Nice to meet you," Heddy said, but the man was staring over Heddy's shoulder at Jean-Rose, her hair in a French twist, her white satin pantsuit glowing in the moonlight. Nelson grinned, his eyelashes long and thick, and tucked his cigar between his teeth. "Did you ever think we'd be at a party like this, Gigi? With the Sunday casserole crowd," he laughed.

Gigi ran a hand along his chest, the top buttons of his shirt undone and the hair so thick it was bear-like. "Well, we still don't belong here," she said. "But we can have some fun." Gigi grabbed his hand, placing his left palm on her right hip and swaying her hips. With his cigar in hand, he moved along with her, doing the merengue.

Nelson threw his head back, laughing like he knew people were watching. "Look at her. She swings like a senora," he told Heddy.

Gigi unfurled herself from Nelson with a dramatic twirl, smirking at Jean-Rose, who was approaching them. "Well, Nelson, look who we have here. The island's newest-named saint."

"Nelson?" Jean-Rose tried to hide her surprise but her breath caught.

Nelson pushed the nub of his cigar out in an ashtray, fanning the smoke away from his face. "You did well for yourself, *querida*." He pulled her into an embrace, and they hugged like people did in movies, going on a beat too long.

Jean-Rose seemed struck by lightning. "It's been years. I can't remember the last time . . ."

He kissed her hand, letting his lips linger near her princess-cut diamond wedding ring. "Let's not think of that day."

Gigi put her arm around Nelson's broad shoulders. "You look as good in this suit as you did at the altar. I swear, this man doesn't age."

Jean-Rose's nostrils flared. "I wish Gigi'd told me you were coming. I wish Gigi'd told me *she* was coming."

"I thought she did." His eyes sparkling, Nelson took Jean-Rose's hands in his again, sizing her up. "You are happy, though. And that is what matters. It seems you chose well."

Jean-Rose seemed to forget Heddy and Gigi were beside them. "I heard about the supper club. Your parents must be proud."

He seemed disappointed by what she'd said; perhaps he'd wanted to tell her. "But you never visit. I want to show you."

Heddy kicked Gigi's yellow kitten heel, whispering, "What is happening?" Gigi tilted her head toward Heddy's shoulder, shrugging, but her grin was mischievous.

Ted, who'd been drinking heavily in an act of defiance since Jean-Rose asked him not to drink at all, came to his wife's side. "Do you know each other?" he slurred. His voice snapped Jean-Rose out of her trance, and she elbowed her husband off her arm, placing a hand on her silken hip.

"I was so sorry to hear about your rejection from the Island Club, Gigi—I tried to make a case to the board for your admission, I did, but apparently, you didn't meet our decency standards."

Gigi stilled a twitch in her lip. "Is that so? Because I pulled my application weeks ago." She purred. "Is that all you got?"

"How dare you come to this party. You think this is funny?" Jean-Rose angled her body so Nelson was back in Gigi's vision; he tipped his hat, shadowing one half of his face. "You don't think this isn't cruel?"

Nelson blew Jean-Rose an empty kiss, strutting past her, his shiny black shoes clip-clapping through the hush of the crowd. "I'm sorry, *bella*—Gigi said you wanted to see me."

Gigi smoothed the fronts of her pedal pushers, strands of silver woven in the fabric. "Don't let her think you're not welcome, Nelson. She doesn't have anything over us anymore . . ." Gigi bent down, so she was eye level with Jean-Rose, her cheekbones caked with foundation, her peach blush shimmering under the lights. "And it's killing her."

"Get out," Jean-Rose said, studied measure in her voice. She looked around her, smiling at the other guests. The bartender, who'd been putting on a show juggling liquor bottles, set them carefully on the bar top.

Heddy knew she should go back to the dishes, but something percolated inside of her. Was it anger? Resentment? Or was she simply excited that someone was standing up to Jean-Rose? Words started coming to her, then sentences. She wanted in on this fight, but why? It wasn't *her* past or *her* friendship.

Gigi glanced at the partygoers, winking at Susanne, but Susanne crossed her arms. "Can't we be grown-ups?" Gigi said, wiggling her curvaceous behind. Someone whistled, pleasing Gigi.

"Get out. Now." The album had finished and it skipped, the needle hitting into the center of the turntable, repeatedly bleating through the speaker.

Gigi looked down her nose at Jean-Rose. "What happened to you?"

Jean-Rose didn't look away, clenching her fists. "I grew up. I got married, had kids. Stop hating me for having the life you wish you had."

Gigi cocked an eyebrow. "Is that what you think?"

"I'm sorry I've always been the prettier one. The popular one. The daughter your mother wished she had. I'm sorry I landed Ted, and that your famous boyfriend is cheating on you."

Gigi blanched; the actor's latest affair and rumored divorce had been in the papers the day before, even Heddy saw it. "You and your sad sorry self. You think anyone wants what you have?" Gigi's wicked laughter ricocheted through the crowd. "Oh, Jeannie. The ego on you, the false sense of purpose. Always pretending you feel sorry for everyone. Why don't you look in the mirror? See who everyone feels sorry for."

With anger pinching her face, Jean-Rose shoved the actress backward into a picnic table, and Gigi, despite being bigger, lost her balance. "Get out *now*."

"That's enough, Jean-Rose," Ted said, draping his arm around her back, breathing heavily by her bosom. "We have guests."

Gigi, still facing Jean-Rose, poked at her bare clavicle with her pointer finger. "Why did you take Teddy's toy away? Scared that he might be a little too much like daddy? Your damn babysitter had to fetch it from the garage just so he'd stop crying himself to sleep."

"You what?" Jean-Rose stiffened, sneering at Heddy.

Footsteps pounded into the yard, dress shoes on stone. Heddy thought Nelson Cruz was back, but it was Ash standing before her now, breathless.

"I need to talk to you," he said. Ash realized then that he'd walked into something awkward, registering the rage on the women's faces, while tugging on Heddy's arm, trying to steer her away. Ted looked dazed, and she wondered if Ted knew about Ash, but then he ran toward the bushes, emitting the unmistakable spray of vomit.

Heddy planted her sandals firmly on the patio. Safety pin and all. "Are you here to sell more bogus real estate developments?"

"You hate me, I get it, but listen." He looked greasy, his hair disheveled.

"Tell them who you really are. Why you're on this island." Now it was her voice that sailed out over the crowd, and at once, there were whispers.

He shook his head, like she didn't get it, crestfallen and his tail between his legs. "Heddy, stop. You need to come with me."

Jean-Rose grit her teeth behind a smile. "Get back to the dishes, Heddy. That is why I pay you."

Heddy shirked from her, from Ash. She was done with all of them: "I'm sorry, Jean-Rose, but . . . But he's worse than you thought."

The lipstick in the corners of her boss's lips had smeared, giving her the appearance of a deranged clown. "No, dear, he's exactly what I thought. And he's done with you, isn't he?"

Ash grabbed Heddy's shoulders, shaking her to attention. "Heddy, listen to me. It's Ruth."

Heddy blinked twice, letting what Ash said register. *Ruth.* Fear swept over her. Had her mother passed away?

Gigi lit a cigarette, blowing a plume of smoke into Jean-Rose's face. "Why do you try to hurt her? She's just a girl."

"Well, she provided you nothing but amusement." Jean-Rose gestured toward Heddy.

Gigi tucked Jean-Rose's bra strap back under the tank of her pantsuit. "You are a miserable thing, aren't you?" There was a murmur in the crowd, the crackle of the firepit, unfamiliar faces holding sticks with meat on them, waiting for the show to go on.

Jean-Rose twisted the emerald pendant at her neck. "No matter how big your house. No matter how many movies you make. You're an actress, not a Rockefeller, and on this island, you may as well be a whore."

"Bravo," Susanne barked, and she shifted awkwardly when no one else applauded.

"Is that what the Academy voted last March? That I'm a street-walker?" Gigi sounded charmed, scanning the crowd for a response, summoning up a few delayed chuckles.

"You're all so curious about her," Jean-Rose told the partygoers. "Well, I *know* her. Oh, I know her. I was there the day she termi-nated a pregnancy—a pregnancy!—because she couldn't keep her legs closed."

Gigi's eyes bulged, her lips falling open with surprise and disgust—or was it betrayal? She inhaled and exhaled, her gaze bor-ing into Jean-Rose like a drill. Then with bravado—and plenty of cleavage—Gigi's face changed to something wicked, and Heddy wondered what she'd say next. But she said nothing. The muggy air hung like wet towels, waiting for words to cut it; the American flag on the porch flapped in the breeze, the turntable still skipping.

"Heddy, please," Ash said, tugging on her elbow, her hands on her hips. The words raced through Heddy's mind. *Nasty. Entitled. Superior. A complete bitch.* No, that wasn't it. What did she want to say?

Heddy cleared her throat.

"Jean-Rose," she said to her boss, who, having turned her back on Gigi, apologized to guests for the "rude interruption."

"Jean-Rose." Heddy, louder this time, waited for her boss to turn, this woman who pretended to be her booster, then accused her of stealing. Who wanted everyone else's heart to break simply because her own heart broke long ago.

"Heddy, go back to the kitchen," Jean-Rose said, her silver heels pert and aligned.

Emboldened by the chorus in her head, by all the people who ever said no or looked at her like she was less than, Heddy cleared her throat a second time, taking Gigi's hand. She felt heat building in her chest, ideas forming in her mind. Heddy hated Ted, yes, but she'd come to hate Jean-Rose and Ted as a couple even more. And Jean-Rose was so selfish, so cruel and uncaring to everyone around her, that it was hard to feel sorry for her. She held this power over everyone, even Gigi, and Heddy wouldn't let her crush the actress's spirit, just as she'd tried to break Heddy's own.

"Want to know what I learned this summer?" Heddy let go of Gigi's hand, but she could feel the actress towering next to her. "I learned that money doesn't buy happiness. Or kindness. Or class."

It hadn't come out the way she wanted, feeling contrived, cliché. Heddy stared at the horizon, where a lighthouse beam strobed across the horizon. She searched her heart, clawing for the right words. The truest ones. She found Jean-Rose's eyes again, shadowed in silver, her mascara a perfect fan of long lashes. Even now, her beauty startled her.

"I started this summer thinking I wanted to be you. This perfect life of yours. And I may go home and live with nothing for the rest of mine." The pain of it burned in Heddy's chest, and she bit her cheek. "But here's what I know: You taught me that the most dangerous kind of woman is one without dreams. A woman who plays by someone else's rules rather than her own. Who does what she thinks people want her to do rather than what she wants. And I will never, ever, be a woman who lets someone, no matter how much money they have, make her believe she's not good enough."

Her eyes were damp, her lips trembling, and still the words came. "I'm sorry, but you can't talk to me like that, Jean-Rose. And you certainly can't talk to Gigi McCabe like that. *The Gigi McCabe.*"

Gigi elbowed her, a pleased smile spreading across her face. She mouthed to Heddy: "Good girl."

Ted stumbled back to Jean-Rose, like nothing ever happened, and the sight of him wiping his mouth turned Heddy's stomach. "And you," she said to Ted. Later, Heddy might regret this, she knew it even as she felt her arm go up, but she needed to do it. Her flattened palm sailed through the air, poised to slap Ted's chiseled cheek. Someone gripped her hand, stopping her. It was Gigi.

"Please. Allow me," Gigi said. But instead of Ted, she slapped Jean-Rose, who emitted a yelp. She knew then that Gigi didn't know about Ted's abuse, that no one did but her and Ruth, and she was sorry then that she'd started this.

The faces around Heddy had turned to a concert of scowls, a sea of murmurs, and Heddy felt her knees buckle as Gigi shook out her hand. She leaned on Gigi to steady herself, her vision blurring for a moment before sharpening.

Ruth. She needed her.

Heddy turned to Ash, who was waiting. "Come on," he said.

❦ TWENTY-SEVEN ❦

*R*uth was lying in a man's T-shirt on Ash's couch, her hair wet from the shower. As soon as she saw Heddy, her eyes glistened. She had a bandage on her forehead, a scrape on her cheek. Heddy took her in her arms, rocking her like a child. "Thank goodness, you're okay."

"She died last night." Ruth tried to pull away, but Heddy squeezed her closer.

"Oh, Ruth, I'm so sorry. Why didn't you tell me?"

Ruth collapsed into her; she smelled of shaving cream, perhaps she'd washed with Ash's. "I wanted to be with her, and I thought people would think it odd." Ruth pulled back to face Heddy, wiped at her eyes. "He wasn't even there when it happened. She was choking, trying to breathe. I mean, he made me do it alone. I was so angry, and when he finally came home, I started yelling. I threw a plate. A vase. He lunged at me, and I fell."

Ash folded his arms across his chest, and until now, Heddy hadn't realized there was blood on his golf shirt. Ruth's blood.

Heddy needed to be strong. She wouldn't cry. "Your dad, he did this to you?"

"It was awful, Heddy," she said. "He's all I have, and I hate him."

Heddy cupped her shoulders. "Ruth, we have to get you out of there."

She shook her head. "There's nowhere else for me."

Ash handed Ruth a glass of water, then dropped a small white pill into her hand. "I drove her straight to Doc Rogers, who told her to take one of these once she calmed down."

After swallowing the pill, Ruth lay down, resting her head on a crochet pillow. "Ash called nine-one-one so they'd come for Mom. I wanted to say goodbye one last time, but I couldn't go back there." Ruth scrunched up her face, her eyes welling up.

Heddy held her hand. "How are you doing?"

"I've been preparing for her death for so long." Ruth buried her face into the knit. "And I'm not prepared at all. What am I going to do?"

"Don't worry. We're here now." Heddy covered her with a blanket, caressing her forehead and humming a lullaby—"Hush little baby, don't say a word"—because she didn't know what else to do.

In the kitchen, she and Ash leaned against the cabinets, sitting on the counter, whispering. "She can't go home."

He put his hand over hers. "She can stay until we figure out what to do next." They could hear Ruth's muffled cries in the living room.

"I think I'm going to have to pack my things today, too," she said, banging her head against the cabinet.

Ash hid his smile with a fist. "You certainly put her in her place. Do you want me to come back with you? Maybe I can smooth things out."

She shook her head. "I've gotta face them at some point." Heddy scooted closer to him, and he put his arm around her. "Thank you," she said. "For helping." She could feel his edges against her, pulsing with longing.

"Can we talk?" he asked. "I have things to say."

She shook her head. "Ash, really, it's not the right time." Heddy went to sit with Ruth, even as she slept, wondering what she could possibly do to help.

The house was dark when she stepped onto the porch after midnight, and she crept upstairs, thankful that Jean-Rose's door didn't swing open as she passed.

She needed to write.

August 11, 1962

I am without options: saying those things to Jean-Rose felt necessary—I'd held in everything for too long. But in bringing out those feelings, others have come, too. I will not choose a man who is untruthful, and I won't pretend to love another for what he has. I think of my mother and how lonely she must have been raising me without a husband, and of the betrayal she must have felt when he told her to get out of his life. Is every man a liar?

There's a pattern here of women taking what a man gives her, accepting her position as less than his, but I will not do that. I will not let a man do as he pleases and still slide under his covers . . . I will find my own way.

She soaked her pillow with her wet face, tears pouring out, chewing down her fingernails one by one. Her nerves kept her up most of the night, and at dawn, with her chest muscles sore, she carried a basket of laundry down to the washer. As she loaded it, she sensed someone behind her.

When she peeked over her shoulder, she saw Jean-Rose was without makeup. Her face pale and tired and so utterly different from how she typically looked. "You know, hiring you was a favor. I had someone else. But Beryl, she promised you were charming,"

Jean-Rose said from behind Heddy's back. Beryl, it was hard to bear. She wondered if they'd stay friends, if they'd have anything in common without school.

Heddy tossed in the last sock, shut the washer door, keeping her back to Jean-Rose. "She can be convincing."

"To think you questioned me as a mother. Yelled at me in my own house. At my own party." Jean-Rose's voice was unhinged, and for a moment, her skin prickling with fear, Heddy wondered if she would creep up behind her and strangle her.

Heddy shut her eyes, willing the moment to end. She spun the dial to Wash, waiting for the spray of the water. "I'll be gone as soon as I can find other arrangements."

"You're lucky I honor my contracts or I would throw your stuff on the lawn. You have forty-eight hours to leave, and I'll be sure you never work on Martha's Vineyard again. And New York, too, at least in a household."

Heddy stood tall, even if she still hadn't turned around. "Ruth is okay, in case you're wondering."

"Ruth will be taken care of. I've been helping her family for years," Jean-Rose snapped. The cycle began to spin, and Heddy pressed her hands against the washer. Something made her turn, curiosity, she supposed, and she felt the cool metal of the machine at her back.

"You loved that man, Nelson, didn't you? So why did you marry Ted? I don't get it."

Jean-Rose sighed, leaned against the doorjamb, her eyes puffy and red. She stretched out her fingers, stared at her ring. "You think you're so smart. But I guess I did, too, at your age. Love seems so black-and-white, I'm sure, but with Ted, well, he was the practical one. He was the choice that made my parents happy. When I told my mother about Nelson, she threatened to disown me—my own mother—and she said, 'If I can't accept you being with a Cuban, why would anyone else?' So I didn't go to city hall that day, and Ted and I went for a drive instead. My whole life came down to that drive. It's funny how a moment can mean everything in retrospect."

Heddy nearly hugged her, despite everything. There was sadness in these walls, no matter how perfectly painted their lines. And now that she knew the details of Ash's scheming, the unhappiness in Jean-Rose's marriage, that Gigi had demons of her own, Heddy could see that money couldn't fix a person. It couldn't save someone, or serve as a Band-Aid to whatever wounds a person carried around. It helped keep the lights on and the radiators humming, but it didn't make anyone happier. Whatever had hurt Heddy as a child would always be with her, no matter how much education she received or how high her social standing climbed. She was thankful for the island for showing her. It was a lesson she could have spent her entire life trying to learn.

Footsteps padded on the floorboards upstairs, causing Jean-Rose to wipe her eyes.

"Stay out of my way until you go. I think you'll understand why I'm withholding this week's pay." Jean-Rose trudged up the stairs, greeting the children in murmurs, the television switching on.

They avoided each other the rest of the day. It was so quiet it felt like someone died. With Jean-Rose in her bedroom and Ted puttering in the garage, Heddy encouraged the kids to go for a walk. She led them to Ash's cottage.

Ruth was on the telephone when they arrived, and the children were confused at the sight of her. "I thought you were sick," Teddy said, scrunching up his nose while Anna wrapped her skinny arms around Ruth's legs.

Heddy quieted them, setting down the clean outfit she'd brought for Ruth.

"That was Jean-Rose," Ruth said, when she hung up. "She said I should move into the attic. You're leaving?"

Heddy pulled her away from the children, who were sitting at Ash's chessboard. "Something happened. I said some things." She whispered in Ruth's ear.

Her eyes resembled saucers. "You what?"

Heddy tucked a wisp of red hair behind Ruth's pale ear. "I wish I could take it back."

"I wish I were that brave."

"Ruth, you're an ox. You could haul the world up a mountain."

They laughed, joining the children on either side of the chessboard.

"Mom wanted to be cremated. Will you scatter her ashes with me? Off Katama Beach."

Heddy took her hand. "You can't do that alone." She was supposed to leave in two days; would Ruth have the ashes by then?

"Ash said he would fetch my things. I don't want to see Dad."

Heddy rubbed her arm. "Of course not. Where is Ash?"

"He left with a list. He's a good man, Heddy. I screamed at him when he pulled over, beating him on the chest. He said to breathe, that he wouldn't leave me on the road. He said he'd bring me to you. He told me stories on the drive, kept asking me my name, what day of the week it was. He didn't have to do any of that. He's more than good."

Heddy buried her face in her hands. "I don't know what he is."

She and the kids had one more stop, and when they left Ash's cottage, they turned to the path opposite from theirs.

Karina answered the door of the estate, leading the children to the patio, where they found Gigi dressed in a skirt suit with a hat pinned sideways, a petite fishnet veil over her forehead—clearly about to board an airplane. Gigi hugged Teddy tight, then Anna. She got on one knee. "I'm off to make my next movie."

"*An Afternoon in Central Park*?" Heddy said.

She nodded. "On a set in the Valley. Does she know they're here?"

Heddy shrugged, wondering how Gigi could slap Jean-Rose, then hug her children. "Why are you so nice to them?"

Gigi and Heddy followed the kids to the wide-open lawn, where they were chasing seagulls. "This may sound crazy, but no matter how nasty she is to me, we were little girls together, then best friends. At one time she was the closest thing I had to a sister. Plus, she knew me before this"—Gigi threw her head back, laughing—"maybe she keeps me grounded."

The children begged to play hide-and-seek, so she and Gigi crouched behind the stone grill while the children counted. "Why the sad face, sugar pie? You got the guy—he loves you."

Heddy grimaced. "He most definitely does not. He's a liar and a cheat." How could Gigi know Ash's feelings, and how could Heddy explain what she knew—what he'd done and how it had changed everything between them, even if helping Ruth had endeared him to her.

The kids hunted for them.

"I heard you at the party, when you told me he was a con man." Gigi tilted her head to the side. "So I went to him, out of concern for you, of course, and asked him if there ever was a Coconut Coast. The poor guy drank two shots of Seagram's Seven before he answered. You broke his heart."

Heddy pulled away. "I broke his heart? I suppose you're forgetting that he's the one who concocted this whole romance just to get money out of the Williams."

Gigi batted her eyelashes. "Gosh, I hate unhappy endings. Let's think this through."

After a long look at Heddy's unchanging face, Gigi said: "Haven't you ever made a mistake so big you wanted to crawl into a cave and never come out?"

The children peeked under the pool loungers.

"Sure, but I've never pretended to be someone else."

Gigi arched an eyebrow. "Haven't you?"

Heddy remembered Gigi's party, how she'd loved seeing herself through Ash's eyes. "That was different. I wasn't stealing from people."

"Think about it this way, sugar pie. What he did is just one thing that happened between you, it's not the only thing."

Heddy ducked lower so the children didn't see her as they passed, whispering. "What I want to know is: Why are you on his side? He would have stolen from you, too."

Gigi swatted at a gnat. "Oh, I don't know. I suppose I envy the two of you, finding each other like this. And anyone who wants to screw Ted Williams is fine by me."

Heddy's nose twitched. "I'm with you on that one."

"Anyway, you need to look at why Ash did what he did. He was stealing, yes, but for a noble reason. Think of it as a character flaw, but not an unforgivable one. In *The Cannes Caper*, Kirk Douglas had a double identity—two sets of friends, two apartments—but in the interest of true love, my character ran off with him, and they lived happily ever after."

"That's the movies, Gigi." Heddy sighed. "What if loving me is a con, too?"

Anna and Teddy spotted them, gaily pulling them out of hiding, and moments later, the housemaid appeared with a tray of cookies and a pitcher of lemonade. Gigi's "lemonade" was a rather tall Tom Collins.

Gigi adjusted the high waist of her skirt before sitting down. "God, I wish someone was fighting for me. You know how rare that is? Well, I can tell you. I've had men in my life, Cary included, and when things ended, they ended. This man wants you. You can't buy that."

The sun was blaring. Heddy pulled out her grandmother's hand-kerchief, dabbing at her neck. "People don't change, Gigi. They are who they are." That's what her mother always told her; disappointing men wouldn't behave better just because a woman asked.

Gigi turned Heddy's cheek so she was looking at her. "That's ridiculous, little girl. Think of how much you changed, just in a summer. You thought all these fancy pants had everything. Now you can see right through them." Gigi smacked her lips, shiny with red lipstick, and drank the rest of her cocktail. "Watching you realize that last night. Well, let's just say you've helped me with my next film. Don't misunderstand me. He was wrong, but don't give up so easily." The actress frowned and said something about Anna's knotty hair. "Heddy, can you run to the bathroom and get me a hairbrush?"

Heddy had to use the bathroom anyway, so off to the orange-painted powder room she went. Gigi knocked, startling her.

"Put on the dress, sugar pie. Let's take a photo." Hanging from a towel bar, there was a pale-yellow dress, strapless with a sweetheart top.

"What's wrong with my outfit?"

"Don't be difficult. I like dressing people. And I like happy endings."

Heddy reluctantly put on the dress—cool cotton eyelet—while thinking about how she envied Gigi's ability to change lives like she did clothes. The actress was accustomed to being airlifted out of one role and landing in an entirely different one. If she was stuck in a rut or took on bad habits, she simply changed her ways at the next stop. The downside, of course, is that a life without commitments could be incredibly lonely.

"Hello?" Heddy stepped out onto the bluestone patio, finding it empty.

"Heddy?" A man's voice, a familiar one. Heddy turned to the house, the only sound the swing of the kitchen screen door. She found him near the pool, just as he'd been the night of the party. Ash, handsome in his pressed linen trousers and white collared shirt, sleeves rolled up, and freshly oiled brown saddle shoes.

Ash pushed his fingers through his tousled hair, looking up at her with that dashing look of his, the one that made people look twice. He walked to her, taking her hands in his. He was red-faced and serious, staring into her like she was a reflecting pool, like if he had a penny he'd make a wish on her.

"Truth. My name is John Green. I grew up in Montclair. My family had some problems. I went to Northwestern." He swallowed hard, and she saw his neck then, remembered how it smelled of vanilla aftershave, how smooth his skin. "I stole money from everyone on this island. But then I met a girl. A really *rich* girl."

He took a step closer to her, his voice pleading with her to understand. "But she wasn't wealthy the way you might think. No, but she had everything. She was beautiful and whip-smart, and true, and she looked at me like I was offering her everything she ever wanted. And I was. I would give this girl everything, if she'd let me."

There was music then, Elvis Presley, the song they danced to at Gigi's party. Someone had put a speaker in the screened window, and Heddy let a smile slip because she hadn't expected, or even wanted, any of this. But here he was.

Ash tipped her chin, his finger lingering, then caressing her cheek. "Dance with me?"

He wrapped his arms around her back, and she pressed against him, burying her face in his chest.

"There's so much to say, and I could stand here and try to explain why I did what I did. Bottom line: I screwed up. But Ted, he ruined my family, and he got away with it, so a part of me, every bit of me, wanted to ruin him."

When she opened her eyes, he was staring at her. He looked different to her now. It wasn't just that his tan had turned from golden to burnished; there was age in his face, worry lines on his forehead she'd never noticed. Still, she didn't know what to say. She searched the greens of his eyes for honesty, for goodness, for signs of authenticity. All she could go on was how he looked back at her, into her, like he was lifting a tiny curtain and letting her see what was inside.

"You don't fit with them, kitty kit, with Jean-Rose and Ted and their high-brow friends, and you beat yourself up for it. But you don't need to fit in with them. Because, well, you fit with me."

He kissed her, and she kissed him back, wrapping her arms around his neck. She wished she'd never found that envelope. *Don't fall for this*, snapped a voice inside of her. *He's a goddamned thief.*

Her hands still braided around his neck, she raised her eyes to him. "Where will you go after this? I'm still figuring things out. There's school." As soon as she'd said it, she realized how obvious it was. Maybe she wasn't going back to Wellesley, but she'd go back to college somewhere, earn her degree.

"There's more money, Heddy—it's from Ted, but it's hard to explain why I have it. There's enough for Wellesley. It will help your mother get an apartment. We can get a house, I'll get an honest job in Boston."

She was surprised to hear that he'd come with her. Did men do that—change their plans to accommodate a woman's dreams? "What do you mean, there's money?"

He backed away, holding his hands up like she might shoot. "Now, listen. Don't get upset, but I'm not giving it all back."

She slapped his cheek, feeling ridiculous suddenly in Gigi's yellow dress. She wasn't angry that there was money. She was angry that she wanted it, that as soon as he said it she found herself salivating over it. She needed a job. Her mother needed a job. Ruth needed a way out. All these women, all these needs, and Heddy with no way of helping.

"I'm not going to Brazil." Ash stood in front of her. "And before you leave and tell me I'm a dirty thief, you need to know that Ted Williams and my father had an affair." His eyes seemed like bottomless pools, and he winced, his face wrenching. "I'm ashamed to say that out loud, but it's true. When my father's company was in the red, he went to Ted for help—they were lovers—and Ted agreed to invest. But on the morning of the deal, Ted told my father he'd give him the money but only if he had full ownership over his company. Things got ugly between them, and in a last-ditch effort to save the deal, my father threatened to 'out' Ted to the papers; he admitted as much to my mother, coming clean about the financial trouble, the affair, all of it. The following day police found my father's parked car. He was slumped over the wheel with a bullet in his head, the gun on the seat."

"I'm sorry, but . . ." Heddy couldn't follow his story, not entirely. "But why does Ted need anything? He's got the steel money."

Ash pressed his hands into hers. "Sure, but a rich man never has enough. Ted gets some sick pleasure from buying and dismantling other people's companies, each one adding a notch in his belt. He's greedy, Heddy, and his business is one big . . ."

"Swindle," she said, bewildered.

"Yes, it's terrible but true," he said, staring into her eyes.

Heddy's lips found his then, she could taste him in her mouth, and she kissed him hard to erase all this hurt that she was carrying. She hated Ted, she hated him and his hitting hand, and she hated that he'd hurt this man, the only one she'd ever loved. Because there was no mistaking it: she loved Ash Porter. Her knees buckled with the reality of it. She was about to walk away from him, and why? He was better than Jean-Rose or Ted or any of their crummy friends at the Island Club. He wasn't seeking fame—or fortune. Not really. And even with all his lies, he was somehow truer than anyone else.

Her heart swelled, her fingers tingling as he held her hands, and still, they didn't stop kissing, Ash pushing her against the side of Gigi's house, traveling his lips down her neck, then back up to her mouth. He pinned her arms up over her head, his breath hot on her face, panting, staring at her.

She spoke. "Then why the Coconut Coast. Why this elaborate plan?"

Ash let go of her arms, brushed his fingers along her lips. "I needed a reason to be here, to gain his trust, so I could figure out how to get to him. Edison made it easy. They didn't exactly hide themselves."

Perhaps, it was why he hit Jean-Rose; he hated what he saw when he looked at her.

"We took photographs of them together, and now I'm . . ."

"Blackmailing him."

In the distance, a lawnmower started.

"You're a quick study." Ash smiled. He kissed her forehead. "Yes, and I'm not giving him back a cent, so it's ours. Come to my house tomorrow, six a.m. We'll get on the first ferry out."

"And then?"

"And then we'll choose us. We'll forget about this crazy summer, and only tell our kids the parts that matter: how you showed up on my doorstep one day, how I took you surfing, how you wore a red dress and we spent the night at a movie star's party. How we fell in love."

He kissed her eyelids, and she tried to understand what he was suggesting, what she might agree to. "We'll be the sum of so many parts. So many summers," he said.

Her head was spinning, and she leaned against his pressed shirt, smelling the fabric softener. She wanted to go, and she knew she loved him—she just wasn't sure she could trust him. Still, she walked him to the side of the house where no one could see, pushing him against the cedar shingles and lying into him with her lips, picking up where they'd left off a few moments ago. He started to unzip her dress, but she moved his hand away from the zipper. They made out some more until they tired, coming to sit in the weedy grass, their backs against the cement foundation of the house.

They were quiet for a moment until Ash said, "There's one more thing. I need a favor."

Ah, here was the catch.

"That envelope I brought by a few weeks ago. For Ted. I need you to bring it to me."

"But I can't go in his office," she said. Her tone made clear this was nonnegotiable.

"Heddy, I need it."

"What's inside?" she asked.

He sighed. "It's better if you don't know the particulars."

She inhaled sharply. Is this what it was to love a thief? One minute you're imagining a life of truth and beauty, and in the next, you're drawn into his criminal world as an accomplice.

"Just trust me. He'll get away with everything—I'll go to jail for extortion if I don't get it back."

She crossed her arms. "I'm not doing this unless you tell me what I'm taking."

Ash dropped his head between his knees. "Okay, there are photographs—of Ted with other people, doing things. You don't want to know, honestly. Those are the originals, and my partner, well, he lost the negatives. They're the only pictures we have."

A dog ran down the dunes from Ash's yard, sniffing at the bushes and peeing, then running away. *Barkley?* she wondered. But he had no reason to walk this beach.

"Look, kitty kit, I need you." Ash put his arm around her back. "If I don't get these photos, I have nothing over him."

"I wouldn't even know where to look." Even as she said it, though, she knew she'd do it. She was out of options, desperate and headstrong all at once, and maybe Jean-Rose was right: The rest of one's life could come down to a single moment, and this was hers. Would she accept defeat, not return to Wellesley, get a job in Brooklyn, and let a bad man go free? Or would she punish the man who deserved punishing—Ted was the real thief, the real liar—and help herself and help Ash, the man she was in love with?

"Does he have a safe?" Ash scooted to face her, willing her to think, but her mind wandered. As soon as Jean-Rose went to the club, she could go through Ted's desk. Maybe she'd pretend the kids wanted to play "Daddy's office," and they'd all go in and answer the phone and scribble on paper while she hunted for the envelope. It wouldn't incriminate her, not exactly, and she could play dumb. No, that wouldn't work. She'd have to sneak in.

"I'll try," she said. Even as she said it, she wondered: If she didn't do it, would he still want her?

He let go of her hand and grinned, lifting her chin with his fist. "I love you, Hibernia Winsome." His lips pressed into hers once more, and she heard a round of applause in her head. He'd said it. *He'd actually said it.*

Even if he was a thief, she would love him because he loved her. More than that, she loved him because they would keep each other's secrets. Because they had secrets that bound them.

"I love you, too," she said. Her eyes lingered on him, her thoughts fast-forwarding to them walking off the ferry boat onto the mainland, the two of them hand in hand, a suitcase of money between them. How she'd stand on tiptoe to kiss him—and he'd retreat, an evil look overtaking his face. How he'd leave her standing penniless and alone.

He could be lying about loving her. He could be lying about helping her. She wouldn't be fooled twice.

Heddy returned to Gigi's patio, Ash following her with a bewildered look, and after grabbing her handbag, she shoved it at him. "I'll do it. But you need to put five thousand dollars in this purse. When I give you the envelope tomorrow morning, you give me the cash." She hoped he didn't hear her voice, the way it was trembling.

Ash wasn't sure she was serious. "I should keep the money in my suitcase on the ferry—so we don't get caught—and I'll give it to you when we dock. Don't you trust me?"

It was her turn to cup his cheek in her palm. "I love you, I do, but if I'm going to risk everything, I want a guarantee that I'm going back to school, that my mother can get an apartment, that Ruth will have help. Like you said, money makes us act in unexpected ways."

She stared at him until he blinked.

"I like this Heddy." he smiled. "Okay, deal."

Her job, fetching this envelope, was critical, and he wouldn't leave with the money now, he couldn't, unless he waited for her. Even if Ash tried to slip away to the mainland, she'd have her purse full of cash. Heartbroken, but well taken care of.

"Five thousand," she said.

He traveled his finger up her side, moving along her bosom and up her neck. "Five thousand," he repeated.

When he was gone, Karina came out of the house with a silver tray: "The children are watching television inside." She handed Heddy a simple square of paper.

Call me collect anytime. 213-555-3234. xoxo Gigi

❦ TWENTY-EIGHT ❧

*T*he kids were hard to settle down that evening, the tension of grown-ups always trickling down to the children. Around nine, once Ruth was reading in the attic bedroom, not long after Jean-Rose and Ted left for poker at the Club, Heddy crept into Teddy's bedroom to kiss him goodbye.

Jean-Rose hadn't taken Miss Pinkie away yet, and he snuggled with her under his spaceship blanket. With his lips half-parted in sound sleep, she watched the rise and fall of his chest and wondered how he'd do in life, if he'd be okay. Would he end up like Sullivan, trapped in someone else's dreams?

She left a note on his nightstand: *Just remember that if you lose Miss Pinkie, she'll always be with you, right in your heart where you left her. Miss you already. Love, Heddy.*

In Anna's room, she brushed the curls off the child's sweaty forehead, kissing her. *Anna, You are as strong and powerful as your brother—don't whine for what you want. Demand it. Remember everything. Love, Heddy.*

She went down to Ted's office, turning the study's doorknob only to find it locked. It was never locked. She'd have to climb through the window. The night air was warm and the tire swing still as she descended the porch steps, disappearing behind the hydrangea bushes lining the house. With an initial push, she realized the screen was jammed, but the window wide-open. She jimmied the screen with a stick, worrying about how noisy she was being. Finally, she got it open enough to hoist herself into the room.

The headlights of a car shone through the bushes, and she froze, ducking down inside, fearing they were coming up the driveway. But the car turned. Was it Ash?

Her flashlight scanned the contents of the dark study. His desk had a neat stack of folders, a framed photograph of him and Jean-Rose, a navy sweater tied at his neck. She opened his desk drawers, flipping through the files, pulling out a manila envelope but finding nothing but photocopies of tax returns. She flipped through the hanging folders on the other side: lighthouse donations, house title, bank accounts, correspondence. The latter one was thick, dozens of papers stuffed inside. She thumbed through, thankful when she spotted the envelope with the postmark from Worcester.

There was the creep of headlights up the driveway. They were faraway still, perhaps down by State Road, but they illuminated the towering oaks down the hill. The Williamses never returned before eleven, and she held her breath. She had to get out of there. Heddy made sure everything was in its place, then unlocked the door, stepped into the hallway off the living room, locked the knob from the inside and closed the door.

She ran upstairs, stuffing the envelope under her mattress, startling Ruth. "What the hell is wrong with you?" Ruth whispered, looking up from *Pride and Prejudice*.

Heddy listened for the slam of a car door, but when it didn't come, she exhaled, slowly crawling into bed. She dropped onto her pillow, facing Ruth, knowing this would be the last time they'd have a late-night talk for a long time. "Ash wants me to leave with him tomorrow."

Ruth sat up. "And you're not going?" Ruth's mother was to be cremated and a memorial service planned, and after promising to be there, Heddy felt like she needed her friend's permission to leave early.

Heddy shrugged. "We have to scatter your mother's ashes."

Ruth put the book she had been reading on the nightstand. "So you're saying that you're not going?"

"I think so." She was testing Ruth, pleased by her response; she'd been worried Ruth would be against it, that she'd beg her to stay. She needed Ruth to be okay with this, even if she didn't know the details of the $5,000.

Ruth flounced backward, the springs of the bed squeaking. "Do you think he'll notice if I show up in your place? I could use a little whisking away."

Heddy forced a smile. "He'd be lucky to have you."

Ruth wiped a tear from Heddy's eye. "No, there's something to serendipity. There's a reason I met you this summer. Maybe there's a reason all of this happened."

Heddy looked out the window at Ash's cottage in the moonlight; she could make out the chimney, the angle of the roof. "Maybe."

"You know," Ruth started, her voice wavering. "I have an aunt in New York. Maybe I could stay with her . . ."

Heddy stood on the mattress, and Ruth did, too, sensing the gravity of what she was suggesting.

"I'm not close with her. I think she hates my father." Ruth rolled her eyes. "Who doesn't?"

Heddy was grinning. If Heddy used the money from Ash, she could go back to school. She could give Ruth money for cosmetology school; they could live in Boston, but she wouldn't tell her that yet. She reached for Ruth's hands. "That means you can come with me. When I leave. We can share an apartment."

They started jumping on the squeaking bed. "I want to, but . . ."

"But what?"

Ruth frowned, her freckles dark and red. "What if it's a disaster?"

"What if it's the best decision you ever made?"

They considered that a moment, the hum of the oscillating fan traveling from one side of the room to the other.

Ruth saw Heddy's suitcase open on the desk, all her belongings folded inside, even Gigi's red dress.

Heddy bit her nails. "What would you do?"

"I'd do anything to get the hell off this island, so you know what I'd do."

"But if you were me?" Earlier, she'd mailed Beryl a postcard with one line: *I'm coming back after all!*

Ruth shrugged. "Who cares about you?"

It's why she loved Ruth. She could always make her laugh.

"I promise I'll send for you," Heddy said.

Ruth giggled. "You act like you're my guardian angel." They squeezed each other.

Heddy excused herself to the bathroom, hoping Ruth didn't notice that she'd tucked the manila envelope under her arm. Once she was on the toilet, she pulled out the contents. She had to know what was inside: she flipped through each picture.

The naked form of a man's chest, intertwined with another body, a line of dark hair running down the center of a bare stomach. But it was a detail in the next picture that caught her eye: One man's face was turned away, while the other, shirtless and in jeans, held a Yankees cap. She studied the image, trying to make out his blurry face.

She spotted a familiar pair of dimples. A pair of tortoiseshell glasses square on the man's nose.

Heddy dropped the pictures, stunned. She gathered them up onto her lap, leaning into the photograph once more. It was definitely him.

❦ TWENTY-NINE ❧

*T*he floorboards of Ash's deck groaned when Heddy dragged her suitcase onto it, and from inside, she could hear two men's voices through the open windows. She slid open the screen door, hiding the envelope and stepping beside a large navy duffel, partially unzipped, collared shirts stuffed inside.

"Well, this complicates things," Sullivan said. He dimpled, but there was something else in his smile, too: satisfaction. He held her gaze while transferring bundles of twenties from two black camera bags into a large, open suitcase on the coffee table, as nonplussed as a cashier packing a bag of groceries. "We had bets on whether you'd come."

She looked at Sullivan, then back at Ash. Ash came toward her, kissing her forehead.

"I should have known," she said, her voice distant and hazy, lost in a daydream. "The car pulling out of your driveway that morning when I was swimming. It was Sullivan's. And I saw Barkley yesterday, but I . . ."

That pointed look Sullivan was giving her. He was enjoying this, she thought, he wanted her to see him this way, with this hard edge. Was Sullivan thinking: *I told you to stay away from him* or *This is what you get for not choosing me.* But he . . . she didn't understand.

She looked from Ash to Sullivan and back again. She wondered aloud: "But how?"

"I know, we have some explaining to do. But first, did you find the envelope?" Ash held her shoulders to steady her, and she stared at the three creases in his forehead, how deep they were. There was the possibility that the photos inside could ruin Ted Williams, but what did they mean to Sullivan, now that she knew he was involved, too? Had he disrobed to tempt Ted, to catch him—or did Sullivan, well, was he a homosexual?

Heddy dangled the envelope in front of Ash's fresh shave, and he snatched it. There wasn't any going back. She'd broken into Ted's office. If they were caught, she would be implicated. She couldn't run now, or Ash and Sullivan would follow. This had been her choice.

"He thought he had me, didn't he?" Sullivan wore the smirk of a bragging child, and Ash took her hand, giving Heddy a twirl.

She planted her feet—she didn't want to spin; her head was spinning enough. She was trying to understand what she was seeing.

"Sullivan is your associate?" Heddy said. She tracked Ash as he walked into the kitchen, slipping the manila envelope into the refrigerator. *An odd spot*, she noted. She also noted the pistol on the kitchen table, shiny and silver, lying on its side. The same pistol she'd seen in the bathroom closet. She blinked, then blinked again, until she realized she wasn't blinking, her eye was twitching.

Ash sat her down on the sofa—she wanted to yell: *Stop touching me. What is happening?*—but she let herself be moved, uncertain what it meant that these two men were standing in the same room. That they were in on this together.

She tried to stop looking at the gun, but like a magnet, her eye kept finding it.

Her summer could have gone differently. If she'd taken the job as a camp counselor in the Catskills, she might have fallen in love with the mountains rather than a man. She would have spent her mornings swimming in the lake or hiking the surrounding forests. The people would have compared the height of the trees, bragged that they saw bear prints and praised the fresh air the way people on this island spoke of money and the sea. But if she hadn't come here, if she hadn't met these two men and been drawn into this crime, she wouldn't be returning to school. She wouldn't be in love.

"We wanted to tell you," Ash said. He intuited that she was uneasy, and he crouched down on his knees to face her, his eyes pleading, like he needed forgiveness. "This will all be over soon, and it will be me and you, kitty kit."

"*He* wanted to tell you." Sullivan retorted, zipping the hard-shell suitcase closed. He took off his Yankees hat, smoothed his hair. "It was a coincidence that I met you at the park, that Jean-Rose set us up. That wasn't planned."

"But Peg?" Ash retrieved her purse from the console, handing it to her, and Heddy could feel its weight in her lap. She'd need to count it. "Sullivan, what are you doing here?"

The handle of the gun was silver, smaller than she thought pistols were. Heddy wondered if she could hold it. If she needed to get to it, she could hop over the back of the velour couch. It was the most direct way.

Sullivan fell back into the couch beside her, sighing, leaning forward on his elbows and dropping his head into his hands. "Peg thinks it's on, but she'll figure out it's not."

"Oh, Sullivan." Heddy felt sorry for him. She supposed she always had. Perhaps that's why she couldn't love him, or perhaps it was something else, some distance she hadn't been able to pinpoint.

Maybe it made sense now that he was in those pictures. She took his hand, clammy and wet, and he squeezed hers in return. He was pretending to be brave.

"Do you swing toward, you know," she whispered, tilting her head to Ash. "Men?"

"God no." He laughed almost too hard, intuiting her anxiety that he'd faked his interest in her. "But we needed to get on the inside and get photos of them, so I joined in. Why not, right? I'll try anything once, although I'm not sure I'd do it again." He paused, then blurted: "You know, I really did like you."

Ash, burning Coconut Coast brochures in the fireplace, shot them a look. "Remember who she's leaving with," he snapped. This made Sullivan inch away, his leg bouncing up and down, earthquakes on the inside rumbling on the outside.

"How do you even know each other?" Heddy asked.

The day she saw Sullivan's car at Ash's house. Had they been concocting their plans at Ash's breakfast table? If she'd arrived only moments earlier, would she have seen them together? The awkwardness that must have ensued once she was juggling dates with the two of them, and then later, once she'd chosen Ash. She felt guilty in her duplicitousness now that she faced them; they'd known what she was up to all along.

"We met at a bar in Florida," Sullivan said, with the amusement of someone starting a good story. "Ash was going on about some guy Ted Williams who screwed his family. I told him, 'Boy, do I know Ted Williams.'"

"I gave you a black eye," Ash said. She opened the clasp of her purse and peeked inside to see the cash. Ten bundles of twenties. Now she knew she'd done the right thing.

"Sullivan, you don't need this." She closed her purse, fastening it shut. "You could leave now. You could go back to your life. You have everything."

But Sullivan ignored her. "Don't you see? Mother can't tell me what to do anymore." He patted the front of the Samsonite suitcase, a tiny silver lock dangling from the zipper. "This is all I need, Heddy. I'm taking Ash's ticket to Brazil. It'll be me, a mojito, playing Latin jazz whenever I want."

She wondered if the gun was loaded. She rubbed her temples. "You were always telling me to stay away from Ash. But it was you, too."

Ash's voice, direct, at Sullivan: "We're square?"

"Fifty-fifty, minus her share," Sullivan nodded. She imagined him in São Paulo playing his sax, how solitary that life seemed already. He turned back to Heddy: "You could come with me."

Ash lunged at him: "You little shit." A slam of a body on the floor, two men rolling like children, each one trying to free a fist to slam into the other. She ran to the kitchen table, positioning herself so her back was to the gun. She didn't want one of them to grab it.

"You can't blame me for trying," Sullivan coughed out. "I like her, too, man."

Heddy whistled sharply, like she'd do to the kids. "Stop it. You're like damned children."

They stood, holding their hands up, backing away from her, like they were stunned. "It's bad enough what you did, but to fight like this is appalling," she said.

There was a subtle tilt in Ash's head, a gentle nod, like he was trying to tell her something. She looked at Sullivan to see if he was up to something, but they were both looking behind her, like someone was standing there.

Heddy's heart struck with fear thinking of the children. Had one of them followed her to the cottage without her realizing it?

Something clicked at her side, and curious, Heddy turned around, her breath slipping when she saw him. Ted, gripping the gun, Ash's gun, pointing it at all three of them. She backed up, instinctively raising her hands, banging into a kitchen chair.

"I told you not to go in my office," Ted barked. Heddy stared into the eye of the pistol, willing whatever was inside to stay there. "Doing their dirty work, eh? Jeannie was right about you, you little slut."

The words shot through her ears. Because even if she was frightened, even if she let herself get caught up in this mess, she'd spent a summer longing for Ted to treat her as a daughter. Now he was pointing a gun at her. Heddy lowered herself into the kitchen chair, thankful to feel the cushion under her, but she couldn't stop looking at the gun, which Ted roved back and forth between the three of them. If she could have run, she would have, but Ted, in his striped golf shirt and pressed khakis, blocked the front door.

"And you two, this ridiculous scheme." Ted's finger was on the trigger, but the gun was pointed at Sullivan. "Give me the photos, and give me my goddamned money. The entire fifty thousand you squeezed out of me."

"Heddy knows where the photos are, don't you?" Sullivan coaxed.

Ted pointed the eye of the gun at him, and Sullivan nodded her along; she could see sweat glistening on his forehead, his cheeks flush with adrenaline. "Why you're in on this, Sullivan Rhodes, I'll never know," Ted seethed.

"Go ahead, kitty kit," Ash said, motioning to the kitchen. "Get the envelope you brought us. It's right where you left it." She tried to understand what he was saying, why he was saying it, what he wanted her to do. Was he telling her to give him the manila envelope or did he want her to distract Ted so that he and Sullivan could overtake him?

"You heard them. Get up, you penniless piece of shit," Ted said, pushing her off the checkered pattern of the cushion and smacking the side of her head with the gun. She yelped, knowing now what Jean-Rose must feel when he hit her, a combination of adrenaline, hatred, and gratitude. Gratitude because if he'd just go far enough, it would all be over. He pressed the barrel of the gun into her back, nudging the metal harder against her spine, before pointing the gun back at Ash and Sullivan, who were still standing, hands up, behind the couch. She cast her eyes to the linoleum floor, knowing Ted's temper, hearing her shallow breath, sensing this was on her. She pictured Jean-Rose, how she could distract Ted when he got angry, confuse him by talking circles around him.

"It's just that . . . ," she started.

A vein in Ted's neck bulged, and he whacked her cheek with the gun. "Get me the damn photos."

Pain whiplashed through her face, and she put her hand there, feeling blood. She glanced at Ash while walking to the kitchen, and at the avocado green stove, she began to cry. As she reached for the handle of the kitchen drawer, her hand trembling as it wrapped the metal, she didn't know what he'd do next, when he saw that there was nothing but forks, spoons, and butter knives inside.

"It's not here." She cleared her throat, ready to flinch.

"I'm not an idiot," Ted said. He jabbed her in the back again, harder, and she felt a burning ring where the gun pulsed. She thought of the violence she heard at night, how Jean-Rose muffled her cries. What was he capable of? She reasoned that Ted wouldn't kill them, not here. It was too big of a mess, there would be too many questions, and he still wouldn't have what he wanted. She'd stick with her plan to stall, give the boys a moment to figure something out.

"Ash put it in here. I saw him. He said he wanted it by the knives so if anyone tried to steal it, there was protection. Now I'm not going to take out one of these knives and do anything funny, but I can tell you, as someone who worked in your home and tucked your kids in at night, that envelope is not where he left it." She tried to read Ash's expression, but he was watching her. Did he expect her to pull a knife out of the drawer and hold it to Ted's throat? She wouldn't; not ever. She mouthed: "Do something," but Ash darted his eyes away.

Ted slammed the gun down on the counter, and she startled. He yanked the drawer harder, fishing his hand around in the back, cursing when he poked his finger on a metal corkscrew. He tossed it out, leaning down to look inside the drawer, and in his haste, he pulled it out all the way, causing the entire tray of silverware to fall with a deafening clatter at his feet.

"Fuck," he hollered, reaching for the gun, but Heddy already had her hand on top of it, sliding the cool metal nose toward her, secured under her palm. She and Ted locked eyes, and she could tell she'd surprised him. He could have tackled her for it—she would have handed it to him if he'd demanded—but Ash was already on top of him, pulling his arms behind his back and holding him there.

Ted's face contorted and he snarled: "Don't send those photos to anyone."

"I'm not putting them in the paper—I don't give a shit that you've got a thing for the boys." Sullivan, acting like a cocky teenager, folded his arms, his smile curt and dismissive. "But if you ever threaten me again, I'll do it. I swear I will."

Heddy tried to imagine how Jean-Rose would save face if the compromising photos of Ted were released, if someone had the gall to print them. Rather than avoid social situations or cry alligator tears, Jean-Rose would simply deny it was him altogether. She could see her already: Surrounded by a group of fashionable women, Jean-Rose's eyes gleaming with confidence, telling the story about how the guy in the picture *looked* so much like Ted—it was uncanny, really—but she could guarantee that it wasn't Ted. She'd wink, reassuring them that when it came to the bedroom, Ted was nothing short of a tiger. She'd explain that someone created the photos for blackmail, and that part would be true.

Ted struggled to get out of Ash's grip, a sweaty lock of hair stuck to his forehead. "You don't even have proof. Those photos could be anybody."

At that, Sullivan walked to the fridge, pulled out the envelope and fished through a stack of pictures until he found a damning photograph of Ted engaging in an act that made Heddy blush.

Ash rolled his eyes. "Sully, there's dock rope in the shed. Grab it. We'll tie him up."

Her boss, the very man whose shoes she'd shined, whose cigar smoke she'd inhaled, she was going to stand in this room and watch him be tied up. And then what? She licked her lips.

Heddy held the gun higher, aimed right at Ted's cheek, which was pressed against the wall, Ash's arms so tight that Ted couldn't move.

With the rope in hand, Ash pinned him down on the couch, Ted's collared shirt twisted around his waist, his frame collapsed on the soft cushions, his breath quick and heavy.

"You probably don't remember me," Ash said, shoving him in the back with his knee and tying his hands together. "But I know you remember my father—Edward Green—and you definitely remember how you stole his company out from under him, you son of a bitch."

"I don't know what you're talking about."

"Sure, you don't," Ash barked.

"But my children. If those photos get out, it will destroy them."

"You don't care about your children," Heddy snapped. Still holding the gun, feeling power in the grip, she bent down on one knee so she was in front of Ted. How tall he seemed to her when she stepped off the boat, when he carried her suitcase to the car and told her to call him Ted. How his hair blew back from his temples on the car ride home, how Jean-Rose snuggled into him, batting her long, curled lashes at his profile. How he swung his golf clubs over his shoulder, a boyish grin on his face.

Heddy pressed the gun between Ted's angled eyebrows, and she felt her teeth grinding, her finger pulsing on the trigger. Ted squeezed his eyes tight, and in his place, she saw the face of the man who was her father, the man whose Long Island house she'd stood outside a year before. She pressed the gun harder against Ted's forehead, just as he'd done to her, and spoke in a hush.

"You can pull on pressed slacks and sip a martini and tell yourself you're fancy because you swing with a golf club. But you're a coward and you're weak, and if we find out that you hit Jean-Rose ever again or lay a hand on those children, those photos are going straight to the papers."

Ash grabbed the gun out of her hand, zipping his duffel bag closed over the manila envelope. "Let's go, kitty kit," he said.

They left Ted there, tossing the suitcases and duffels into Ash's truck, not caring how he found his way home. Ash peeled out of the driveway, but with the cottage still in view, he slammed on the brakes. "We need to find a boat."

"The ferries are too risky now," Sullivan said. "If Ted gets out before we leave, he could have us stopped."

"But the envelope," she said. "I thought he couldn't."

Ash tapped his fingers on the steering wheel. "We'd be found with suitcases full of money, and the cops could be paid off for the pictures. Ted's a local hero. No cops."

Heddy thought about the whaler she and Ash took out that night, but if it were that easy, Ash would have suggested it.

"Gigi," she said. "Gigi has a boat."

Sullivan shook his head. "No movie star is going to tangle with this."

"I—I—I need to use the phone." She dug through her wallet, finding the slip of paper with Gigi's number. "Let me try her."

She refused to go into the cottage alone, so they all returned, Ash and Sullivan sitting on either side of Ted, who was spitting out empty threats.

Heddy cradled the kitchen phone with her chin, listening to the ringing on the line, a series of tinny bells sounding into an echoing valley. Each time the line went through, a recorded voice—was it Gigi's? the connection was too warbled to tell—prompted her to leave a message. Heddy had heard of these contraptions that took messages like secretaries—answering machines, they were called—but she'd never actually encountered one.

She dialed the number for the fourth time, willing Gigi to pick up. After a minute, she heard a mumbled hello. Heddy glanced at her watch: seven thirty in the morning. That meant that in Los Angeles, it was four thirty.

"Sorry, it's early, but it's me." The line went dead. Gigi had hung up on her. She dialed Gigi's number one more time. The line clicked after one ring.

Heddy stretched the cord and stepped outside so Ted couldn't hear. "Don't hang up. It's me. Heddy."

"Jesus, girlie, it's the middle of the night here." Gigi coughed.

Heddy couldn't talk fast enough. "I'm sorry. I'm really sorry, but remember the happy ending? It's going to happen. It *can* happen. But I need your boat. I need to take it right now. But you can't report it missing."

Heddy heard something fall, the sound of Gigi picking it up. "Hold on, hold on for a minute. Let me sit up." She heard Gigi yawn. The snap of a lighter, the deep inhale of a cigarette. "You need my boat?"

She was beginning to think it was a long shot. "Yes, but don't report it missing. We'll leave it on the other side of the sound. I can explain more later. As soon as I get home." She paused. "We got Ted. He's a terrible person, Gigi. There's things you don't know."

She heard Gigi chuckle, and Heddy imagined her friend, her long legs crossed, sitting at the center of a pile of satin sheets, her hair tousled, grinning at the phone. "You are bad, bad, bad, Hibernia Winsome." Of course, Gigi would enjoy this, and it embarrassed Heddy a little but also pushed a proud grin onto her face.

"I'm serious. Your boat. Can I take it?"

"The keys are under the passenger seat," Gigi said. "But you know that. Why did you call?"

"What if your housekeeper called the cops? And, well, I called because I'm going to write this. A screenplay. About all of this. I wanted to tell you that."

"Heddy?" Ash poked his head out the screen door; he motioned for her to hurry.

Gigi hadn't said anything, and the quiet hung between them.

"I have to go," Heddy said.

"I'd be happy to read it. I love you, little girl." Gigi said.

Heddy bit her lip. "I love you, too." She hung up the phone and grinned at Ash. "Let's go."

They'd have to walk to the boat, so they carried suitcases along the sandy path to Gigi's enormous lawn, Ash always looking behind them. Heddy kept her eye on Gigi's long private dock on the horizon, pulling and tugging her suitcase, until the dock creaked underfoot, a lone seagull flying off, leaving a splatter of white excrement in its wake.

"That's good luck," Heddy said, although both men were too busy heaving the duffel bags and suitcases onto the polished mahogany speedboat to notice.

Heddy faced Gigi's house, remembering how it had twinkled the night of Gigi's party. The island looked so different to her than when she first arrived. Those first few days, she'd been in awe, filled with a sense of wonder at what the summer held for her. But then she'd sat on this very dock and learned that life isn't always as it is in the movies. And that didn't matter, as long as life was what you wanted it to be.

A tickle of salt filled her nostrils. She shielded her eyes from the blazing sun and maneuvered herself onto the boat, fishing the key out from under the seat. Ash put his hand out for it, but she inserted the key into the ignition and started the engine, positioning herself at the steering wheel, her butt on the edge of the white leather seat.

"I'll drive," she said, feeling for her purse, the money, at her feet. Cocking her head and pausing at the sight of Ash beside her, she realized that she wanted him with all her heart, but she didn't need him. She didn't need any man. Because she was in charge of her life now, and no one would tell her what to do ever again. No one would stop her from going to school or writing a script. No one would trap her in the outdated notion that you had to be who men told you to be. Maybe Jean-Rose was right all along when she said that Heddy was capable of so much more. Because she was. She'd surprised all of them, most of all herself.

Ash leaned down to kiss her shoulder, while Sullivan settled into the cushioned bench upfront, his arm draped around the empty seat. "I'll find my way from the other side," he said.

She could see the mainland already, the sandy beaches and green hills waiting for them across Vineyard Sound.

"I'll call Ruth from a payphone at the dock," she told Ash. "I put an envelope for her in your kitchen drawer." When they'd gone back inside, she'd stuffed in a wad of cash. It was enough to get Ruth to Boston.

Heddy revved the engine. There was warmth in the salt air, and she pushed the boat into drive, her hair blowing back as she zipped the vessel across the water. She put her arm around Ash's waist, and he pulled her close to him.

This was it. She'd known it when she'd arrived this summer, hadn't she? This would be the summer to change everything.

Ash leaned in to say something, but she couldn't hear him. She stared out at the rippling blue sea, a couple of drag fishing boats crisscrossing the horizon, a ferry sounding its departure. There it was in front of her: The whole wide world.

She was going on adrenaline, and if Sullivan hadn't been with them, she might have pulled her yellow tank over her head and straddled Ash right then and there. Still, she warned herself, she'd never go overboard in her loyalty, in how she rearranged her life for him. She mumbled something back in his ear, and when he yelled "What?" over the roar of the boat's engine, she yelled back, taking in the green of his eyes, and feeling a ping somewhere she couldn't locate, noting how the tingling spread into her head. "I'll only take so many risks for you. I won't . . ."

And then he kissed her deeply, square on the lips. She thought it was to silence her, until he pulled away, grinning. "I'll never ask," he said.

She knew then that he was hers, and together, life would be wonderful and all her own.

ACKNOWLEDGMENTS

Writing historical fiction is an overwhelming endeavor not only because you are trying to tell a great story but you're hoping to do so while set in a time period you didn't live through. Even if I've spent two weeks of every summer on Martha's Vineyard, I didn't live there in the summer of 1962; and even if I love the island like a local, I wouldn't dare call myself an islander. But that's the fun of fiction. I could dream up 1960s Martha's Vineyard and send my WASPY characters to some of my favorite places, spending my days on the island even while I wrote at home in the dead of winter.

Some details in the novel are inspired by fact: The beach club is very loosely based on the East Chop Beach Club. The Katama Airfield was around in the '60s, even if the hipster restaurant where Sullivan plays sax is not. The towns, lighthouses, and beaches are real places you can still visit today. Other elements of the story are products of my imagination, like the restaurants and shops that my characters frequent, what their houses look like, how fancy their clothes. I took creative freedoms featuring famous island residents Carly Simon and James Taylor, who were very young seasonal residents on the island back then, just getting their feet wet in music. Much of my research came from articles culled from the detailed archives of the *MV Times* and the *Vineyard Gazette*; both papers have published numerous stories about the island's history and provided endless fodder as I was writing.

There is a storied house on the island that inspired the novel. On a small stretch of beach just outside Vineyard Haven, there's a house that you can still rent called "The Swindle." At one point in the 1950s, there were three houses there: the first owned by a famous stage actress Katherine Cornell, the second by Helen Pratt Philbin—granddaughter of Charles Pratt, one of the founders of Standard Oil. In between them in the third house lived a bachelor who fell on hard times in 1953 and approached his wealthy neighbors to buy his place. They declined, and everyone returned home for winter. But the following summer, the two women arrived at their grand estates to find that the bachelor had painted his house an offensive blue. The women found it so garish that they paid him $20,000 to take the cabin off his hands. As the story goes, they were "swindled" into buying the cottage. After reading about the Swindle rental in a glossy real estate magazine, the idea for the novel took root. Immediately, the characters of Jean-Rose and Gigi McCabe came to mind. They would live in the enormous houses on either side of the fishing camp, with a handsome young swindler—Ash Porter—in between.

Summer Darlings would not exist without my extraordinary teachers at the Writing Institute at Sarah Lawrence College, Jimin Han and Pat Dunn, who were my earliest readers and champions. You too, Eileen Palma! It takes a village to write a novel, and this one would not be what it is today without the careful reads of those who read early drafts and offered critical feedback. Thank you to Diane Foster, Chelsea Foster, Jean Huff, Carolyn Lyall, Kim Leibowitz, Laura

Bower, Molly Pease, Sara Farnsworth, and Meredith Mialkowski, in particular, who read the book too many times to count.

From the moment I sat down with my agent, Rebecca Scherer, at a publishing conference, I knew I'd found someone special. Rebecca read a very early draft of this book and she believed in it from the start, even when my characters didn't yet feel like real people. And then she read another draft and another, each time pushing me to fine tune the story. And as such, she's felt like an editor, an agent, and a friend.

To my fantastic and whip-smart editor at Gallery Books, Kate Dresser: Thank you for helping me write my best book. I am grateful for your energy, insight, and wise counsel because without it we wouldn't have been able to elevate the manuscript into the novel it is today. Most editors tell a writer how to fix their work, but Kate's provocative questions encouraged me to take the manuscript in new directions while hardly changing the backbone of the story itself.

When I started writing this book a few summers ago, my little girl, Emerson, was a baby, and my son, Harper, was six. And as every writer knows, the act of putting down words on a page can be isolating. You disappear into your head as often as you disappear into the next room to write. Thank you to my kids for their patience, and for encouraging me in that sweet way that children do, regurgitating some of which I've instilled in them: You can do it, Mama.

Thank you to Fiorella Calvo, my longtime babysitter. Your love for my children isn't lost on me, and I appreciate all that you do for us, just to give me dedicated time to focus and write.

Thank you to my mom, who showed me from a young age that women can be strong writers; and my sisters, Erin and Chelsea, for making me laugh and cheering me on; and my father, who encouraged me to come to his house to chop wood whenever I was feeling stressed. I declined.

My grandmother, Marie Foster, a former dancer, had an air of glamour that captured my heart as a child. I heard her voice many times while writing.

To my best friend and husband, John Vargas. I owe this entire grand adventure we call a life to meeting you in college all those years ago. Coming of age with you has been my greatest joy. Remember all of those early morning talks in the kitchen where you reassured me that we would see this thing through? You were right. You always are. I love you.